TO BIN

CAROL MARI

THE FIREFIGHTER TO HEAL HER HEART

BY
ANNIE O'NEIL

MILLS
BOON

Carol Marinelli recently filled in a form where she was asked for her job title and was thrilled, after all these years, to be able to put down her answer as 'writer'. Then it asked what Carol did for relaxation. After chewing her pen for a moment Carol put down the truth—'writing'. The third question asked: 'What are your hobbies?' Well, not wanting to look obsessed or, worse still, boring, she crossed the fingers on her free hand and answered 'swimming and tennis'. But, given that the chlorine in the pool does terrible things to her highlights, and the closest she's got to a tennis racket in the last couple of years is watching the Australian Open, I'm sure you can guess the real answer!

Annie O'Neil spent most of her childhood with a leg draped over the family rocking chair and a book in her hand. Novels, baking, and writing too much teenage angst poetry ate up most of her youth. Now, quite a few years on from those fevered daydreams of being a poet, Annie splits her time between corralling her husband (and real-life Scottish hero) into helping her with their cows or scratching the backs of their rare breed pigs, and spending some very happy hours at her computer, writing. Find out more about Annie at her website: www.annieoneilbooks.com

BABY TWINS
TO BIND THEM

BY
CAROL MARINELLI

First published in Great Britain 2015
by Mills & Boon, an imprint of Harlequin (UK) Limited,
Eton House, 18-24 Paradise Road, Richmond, Surrey, TW9 1SR

© 2015 Carol Marinelli

ISBN: 978-0-263-24693-3

Dear Reader,

Sigh…

I completely *loved* writing this book. The only down side to loving my hero, Dr Guy Steele, so much is that he has spoiled any future relationships—because I will for ever be thinking *Steele wouldn't have said that…* or *Steele wouldn't have done that…* Yes, he's really that delicious—just so assured and sexy, yet nice.

I'm actually jealous of my own heroine!

Happy reading!

Carol x

Books by Carol Marinelli

Unwrapping Her Italian Doc
Playing the Playboy's Secret
200 Harley Street: Surgeon in a Tux
Tempted by Dr Morales
The Accidental Romeo
Secrets of a Career Girl
Dr Dark and Far Too Delicious
NYC Angels: Redeeming the Playboy

**Visit the author profile page
at millsandboon.co.uk for more titles**

Praise for Carol Marinelli

'A compelling, sensual, sexy, emotionally packed, drama-filled read that will leave you begging for more!'
—*Contemporary Romance Reviews* on
NYC Angels: Redeeming the Playboy

CHAPTER ONE

Before

'YOU PAGED ME to see a patient.'

'No, I didn't.' Candy, holding an armful of sheets, smiled when it would have been far easier to stand there and gape. He was stunning—tall, slender, wearing a suit and a tie. His dark brown hair was cut short and his voice was so deep and commanding that it stopped Candy in her tracks. She met his chocolate-brown eyes fully and it took a moment to respond normally. 'Who are you here to see?'

'A Mr Thomas Heath.'

Candy walked over to the board. Emergency at the London Royal Hospital was quiet this afternoon but as she was in Resuscitation Candy didn't know which patients were in the cubicles. After a quick scan of the board, she located Mr Heath. 'He's in cubicle seven. Trevor's the nurse looking after him. He must be the one who paged you.'

'Thanks for that. By the way I'm Steele.'

'Steele?'

He watched as her very blue eyes moved to his name

badge. 'Well, Dr Guy Steele, if you'd prefer to be formal,' he said.

'Steele will do.' She must look like a dental commercial, Candy thought, for she simply couldn't stop smiling at him. He must be thirty or mid-thirties, which was a lot more than her twenty-four years, and he was also way older than anyone she had ever fancied, yet he had this impact, this presence, that had Candy's heart galloping in her chest.

'And you are?' he asked.

'Candy. Candy Anastasi.' She watched a smile twitch on his lips as she said her name. 'I know, I know, I should be tall, leggy and blonde to carry off a name like that!' Instead, she was short and a bit round with long black ringlets and piercing blue eyes. 'There's a story there.'

'I can't wait to hear it, Nurse Candy.'

He had the deepest voice that she'd ever heard. Like a headmaster, he was stern and bossy, yet it was all somehow softened by a very beautiful mouth that she could barely drag her eyes from. 'You'll never hear the story of my name,' Candy said.

'Oh, we'll have to see about that.'

Had they been flirting? Candy wondered as sexy-as-hell Steele walked off.

'Who's that?' Kelly said as they started to strip one of the resuscitation beds.

'Steele!' Candy said in a deep low voice, making Kelly laugh. She continued speaking gruffly while they bent over and tucked the sheet in. 'Or Dr Guy Steele if we want to be formal and, young lady, I'm going to make your eardrums reverberate with my deep—'

'Nurse Candy?'

Candy froze when she realised that Steele was behind her.

'Could I borrow your stethoscope?' he asked.

She laughed at being caught impersonating him and turned around and took her stethoscope from her neck and held it out to him, yet pulled back as he went to take it. 'You can,' she said, the stethoscope hovering. 'Just so long as you stop calling me Nurse Candy.'

He just took the stethoscope, smiled and walked off.

They made up all the beds and checked the crash trolleys and then gave up pretending to be busy, given that Lydia, the manager, was in her office. Instead, they took a jug of iced tea to the nurses' station, where Steele was tapping away on the computer. It was a lovely early summer day but the air-conditioning was struggling and it was nice to sit on the bench and gossip, though Steele had a couple of questions for her.

'How do you get into the pathology lab to check results?' he asked, not looking around.

'You've got your password?' Candy checked.

'I have and I've got into...' He tapped again. 'Got it.'

'Have you told your parents about Hawaii yet?' Kelly asked Candy, resuming the conversation they'd been having in the kitchen as they'd made their drink.

'No.'

'You go in four weeks' time,' Kelly pointed out.

'They might not notice that I've gone,' Candy said hopefully, then let out a sigh. Her parents were Italian, strict and very prone to popping over to her flat unannounced. They also spoke every day on the phone. 'I know I'll have to tell them or I'll be listed on Interpol as a missing person.'

Candy had, on a whim, booked a holiday to Hawaii.

Well, it hadn't been purely on a whim—she had already been aware that she needed to get away when the info-mercial had appeared on her screen with a very special offer for the first ten callers. She'd been tired, a bit jaded and upset over a stupid fling with Gerry, one of the head nurses here. Thankfully he was in Greece for a couple of months, which spared Candy her blushes, but when she'd reached for the phone and, lucky her, been amongst the first ten callers, she'd known she needed this break.

She couldn't wait for two weeks in which to lie on a beach and explore the stunning island at leisure while she attempted to sort out a few things that were on her mind.

'They're going to freak when I tell them,' Candy admitted. 'They know that I can't really afford it.'

'It's all paid for?' Kelly checked, and Candy nodded.

'All except for spending money, but I've just spoken to the hospital bank and I've got loads of shifts. Actually, I haven't got a single day off until I fly.'

'Where are your shifts?'

'In the geriatric unit.'

Kelly pulled a face. 'Yuk.'

Candy didn't mind. She had enjoyed working in the geriatric unit during her training and was really grateful for the extra work. Even if she was exhausted at the prospect of nearly four more weeks without so much as a day off.

As her parents would point out, when she finally got around to it and told them about her holiday, it was fool-ish to be working extra shifts because you were so tired that you needed a break—but Candy just wanted to get away for a while.

'When do you start working there?'

'The weekend. I'm working Friday night and then I've

got a four-hour shift on Sunday morning, then back here Monday.'

'Okay.' Steele turned around. 'I want Mr Heath pulled over to Resus. He needs to be monitored while I start him on some medication. His bloodwork's dire.'

'Sure.' Candy jumped down from the bench and she and Trevor brought Mr Heath over.

Candy wrote his name on the whiteboard and turned to Steele. 'Sorry, what specialty is he under?'

'Geriatrics,' Steele said, then he gave her a thin smile. 'Yuk!'

Candy's cheeks went pink; she wanted to point out that she hadn't been the one who had said that.

'It's okay,' Steele relented when he saw her uncomfortable expression. 'You hit a nerve—I hear that sort of thing a lot.'

'So are you a new geriatric consultant?' Kelly asked, but Steele shook his head.

'No, I'm only here temporarily. I'm covering for six weeks while Kathy Jordan is on extended leave.'

'Just six weeks?' Kelly asked shamelessly.

'Yep,' Steele said, and walked off.

'Wow, talk about bringing the schmexy into geriatrics,' Kelly said. 'And you're going to be working there, you lucky thing. I bet you're not complaining now.'

She hadn't been complaining in the first place, Candy was tempted to point out.

They soon paid for the lull in patients because, not an hour later, the department had filled and she and Kelly were busy in Resus, Kelly with a very ill baby and Candy attempting to calm down Mr Heath. He was rather shaky from the medication and was getting increasingly distressed and trying to climb down from the resuscitation bed.

'The medicine makes your heart race, Mr Heath,' Candy tried to explain to the gentleman. 'It will settle down soon...' But he couldn't understand what she said and kept trying to climb off the bed so Candy tried speaking louder. 'The medicine—'

'You do it like this.' Steele saw that she was struggling and came over. 'Mr Heath!' he boomed.

The people in the Waiting Room surely heard him, Candy thought as he gave the same explanation to Mr Heath that she had been trying to give. The gentleman nodded weakly in relief and then lay back on the pillows. 'Good man,' Steele barked and smiled at Candy and, in a comparatively dulcet tone, added, 'I have the perfect voice for my job.'

'You do,' she agreed.

'So you're going to be doing a few shifts up on the geriatric unit?'

'Yep.'

'For a holiday that you can't really afford?'

'I know,' Candy groaned.

'Well, good for you,' Steele said, and Candy blinked in surprise. 'Okay, once Mr Heath's medication has finished I want him monitored for another hour down here. Then everything's sorted for him to be admitted. We're just waiting on a bed, which might be a couple of hours. I've spoken to the ward and they have said that they'll ring down when they're ready for him to come up.'

'Ha-ha,' Candy said, because there was no way that the ward was likely to ring down. Instead, she would have to chase them and push for the bed to be readied.

Steele well understood her sarcastic comment. 'Well,

I hope that they do ring down in a timely manner. I'm less than impressed with the waiting times for patients to get into a bed at the Royal.'

With that he stalked off, possibly to return to whatever fluffy white cloud he'd just drifted down from, Candy thought.

She'd never, ever been so instantly captivated by someone.

Candy left Kelly watching Mr Heath when she was told to go for her lunch break. She'd forgotten to bring lunch so she bought a bag of salt-and-vinegar crisps from the vending machine and put them between two slices of bread and butter. Sitting down in the staffroom, she smiled at Trevor, who was having his lunch too, and checked her phone. Yes, her parents had called, wondering why she hadn't been over.

She'd tell them about Hawaii tonight, Candy decided. Just get it over and done with and then maybe then she'd feel better. Yet she was incredibly tired and really just wanted to go home, have dinner and an early night.

'Here!'

That delicious voice tipped her out of introspection and she looked up at Steele, who was holding a stethoscope, which she took from him.

'Thank you,' Candy said, 'though you didn't have to rush to bring it back down. It's only a hospital-issue stethoscope.'

'Oh,' Steele said. 'I thought I'd pinched yours. Still, it doesn't matter, I was coming down anyway. I'm waiting for a patient to arrive—a direct admission from her GP, though she's refusing to go straight to the ward. She's just agreed to a chest X-ray and some blood tests, and then she thinks she's going home!'

'Thinks?' Candy asked as Steele sat down beside her and stretched out his long legs. It was nice that he sat down next to her when there were about twenty seats to choose from. She turned and smiled as he spoke on.

'Her GP is extremely concerned about her. He thinks there's far more going on than she's admitting to. Macey has had the same GP for thirty years and if he's worried about her then so am I. He thinks she's depressed.' He turned and looked right into her eyes and Candy felt her heart do a little flip-flop. 'It's a big problem with the elderly.'

'Really?'

Steele nodded and looked at what she was eating. 'That looks so bad it has to be good.'

'It's fantastic,' Candy said, and ripped off half her sandwich and gave it to him. 'The trick is lots of butter.'

'That's amazing!' Steele said, when he'd tasted it.

'I'm brilliant with bread,' Candy said. 'Toasted sandwiches, ice-cream sandwiches, beans on toast...'

'I thought a nice Italian girl like you would be brilliant in the kitchen.'

'Sadly, no,' Candy said. 'I'm a constant source of concern to my mother. Anyway, who said I'm nice?'

They smiled.

A smile that was just so deliciously inappropriate for a man you'd met only an hour or so ago. A smile she had never given to another man before and, really, she had no idea where it had come from.

Candy Anastasi! she scolded herself as she looked into those dark brown eyes.

Step away from the very young nurse, Steele told himself, but, hell, she was gorgeous.

Lydia came in then and they both looked away from

each other. Lydia was waving a postcard of a delicious aqua ocean and Candy found that she was holding her breath in tension as Lydia read out the card. 'There's a postcard from Gerry. It reads, "Glad that none of you are here."'

Lydia gave a tight smile as she pinned it on the board and Candy just stared at the television.

Was that little dig from Gerry aimed at her?

'When is he back?' Trevor asked.

'End of July, I think.'

Lydia's voice was deliberately vague and Candy knew why. Gerry, the head nurse in Emergency, had been strongly advised to take extended leave.

Gerry was one of the reasons that Candy wanted a couple of weeks on a beach with no company.

Candy's parents had freaked when, at twenty-two, she had broken up with a man they considered suitable and had declared she was moving out. They had been so appalled, so devastated at the prospect of their only daughter leaving home that Candy had ended up staying for another year.

She'd simply had to leave in the end.

Her mother thought nothing of opening her post. She constantly asked whom Candy was talking to on the phone and when Candy pointed out she was entitled to privacy they would ask what it was she had to hide.

Last year she had moved out and, really, she had hardly let loose. She'd had a brief relationship with Gerry when she'd first moved into her flat but that hadn't worked out and she had been happily single since then.

A couple of months ago, aware that Gerry was having some problems, she'd agreed to go out for a drink with him.

It had resulted in a one-night stand that had left Candy feeling regretful. Gerry had been annoyed to find out that their brief relationship hadn't been resumed.

It was all a bit of a mess, an avoidable one, though. Candy was just grateful that no one at work knew about that regrettable night and Candy wanted it left far behind.

'You'll be sending postcards soon,' Steele said, but Candy shook her head.

'I won't be thinking about this place for a moment.'

That wasn't quite true, though. She would be thinking about work—Candy was seriously thinking of leaving Emergency.

CHAPTER TWO

JUST AS SHE RETURNED from lunch she was informed that Steele's patient was here but refusing to come inside the department and had requested, loudly, that the ambulance take her home.

'I'll come out and have a word with her,' Candy said as Steele was taking a phone call. She headed out to the ambulance and was met by a teary woman who introduced herself as Catherine, Macey Anderson's niece.

'I knew that she was going to do this,' Catherine said. 'It's taken two days to persuade her to come in. She used to be a matron on one of the wards here, and still thinks she is one.' Catherine gave a tired smile. 'She was in a few months ago and she was just about running the place by the time she was discharged.'

'I want to go home,' Macey shouted as Candy came into the back of the ambulance.

Macey was a very tall, very handsome woman, with wiry grey, curly hair, a flushed face and very angry dark green eyes. She had all her stuff with her, a huge suitcase, a walking frame and several other bags.

'Mrs Anderson—' Candy started, but already she was wrong.

'It's Miss Anderson!'

'I'm sorry, Miss Anderson. I'm Candy Anastasi, one of the nurses in Emergency, and I'm going to be looking after you today.'

'But, as I've told everyone, many times, I don't *want* to be looked after,' Macey retorted. 'I want to be taken home.'

It was all pretty hopeless. The more they tried to persuade her to come into the department the more upset Macey became. The last thing Candy wanted to do was wheel her through when she was distressed and crying and so, instead, she tried another tack, wondering if, given that Macey had once been a matron, she might not want to get another nurse in trouble.

'Dr Steele is already here to see you,' Candy said. 'He's been waiting for you to arrive. Am I to go in and tell him that I can't get you to come into the hospital?'

Macey looked at her for a long moment and then she looked beyond Candy's shoulder and Candy knew, she simply knew, that it was Steele who had just stepped into the ambulance.

'Is there a problem, Nurse? Only I've been waiting for quite some time.' His low voice sounded just a touch ominous and Candy met Macey's eyes for a brief moment.

'No,' Macey answered for Candy. 'They were just about to bring me in.'

'Good,' Steele said. 'Then I'll come and see you shortly, Miss Anderson.'

As he headed back into the department the paramedics lowered the stretcher to the ground and Candy found out perhaps why it was that Steele was so sharply dressed. 'At least he's not twelve and wearing jeans,' Macey muttered.

Candy smiled—yes, Steele's appearance and authoritarian tone had appeased Macey.

They took Macey into cubicle seven, aligned the stretcher with the trolley, and Candy positioned the sliding board that would help to move the patient over easily. 'We'll get you onto the trolley, Miss Anderson.'

'I can manage,' the elderly lady snapped, 'and it's Macey.'

'That actually means she likes you,' her niece said, and gestured with her head for Candy to follow her outside.

'I've got this,' Matthew, a very patient paramedic, said, and Candy went outside to speak with Catherine.

'It's taken two days for her GP to persuade her to come in,' Catherine said. 'Honestly, I'm just so relieved she's finally here. She's got a temperature and she's hardly eating or drinking anything. She doesn't take her tablets or if she does she gets them all wrong…'

'We'll go through all of that.' Candy did her best to reassure Macey's niece.

'She's so cantankerous and rude,' Catherine said, 'that she puts everyone offside, but she's such a lovely lady too. She's always been on her own, she's never had a boyfriend, let alone married, she's so completely set in her ways and loathes getting undressed in front of anyone. You're going to have a battle there…'

'Let us take care of her,' Candy said, 'and please don't worry about her saying something offensive. Believe me, we'll have heard far worse.'

'Thanks.' Catherine gave a worried smile and they went back inside. The cubicle was pretty full, with Macey's huge bag and walking frame, and Candy had a little tidy up. 'Why don't we first get you into a gown and then—'

'Get me into a gown?' Macey shouted loudly. 'You haven't even introduced yourself and you're asking me to take my clothes off.' Candy said nothing as Steele came into the cubicle. She had, in fact, introduced herself in the ambulance. 'You're not a nurse's bootlace,' Macey said to Candy just as Steele came in.

'Hello, Miss Anderson,' he said. 'I didn't introduce myself properly back there in the ambulance. I'm Steele, or Dr Steele, if you prefer to be formal.'

Candy smothered a little smile as he repeated a similar introduction to the one he had given her. He must have to say it fifty times a day.

He ran through a few questions with Macey as a very anxious Catherine hovered.

'You had a heart attack three months ago?' Steele checked. 'And you were admitted here for a week.'

'All they did was pump me with drugs,' Macey huffed. 'Where were you then?'

'I believe I was in Newcastle,' Steele said.

'So how long have you worked here?'

'Two days,' Steele answered easily.

'You'll be gone tomorrow.' Macey huffed. 'You're a locum.'

'I am, though I happen to be a very good one,' Steele said, completely unfazed. 'And I'm here for six weeks, which gives us plenty of time to sort all this out.'

They went through her medical history. Apart from the heart attack it would seem that Macey was very well indeed. She had never smoked, never drunk, and at eighty still did all her own housework and cooking, with a little help from her nieces, Catherine and Linda. Macey had until a couple of days ago walked to the shops every day.

'It's quite a distance,' Catherine said. 'I offered to do her shopping weekly at the supermarket for her but Aunt Macey wouldn't hear of it.'

'I like to walk,' Macey snapped.

'It's good that you do—exercise is good for you,' Steele said. 'Do you have stairs at home?'

'Yes, and I manage them just fine,' Macey retorted. 'You won't see me with bungalow legs!'

'Right, Miss Anderson,' Steele said. 'I'm going to ask Candy to help you into a gown and do some obs and put an IV and draw some blood. Then I'll come and examine you.' He looked at two blue ice-cream containers that were filled with various bottles and blister packets of medication. 'I'll take these and look through them.'

As Steele went to go Macey called him back. 'I'm not having a nurse take my blood. That's a doctor's job.'

'Oh, I can assure you that you're better off with Candy than you are with me,' Steele said. 'I get the shakes this side of six p.m.'

His quip caused a little smile to inch onto Macey's lips and, after Steele had gone, Candy helped her into a gown while doing her best to keep Macey covered as she did so. But the elderly lady fought her over every piece, right down to her stockings.

'Leave my stockings on,' Macey said.

'Oh, I'll leave them for Steele to take off, shall I?' Candy challenged.

Macey huffed and lifted her bottom but as Candy rolled the stockings down she found out why Macey was so reluctant to get fully undressed—there was a bandage on her leg and around that the skin was very red and inflamed.

'I'll take this off so Steele can take a look,' Candy said. She went and washed her hands and opened up a dressing pack and then put on some gloves.

'Careful,' Macey warned.

'Is it very painful?' Candy asked, and Macey nodded.

'Okay, I'll just put some saline on,' Candy said, 'and we'll soak it off. Has your GP seen this?'

'I don't need a doctor to tell me how to do a dressing.'

Candy soaked the dressing in saline and then covered Macey with a blanket and checked her obs, before heading out to Steele. He was sitting at the nurses' station, going through all Macey's medications. He had a pill counter and was tipping one of the bottles out when Candy came over.

'She's got a nasty leg wound,' Candy said.

'How bad?'

'I haven't seen it,' Candy said. 'I'm just soaking the dressing but her shin is all red and I think it's very painful.'

'Okay.' He started to tip the tablets back into the jar. 'I don't want her left on her own,' Steele said.

'Sorry?'

'I don't like what I'm seeing with these tablets,' Steele said. 'I don't trust her not to do something stupid.'

'Oh!'

'I'll come in and see her now.'

They both returned to the cubicle and Steele examined Macey. He listened for a long time to her chest and felt her stomach, keeping her as covered as he could while he did so, and then they got to her leg.

Steele put on some gloves and took off the dressing and Macey winced in pain. 'Sorry, Miss Anderson,' Steele said. 'How long have you had this?'

'A couple of weeks.'

Steele looked up at Macey. 'That's very concerning. This has developed over two weeks?'

Candy could hear the note of sarcasm in Steele's

voice and watched as Macey stared back at him and then backed down.

'I knocked my leg when I came out of hospital. It's just not healed and it's been getting worse.'

'That sounds far more plausible.' Steele smiled at her. 'Well, that accounts for your temperature!' He took a swab and though he was very gentle the cotton tip must have felt like a red-hot poker because Macey let out a yelp of pain. 'Very sorry, Macey,' Steele said. He put a light dressing over it. 'We'll give you something decent for pain before we dress it properly.' He spoke then to Candy. 'Can you take Macey round for a chest X-ray?'

Just as Candy had finished drawing some blood the porter arrived and Candy went to X-Ray with Macey and Catherine. They were seen relatively quickly but Macey was clearly less than impressed at what she considered a long wait.

Having looked at her X-ray, Steele came into the cubicle and then turned to Catherine. 'Why don't you go and get a drink?' he suggested. 'I'm going to be with your aunt for the next twenty minutes or so—you might as well take the chance for a break now.'

'Thank you,' Catherine said in relief.

'I just wanted to check a couple of things,' Steele said once Catherine had left the cubicle.

'And then I can go home?'

'You're not well enough,' Steele said. 'Now, while Catherine isn't here, I want you to tell me how many you smoke a day?'

'I don't smoke.'

'Miss Anderson, do you want me to bring in your chest X-ray and we can go over it together?'

'Two.' She gave a tight shrug. 'Maybe three a day.'

'We'll say ten, then, shall we?' Steele said, and Candy blinked when Macey didn't correct him. 'I'll write you up for a nicotine patch. How much do you drink a day?'

'I've told you already, I don't.'

'Six broken ribs of varying ages.' Steele smiled at the old girl. 'Come on, Macey. So am I to worry that you're falling down for no reason?'

'I slipped on some ice,' Macey said, 'and I've got a cat that gets under my feet.'

'Fair enough.' Steele nodded. 'So you don't want me to write you down for a couple of shots of sherry at night?' he checked. 'You can have either your own stuff, or the hospital's cheap disgusting stuff. We just need the bottle if you want to drink your own.'

Macey took in a deep breath before saying anything. 'It's in my bag.'

'Good, we'll make sure it's handed over to nursing staff out of sight of your niece.'

Candy stood there feeling a bit stunned but she hadn't seen anything yet. Steele had brought back in the two ice-cream containers that Macey had brought in with her and he started to go through them.

'Macey, you haven't been taking these regularly.' He held up a pill bottle. 'Yet you're not.'

'There's so many. I can't keep up.'

Steele picked up another bottle that had just a couple of tablets in it. 'And these were only dispensed two days ago,' Steele said, 'and there are only two left.'

'I didn't take them,' Macey said in a scoffing voice.

'I know that you didn't or we wouldn't even be having this conversation. So where are they now?'

'I don't know. My niece puts them into a pill box…'

'Macey?'

'I tipped them down the toilet. I don't trust the drug companies.'

'Are you depressed, Macey?'

'Oh, you're going to put me on antidepressants now. You're in cahoots with the drug companies.'

'Are you confused and mixing up your medication or are you ignoring your health?' Steele asked, and Candy stood there, watching him stare right into Macey's eyes. 'Are you depressed, Macey?'

There was a long stretch of silence before Macey answered.

'I'm not confused,' she said. 'Well, sometimes I am with dates and things.'

'But you're not confused where your medication's concerned?' Steele checked.

'No,' Macey said, and Candy frowned at the serious note to Steele's voice.

'Okay.'

'Could you just leave me, please?' Macey asked.

'Not happening,' Steele said, and he took down the edge of the trolley she was lying on. His legs were long enough that he sat there easily. She would need a ladder to do that, Candy thought, and then she stopped thinking idle thoughts as she started to realise the seriousness of this conversation.

'Why did you tip the tablets in the toilet?' Steele challenged gently, and Candy felt the back of her nose stinging as he pushed on. 'Were you scared that you might take them all?'

Macey's face started to crumple and Steele took her hand. 'Look at me, Macey. Are you having suicidal thoughts?' Steele asked bluntly, and after a moment she nodded and then started to cry.

'Well done for throwing them away,' Steele said. 'Well done for coming into hospital and speaking with me.' Candy watched as he wrapped his arms around the proud lady as she started to really sob. 'It's okay.' His voice was very deep but so gentle. 'We're going to look after you…'

CHAPTER THREE

CANDY SLEPT FOR a few hours on Friday afternoon before her first night shift on the geriatric ward and then she got ready and took the Underground into work.

She was actually rather nervous about her night shift. She was so used to working in Emergency that she wasn't too sure how she would go on the ward. She also had a short four-hour shift there on Sunday morning.

It will be worth it, Candy told herself as she stepped into the geriatric unit.

Hawaii, here I come!

The handover lasted much longer than it did in Emergency and the day staff went into far more detail about the patients than she had grown used to. Candy sat as the staff discussed in depth the patients' moods and their ADLs: activities of daily living. Steele was sitting at a desk in the room with his back to everyone but didn't leave as the handover started; he just carried on with whatever he was doing on the computer and offered comment or clarification at times.

Candy knew that she was far, far too aware of him.

The staff clearly liked him. If there was a question they would toss it over to him and he would answer as he typed away.

Elaine, a student nurse, was giving her handover to the night staff, watched over by her mentor, Gloria. Elaine was very bossy and seemed to think she was the only one in the room who knew what she was doing. She had given a sigh of exasperation when Candy had introduced herself and said that she was from the hospital bank. 'Another one!' Elaine had said.

As Elaine gave her handover there were a few times when Candy caught Abigail's eye—Abigail was the senior nurse she would be working with tonight, and they both smothered a smile.

Mr Heath, who had been so unwell the other day in Emergency, was doing a lot better and Candy was allocated to look after him for the night.

She was also given Toby Worthington, a terminal patient who was on a lot of morphine for pain control and, Elaine said, liked to have his radio on till eleven at night and then turned on again at six.

'Then we have Macey Anderson.' Elaine moved on to the next patient.

'I know Macey,' Candy said. 'I was in Emergency when she was admitted.'

'Could you have her tonight as well, then?' Abigail checked and Candy nodded. They went through her history, which was pretty much what Candy already knew. How Macey had been since admission had changed rapidly, though. 'Since she's come to the ward she's been very withdrawn,' Elaine said. 'She doesn't want to eat, or wash. She's on an IV regime but if she continues to refuse meals and drinks she'll need an NG tube. Steele has taken her off a lot of her medications and has also started her on a low dose of antidepressants…' Elaine went through her medications. 'Make sure she takes them and she's not hiding them,' Elaine warned, and Candy nodded. But that wasn't enough for Elaine. 'You have to ask her to lift her tongue.'

'I shall,' Candy said, trying to keep the edge from her voice. Elaine was a funny little thing, with a very long, wide mouth that opened often.

She reminded Candy of a puppet.

'Why does she have to lift her tongue, Elaine?' Steele asked from the computer, and Candy felt her lips stretch into a smile because clearly he had Elaine worked out too.

'To make sure that she's not hiding any under there,' Elaine said, and looked at Candy to make sure that she understood the instruction.

'Thanks,' Candy said. 'I'll make sure that she takes them.'

As Elaine left the room Abigail winked. 'Matron Elaine!'

'Her heart's in the right place, though,' Gloria, the sister in charge of the day shift, said. 'But, oh my, she's hard work. Elaine insists on calling everything by its technical name. The patients haven't a clue what she's asking. Just this evening she asked Mr Heath if she could check for scrotal oedema.' Gloria smiled as she recalled it. 'He said, "Do you mean my balls, dear?" It was too funny.'

They were all very nice and after handover Elaine gave Candy a quick tour of the ward before she headed for home.

Actually, it wasn't that quick—Elaine was incredibly thorough, going through everything in detail when really Candy wanted to get started.

'I think that covers everything,' Candy said. 'Thanks for the tour.'

'I'll just show you where the torches and things are kept,' Elaine said, but Candy looked at the clock and it was already nearly ten. 'Go.' Candy smiled. 'It's Friday night. Enjoy it!'

Elaine gave a little nod and finally headed for home and then Candy went to check on her patients for the night.

Mr Heath was indeed looking better.

'Hello, Candy.' He smiled when she came over and he put down the book that he was reading.

'You remember me?' Candy asked in surprise, because Mr Heath had been so distressed in Resus that he hadn't seemed very aware of his surroundings or able to hear what anybody except Steele was saying.

'Of course I do.'

'Well, it's lovely to see you looking so much better,' Candy said. She then did his obs and gave him his medications for the night and, as she did so, they chatted for a while.

'I'm hoping to go home on Monday,' Mr Heath said. 'My granddaughter gets married next week.'

'How exciting,' Candy said. 'Is it a big wedding?'

'Huge!' Mr Heath nodded. 'She's marrying an Ital...' His voice trailed off.

'Don't stop on my account.' Candy grinned. 'I know what Italian weddings can be like. I must be the only girl in the world who's dreaded her wedding day since she was little rather than dreamt of it.'

Mr Heath laughed. 'Will it be big?'

'You have no idea,' Candy said. 'I have four older brothers, all married, and my mother is itching for it to be my turn. She buys sheets and towels for me when she shops—oh, and washing baskets and the like. I'm all set up!' Candy smiled. 'Apart from the groom.'

It was, in fact, a very friendly ward and the staff didn't

mind that Candy had a few questions every now and then. But as she went to do Macey's medications, Candy frowned and looked around for Abigail, but she was in with Mrs Douglas, who was very sick indeed.

'Problem?' Steele had come onto the ward and was writing up some medication for a patient who wasn't Candy's.

'No, I just want to check something,' Candy said, taking the prescription chart over to him. 'Macey's written up for sherry, but she's on a lot of other medication.'

'No doubt she'll be having the sherry when she gets home,' Steele pointed out. 'Though I don't think you have to worry about it tonight—she's not having her sherry at the moment. She's not really having much of anything.'

He was right. Candy was shocked at the change in Macey. She'd been a fierce, proud woman when she had arrived in the emergency department but now she just lay on her side and stared into space. She didn't say anything when Candy introduced herself and her arm was listless when Candy checked her blood pressure.

'I've got your tablets for you, Macey,' Candy explained, and she helped her to sit up to take them. The old lady took her tablets without a word of protest and then tried to take the water Candy offered, but her hands were shaking terribly so Candy held the glass and helped her take a drink to wash them down. 'Sorry, Macey, but can you lift your tongue for me?'

She lifted her tongue and, yes, she had swallowed all the tablets rather than hiding them. Then she lay back down on the pillow.

'Can I get you anything else?' Candy offered. 'A drink?'

Macey gave a small shake of her head and Candy

looked at the fluid balance and food charts. She was on an IV, and that was, apart from the water she took with her medicines, practically all that Macey was having at the moment.

'Macey,' Candy suggested as she put another blanket on and turned her pillows, 'why don't I get you some milk?'

Her lethargy was troubling. Candy would far prefer her to be shouting at her and telling her that she wasn't a nurse's bootlace.

'Some warm milk,' Candy elaborated. 'I know your hands are a bit shaky at the moment but I can help you to drink it. Will you have some milk?'

Macey didn't say yes but at least she didn't shake her head this time.

Steele looked over and saw Candy hovering, sorting out pillows and blankets on Macey's bed. He half expected Macey to shout for her to get off as she had done when she'd been with the other nurse that afternoon, but he was pleased to see that tonight Macey didn't seem to mind the small attention.

Steele liked Candy, which had certainly come as a surprise to him.

The attraction had been instant, yet Candy was nothing like the women Steele usually dated.

Oh, he dated.

A lot.

Steele went for sophisticated women. He liked women who understood right from the start that this could only ever be a fleeting thing for he was never anywhere long. Six months here, two years there and now just six weeks here.

Steele glanced at the date. He had been here almost a week, so make that five weeks he had left at the Royal.

And Candy was away for the final two of them.

Steele had already done the marriage-and-settle-down thing and it hadn't worked.

Or rather, it had worked, possibly more than he had realised, because ten years on his ex-wife, completely out of the blue, had rung him. Her second marriage had failed and she had suggested that they give it another go. Even before Steele could answer her and say he had never heard a more ridiculous suggestion in his life she had added her little postscript—there was one proviso to them getting back together.

There had been a lot of advances in technology after all.

Ten years on the hurt was there and she had just hit it with a sledgehammer again. His one raw nerve, the one chink in his confident persona, had been exposed again. Steele had promptly hung up on her without response because otherwise he might well have exploded and told her exactly the words that were in his head.

They weren't pretty.

For Steele, finding out that he was infertile had been a huge blow. His wife's response to the news had been devastating.

He made sure now he was never in a position to reveal that part of himself again. He kept things light; he kept things intimate sexually rather than emotionally.

Then he moved on.

Candy walked past just then, carrying a feeding cup, and she went over and helped Macey to sit up.

Candy didn't say anything; she just gave Macey a smile as the elderly lady took sips of the milky drink. That was all Macey wanted for now: no conversation, just a warm drink and the comfort of companionable silence.

Candy was fine with that—she was used to it, in fact.

When she'd been ten, her *nonna* had come to live with them. Candy's job in the morning had been to make sure Nonna got her *biscotti* and milky coffee and then to see her to the bathroom and make up her bed. Candy had loved the mornings—the chatty ones when Nonna had told her all about the village that she had grown up in. The reminiscent ones when Nonna had spoken about falling in love and the parties and dancing. The sad ones—leaving Italy and the death of her husband, Candy's *nonno*. Candy had been comfortable too with the silent mornings, when Nonna had just eaten quietly, lost in a world of her own, as Macey was now.

'Do you want a bedpan?' Candy offered Macey when the milk was gone.

'I'll go…' Macey sighed and pulled back the bed covers.

Glad to see that she was making the effort to get out of bed, Candy helped her with her slippers and got Macey her walking frame and they walked over to the bathroom.

Candy waited outside and when Macey came to wash her hands Candy sorted the taps and squeezed the soap for her. Macey washed her hands very thoroughly. Her nail varnish was chipped and Candy watched her examine her nails for a moment, clearly less than impressed with the state of her hands.

'I'll sort your nails out for you on Sunday,' Candy offered, and then took Macey back to her bedside, where she asked her to sit for a moment. 'Sit there and let me make it up all nice and fresh for you to get into.'

Candy made the bed so nicely that she wanted to climb in it herself. 'You'd better get in quickly or I will.'

'You look tired,' Macey said, and Candy smiled at the first invitation to conversation.

'I am, though I shouldn't be,' Candy said. 'I slept all afternoon.'

She got the older woman into bed, put up the bed rails and tied the call bell to the side. 'Press it if you need anything,' Candy said. 'I hope you have a lovely sleep.'

Candy sorted out her other patients and, by one a.m., when Abigail asked if she'd mind taking the first break, Candy was more than ready for an hour to rest. It would seem she wasn't the only one who needed a doze, because when she walked into the break room there was Steele, asleep on a sofa with the television on in the background.

'Aloha,' he said sleepily, when Candy disturbed him as she took a seat.

'Aloha.' Candy smiled. 'How come you're still here?'

'I'm waiting for some relatives to come in for Mrs Douglas.'

Candy remembered from handover that Mrs Douglas wasn't expected to make it through the night.

'How long is it now till your holiday?' Steele asked.

'Three weeks,' Candy said, and set her phone alarm for an hour's time. She saw the date and that it was now Saturday morning. 'Actually, just under three weeks. I fly on a Friday night.'

'Are you working right up till then?'

Candy nodded and then yawned at the very thought. 'I almost go from here to the airport.'

'Is it just you going?'

'Yep.'

'I thought Hawaii was more a couples' destination,' Steele said, fishing shamelessly.

'I think you may be right but I saw an advert and I

couldn't resist,' Candy admitted and nodded to the television, where an infomercial for knives was showing. 'It was a limited offer, with a huge discount for the first ten to call… I fall for it every time'

'Yep.' Steele nodded. 'And me. I bought the juicer, the chopper and some blender thing until I finally worked out that nothing is going to make me like vegetables.'

'It's one of the perils of working nights,' Candy agreed. 'What looks appealing at two a.m. seems stupid when the parcel arrives. Anyway, I saw the advert for the holiday when I was feeling particularly miserable. It looked absolutely beautiful and I really needed to get away…'

'How come?'

'Lots of things really.'

'Such as?'

Candy hesitated. She hadn't really spoken to anyone about the fact she was considering leaving. She glanced at Steele and realised that by the time she got back from Hawaii he'd be gone, so it really made no difference. 'I'm not sure if I still want to work in Emergency.'

'It must be a pretty stressful job.'

'It is at times.' Candy nodded. 'Though it's not just that. I made a mistake couple of months back.' She didn't elaborate; instead, she lay down on the sofa, determined to squeeze in some sleep during her break.

'A professional mistake?' Steele probed, and Candy let out a small laugh at his very direct question.

'No, it was a personal one.'

'Do tell.'

'No way.'

'So there are two things I have to find out about you now,' Steele teased. 'The story behind your name and the mistake that Nurse Candy made.'

'You can try, but it won't get you anywhere,' Candy said, and closed her eyes. 'I'm going to have a little rest.'

'Hopefully you talk in your sleep.'

She smiled with her eyes closed and was mildly surprised when after a moment or so Steele continued to speak.

'We all make mistakes, Candy,' he said. His lovely deep voice was soothing and broke into her semi-doze. 'If I've learnt one thing in this job, it's that everyone makes so-called mistakes and also that everyone wastes way too much time regretting them.'

She opened her eyes and looked at him. 'You really do like your job,' Candy said, and it wasn't a question, more an observation, and Steele nodded.

'I really do.'

Yes, she should sleep and her aching body might regret it later but she chose to forgo the full hour of sleep just to find out a little more about him. She lay there and peeked over to Steele, who was still looking at her.

'Did you always want to work in geriatrics?'

'Not really,' Steele said. 'It sort of found me, I guess. I was pretty much raised by my grandmother...'

'Are your parents...?' Her voice trailed off and Steele grinned.

'They're not dead.'

'Good.'

'My parents are both doctors and were very serious about their careers. I was a late accident. I don't think they ever really wanted to have children. My mother was a top thoracic surgeon—which means she had balls.'

Candy laughed.

'My grandmother looked after me till I went to boarding school and in the holidays I stayed with her.' He saw her frown. 'My parents are good people. They were just very, very focused. Anyway, when I went to my grandmother's for Easter one year, she was very confused. Just completely off the wall. I rang my mother and she pretty much would have had her shipped off to a nursing home that day.'

'Really?' Candy said.

'Really!' Steele nodded. 'But the GP came and it turned out all she had was a urine infection. He explained the confusion it could cause in the elderly. Anyway, two days later she was completely back to herself. It just stayed with me, I guess.'

'My *nonna* lived with us.' Candy yawned. 'I think my mother thinks she'll be living with me...'

'Did your mother work?' Steele asked, and Candy shook her head. 'You do, though. You have a career.'

Candy looked at him. Right there, right then, she felt as if he knew the wrestle in her heart because though she loved her parents they clashed a lot as Candy struggled to be independent when they didn't want her to be. 'I do have a career,' Candy said, 'and I had to fight to have one.'

'Have your rest.' He smiled and Candy nodded.

She'd had to fight to simply be here, Candy thought as she closed her eyes. Her parents had wanted her to marry Franco, and for her to work in the family business. They hadn't understood that she'd wanted to study to become a nurse.

Candy fell asleep but it felt about twenty seconds later that her phone bleeped and told her that her hour was up and it was time to go back to work. The staffroom was empty and when she went round to the ward Steele wasn't there either.

She liked him.

Candy knew it properly then because she preferred the feel on the ward when he was around.

The rest of the night flew past quickly. Candy helped out with Mrs Douglas while Abigail took her break and then it was time to start her morning routine. At seven-thirty, after handover, Candy said goodbye to her patients and told Macey that she would be in tomorrow morning and, if Macey liked and Candy had time, then she would do her nails.

Macey said nothing.

As Candy walked along the main entrance corridor she saw Steele on his way into work. His hair was damp from his morning shower and he was wearing a dark grey suit and fresh shirt, though he hadn't yet done up his tie. He was standing looking at one of the pictures that lined the corridor, images of the hospital and the changes over the years. Renovations were taking place throughout the Royal.

'What are you looking at?' she asked.

'Come and see,' Steele invited, and as she stood beside him he started to do up his tie. 'Do you recognise anyone?'

Candy peered at the image that he had been focused on. It was a group of nurses and doctors standing in the gardens at the rear of the hospital. It looked like a presentation had just taken place as some of the nurses were sporting medals. Candy smiled when she saw the long dresses and aprons that the nurses were wearing as well as their hats and capes. Then she saw just who it was that Steele was looking at. 'Oh, my goodness, it's Macey.'

'It is indeed.'

She had the same wild curly hair, though it was tamed

by a frilly white cap. Her cheekbones were high and her lips, though smiling, looked a touch strained. Her cape was around her shoulders and Candy smiled at the red cross that it made on her chest.

She looked incredibly young but certainly it was Macey.

'Do you think she'll come out of her depression?' Candy asked.

'Now I do.'

'What do you mean?'

But Steele didn't answer her directly. 'You were very good with her last night. I'm glad she had a drink and got up to the bathroom. How was she this morning?'

'Still very quiet, but she had another drink and I made her *biscotti*, which she ate.'

'*Biscotti?*'

'Biscuits in warm milk, all mashed in.' Candy smiled and then groaned as her stomach rumbled just at the thought. 'Now I've gone and made myself hungry, I'll have to have some when I get home.'

'Did you feed her?'

'I did.' Candy nodded. 'She's very shaky.'

'It's all the new medications,' Steele said, 'and a lack of sherry, but it should soon start to settle down.'

'How did you know that she was drinking?'

'Because drinking is incredibly common in the elderly. Far more than people realise. It's not all bad.' Steele smiled. 'Macey can't ask her niece to get her four bottles of sherry a week, or however much it is that she actually drinks. At least it keeps her walking to the shops each day. I admit that I worry what will happen when my oldies all discover online shopping.'

Candy realised she was doing her dental commercial smile at him again.

He made her smile.

'I'm going home.' Candy hitched up her bag. 'I'll say goodnight because it's night-time to me.'

'Have a good sleep,' Steele said, 'and don't talk too much.'

'I *don't* talk in my sleep.' She smiled back at him. 'At least, I don't think I do.'

As she walked off his deep voice caused her shoulders to stiffen.

'Make that three things that I have to find out about you.'

Oh, my God, Candy realised.

They *were* flirting.

More than that, she was considering revising her recently put in place rule—to never again get involved with someone at work.

He was *that* good.

CHAPTER FOUR

'CAN I HAVE a hand to turn Mr Worthington, please?' Candy asked Elaine the following morning.

She had slept all of Saturday and had then got up for dinner and gone out for a couple of hours with Kelly, only to be in bed by ten and asleep again in a matter of moments.

And she was *still* tired.

Elaine was very brusque and efficient and they soon had Mr Worthington turned. 'Why isn't his radio on?' Elaine asked, turning it on. 'Toby likes to have his radio on, especially on a Sunday morning. I wrote it down in his care plan.'

'Sorry,' Candy muttered as Elaine marched out.

As bossy as she was, though, Elaine's heart really was in the right place because Toby started humming a little as Candy shaved him and all too soon she found herself singing along to the Sunday morning hymns. It made Toby smile and his eyes encouraged her and he even started singing along to some of the choruses, which only made Candy sing louder.

'Mr Worthington!' Gloria popped her head in. 'Your family are here to see you.' She smiled at Candy. 'They'll be pleased to see him looking so cheerful. Steele was just having a word with them.'

Candy quickly tidied up the room and moved the trolley out of the way as Toby's family thanked Steele and then smiled at Candy as they made their way in.

'Did you enjoy your little singalong?' Steele asked when she came out.

'Actually, I did,' she said, 'although I'm not sure quite what Toby would have to say about it if he was able to talk.'

'Oh, I'm sure that, with the amount of morphine he's on, your voice sounded pretty fantastic.'

'Are you telling me that I'm tone deaf?'

'Ooh, just a touch,' Steele teased, but it didn't faze Candy.

'I'm going to sing louder next time.'

They would have chatted for longer but Matron Elaine was back and ready to move things along. 'Come on, Candy, we're falling behind. I'll help you with Macey.'

Candy would really prefer that she didn't.

'Have fun!' Steele said as Candy rolled her eyes.

The strangest thing was, though, that Candy did enjoy herself.

In fact, she had more fun then she'd had in a long time and so did Macey!

'Good morning, Macey.' Candy smiled as she pulled the curtains around the bed. 'Would you like to have a shower?'

Macey gave a slow shake of her head.

'Well, Elaine and I will give you a wash in bed, if that's okay, and we'll give you some nice fresh sheets and things. Then I'll do your leg dressing.'

'I'll do Macey's leg dressing,' Elaine said. 'I need to practice my aseptic technique.'

'Sure,' Candy agreed, and then spoke to Macey. 'Would you like me to wash your hair? We can do it in bed. I just need to take the bedhead off. It might make you feel a little bit better,' Candy pushed gently, but again Macey shook her head.

Elaine had everything set up on the trolley to wash Macey and she was busy collecting sheets and pillow-cases for the bed change as Candy washed Macey's face. She then offered her the cloth to wash her hands but Macey didn't take it so Candy washed Macey's hands in the bowl. 'I'll take that nail varnish off in a little while and do your nails.'

'There isn't time to do nails,' Elaine said as she re-turned.

'I'll do it on my coffee break,' Candy said as they turned Macey and washed her back. Elaine was start-ing to seriously get on her nerves. 'I like painting nails.'

Delightfully, though, as Macey was turned back from her side she caught Candy's eye and gave her a tiny wink. This showed Candy she was coming back to the world and that Macey understood how difficult Elaine might be to work with.

She returned the wink and soaped up the cloth again.

'Would you like to wash yourself down there?' Candy offered, so that Macey could wash her private parts her-self, but both Candy and Macey blinked at the same time when a loud voice interrupted them.

'No!' Elaine said. 'We do not speak down to our pa-tients. You are to call it by its proper name.'

Candy shared a brief *yikes* look with Macey.

'I apologise, Macey,' she said, looking into Macey's

eyes as they both tried to fathom what it was that she was supposed to say.

'Would you like to wash your private parts?' Candy offered and saw Macey's lips start to twitch into a smile, especially when Elaine chimed up again.

'No!' she said. 'You're to call it by its proper name.'

Given that Candy was the qualified nurse, she could have told Elaine to simply be quiet, but there was a glimmer in Macey's eyes that hadn't been there for a long time and, Candy guessed as they shared a smile, she was more than happy for the exchange to continue.

Macey presumably had a nurse's sense of humour after all.

'I'm sorry, Macey,' Candy said again as she stretched her brain as to what she should say. She rinsed out the cloth again and then mouthed to Macey, 'What do I say?'

Macey offered a tiny shrug.

Was she supposed to ask if she wanted to wash her vagina? 'Macey,' Candy said, and cleared her throat. They stared seriously at each other, though they were both laughing on the inside. Each knew the other's thoughts. 'Would you like to wash your genitals?'

'No!' Elaine, clearly incensed by Candy's apparent ineptitude, took the cloth from Candy. 'This is how you do it,' Elaine said, and soaped up the cloth again. 'Macey,' she said, holding out the cloth, 'would you like to wash your muffy?'

Macey and Candy cried from laughing.

Not in front of Elaine, of course, but as Elaine went to set up for the leg dressing Candy had to wipe the tears from Macey's eyes as they tried to keep their laughter quiet.

They clearly didn't succeed because Steele popped his head in.

'Did Elaine do her muffy thing again?' he asked.

'She did.' Candy grinned. 'Has she done it before, then?'

Steele nodded. 'Somebody has to tell her that that's not the technical name for it.' Steele grinned. 'Please, God, it's not me.'

'She'll be a wonderful nurse,' Macey said, still smiling. 'At least she's thorough.'

Candy was told to go for her coffee break and so she made a mug of coffee and put it beside Macey's bed, ready to set to work on her nails.

'Have your break,' Macey said.

'I honestly like painting nails,' Candy said. 'I do my mum's every week and I just wish I had four sisters instead of four brothers. It really does relax me.'

She held up a bottle of coral nail polish. 'Is that colour okay?'

Macey gave a small nod.

Macey sat quietly as Candy set to work. Candy didn't chat very much because she really was concentrating. There was something so soothing about painting nails that she truly did enjoy doing it. The immediate improvement was instantly gratifying and having nice nails was also a very easy lift to the sprits.

'Four brothers?' Macey said suddenly.

'And then came a daughter.' Candy gave a wry smile.

'Are they very strict?'

'They are but they're also very lovely. I know that I really have nothing to complain about, but...' Candy shook her head. 'I'm still plucking up the courage to tell them that I've booked a holiday to Hawaii. They're not going to be pleased.'

'Why?' Macey asked. 'Because you're going with your boyfriend?'

'I don't have a boyfriend,' Candy said, taking Macey's other hand and starting to work on those nails. 'That won't appease them, though…me in America on my own…'

Macey looked across the ward and saw that Steele was looking towards them, or rather at Candy. When he realised that she was watching him he gave her a very brief smile and then looked away.

She might not say much but Macey knew everything that went on in the ward.

'There,' Candy said, finishing off and admiring her handiwork. 'Let them dry for a little while before you do anything.'

'No washing my muffy for the next half-hour, then,' Macey joked and smiled at Candy as she rested her head back on the pillow. 'Thank you, my dear.'

As she went to take her mug through to the kitchen Candy passed Steele. 'What time do you finish?' he asked.

'Eleven-thirty,' Candy said.

'Do you want to get lunch?'

He'd completely sideswiped her but, then, Candy thought, he had been doing that since the moment she'd clapped eyes on him. 'The canteen?' she suggested.

'If you like but I think we can do better than the canteen.'

Oh!

Did she want to have lunch with the sexiest man she had ever met? There really wasn't an awful lot to think about.

'Yes,' Candy said, 'that sounds great.'

'Good.'

'But aren't you on call?'

'My registrar can earn his keep for a couple of hours,' Steele said.

Wow.

There really was no messing with Steele; she had never really known anyone as direct as him before.

'Anyway,' Steele added, 'I've got a few questions that I'd like to know the answers to.'

'Question one,' Steele said as they sat in a very nice café that was just a short drive from the hospital. 'I want to know about your name—Candy?'

'You'll never know,' Candy said as she looked through the menu. 'It's the reason I'm never getting married. It's the reason I'm going on holiday alone. No one is allowed to see my passport!'

'I'm determined to find out.'

'You can be as determined as you like.' She smiled. 'It doesn't mean that you'll get anywhere, though.'

'What do you want to eat?' Steele asked.

'I would like…' She looked through the menu. What would she like? 'I fancy a roast.'

'Have a roast, then.'

'I shall.' Candy nodded. 'A Sunday roast is exotic to me. It was pasta and pasta and more pasta when I was growing up.'

'Well, I'll have the pasta, then.' He smiled, glad to be out with someone who seemed to enjoy their food. 'That's exotic to me.'

'Please.' Candy rolled her eyes.

'Okay, second question—what was the mistake?'

Candy let out a breath; if this was leading anywhere,

and it felt as if it was, then possibly she ought to tell him. Or possibly not, given that Steele would be long since gone by the time Gerry returned from Greece.

It wasn't just a question of that, though. She liked Steele's eyes, she liked his smile, she liked that she felt she could be honest with him. It would be such a relief to share what had been eating her up for these past couple of months.

'Have you ever slept with an ex?' Candy asked, quite sure, as she did so, that she was blushing from the roots of her hair to the tips of her toes.

'Doesn't everyone sleep with their exes?' Steele checked. He was so at ease with it all that she let out a breath that she felt as though she'd been holding in since it had happened.

'Well, I've only had two exes, and I only made that mistake with one of them.'

'Actually,' Steele added, 'I've never slept with my ex-wife. I knew from the day we broke up that we were done.'

He saw her swallow. And swallow Candy did—she had certainly thought him worldlier than her and that he had been married and divorced confirmed it.

'You sound bitter,' she said, and was somewhat surprised when he didn't deny that he was.

'I am a bit when I think about it, which I don't often do.' He smiled. 'She rang a few weeks ago and asked if we might consider getting back together. I long ago decided that I would never settle down with anyone again.'

He didn't reveal the initial reason for their break-up. There was no point. There was no need for in-depth explanations about his infertility, given that he wasn't going to be hanging around in any one place or in anyone's space for too long.

Though perhaps he needed to make that a little clearer to Candy, he realised. She was seriously gorgeous. The attraction had been instant for both of them, of that there was no doubt, but she was several years younger than him and a lot less jaded and he did not want to cause hurt.

'So you slept with your ex?' Steele checked, and she gave a glum nod.

'Do you know Gerry?' Candy asked. 'One of the head nurses in the emergency department.'

'I've never met him,' Steele said. 'But I heard a bit about him when I was looking into the waiting times in Emergency. He's an arrogant jerk apparently.'

'That's Gerry!' Candy rolled her eyes. 'He didn't used to be. He got beaten up by two patients a few months ago and it seems to have changed him.'

'He's the one currently in Greece?' Steele checked. 'The one who wrote "Glad you're not here" on his post-card?'

'That's the one.' Candy nodded. 'When I first moved out of home last year we went out, though not for very long.'

'You only moved out last year?'

'Believe me, twenty-four years of age is way too early in my family, unless it's to get married. I should only have moved out to marry the boyfriend they had sort of pressed onto me... Instead, I dumped him and rented a flat.'

'That would have been tough,' Steele commented.

'Yes, it caused a lot of arguments with my parents and I mean a *lot*, but in the end it was far easier to do that than marry someone just because my parents considered him suitable. Anyway, Gerry helped me a bit with the move, given that my parents were sulking. We went out for a while, like I said, but pretty quickly I ended it. That was last year but he's been having a few problems of late. He asked if we could go out for a drink a couple of months ago…' Candy gave an uncomfortable shrug.

'One thing led to another?' Steele checked, and she nodded.

'It was a complete mistake on my part—he thought that signalled we were back together and he wasn't best pleased to find out we're not. Since then he's been making things difficult for me at work. No one knows that we slept together again, thank God.' She looked at Steele, surprised she could meet his eyes after her big revelation. 'It should serve as a reminder—never get involved with anyone from work.'

'Too late,' Steele said. 'I think we both know we're heading for bed—guilt free.'

He liked it that she blushed and he liked it even more that she didn't disagree with him. Now was the time to make it clear that, though this could be incredibly pleasant, there was no question of it lasting for very long.

'I can assure you that I won't turn into a monster when we're over,' Steele said, not very gently spelling it out for her. 'I have very many exes who will tell you the same.'

Candy sat there as a delectable plate of roast beef, with all the trimmings, was placed in front of her. She was glad of the chance to think over his words rather than react immediately to them as she smiled and thanked the waitress. Steele was sitting there basically telling her that he was a playboy and warning her that before they started they had a use-by date hanging over them.

The strange thing for Candy was that she didn't mind. His openness was, in fact, refreshing. She was tired of games, tired of pretending she was enjoying herself. Tired of simply going along for the sake of going along. Gerry had got way too serious too soon, and Franco had been happy to marry her before they'd had so much as a coffee. She had been brought up with the expectation that any man she dated was a potential husband and had to somehow be a suitable provider. It drove Candy insane. She wanted to be twenty-four, she wanted to have fun, and with Steele she could. With him it was different—there were no games, just pleasure to be had with no expectation or end aim. There was something so unique about him, something that said she *deserved* to have sex with him at least once in her lifetime.

'What are you smiling at?'

'My thoughts,' Candy said. 'And they're not for sharing.'

'Would your parents be disappointed in you if they knew what they were?'

'Very.' She smiled.

'Good.'

'So you're here for six weeks?' Candy checked.

'Five now,' Steele said, 'and the last two of them without you, given that you'll be off on your holiday.'

Getting over you, she thought.

But, oh, at least she'd get to be under him.

That was the only sex Candy knew.

'Then where will you be living?' she asked.

'Kent,' Steele said. 'It's an amazing opportunity. I'm overseeing a complete overhaul of their geriatric department. I'm implementing an acute geriatric unit, where all medical patients will be admitted first.'

He had such energy for his job. Candy could hear it in every word he spoke. They had the loveliest lunch, chatting about work, about them, oh, about lots of things, but then Steele said he had to get back.

'I'm speaking with Macey's nieces at two. I'll give you a lift home…'

'I don't need a lift,' Candy said. 'I'm only two stops away.'

'You're sure?'

'Very.'

'So how will I know where you live when I come over to take you out tonight?'

'Where are you taking me?' Candy smiled.

'I haven't decided.' Out on the street he took her wrist and turned her to face him. 'Where would you like to go?'

Bed, she wanted to answer, when she had never felt or given that answer before. 'I'll leave it up to you. Though I warn you, I'm pretty wrecked. Night duty hasn't left me at my most sparkling.' She told him her address and he tapped it into his phone. 'I'll see you tonight about seven?'

'Sounds good.'

It was the middle of the day, there were people everywhere and yet when he took her in his arms it could have been the end of the most romantic night.

'Thanks for coming to lunch.'

'Thanks for asking me.'

It was a very new thing to her, to be somewhere simply because she wanted to be. It should be wrong, except it felt completely right. He was older, wiser and sexier than she had ever dealt with and she was more turned on than she had ever been in her life, and he hadn't even kissed her.

That was about to be corrected, though. Her heart was galloping even more than it had the first day they'd met. Right now it was almost leaping out of her throat in anticipation. An anticipation she had never known because when their lips met it seemed to set off a chain reaction. *This is what a mouth should feel like*, Candy thought, and *This is what a tongue was surely designed for*, she decided as his stroked hers.

Yes, there was a building anticipation because when first his body melded with hers Candy couldn't help but wonder what it would feel like if his hand moved a little higher, or how it would be if she moved in a little closer. Each question was answered—the sound of the traffic dimmed as their kiss intensified. She had never been kissed expertly before and his hand moved just a little higher than her waist to the edge of her rib cage and she ached for it to move higher still. His mouth, the pressure of his lips, the constant beckon of his tongue made her move in closer and she felt breathless.

Both rested their foreheads on the other's for a moment. Trust time to make things complicated, because if it had been nearly two a.m. they would be racing home right about now.

It was daylight, people were talking, a lazy Sunday afternoon was going on all around as they pulled back and met each other's eyes.

'Tonight' was the unspoken word between them.

Candy had never really looked forward to the night in that way before.

'I'm going to be late for my meeting,' Steele said as she got back to his mouth.

'You can be two minutes late,' she said.

She just needed one more taste.

CHAPTER FIVE

THANK GOD THAT she'd just had her period.

It had used to be Candy's excuse not to have sex, but as she had a lovely long bath and shaved and plucked and buffed her body into suitable Steele shape, she was grateful for that fact.

Yes, her Catholic guilt was hovering there in the background but she told it to please be quiet as she took her Pill.

She still hid them in her handbag. It was a matter of habit and her mother would freak, just completely freak, if she knew that Candy was on it. She'd come off it last year but, given what had happened with Gerry, she had gone back on it. She and Gerry had used condoms but what had happened had been such a surprise that she did not want to take any risks.

She hadn't gone home after lunch with Steele; instead, she'd dashed to the shops and bought fabulous underwear that she was now tearing the labels off. There was a silver-grey bra that gave her the best cleavage ever and silver panties that made her dimply bottom look fantastic. In fact, she was so impressed with them that Candy had bought a set in purple also.

She'd always felt fat, but she felt curvy now.

I'll regret it later, she promised her conscience as she looked in the mirror.

Just not yet!

With no idea where they were going Candy decided on a pale shift dress that would look casual with ballet pumps or fab with heels.

It didn't work with her new bra, though.

Second go.

A grey wraparound dress worked better, though showed a little more cleavage than her parents would consider suitable.

Perfect!

Not big on make-up, Candy put on some mascara and a slick of lipstick and when there was a knock at the door she was nervous, but nicely so.

'You're no help,' Candy said as she let him in and he handed her a bottle of wine. Steele was wearing black jeans and a black shirt. He looked incredibly handsome and had that air about him that meant he was suitably dressed for any venue.

'Meaning?' Steele asked.

'I was trying to decide whether to wear flats or heels given that I don't know where we're going.'

'We're going to the movies,' Steele said. 'I figured it might be nice if you're tired—though we shan't be making out in the back row. I like watching a film properly.'

'What are we going to see?' she asked. The movies was possibly the nicest place he could take her if they *had* to go out. It would be nice to turn her brain off for a couple of hours.

'Two choices,' he said. 'One is very dark, apparently funny in part. One is very sad… See what mood you're in.'

'I don't mind,' she said as she led him through her lounge and put the wine down on the bench of a very small kitchen.

'So this is what all the arguments with your parents were about?' Steele said, looking around the living room of her small but cosy flat. The front door opened to the living room. Off that was a small kitchen and to the side a hall that led to the bathroom and bedroom. 'It's nice.'

'I love it,' Candy said. 'It's a ten-minute walk to the Underground, a five-minute walk to my favourite Indian restaurant.

'We can eat before or after...' Steele said.

The thought of Indian before sounded too good to pass up, but then other senses were calling, the attraction wafting between them as potent as any delicious aroma from food.

Candy knew she was eons behind him sexually. She wanted to have slept with him, in part to have jumped that hurdle without knocking it over, in part just to dive onto the track...

And Candy usually hated even the thought of sport, but, oh, he was handsome.

And he was here.

'Do you want a glass of wine?' she offered, even though he'd brought it, but Steele shook his head.

'Not for me,' he said. 'I'm driving. You have one, though...' He went to open the bottle he'd brought but she stopped him.

'Not for me.' Candy shook her head. 'I don't really drink and anyway I'm on early tomorrow. I'll just get my shoes.'

She went to her bedroom and put on flats but as she came out Steele frowned.

'What happened to the heels?'

'For the movies?'

'For me.'

She smiled and went and put on said heels, with Steele watching her from the doorway.

He made her shiver. If Gerry had stood watching her she'd have found it invasive, but with Steele she just wanted to strip off her dress, pull back the covers on the bed and climb in.

She could feel his eyes on her calf muscles and then on her bum and she turned and it was nice to feel provocative. It was something she had never felt before. He made her feel like this.

And he made her want to kiss him.

It was as simple as that, as natural as breathing to stand in the doorway of her bedroom and wrap her hands behind his neck and share a kiss for no other reason than they both wanted to. She didn't feel naïve or inexperienced with him. There wasn't enough space in her mind for those sorts of thoughts because it was filled instead with pleasurable ones as they got back to where they'd been on the street in record time.

Steele's hand did move higher than the base of her rib cage this time. He was stroking the underside of her breast as they kissed, and her nipples hardened and ached for his fingers to attend to them. She had one hand at the back of his head, just to feel his silky hair, not for pressure for there was plenty of that from Steele, and she had the other on his bum. His buttocks were taut and she checked again. Yes, they were still taut and it was that hand that demanded he press into her.

His moan to her mouth as he did so, his hand at the

tie of her dress, told Candy there was no way they would be making the movie.

It was evening, not even semi-dark, and that was seriously uncharted territory for her. End-of-evening sex was all she was used to.

But this wasn't, oh, okay, then, it had been a week after all. This was, let me get this shirt open and this zipper down because I need you to take me now.

Her dress was open, his shirt too, and his fingers were at the back of her bra, ready to undo it, and Candy could barely breathe at the thought of their naked chests pressed together and his hot hands roaming her. She'd never had sex standing, never considered it, because she wasn't the tall, leggy version that a good Candy should be. She was a shorter, chunkier one, who any second now was going to scale Steele's body with the grace of a feline. It was that essential, that natural, that...

'Ignore it...' Steele said as there was a loud rap on the door.

'No...' She could barely breathe now but for a different reason. It was her father's very loud knock and she froze for a second.

'It's my parents.'

'Just ignore it,' he said again.

'They'll let themselves in.'

That her parents had a key came a close second to a bucket of water—actually, it beat the bucket of water because Steele was dressing her and himself with his hands as Candy stood there.

Then he chose to concentrate solely on her for now.

He did up her dress, a little loosely, and wiped off some lipstick and wished the flush on her cheeks would fade by the time she got to the front door. She looked as if she'd just come, or had just been about to. Her nipples were like the dials on his washing machine. Even her lips were swollen.

'Breathe,' Steele said.

'If they find you here…' Candy shivered as he knelt down and changed her heels to flats as there was another knock on the door.

'Will they have us married?'

'You have no idea.'

'Where do you want me?' Steele smiled.

'On my bed.'

'That's what I like to hear,' Steele said, then stopped joking. 'Are they likely to come in here?'

'I hope not.' Candy let out a breath. 'Probably not.'

'Relax,' he said as she closed the bedroom door on him and went to greet her parents. He checked under her bed and he could possibly fit there but first he smiled as he saw the scissors and labels from her brand-new underwear.

She was seriously gorgeous, Steele thought as he did up his shirt and wiped lipstick off. He was unused to thinking *seriously* anything about his dates yet she was so lovely, so focused on fighting for her independence and living her life and yet so kind.

Actually, right now, as Candy opened the front door all she was was stressed!

There were her parents buckling under the weight of jars filled with home-made tomato sauce.

'I said I'd pick them up next week,' she said.

'Why are you all dressed up?' her mother asked, instantly accusing.

'Because I'm just about to go out,'

'You need to wear a top under that dress!' Her mother warned.

They walked through and put the jars of tomato sauce on the bench and Candy got out the coffee machine. There was no such thing as her parents coming over and them not having a coffee, though her father's eyes lit up like a Christmas tree when he saw the bottle of wine on the bench and Candy poured him a glass.

'Where are you going tonight?' her father asked.

'To the movies with a friend.'

'What friend?' her mother checked.

'Kelly.' Candy glanced at the clock. 'Ma, I really do need to get going soon.'

'We've barely seen you these last few weeks.'

They chatted in Italian for twenty minutes or so. Candy had promised herself that the next time she saw them she'd tell them about her trip to Hawaii, but with Steele hiding in the bedroom she chose not to. It was not a conversation that would take twenty minutes—it would be an entire evening of tears and threats and shouting.

Her dad's wineglass was empty, her mum's coffee was gone and though they looked settled in for the evening and her father would no doubt love another glass of wine, Candy stood. 'I'm already late for Kelly,' she said. 'I really am going to have to get ready.'

She felt guilty kicking them out, and then cross that she'd had to. Couldn't they simply ring before they dropped around?

They'd be offended if she asked them to.

Talk about kill the mood, she thought once they had gone and she headed to her bedroom. Steele was lying on her bed, his legs crossed and reading her book.

'I'm so sorry about that,' she said.

'Why?' Steele shrugged. 'Your parents dropped around. It's no big deal.' He smiled at her as she came and sat on the bed beside him. 'I understand, though, that it would be a big deal if they found me here.'

'Thanks.' Candy smiled.

'Do they drop around a lot?'

'They do,' she said. 'They don't drive and, as a sweetener, when I moved out I said I was only moving nearby, which was a big mistake.' She let out a long sigh. 'Another one. I seem to be making rather a lot of them lately. Have I made us late for the movies?'

'I haven't even got the tickets,' he said. 'I didn't know if you'd like the idea.'

'I do,' Candy said, 'I haven't been in ages.'

'I go all the time,' he said. 'Well, not all the time, but I guess going to the movies, for me, is like reading a book is to you. I usually go on my own,' Steele said. It had surprised him that he'd considered taking Candy along. He really did prefer his own company when watching a film.

'How come you go alone?' she asked, gently poking him in the ribs as he lay there. 'Don't you have any friends?'

'I have a lot of friends but not any I'd want to go to the movies with. You should try going by yourself,' he said. 'I loathe trying to concentrate while getting the *What the hell did you bring me to this for?* vibe coming from my right or left.'

Candy started to laugh. 'I get that with my friend Kelly.' She told him about the time she'd suggested to Kelly that they see what Candy had thought was a romance and he laughed as she described Kelly's reaction as she'd sat beside her, watching someone being tied to the bed.

'She said I was never allowed to choose the movie again,' Candy said, and then she looked down and saw that her hands were now on his chest and fiddling with his buttons and that his hands were playing with her hair. It was as if their bodies were having a little conversation of their own as they carried on talking.

His hand pressed the back of her head a little and she started to kiss him. Her heart was still hammering a bit from her parents' unexpected visit, and a long, slow kiss did nothing to calm it down, but slowly the turmoil of the sudden invasion by her family was fading.

His shirt was open again and beneath her hands were lovely flat nipples that she could not stop stroking, and her dress was open again and how she wished she had a front-opening bra, because she did not want to move her hands from his skin to get naked.

Steele peeled off her dress as she sat over him.

Till this point, till this evening, she had always felt that brief moment of judgment as she undressed. She felt only adoration now; she didn't even try to define what was going on in her head as her dress slid off. She did not care what he thought, safe in the knowledge he thought only good things.

He did think only good things. More used to slenderness, he adored her generous curves and her ripe breasts spilling as he undid her bra, but more giddying and satisfying was the mutual eagerness, as if they had somehow known this was where they were leading.

'I've got something I ought to tell you...' Steele said, pulling back.

'What?' she breathed. 'What do you have to tell me?'

He smiled at the dart of concern in her eyes.

'I'm not sleeping with you till I hear about your name.' His hand stroked one generous breast. 'Tell me,' Steele said.

'No.'

He pulled her onto him and then flipped her onto her back and she lay looking up at him, aching for his kiss. She had already kicked off her ballet pumps. All she had on were her panties and it was he who looked down at her now.

'I'm never going to tell you,' Candy said.

He stood and picked up his shirt.

'Come on,' he said. 'Get dressed.

'That's bribery.'

'Yep.'

Well, two could play at that game. 'Fine,' she said, half-heartedly sitting up, putting her legs over the bed and reaching for her clothes. 'Let's go and get something to eat...'

She picked up her bra and Steele took it from her hands.

He placed it beneath her breasts and did it up at the back and while he did so she could feel his breath on her shoulder and she was more than a little aware of his erection through his trousers. He took one of her breasts and gently stuffed it into the fabric but his hand stayed in there, stroking her, teasing her, and she sat still as his lips started to nuzzle the other one, licking and sucking at her nipple, stretching it with his lips as her hands moved to his head and urged him for more contact. But then he stopped. She looked down as he went to tuck her wet, very aroused breast back into her bra, and she decided he was cruel, so cruel that she knew if she didn't relent they would be sitting eating a curry or watching a movie about half an hour from now.

'Okay.' Her voice was all husky and she didn't really recognise it as hers. She cleared her throat, but it still sounded the same.

'As you know, my parents are Italian,' Candy said, and her head was on his shoulder as he unhooked her bra again.

'Okay.'

'Strict,' she said. His hands were now on her hips and she lifted her bottom to allow for him to take her panties down.

'Go on,' Steele said, which was contrary to his words because he was kneeling with his mouth on hers as she spoke.

'And they chose the most beautiful name that means pure and innocent…' she said, and she felt the stretch of his lips on hers as he smiled as she told him what she had sworn she wouldn't. 'And then when I hit my teenage years I noticed that people started to snicker and…'

'What is it?' Steele asked.

'What's the medical term for thrush?'

He pulled back and smiled. 'Candida.'

'Which is why I became Candy. Sadly, not to my parents. They still insist on calling me by my full name.'

'Were you teased?' he said to her mouth as his hand parted her thighs and his fingers slipped inside her.

Mercilessly.

'Poor baby…' Steele said.

'Oh…' Candy moaned, her thighs quivering.

He felt her thighs clamp around his hand and her head rest on his shoulder and there was that blissful choice whether to feel her come now or dive in for the pleasure.

Greed won.

He removed his hand and she let out a small sob of frustration combined with bliss as he stood and she sat naked, a breath away from him as he slid down his zipper and undressed. He handed her a condom and she shook her head.

'You do it.'

'You.'

Okay, she was bad at this part, except his erection was at her cheeks and she was licking her lips as she undid the foil. She had never seen something so lovely, so fierce, so tempting, and the quicker she did this and the quicker she came were very good incentives to get it on.

She played for a moment, loving the feel of him naked in her hands, teasing him with hot breaths to the head, cupping him in her hand.

'Candy.'

His voice was deeper, if at all possible, impatient and deliciously stern, and she would have loved to find out what might happen if she teased him further, dragged this out a little longer. Instead, she briefly looked up at chocolate-brown eyes that made her feel as sexy as hell.

'Put it on,' he said.

She did as she was told, unravelling it along his lovely thick length and deliberately taking her time, loving the sound of his sharp breathing and then the impatient way he pushed her hands away when the job was done.

He pushed her shoulder lightly and it was like dominoes falling, because she toppled back on the bed and he lifted her legs abruptly for daring to keep him waiting. She was compliant, wonderfully so. *Talk about boys to men*, Candy thought as he seared inside her and then she wrapped her legs around him. It was like comparing apples to oranges. He knew exactly what to do as he moved deep inside her. His erection was so strong and fierce that each thrust took her to a place she had never been before.

'I'm going to come,' she said almost in apology, watching, feeling, arching to the bliss of him searing inside.

'I think that's the point,' he said, trying to hold on, revelling in the tight grip of her muscles and the tension of her as she came. It was so deep, so heavy, so intense that Candy briefly wondered if she'd even had an orgasm before.

He kept making love to her through it. She wanted to catch her breath, but then she didn't, for she loved the feel of him taking her as she came. Then she lost her head a little, stopped thinking about anything other than a very small bedroom and a whole lot of pleasure. Steele was looking down at her and then he stilled and she sobbed in pleasure as he started thrusting faster and released into her. To not come again would have proved impossible, to feel his tension release, to see this beautiful man above her and feel him come deep inside shot her into orbit again, her hand pushing at his chest, at the delicious hurt of a sensitive orgasm.

No regrets, never, she swore as, still inside, he collapsed onto her and they breathed their way back to consciousness.

He lay there, inhaling the scent of her hair, feeling her legs loosen and lower to the floor, and he knew this was different. Never had he been more perfectly matched in the bedroom. Her inexperience counted more than she knew for she melded to him, moulded to him. It was all he could do not to gather her things and carry her home.

And then normal service returned to his brain and he kissed her instead of saying the thoughts in his mind.

They ate at her favourite takeaway. A Formica table and cheap plates yet they fell on their food like savages, rather aware that sustenance might be needed later in this night, and then they headed for the movies.

'Sad or dark?' Steele offered.

'Dark,' Candy said.

They went to the blackest, grimmest, yet funniest film. He did watch it intently, yet the only reason he couldn't concentrate fully wasn't the *What the hell did you bring me here for?* vibe.

It was the *I really have to touch you* vibe that was coming from him.

'Stop it,' Candy said as his hand moved up her warm thigh and his mouth went for her neck. 'Concentrate.'

Futile words.

They were like teenagers, and that had been a long time ago for Steele and never for Candy. Those years she'd been keeping Franco at arm's length, not dropping her popcorn on the floor and necking.

'I'm going to have to come and see this alone.'

'So am I.' She smiled and got back to kissing him.

This was heading for morning, Steele knew.

This was heading to tomorrow evening and tomorrow night and the next morning too.

He had this vision of her parents arriving on the doorstep as her legs were behind her ears.

'Come back to mine tonight,' he said between kisses.

'Yes, please,' she agreed.

They weren't ready to be apart any time soon.

CHAPTER SIX

'How are you, Miss Anderson?' Steele asked the following Monday morning as he did his rounds.

'Macey.'

'How are you feeling, Macey?'

'A bit better.'

'That's very nice to hear,' he said as he examined her.

'How was your weekend?' Macey asked him.

'It was very nice,' he said, and she gave a soft smile.

He and Candy had been with each other for a week now. It had been the most intense week of either of their lives. Every available moment they had was spent together. Perhaps, aware how limited their time was, they were determined to make every moment count and were completely into each other. They were both exhausted but in the nicest of ways—between work and sex and eating, and dancing and drives at night just so Candy could find out what it was like to do it in a car, they were sleep deprived and loving it.

'Is Candy on this morning?' Macey asked, oh, so casually.

Steele answered a beat too late. 'I'm not sure what nurses are working this morning.'

'Well, I hope that she is. I haven't seen her for a few days.'

'I think she works in Emergency as well,' Steele said. 'From memory.'

'Does that mean that I won't get to see her again?' Macey fretted, or rather pretended to fret.

Steele knew when he was being played and he didn't mind a bit; he liked it that Macey was starting to notice things that were going on around her. 'I think Candy might be on duty later in the week.'

'Oh, that's good to know.' Macey smiled.

He had, on admission and again last week, interviewed Macey extensively and she had revealed nothing more but Steele pushed on. He knew where they were heading.

'I saw your picture in the corridor,' he said. 'They're putting up pictures of the history of the hospital as a part of the renovations. Emergency is getting a makeover at the moment and so too is the entrance corridor.'

Macey said nothing at first. She didn't want to hear about the changes to the hospital she had loved. It had been such a huge part of her life. 'I don't like hearing about renovations,' she said finally. 'I like remembering it as it was.'

'Things change,' Steele said. 'Not all things, though. Anyway, I saw you in one of the photographs. It looked as if you were getting a medal or a badge in the gardens…'

Macey's eyes filled with tears as she remembered those days.

'Can you talk to me?'

She shook her head.

'I want to see if I can help.'

'Well, you can't.'

'Okay.' He knew not to push her. Macey was starting

to come out of her emotional collapse a little. The medicines were starting to help and she was engaging with the nursing staff and the occupational therapist.

He knew there was more, though, and that night he told Candy as he cooked them a stir-fry.

'Macey's holding out on me.'

'Maybe not,' Candy said.

'Oh, I'm pretty certain that she is.'

'How do you know?'

'I just know.' He smiled. 'Can you pass me the oyster sauce?'

She jumped down and went to the cupboard and got it for him.

'I hate this kitchen,' Steele said. 'It's really badly thought out.'

'I hate kitchens, full stop,' she said. 'You like cooking?'

'Not really,' he said, 'but I like eating.'

'Did you…?' Candy stopped. She'd been about to ask if he'd done the cooking when he'd been married. It was, she guessed, a no-go area, so she swiftly changed what she had been about to say. 'So why did you buy it if you hate it so much?

'It's just a serviced apartment.' Steele answered her question while knowing what she'd been about to say. He was used to avoiding such subjects with women he dated but Candy, or rather his feelings for her, was unlike any he had known and he was starting to come to grips with answering the tricky questions for her. For now, though, he was glad she had changed what she'd been about to say. 'All my stuff is in storage. Which is why I have to work out things like the coffee machine.'

'Oh! I thought you just need glasses. Well, I guess that accounts for the terrible pictures on the walls.'

'I was about to say all my stuff is in storage apart from the pictures,' he said, and then grinned at her pained expression. 'Joke.'

'Thank goodness.'

She opened the bottle as he stirred in the beef. The smell was incredibly strong, and she headed to the sink for a drink and took a few breaths, not wanting to show how the smell had affected her.

Tiny spots were dancing in her eyes and she was sure that if she said anything then Steele would simply tell her, as her parents had, to cut down on the extra shifts that she was working.

'Are you okay?' he asked.

'Fine,' she said as she ran a glass under the tap. 'I'm just thirsty.'

'You're wrecked,' Steele said. He turned off the wok and came over and turned her to face him. 'You need an early night.'

She smiled up at him. 'Our early nights are possibly the reason that I'm so tired.'

'I'm serious,' he said. He looked at her pale features and felt a touch guilty that she had been burning the candle at both ends. 'Why don't you go to bed?' he suggested. 'To sleep—a decent sleep.'

'It's seven o'clock.'

'Go to bed,' Steele said, 'and I mean to sleep. You need it.'

'I think I might.'

Because they could, because they were both tired, for no other reason than they wanted to, when Steele had served up their meals they headed to the bedroom, stripped off, Steele closed the curtains and they ate dinner in bed while watching the news. Candy felt very spoiled and very lazy as he took their empty plates through to the kitchen.

'I don't think I've been to bed at this time since I was seven years old,' she said as Steele climbed back into bed. 'I used to beg to stay up then!'

'Do you want to watch a movie or just go to sleep?' he asked, and they shared a very nice kiss.

'I just want to sleep.' She sighed, wriggling down in the covers and getting comfortable with him.

'Then do.'

She lay on his chest, delighted with their early night, feeling the lovely crinkly hair on his stomach and wondering if she'd ever been happier. 'I love your stomach,' Candy said.

'If you want to sleep you'd better stop playing with it, then.'

She didn't.

She thought back to what she'd been about to ask in the kitchen. Whether Steele had done the cooking or if his wife had was irrelevant, she knew. There was other stuff she'd like to know, though. 'Can I ask you something?'

'You can,' he said, staring into the semi-dark and sort of knowing what was coming and wondering how he'd answer it.

'Why did your marriage break up?

'We just didn't work out,' Steele said. Then he went to add his spiel about they'd been too young, or they'd just grown apart, yet he and Candy had always been honest with each other. They were *so* honest with each other that it sometimes took his breath away. Which meant he didn't want to be evasive now, yet he had never told anyone the reason for the break-up. He'd never told anyone apart from his ex-wife that he was infertile.

And when he had told Annie, she hadn't taken the news well.

'I haven't really talked about it before,' Steele admitted.

'Were you a wife basher?' Candy whispered.

'No.' He laughed.

'Then it doesn't matter,' Candy said, and gave him a light kiss on the chest. 'You don't have to answer.'

He wanted to, though.

'Annie and I got married when I was twenty-three and she was twenty-six. We'd been going out for years,' Steele said. 'We bought the house, the dog, all good...'

Candy didn't like that.

It was funny but she felt the little stiffening of her body as he gave his past a name and an age but then she breathed out through her nostrils and lay there, waiting for him to continue. 'Then Annie decided, or rather we both decided, to start a family.'

'She decided or both?' Candy checked.

'I thought we should wait but Annie really wanted children so we went for it but nothing happened,' Steele said. 'And then nothing kept on happening. I went and had a test—they usually check for issues with the guy first as it's far less invasive—and so we found out, pretty much straight away, that the problem was me. I'm infertile.' He waited for her to stiffen again, or some sign of tension, or what, he didn't know, but instead she looked up at him through the darkness. '*That's* why you broke up?'

'Pretty much. Annie was devastated. I mean, the news completely sent her into a spin.'

'You broke up just because of that?' Candy asked. She really didn't understand.

'It causes a big strain in a marriage. Then there was all her family and how they dealt with the news.' Steele let out a sigh. 'Can you imagine your family's reaction if you told them that your husband was infertile?'

Candy thought for a moment and she could and so she answered him honestly. 'One, I'm not very keen on getting married...'

'Come on.'

'Seriously, I'm not,' she said. 'Two, I wouldn't tell them—it's none of their business. I might tell them that *we* were having problems if they nagged enough.' She thought about it some more. 'Steele, I do everything I can not to discuss sex and such with them—I still hide my Pills in my handbag.'

'I guess.' He smiled. 'After all, you hid me in the bedroom.'

Candy nodded to his chest. 'So I certainly wouldn't be discussing my partner's sperm count with them.'

Steele gave a low laugh.

'You said that she'd been back in touch?' she ventured.

'Yep, her second marriage has broken up and she asked if I would consider giving us another go, though with one proviso—there have been a lot of advances in technology apparently...'

'What a cow!'

He smiled. 'My thoughts at the time—well, a little less politely put in my head. I just hung up on her.'

'You didn't consider it.'

'I don't love her any more,' he said. 'I haven't for a long time.'

He looked a little more closely into the timeline of his

marriage and divorce, something he rarely did. 'When I found out that I probably couldn't be a father and Annie had wrapped her head around the news, she lined us up for this battery of tests and investigations. She started to talk about donor sperm and, to be completely honest...' Steele hesitated; it hurt to be honest at times. 'I think I knew then that we had more problems than my infertility.'

'Like?'

He had never really examined it. He'd just shoved that into the too-hard basket, but lying there, her fingers on his stomach and her breath on his chest, he felt able to go further. 'Well, I'd always planned on being the complete opposite to my parents with my children. I didn't want boarding school or that sort of thing. I wanted to be a real hands-on father. When we first started trying to have a baby, though I thought we were maybe jumping in rather too soon, I was also looking forward to it. I think we all assume, or at least I did, that I'd be a parent one day. When I got the results I suddenly lost all that. I told Annie and she sobbed and she cried and then she had to go to her family and wail with them. It went on for weeks, and do you know what, Candy?'

She heard the bitterness in his voice and now she could understand it. 'What?'

'I was feeling pretty awful at the time. Seriously awful. I wanted some time to get my head around it. I wanted to process the knowledge that I couldn't have children. In hindsight we'd had it really good till that point. We'd never had to deal with anything major. And when we did, I found out that I didn't like the way Annie dealt with the difficult things that life flings at us at times. She made it all about her, not even about us. It was all about

Annie. I tried to understand where she was coming from, yet she never did that for me. I think I fell out of love. If I was ever properly in love in the first place...' he mused. 'So, yes, while I've always thought that it was infertility that broke us up, I don't think it's that neat.'

He loved it that she was still there. She hadn't even jolted when he'd told her. Maybe because they were temporary, Steele pondered. Maybe because she wasn't worried about his ability to make babies, but it was nice to have said it and to have got such a calm reaction.

'Was she blonde?' Candy asked, and it made him smile.

'No.'

'Tall and leggy?'

'Go to sleep.' He was really smiling now as he kissed the top of her head.

'Can I ask another thing?' she said sleepily.

'You can.'

'Why are we using condoms?'

'Because I always have.'

'So have I.' She gave him a little nudge and Steele lay there smiling at the potential reward for his little confession. 'Well, they do say that every cloud has a silver lining.'

Candy didn't answer.

She was fast asleep.

CHAPTER SEVEN

CANDY HAD NEVER slept better than she did when Steele was beside her. His breathing, his heartbeat, the way he held her through the night were like a delicious white noise that blocked out everything else other than them. They wrapped themselves around each other, then unwrapped themselves when they got too hot and then when they got too cold found the other again. It was a seamless dance that lasted a full ten hours and had them on a slow sultry simmer that, by morning, started to rise to boiling point.

Candy awoke slowly, face down on the pillow and with her arms over her head. Steele's arm lay over her waist. The scent in her nostrils was Steele and as she started to wake up she remembered what they had been talking about before she'd fallen asleep. She knew it wasn't something that he'd discussed with others and the privilege of him confiding in her gave her a warm feeling. She loved it that he'd told her. She loved lying in bed next to him and feeling him start to wake up. She loved every minute of her time with him.

She felt his hand roam her spine. Steele's slow, lazy explorations made her melt into the mattress. It was as if each vertebra, right down to the lowest, was an individual treasure worth examining. His hand moved up her back and then to the exposed flesh on her side. Her rib cage received a significantly slower perusal, and his fingers found the softness of her flattened breast. She wanted to lift herself up to let his hand in but he rolled heavily onto her. His mouth buried beneath her hair, reaching for her neck, and then kissed his way to her ear.

'You do talk in your sleep.' His lovely voice greeted her ear and was just as effective in turning her on as his hands.

'Don't believe a word I say.' Candy smiled as he whispered to her the rude things that she *hadn't* said.

'How are you feeling now?' he asked, because it had been a very long sleep after all.

'Better than I ever have,' she admitted. 'I never want to move.'

'Then don't.'

There was a thrill low in her belly and Candy, who had never, till Steele, had morning sex, was fast becoming a fan as, still face down on the pillow, she felt Steele's delicious weight come fully on top of her.

Temptation beckoned as she parted her legs just a little, closing her eyes as his fingers checked that she was ready, which of course she was. Clearly last night's conversation was still on his mind because there was no pause in proceedings to reach for a condom and put it on. Instead, she felt his naked warmth nudging her.

He entered her slowly and Candy let out a moan and so too did Steele, because to feel her wet warmth along his length was intimate, way more intimate than he had been in a very long time.

His mouth was at her ear. 'Cross your ankles,' he said.

Candy did so and she thought she might collapse with

the pleasure as together they started to rock—she could feel every long generous inch of him, hear his ragged breathing. Her face was red and sweaty in the pillow, and Steele took her hand and placed it between her legs and got to work on her breasts.

Oh!

She'd feel guilty later, Candy decided, but he didn't seem to mind a bit that she touched herself. They were barely moving, just rocking, his mouth was at her ear, his fingers stretching her nipples, and then his fingers slid down and took over from hers.

'You're bad for my conscience,' she said.

'No conscience needed,' he said.

He could go for ever like this.

Usually.

Her buttocks were so soft and ripe and they started to lift and press into his groin, and the soft muffled moans of pleasure had Steele tip just as she did and it was bliss to feel him come unsheathed inside her.

'Oh…' Candy lay feeling his weight on her and never wanting him gone. Even the alarm clock that was going off seemed a mile away.

'Can you wake me up like that tomorrow?' she said.

'I can.'

He rolled off and they lay, Candy still on her stomach, facing each other, and sharing a smile.

'I'm going to try and swap so I can get this weekend off,' Steele said, because she flew out the following Friday. 'It's not long now till you go.'

She didn't want to go.

Well, she did, because she was probably going to spend the entire first week of her holiday in bed. With all these extra shifts and sex marathons she was looking forward to sleeping round the clock.

She just wished that her holiday was scheduled for after he'd gone.

Then she stared into his eyes and wondered who she was kidding because she knew that she was going to spend her entire holiday sobbing. Despite starting off with the best of intentions to keep things light, to simply enjoy, Candy knew she was in way over her head. Her feelings for this man were so intense, so instinctively right that she simply could not imagine how she was possibly going to begin to get over him.

'Steele…' She took a breath. She wasn't sure if what she was about to say would sound too pushy, but she'd never held back from the truth with him and she chose not to now. 'Why don't you come for a few days?'

'To Hawaii?'

'Yes.' Candy nodded.

'I don't want to intrude on your holiday…'

'It wouldn't be intruding. It would be nice if you came in the middle. You've got a long weekend coming up.'

'It would be nice,' Steele said. 'I'd be pretty wrecked, though.'

'Well, I'll have slept for a week by the time you get there,' Candy said. 'I'll have enough energy for both of us. Think about it,' she offered, and then she climbed out of bed and grimaced when she saw the time. 'I'm going to be late. I'll have a quick shower and then I need to stop by my flat.'

'I'll drive you in,' Steele said. To keep things well away from work Candy was still taking the Underground and he watched the little flash of worry flare in her eyes.

'We might be seen,' she said. 'Steele, you've no idea how gossip spreads at that place.'

'I'm sure I do.' He smiled. 'It doesn't bother me if we're seen, unless of course it's a problem for you.'

She thought about it for a moment. 'Actually, no.'

'I can have broken your heart and put you off seeing anyone for ages after I've gone.' Steele grinned, giving her an excuse to give to Gerry if he pushed her to go out with him when he returned from Greece. But then Steele met her eyes and his tone changed slightly and she, though late for work, stood there in the bedroom and felt her heartbeat quicken. 'You could even say you were still seeing me,' he said, and they just looked at each other.

'I guess he wouldn't know either way,' Candy said, though something told her this conversation had little to do with excuses to give to Gerry.

There were two, possibly three, conversations going on.

That Steele would be gone and that Candy could say what she liked about them if it made things easier for her with Gerry.

That he would be gone, Steele thought, and he was saying that possibly this might last longer.

That he would be gone, Candy thought, and she didn't want him to be.

'Get ready,' he said.

They stopped at her flat and Candy quickly changed into jeans, which was what she usually wore for arriving at work, and rubbed some serum into her hair as she chatted to Steele.

'We came back here for this?'

'I can't leave home without it,' Candy said, trying to

tame her long wild curls. 'I should buy another bottle and leave it at yours.'

'Why don't you just pack some things now and put them in my car?' Steele said, and she hesitated because she'd been thinking exactly the same thing. 'It would save us dashing back and forth all the time.'

She packed a case and they loaded it into his car and drove to work. It was all so new, so exciting that neither could help smiling.

As they pulled into the staff car park, Louise, a midwife who had done a stint in Emergency last year, was walking past. She and Candy had got on well. Louise was blonde and gorgeous and rather pregnant and she waved to Candy and gave a little wink.

'We're public knowledge now.' Candy smiled as she waved back, because Louise was a terrible gossip, which was surprising, considering that she was married to Anton, an obstetrician whose middle name was discretion.

'I'm fine with that,' Steele said.

He had long ago stopped playing games and this felt nothing like a game with Candy.

'We'll keep it discreet on the ward, though,' Candy said, because she was working on the geriatric unit today till lunchtime.

'Yes,' Steele said. 'I just don't want to be dropping you at another entrance and things. Come back to mine after work. I've got a meeting at six, though,' he continued, 'so I won't be back till about eight.'

'I'll have bread waiting in the toaster for you,' Candy said as he peeled off a key, which he had never done before. She snapped it onto her key ring as if it was no big deal.

It was a big deal. Both knew it. It was way too soon, but in other ways it was not soon enough.

Neither knew where this had come from or fully what it was.

They were planning holidays, her suitcase was in his boot, his key was now in her bag and they were kissing in the front seat as if one of them had just stepped off a plane after a year's absence. When she pulled back from his kiss, she returned to her question from before she'd fallen asleep. Candy was curious about his ex-wife and that spoke volumes in itself.

'*Was* she tall and leggy?' Candy smiled, watching him cringe just a little as he shook his head.

'Gamine?' Candy ventured. 'Please say no.'

'Not gamine *exactly*...' Steele said, and she groaned.

'Careful, Steele,' she warned. 'You may live to regret your next choice of words.'

He just smiled as they got out of the car.

There was nothing about their time together to regret.

Just that it was running out.

CHAPTER EIGHT

'I'M GOING TO take off your dressing, Macey,' Candy said. 'Steele wants to have a look at it.'

'Are you working tomorrow?' Macey asked, because Candy only had a four-hour shift and finished at lunchtime.

'I am, but I'm working down in Emergency.'

Macey was improving. Her medications were starting to kick in and she was engaging with the staff and other patients. She was also taking her meals unaided but she was still far from the feisty woman who had arrived in Emergency.

Steele came in just as Candy had got the dressing off. It was clearing up but it was very sloughy and still a bit smelly and as she saw it, Candy blew out.

'I'm just going to get the phone,' she said, even though it wasn't ringing, but she felt a bit sick. 'I won't be long.'

'I was like that,' Macey said to Steele, 'when I was...' Macey quickly changed what she had been about to say mid-sentence. 'When I was nursing.'

'No, you weren't,' Steele said. 'You weren't some young pup who couldn't stomach a bit of pus.'

Macey looked at him.

He knew. She was sure of it.

Steele did know because he had seen the cape carefully held to hide Macey's stomach in the photo in the entrance hall. He'd also done a little delving and it would seem that Matron Macey Anderson had gone to Bournemouth to recover from polio, though she'd made no reference to it when Steele had asked her for her medical history.

Tell me, his eyes said as Macey's own eyes filled with tears. Steele sat on the bed and took her hand. 'Talk to me, Macey.'

'When I was *carrying*, I was like that.' She started to cry as a fifty-five-year-old secret was finally released and Steele let her cry. He passed her tissues from her locker, not saying a word as Macey wept.

As Candy came in to do the dressing he briefly looked up to her. 'I've got this, thanks,' he said.

Candy saw that Macey was upset and left them.

When Macey stopped crying, he didn't press her for more information; instead, he did the dressing on her leg and afterwards he sorted out the covers. 'Do you want a cup of tea?' he asked.

'I'd like a sherry.'

'I bet you would,' he said. 'I'll be back in a moment.'

He took away the trolley, leaving Macey alone for a little while to gather herself. He left the curtains closed around her.

Candy was having a glass of water at the desk and he asked her for the keys to the cupboard where the sherry and things were kept and poured Macey a glass.

'Is she okay?' Candy asked.

'She will be. I'm going back in to talk to her,' Steele said. 'Macey saw you get a bit dizzy and has got you down as pregnant. I told her you're not and that they don't build nurses as strong these days.' He gave her a grim smile and then explained what was happening. 'As it turns out, she had a baby.'

'Oh…'

'Macey has never told anyone until now so it's a huge deal to her. I'm just giving her a few moments to gather herself,' Steele said, 'and then I'm going to go in and speak with her. Would you tell Gloria to make sure that we're not disturbed?'

'Sure.'

'If she has any visitors…'

'I'll say that the doctor's in with her.'

'Thanks.'

He walked back behind the curtains. Macey had stopped crying and she gave Steele a watery smile.

'Sorry about that,' she said.

'Why should you be sorry?' Steele asked, handing her the glass of sherry. 'I'm glad that you told me. Would you like to talk about it?' he offered.

'I don't know how to,' Macey admitted. 'It's been a secret for so long.'

'Not any more,' Steele said. 'It might help to talk about it.'

'I got pregnant when I was twenty-seven,' Macey said. 'He was married. I was never much of a looker and I suppose I was flattered. Anyway, my parents would have been horrified. They would have said that I was old enough to know better. We're never old enough to know better when it comes to matters of the heart, though. Instead of telling them, I confided in one of the matrons here. I thought she'd be shocked but she was more than used to it and took care of things. I was sent down to Bournemouth to have him. Everyone thought that I had polio and that was the reason I was away so long. Instead, I had my son and he was handed over for adoption.'

'I'm sorry, Macey,' Steele said. 'That must have been so painful.'

'It still is.' She nodded. 'I was very sick when he was delivered. I did everything I could not to push because I knew that as soon as he was born he would be taken away. I passed out when he was delivered and I never got to hold him and I never even got to see him. When I came around the next day I asked if I could have just one cuddle but I was told it was better that way. It wasn't.'

'Have you ever tried to look him up or make contact?'

'Never,' she said. 'I've thought about it many times but I didn't want to mess up his life if he didn't know he was adopted. I was told that he had gone to a very good family and that I was to get on with my life. I came back to work and threw myself into my career, but I've thought about him every single day since.'

'And his father?'

'I had nothing to do with him after that,' Macey said. 'We worked alongside each other for a few years afterwards. I think at first he thought he could carry on with me as before but I soon put him right. I told him to concentrate on his marriage. I'm very ashamed that I had an affair with a married man.'

'Try not to be ashamed,' Steele suggested. 'Perhaps it would be better to view that time with remorse but do your best to leave the shame out of it.

'I know you must have felt very alone at the time but I can tell you from all my years doing this job that what happened to you happened to a lot of women from your generation.'

'He was married, though.'

'You weren't the first and you certainly won't be the last person to have an affair with a married man. My guess is you've more than paid the price.'

'I have.'

'Forgive yourself, then,' Steele said. 'Have you thought about discussing what happened with your nieces?'

'Sometimes,' Macey said. 'I wake up some nights, imagining them finding out what happened after I'm gone and not being able to speak about it with me.'

'Maybe consider speaking with them again,' Steele suggested. 'And if you want help telling them, or if you want me to do it for you, let me know.' He watched as Macey frowned, though it wasn't a dismissive frown. He could see that she was thinking about it. 'And if you never want to discuss it again, then that's fine too.'

'I might think again about telling them…' she said. 'There's just so much guilt. Sometimes when I'm enjoying myself I feel that I don't deserve to.'

'Let the guilt go, Macey,' Steele said. 'You are allowed to be happy.'

Candy sat at the nurses' station, staring at Macey's curtains, but, though usually she'd be curious, right now she wasn't wondering what was going on behind closed curtains.

Steele's throwaway comment about Macey thinking that Candy was pregnant had immediately been disregarded but now a small nagging voice was starting to make itself known.

She felt *so* tired.

Seriously tired.

There were many reasons that could account for that but the usually energetic Candy could barely walk past a bed without wanting to climb into it.

And she *had* felt sick a couple of times.

Actually, she'd had a bout of stomach flu a few weeks ago. Or she'd assumed it was stomach flu.

But she'd had her period, though it had been light, but she was sure that was because she had gone back on the Pill.

God, was it that fabulous bra that had given her such cleavage?

Stop it, Candy told herself.

Except she couldn't stop it.

'How is she?' she asked, when Steele came out from behind Macey's curtains.

'She's having a cry so keep them closed.' He told her a little about it. 'She doesn't want her nieces to know at this stage but at least she seems to be thinking about telling them.' He frowned at Candy's distraction. 'Are you okay?'

'I'm fine,' she said.

She wasn't, though.

Macey's words had seriously unsettled her.

Candy did her best not to let them.

She headed for home and looked around her flat. She opened the fridge to sort out the milk and things but let out a moan when she saw that it had already been done.

Her parents had been around.

Candy looked at a letter on her kitchen bench and saw that it had been opened.

It was her bank statement.

And there were flashing lights on her answering machine that Candy knew would be messages from her parents—they were really the only people who called her on her landline.

Candy took a breath and called her mum. She sat for

five minutes wondering why it had to be like this as her mum demanded to know where she'd been and what she'd been doing.

'I've been really busy with work,' she said, loathing that she had to lie and then deciding not to. 'I've been doing a lot of extra shifts,' she explained, and took a deep breath. 'I've booked a holiday. It was a last-minute thing.'

'Where?'

'Hawaii. I go next Friday for two weeks.' Candy closed her eyes and tried to answer in calm tones as the questions started.

'I'm going by myself,' Candy said. 'I just felt that I needed to get away.'

No, she couldn't afford it and as she was told that Candy thought of the first day she had met Steele, who had simply said, 'Good for you.'

'Mum,' Candy interrupted. 'I'm going on holiday, I want to go and I'm not going to argue about it with you.'

'You listen—'

'No,' she said. 'I love you very much, you know that I do, but I'm not going to run everything that I do by you.'

It hurt to have this discussion but she knew it was way overdue. She knew they loved and cared for her and that they expected to be involved in every facet of her life. It just wasn't the way Candy wanted to live any more.

'Ma, I'm not arguing,' she said. She took a breath, wanting to tell them to please ring in the future before dropping around. She wanted to ask for the return of her keys but baby steps, Candy decided, so she dealt with that morning's events. 'Mum, I don't want you opening my mail and I've told you over and over that I don't want you coming around and letting yourself in when I'm not here.'

She meant it. So much so that when her mother pointed

out she was just trying to help and, anyway, she'd need someone to take care of the flat while she was in Hawaii, Candy snapped in frustration. 'It's not a stately home that needs taking care of. It's a one-bedroom flat!'

It didn't go well.

Candy knew her requests would be, as always, simply ignored so after she put down the phone she did what she didn't want to but felt she had to.

She made a trip to the hardware store, but not just for locks. She also bought a drill.

Then she had to go back to the hardware store a second time because after numerous attempts her shiny new drill wouldn't screw in a nail but a very nice guy explained what a drill bit was for!

She loathed that she'd done it.

She loathed more than that that she'd had to, but she had realised that despite the move she hadn't really left home. Her parents saw her flat as a bedroom with a slightly longer hall to walk down. Candy thought of Steele hiding in her room that night and knew that was the reason they stayed at his place.

No, Candy thought as she turned the new lock on her door and then headed for Steele's, it was her life.

It was a long day for Steele.

A very long day.

He stopped by Macey's bed at the end of his shift and she asked if he would speak with her niece when she visited tomorrow.

'Of course I will,' Steele said.

Then he had a meeting to sit through, which really had nothing to do with him, given that he'd be gone in a few weeks. Not that it stopped him putting his point across about the lengthy waits in Emergency. Oh, and a few other things too.

By nine he should be more than ready for home but for once Steele was tentative.

There was no bread waiting for him in the toaster.

Steele walked through his apartment and put Candy's case, which he had bought in from the car, down in the hallway. He knew she was here and he knew where she probably was.

He walked through to the bedroom and, sure enough, there was Candy, fast asleep in bed with the light still on. He looked at her black curls all splayed out on the pillow and he looked at the dark circles under her eyes and he stood there for a full two minutes, watching her sleep deeply.

Steele made his own toast and then had a shower and tried to watch a film. It was a film that he had been meaning to watch for ages but, unusually for him, he couldn't concentrate.

There was something else, far deeper, on his mind.

He turned off the television and lights and got into bed next to Candy, and she rolled into him.

'Sorry,' she said sleepily. 'I saw the bed and couldn't resist. When did you get back?'

'Just now,' he said, though it had been a good hour.

'I changed the lock on my front door.' Her voice was groggy with sleep.

'Good for you,' Steele said. 'Go back to sleep.'

She did.

He didn't.

Instead, he lay staring at the ceiling.

Yes, there was a lot on his mind.

Macey's words had now seriously rattled him too.

CHAPTER NINE

After

CANDY WOKE IN Steele's arms and listened to the sound of his breathing.

She wanted him to wake and roll over and make love to her. She wanted the pregnancy thought in her head to be obliterated by his kiss.

Then she didn't want his kiss because she felt sick.

Candy's mind flicked over the past few weeks.

Yes, she'd been sick last month, but it had been one of those bugs.

Surely?

She really felt sick now and she crept to the bathroom and tried to throw up as quietly as she could.

It was exhaustion, Candy told herself, brushing her teeth and then showering, but when she glanced in the mirror she could see the fear in her eyes.

Steele lay there listening to Candy flush the toilet to drown out her gags and he blew out a breath.

'Morning,' he said a few moments later, when he came in and she was already in the shower.

'Morning.' Candy smiled but she couldn't quite meet his eyes.

There was an elephant in the room that they both chose to ignore and they dashed around, getting dressed, finding keys, exclaiming they were running late when really they were actually doing quite well for time.

There was the first uncomfortable silence between them as Steele drove Candy and the massive elephant in the car to work.

There was no frantic kissing and they walked through the car park in silence, Candy making the decision to do a pregnancy test as soon as she got there, Steele wondering what the hell he should say.

If anything.

The sound of an ambulance siren had her look up and she saw Lydia standing in the forecourt, frantically gesturing for her to run. Clearly there was something big coming in.

'I've got to go,' she said.

'Go!' Steele said, and he watched her run through the car park and to the forecourt, where not one but three flashing-light ambulances were now pulling up. Kelly ran past him too and as Steele walked up the corridor the anaesthetists and trauma teams were running down it towards Emergency.

Candy, Steele thought, was in for one helluva morning.

She was.

She raced into the changing rooms and stripped off her jeans and T-shirt and got into scrubs as Kelly did the same.

'What is it?' Kelly asked.

'Multi-traumas.' Candy passed on the little Lydia had told her as she'd dashed past. 'Four of them.'

'Four are coming here?'

It was rare to get four all at once but apparently there

were several more critically injured patients going to different emergency departments. A high-speed collision, involving several vehicles, meant there would be nothing to think about other than the patients any time soon.

It was on this morning that Candy fell back in love with Emergency.

Yes, it was busy and stressful but it was what she loved to do. Helping out with a little girl who had looked dire when she'd first arrived but who was now coughing as Rory, the anaesthetist, extubated her was an amazing feeling indeed.

'It's okay, Bethany,' Candy said as the girl opened her eyes and started to cry. 'I'm Candy. You're in hospital but you're going to be okay.'

Thank God! She looked up at Rory, who gave her a wide-eyed look back because it had been touch and go. Bethany had had a chest tube inserted as her lung had collapsed in the accident and her heart hadn't been beating when she'd arrived in the department.

To see her coughing and crying and alive, Candy knew why she'd fought so hard to do a job she loved.

Rory and the thoracic surgeon started talking about sedation and getting Bethany up to ICU, and it all happened seamlessly.

'Busy morning?' Patrick, the head nurse in ICU, smiled when Candy came up with her patient.

'Just a bit.'

'You look exhausted,' Patrick commented. 'So this is Bethany?' He looked down at the little girl, who was sedated but breathing on her own. He nudged Candy away for a moment. 'I'm going to put her in a side room. I thought about putting her next to Mum but I think it's going to scare her more for now.'

'How is her mum doing?' Candy asked, because she had been so busy working on Bethany that she didn't really know what was going on with the rest of her family.

'Won't know for a while,' Patrick said. 'They'll keep her in an induced coma for at least forty-eight hours. Is it settling down in Emergency now?'

'I don't know,' she admitted. 'I haven't looked up yet.'

'Go and grab a drink,' Patrick said.

He was nice like that and Candy headed round to the little staffroom and had a quick drink from the fridge, pinched a few biscuits and then headed back to the unit.

It was quiet. One elderly man was being wheeled in on a stretcher and Candy rolled her eyes at Kelly as she walked into Resus to start the massive tidy up.

It was going to be a big job.

'Let's get one bed completely stocked and done,' Kelly said, 'just in case something comes in, then we can deal with the rest.'

They got one area cleared and restocked and were just about to commence with the rest when Lydia came in.

'I've asked if everyone can come through to the staffroom.'

'Now?' Candy checked, because there was still an awful lot to do.

'Just make sure that one crash bed is fully stocked,' Lydia said, 'and then come straight through. I need to speak to everyone.'

Steele's morning flew by too.

He had a video meeting with some of his new colleagues in Kent and arranged to go there next Thursday as he wanted to see how the extension was coming along.

He also had a house lined up with a real estate agent and wanted to take a second look.

Mr Worthington passed away just after eleven, his radio on, his family beside him. Steele spent a good hour with the family afterwards in his office at the end of the ward.

As they left, instead of heading back out, he sat and thought about Candy. He didn't know how he felt and he didn't know what to do.

He looked up when there was a knock at the door and he called for whoever it was to come in then remembered that he'd asked Gloria to send Macey's niece in once the Worthington family had gone home.

'Hello, Dr Steele.' Catherine smiled. 'Gloria said that you wanted to talk to me.'

'I do,' he said. 'Come in.'

'Aunt Macey has just gone for an occupational therapy assessment,' Catherine said. 'It's nice to see her walking again.' She took a seat and then looked at Steele. 'It's bad news, isn't it…?' she said, and her eyes filled up with tears.

'No, no.' Immediately Steele put her at ease. 'I haven't called you in to break bad news about your aunt's health.' He watched her let out a huge breath of relief. 'Her physical health anyway,' Steele amended. 'But as you know, Macey's been depressed.'

'She seems to be getting better, though,' Catherine said. 'The tablets seem to be starting to work.'

'They are,' Steele said. 'She's talking a bit more and engaging with the staff. The thing is,' he said, 'it isn't just medication that your aunt needs at the moment. She's asked that I speak with you. There's something that's upsetting her greatly and it's been pressing on her mind.'

'I don't know what you mean.'

'Your aunt has something she wishes to discuss with you, a secret that she has kept for many, many years, and it's one she doesn't want you to find out about after her death…' He told her that Macey had had a baby more than fifty years ago and that he'd been given up for adoption at birth, but Catherine kept shaking her head, unable to take in the news. 'We'd have known.'

'Very few people knew,' Steele said. 'That's what it was like in those days.'

'But my aunt's not like that…' Catherine said, and then caught herself. 'When I say that, I mean she's so incredibly strict—she's always saying that women should save themselves and…' She stopped talking and simply sat there as she took the news in. 'Poor Aunt Macey. How can we help?'

'I think speak with Linda and then perhaps you can both come in together. Talk it over with Macey, maybe ask if she wants to look for her son, or if she simply wants it left. Her fear is that you'll find out after her death, whenever that may be, and you might judge her.'

'Never.'

'I know it's a shock,' he said.

'It is.' Catherine smiled. 'My mother would have had a fit if she knew. Is that why she's been depressed?'

'I think it's a big part of it,' Steele said. 'Maybe when she's got it off her chest and spoken with her family, things can really start to improve.'

He was about to head down to Emergency to check to see if his new admission had arrived, but before he left he quickly checked some lab results and then scrolled through his emails. Then he checked the intramail as they were hounding him to go and get another security shot for his lanyard. He saw an alert that the Emergency Department had been placed on bypass and let out a sigh of frustration, because he really didn't want his patient ending up in another hospital.

He clicked on the intramail and, for a man who dealt with death extremely regularly, for a man who usually knew what to do in any given situation, Steele simply didn't have a clue how to handle this.

We are greatly saddened to inform staff of the sudden death of Gerard (Gerry) O'Connor, a senior nurse in the Emergency Department.

Gerry passed away after sustaining a head injury in Greece. Currently the Emergency Department has been placed on bypass as his close colleagues process the news.

He blinked when his pager bleeped and saw that his patient had, in fact, arrived in Emergency.

Steele considered paging Donald, his registrar, to take it. He wanted some time to get his head around things.

Yet he wanted to see how Candy was.

Steele walked into the war zone of Emergency. Resus was in shambles, though some staff, called down from the wards, were trying to tidy it up.

There were just a few staff around and he was surprised when, after checking the board, he walked into the cubicle where his patient was, to see Candy checking Mr Elber's observations.

'I'm Steele,' he said to his patient.

'Dr Steele, if you want to be formal.' Candy smiled at the elderly man as she checked his blood pressure. She was trying to keep her voice light but Steele could hear the shaken notes to it.

'I thought the place was on bypass,' he said to her as she pulled off her stethoscope.

'Mr Elber arrived just before we closed.'

'Can I have a brief word?' he said, and he watched her eyes screw up at the sides a fraction but she nodded and followed him outside.

'I'm so sorry,' Steele said, but Candy shook her head.

'Please, don't.'

'Candy—'

'Please, don't. I can't talk about it. I think I'm going to go home,' she said. 'Lydia offered.' She thought about it for a moment. 'I think I just want to go home.'

'Come round tonight,' Steele said, 'or I'll come over to you.'

'I don't want you to,' Candy said. 'I don't want to sit and cry over my ex with you. It's too weird.'

'It's not,' he said, but he didn't push it. 'Call me if you change your mind.'

'Thanks.'

Candy headed off and spoke with Lydia and said that, yes, on second thoughts, she was going to go home.

The news had come completely out of the blue. All the staff were stunned. Candy had headed straight back out to the department, not really knowing what to do, when she'd seen that Mr Elber was sitting on a trolley and had been pretty much left to himself.

Now the complete numb shock that had hit her after finding out that Gerry was dead was wearing off and she was very close to tears.

And very scared too.

She changed and as she headed out of the department she saw Louise walking in on her way to work.

'Candy.' Louise came straight over. 'I just heard about Gerry. It's such terrible news…'

Candy started to cry but as Louise wrapped her in a hug, feeling Louise's pregnant stomach nudging into her was just about the last straw.

'I know you had a bit of a thing going on last year,' Louise said. 'It must be so—'

'Louise,' Candy begged, 'it's not that that I'm crying about.' Well, it was, but she certainly wasn't about to tell Louise the entire truth either. 'I think that I might be pregnant and I don't know what to do…'

'Come on,' Louise said, and led her to the canteen. There were groups sitting and talking, some from Emergency and in tears, so it didn't look out of place that Candy was crying.

Louise went and got them both drinks and then came over.

'How late are you?' Louise asked, knowing full well that Candy was seeing Steele—she'd seen them in the car after all.

'I'm not late,' Candy said. 'But I've been feeling sick and I'm so tired…' She knew it didn't sound much to go on. The awful thing was that she *knew* that she was. 'I simply can't be pregnant,'

'It will be okay,' Louise said. As a midwife she was extremely used to a woman's shocked tears when they first came to the realisation that they were pregnant.

'I don't think it can be,' Candy sobbed, 'and I can't tell you why.'

Louise sat and thought for a moment. If Steele was

only here for a few more weeks, which was what she'd heard, then it wasn't any wonder that Candy was upset.

'I don't know who to talk to,' Candy said, and then blew her nose and told herself to get it together.

'Can you talk to me?' Louise offered. 'Do you want to do a pregnancy test? I'll come with you.' When Candy said nothing Louise pushed on. 'Could you talk about it with Anton?' Louise asked. Anton was Louise's husband and one of the most sought-after obstetricians in London. 'I was just on my way to have lunch with him so I know that he's got time to see you.'

Candy nodded.

It was time to find out for sure.

Louise took out her phone and sent a text and a few moments later she got a response. 'He says to come to the antenatal clinic and he'll see you. I'll take you over there now.'

'People will wonder what I'm doing in the antenatal clinic.'

'People will think we're just two friends catching up for lunch,' Louise said. 'Don't be so paranoid.'

As they arrived at the clinic Candy felt a moment's reprieve as she looked around at the pregnant women all sitting waiting for their turn to be seen.

She was overreacting, she told herself.

This world didn't apply to her.

'You might as well come in,' Candy said to Louise as they arrived at a door that had a sign with Anton Rossi written on it. 'He'll only tell you what's happening anyway.'

'God, no.' Louise rolled her eyes. 'Unfortunately for me Anton's all ethical like that. If you tell him not to tell me, then wild horses wouldn't drag it from him! You don't have to worry about that.' Louise gave her a lovely smile. 'But if you do want to tell me then I'm dying to know!' She gave Candy a cuddle just before she went in. 'You'll be fine.'

Candy really hadn't had anything to do with Anton before this. She just knew him by reputation and had seen him occasionally when he'd come down to Emergency to review a patient there.

'I'm sorry to interrupt your lunch break,' she said. 'Thank you for seeing me so quickly.'

'Louise said that you were very upset.'

Candy nodded. 'I know that everything is confidential but the thing is, this is terribly delicate and—'

'First of all,' Anton interrupted, 'you are right— everything you tell me is completely confidential. I never gossip.'

'Thank you.'

'I'm not even taking notes. Do you want to tell me what's happening?'

'I think I might be pregnant,' Candy said. 'The thing is, my partner...' She didn't even know if Steele was that but she pushed on. 'It can't be his.'

'Because?'

'He's infertile.'

'Have you been seeing someone else?' Anton asked gently—he was used to that being the case—but Candy shook her head.

'I've only been with my current partner for a couple of weeks. We weren't supposed to be serious, but...' It sounded so terrible put like that but Anton's eyes were sympathetic rather than judgmental. 'I had a one-night stand with my ex a couple of months ago.' She thought back. 'Three months, maybe. We used condoms.'

'Nothing is fail-safe,' Anton said.

'I went on the Pill afterwards,' Candy said. 'I wasn't expecting anything to happen again but I just decided I wasn't coming off it. I have had my period.'

'A normal period?' Anton checked.

'It's been light but I thought that was because the day I got it I started the Pill.'

'The first thing we need to do—' Anton was very calm '—is to find out if you are indeed pregnant.'

He gave her a jar and a few minutes later she sat in his office and she knew, she simply knew that she was. A few moments later Anton confirmed it.

'Candy, you are pregnant.'

He let it sink in for a moment.

'How do you think your partner will react?' Anton asked.

'I don't think I'm going to find out,' Candy said, and she just stared at the wall. 'There's really no point telling him. We both agreed from the start—'

'What about the father?'

Oh, that's right. Candy's brain was moving like grid-locked traffic. It was like telling a joke and forgetting the punch line, because she hadn't told Anton the good part yet. 'You know Gerry, the head of nursing in Emergency…'

'Oh, Candy.' Immediately he took her hand. Anton didn't gossip—in fact, he had been in this office all morning—but he had seen the email twenty minutes or so ago informing everyone that Gerry had passed away while on holiday in Greece and that Emergency was on bypass.

'I don't know what to do.'

'Of course you don't know what to do at the moment,'

he said. 'This is all too much of a shock. How long have you been worried that you might be pregnant?'

'Since yesterday,' Candy said. 'A patient said something. I know I'm a bit overweight, it just...'

'Hit home?'

Candy nodded.

'I knew you were pregnant before I did the test,' Anton said, which concerned him a little as it did not seem to fit with her dates. 'We could do an ultrasound now, here, and see exactly where we are,' he suggested. 'Are you ready to do that?'

She nodded.

'Go to the examination table and undo your jeans. He came over and had a feel of her stomach but said nothing—though he was starting to think that Candy would soon be in for another shock.

He squeezed some gel on and turned the machine away from her. 'Can you turn the sound off, please?' Candy said, because she didn't want to hear its heartbeat.

'Of course I can.'

He took a few moments, running the probe over her stomach and pushing it in over and over.

'I really am sorry to interrupt your lunch break,' Candy said, more for something to say because she was dreading the next conversation.

'My wife would have been nagging me to do an ultrasound on her anyway.' He smiled and then he looked across at Candy. 'I shan't be discussing this with her.'

'Thank you.'

He had finished.

'Stay there,' Anton said as she went to sit up. 'You are close to thirteen weeks pregnant, which means conception was eleven weeks ago.'

'I've had my period, though.'

'Breakthrough bleeding,' Anton said. 'Nothing to worry about. All looks well on the ultrasound. Obviously your hormones are everywhere right now.'

'Would the Pill have harmed it?'

'No. Many, many women I have seen have taken the Pill while not knowing that they are pregnant. You've had no symptoms?' Anton checked.

'Not really.' Candy shook her head and then lay and thought back over the past few weeks. 'I had what I thought was a bug and I've felt sick a couple of times and been a bit dizzy, but I never really gave it much thought.' She looked up at Anton. 'I've been so tired, though. I mean *seriously* tired. I actually booked a holiday because I was feeling so flat.'

'Candy,' Anton said gently, 'I'm not surprised that you have been feeling exhausted—it's a twin pregnancy.'

It was just as well that he had kept her lying down.

Candy lay there, stunned, trying and failing to see herself as a mother of twins. Finally she sat up and when she took a seat at the desk Anton gave her a drink of water.

'I don't know what to do.'

'As of now,' he said, 'I would expect that your mind is extremely scattered. Is there anybody that you can talk to about this?'

'Not really. My parents will freak,' Candy said, panicking just at the thought of telling them. 'I can't tell anyone at work or it will be everywhere.'

He nodded in understanding but he was practical too. 'You are going to start showing very soon—in fact, you are already,' Anton said. 'I could feel that you were pregnant before I did the ultrasound. Your uterus is out of the pelvis and you will show far more quickly with twins.'

'I can't have it, Anton,' Candy said, but then she started to cry because it wasn't an it. It was a *them*.

'Candy, you do need a little time to process this news but you also need to come and see me next week. You don't have much time to make a decision. I do want you to take the time to think very carefully about this.'

She didn't need the time. In that moment, she had already made her choice.

'I can't…' Candy said, and then took a deep breath. 'I'm not having an abortion.'

'Well, you have a difficult road coming up,' Anton said, 'but I can tell you this much—I will be there for you and in six months from now you will have your babies and today will be just a confusing memory.'

'Thank you.'

They chatted some more and Candy told him that she was booked to go to Hawaii next week. 'Can I still go?'

'Absolutely!' he said. 'It will be the best thing for you. Let your insurance company know. Put me down as your obstetrician. I do still want to see you next week, though. You need to have some blood tests and I want to go through things more thoroughly with you. Right now, it's time for the news to sink in.'

Poor thing, Anton thought as she left his office. He had looked after many women whose partner and even ex-partner had died and knew that it was a very confusing time.

He smiled as there was a knock at the door and Louise came in. 'How was she?'

'She's fine,' Anton said, and then rolled his eyes as

Louise picked up the gel. 'Step away from the ultrasound machine, Louise.'

'Please,' Louise said. 'It's wide awake. I can feel it kicking.

'Because it probably knows its lunchtime,' Anton said. 'Come on, I would actually like to get some lunch.'

'Is Candy okay?' Louise shamelessly fished as they walked down to the canteen. Anton absolutely trusted his wife but part of what he adored about her was that she could not keep a secret and so, to be safe, he said nothing.

'She's on with him…' Louise nudged.

'Who?' Anton frowned.

'The sexy new geriatrician that just walked past,' Louise explained. 'Candy is on with him.'

He loathed gossip, he truly did, but, unusually for Anton, he turned his head.

He felt sorry for her new partner too and tried to imagine how he would feel if his gorgeous wife had already been pregnant when they'd met.

Anton was man enough to admit that he didn't know.

Candy stepped into her flat and put down her handbag and she didn't know where to start with her thoughts.

Just after seven there was a knock at the door and Candy opened it to the angry questions and accusations of her parents.

'Where were you?' her mother asked, and demanded to know where Candy had been last night and the night before that.

'We came over and you were not home.'

'Please, not now,' Candy said.

Yes, now.

'For the last two weeks you are hardly home. We call

around and the lights are off. We telephone and you don't pick up.'

'I'm twenty-four years old, Mum,' Candy said. 'I don't have to account for my time…'

She might as well have thrown petrol on the fire because all the anger that had been held in by her parents since Candy had moved into her flat came out then.

She was heading for trouble, her mother warned.

They didn't raise her to stay out all night.

Who was she going to Hawaii with?

Candy thought of Steele then and stood there, remembering the beginning of tentative plans.

How much simpler life had seemed then.

'I'm not discussing this,' Candy said. 'I'm very tired. It's been an extremely long day.'

She simply refused to row.

When they finally left she stood in the hall.

No one understood. Her friends at work thought she was ridiculous to worry about what her parents might think, but she did. Candy loved them. She just didn't know how to be both herself and the daughter they demanded that she be.

Imagine telling them that the she was pregnant.

She simply could not imagine it.

Not just pregnant, but pregnant with twins and the father was dead.

Candy dealt with things then as any rational, capable adult would.

She undressed, climbed into bed and pulled the covers over her head.

CHAPTER TEN

'Hi.'

Steele could hear the tension in her voice when Candy called him on Saturday, though she was trying to keep her voice light.

'Hi, Candy.'

'Is it okay if we give it a miss tonight?' she asked. They had planned to go to a stand-up comedy and the tickets had been hard to come by.

'Of course it is,' he said. 'I doubt you're in the mood for laughing out loud. Do you want me to come over?'

'I'd really just like a night on my own,' she said.

Another one.

And then another.

And then another.

On Tuesday, four days before she flew, Steele saw her briefly in the admin corridor. She was coming down from Admin, where she had been trying to sort out her salary for her annual leave when she bumped into him.

'How are you doing?' he asked.

'I'm fine,' she said. 'I actually can't stop and speak. Lydia has messed up my annual leave pay and I've been trying to sort it out.'

He walked in the direction of Emergency with her. 'How's the mood in Emergency?'

'Pretty flat,' Candy said. 'His funeral is being held in Sunderland, where he's from, but the hospital is holding a memorial service for him. They're naming the new resuscitation area after him,' She gave a tight smile. 'Thankfully I'll be in Hawaii when it's held.'

'Thankfully?'

She shook her head. She really didn't want to discuss how mixed up she was feeling right now, especially with Steele. She had considered changing her holiday so she could attend the memorial service but the thought of facing his parents there was too much for Candy. While she knew she had to tell them, she wanted to get her own head around it first. As for them naming Resuscitation after him! Well, the thought of wheeling patients in and out of Gerry's Wing, day in and day out, had her stomach in knots.

Then she turned and looked at the man she was quite sure she loved with all her heart and she wanted to break down and tell him. She wanted the pregnancy to go away and to be back to where they had once been, but it certainly wasn't Steele's problem so she gave him a very tight smile. 'I do have to go.'

He nodded and watched her dash off.

Leave it, the sensible part of his mind said as he headed back to the geriatric unit and went and hid in his office.

He was certain now that Candy was pregnant. In a matter of days her body had changed and she was completely unable to meet his eyes.

He was roused from his introspection by a tap at the door and he called for whoever it was to come in.

'Sorry to trouble you.'

'No trouble at all.' Steele smiled at Catherine, Macey's niece and another woman.

'This is my sister, Linda.'

'Good afternoon, Linda.' He expected Linda had some questions, that they perhaps wanted to know how best to broach things with Macey. But, as Steele found out every day in his job, there were always surprises to be had.

'When Aunt Macey had her heart attack,' Catherine started, 'Linda took care of her home, fed the cat, that sort of thing…'

'I see.'

Linda spoke then. 'A letter came while she was in hospital. I was doing her mail and paying her bills so she didn't have to worry about being cut off. I opened this letter and it was from a charity that deals with adopted children. It explained that Macey's son wanted to make contact. I didn't know if it would make things worse. She was so sick…'

'Of course you didn't know what to do,' he said.

'I didn't even tell Catherine,' Linda said. 'I just didn't know what to do with the news. I spoke to my husband and he suggested that we wait till Aunt Macey was feeling better. Really, though, she's been slowly going downhill for so long…'

'Do you have the letter with you?' Steele asked, and she nodded and handed it to him.

'He wants to make contact,' Linda said. 'I feel bad for not telling her.'

'Don't feel bad,' Steele said. 'It could have been an awful shock for her, though now I think it will be very welcome news. Why don't you go in now and speak with her? Facing it will be hard and I'll be around if she gets upset but, to be honest, I think it will be a relief.'

He did hang around, but all seemed calm with Macey. He sat at the desk next to Elaine. He could see Macey and her nieces talking earnestly and at one point Macey actually laughed.

'It's good to see her laughing,' Steele said, and turned and smiled at Elaine.

'Sorry?'

'Macey,' Steele explained, then he saw Elaine's swollen eyes. 'Are you all right, Elaine?'

'I am.' She gave a small shake of her head. 'I'm worried about my assessment.'

Steele frowned. 'Elaine, you're doing really well. I know I'm not a nurse, but I do know how well you look after the patients.'

'Even if I get my words wrong at times,' Elaine said, because Abigail had had a small word with her about the muffy thing.

'Even if you get your words wrong.' He smiled, and was pleased to see that she did too. 'Is there anything else on your mind?'

'No.' She shook her head and stood up and left him sitting alone.

Steele looked over again at Macey and her nieces and knew it was time for him to take his own medicine.

It was time for him to face things.

When he arrived in Emergency he saw the smudges beneath Candy's eyes and she was still refusing to meet his gaze.

Direct as ever, Steele asked the question. 'Are you avoiding me?'

She stood there and went to lie to him, to say of course not, or whatever, but his beautiful eyes demanded the truth so she nodded. 'Yes.'

'Can I ask why?'

There was no point in telling him about the pregnancy so she made up an excuse. An excuse that was partly true. 'I've been a bit mixed up about Gerry and I had a big argument with my parents. They've realised that I've been staying out at night…'

'Really?' He looked at her for a long moment. He knew she was lying, knew how she'd fought for her independence and knew too that she wouldn't give in to them.

'I think we should just leave things,' Candy said. 'I don't want to upset them.'

'I don't believe you,' he said. 'While I understand you might need a bit of space after what's happened to Gerry, I don't believe that's it.' When Candy didn't respond he pressed on. 'Do you know, one thing that I've really enjoyed about our time together is how honest we have always been. It's fine if you want to end things, but at least tell me the reason why.'

'Can we go somewhere private?' she asked.

'Sure,' he said, his voice clipped. 'My office?'

They walked through the hospital in silence and then onto the geriatric unit and it felt to both of them as if they were walking to the gallows—which they were, for this killed them.

Through the ward they went and to his office at the end, and Macey watched their strained faces as they passed by.

Candy stepped into his office and didn't take a seat. She had a feeling she wouldn't be here for very long.

'Do you want to tell me what's going on?' he invited.

'Not really,' she said.

'Okay. *Are* you going to tell me what's going on?'

'I'm pregnant,' Candy said.

For Steele it was the strangest sensation. Ten years ago he had wondered how he might react when the woman he was crazy about told him such news.

Now, ten years on, the woman he was seriously crazy about was telling him such news.

'With twins,' she added.

He hadn't been aware that she'd brought a cricket bat with her when she'd come into the office. Of course Candy hadn't but it felt like that as she added her little postscript and he was left with one thought, one regretful, sad thought.

They're not mine.

'They're not yours,' she added, like an echo to his brain, and Steele snapped his response, in his gruff, low voice.

'I think I'd already established that, thank you.'

Yes, he actually felt as if he'd been knocked on the back of the head because his reactions, his words did not belong to the man he knew he was, yet, concussed by the impact of her news, he continued to speak. 'What do you want me to say here, Candy?'

'I don't know,' she admitted.

He honestly did not know how to react. Was he supposed to step in and say, *That's fine, darling, I'll raise his babies*? Or, *How convenient, Candy*, he should perhaps say with a smile, *given that I shoot blanks*. Or was he supposed to say that it was no big deal?

It was a massive deal.

He should, Steele knew on some level, take her in his arms and tell her that things would work out, that she could get through this.

His arms couldn't move, though, and his mouth was clamped closed so that no words could come out.

'I'm going to go,' she said.

'Wait.'

'Why?' Candy answered. 'Steele, we agreed to three weeks. We managed two. I was hoping to get through this week without telling you.'

'But you have.'

'Because you're right—we *have* always been honest. Yes, I've been avoiding you. I didn't want to spoil what we had.'

'Have you told your parents?'

Candy shook her head.

'Have you told anyone?'

'I have now,' she said, and she looked straight through his eyes and to his heart. 'I've got the hardest part out of the way now.'

And telling Steele *was* the hardest part. Her parents, Gerry's parents, all of that she would deal with in time, but this part hurt the most.

'I'm going to go,' she said again. 'If you could drop my case off that would be brilliant. Just leave it at the door.'

She walked out then and he sort of came to and opened his office door and stepped onto the ward. There was Candy, walking out quickly, and he closed his eyes in regret for his lack of response. Then he turned and saw that Macey was watching him.

No, Steele did not smile.

Instead, he walked up to the nurses' desk. 'I'm going home,' he said to Gloria. 'Page Donald if you need anything.'

CHAPTER ELEVEN

IT WAS A long lonely night for both of them.

Candy woke in her flat and was more tempted than she had ever been in her life to ring in sick this morning. She had a shift on the geriatric ward, her last one. She was desperate to avoid Steele yet she wanted somehow to see him. And to see Macey too and say goodbye.

Then she had two more shifts in Emergency and then she flew to Hawaii.

Alone.

Or rather not alone—she ran a hand over her stomach and felt the edge of her uterus.

She had no idea how she felt about being pregnant.

No idea how to tell her parents or friends or anyone.

Right now, none of it even seemed to matter.

She loved Steele.

It wasn't like the crushes she'd had on other men, which Candy was rather more used to.

It felt so much deeper than that, like an actual concrete thing that now resided within.

Except the twins resided within also.

Twins?

As he did up his shirt that morning Steele was thinking about them too.

He was also thinking about her words—how telling him had been the hardest part.

He knew how impossible her parents were and he knew telling Gerry's parents would be supremely difficult.

Yet telling him…

As he did up his tie, he found himself closer to tears than he had been at his marriage break-up. Closer to tears than he had been at his grandmother's funeral.

In fact, Steele wasn't even close to tears—he was sitting on the edge of the bath in a serviced apartment, bawling his eyes out, for the fact they were over and the grief that her babies were not his. He'd never cried. Even when he'd found out that he couldn't have children, Steele hadn't broken down. He'd been too busy mopping up Annie's tears. Now, ten years later, he let out what had long been held in. He cried alone.

He was as nice to himself as he had been to Macey.

At seven a.m. it was a bit early for sherry but he made a strong mug of tea and put in extra sugar and then sat and thought what best to do.

He could avoid Candy, Steele knew. He could call in sick today. He had a day off tomorrow and then it was just her final shift in Emergency on Friday—he could send Donald to deal with anything that came up in Emergency, and he would never have to see Candy again.

He couldn't do that, though.

'Morning,' he said as he came into the kitchen on the geriatric ward, and there was Candy, making a mug of tea.

'Morning,' she said, though she brushed past him pretty quickly and headed off for handover.

Steele headed into his office and checked his emails.

Oh, joy.

There was Gerry.

His smiling face was surrounded by flowers, and Steele, along with the entire hospital—as long as cover could be arranged, of course—was invited to attend the memorial service next Tuesday and the naming of the resuscitation area as Gerry's Wing.

Candy was trying to get her head around that terrible name too.

Lydia, who had been on the edge of taking disciplinary action against Gerry, was now talking about him as if he'd been an angel—an angel with one wing—a wing named after him that Candy would work in, walk through, deal with day in and day out...

As Candy helped Macey shower, she was wondering how the hell she could continue to work there. Kelly had given her an odd look in the changing room yesterday and a little huddle at the nurses' station had suddenly gone very quiet when she had approached.

No one had had the nerve to outright ask her. Candy was quite plump and they were clearly trying to work out if she'd been hitting the doughnuts or if indeed she was pregnant.

Imagine them knowing she was pregnant by Gerry.

'You're very quiet this morning,' Macey said as Candy turned off the taps and helped her to get dried and dressed.

'I'm sorry, Macey, I was miles away.'

'Dreaming of Hawaii, no doubt,' Macey said. 'Are you looking forward to your holiday?'

'I am,' Candy said. 'I fly on Friday night.'

'It's Wednesday today.' Macey smiled. 'I think for the first time in years I actually know what day it is.'

'You're so much better,' Candy commented, as Macey dressed herself with just a little help. When they got back to the bed, Candy would remove Macey's dressing for Steele to have a look at her leg ulcer, which was doing much better. After lunch, Macey would lie on the bed for a couple of hours' sleep, but apart from that she sat in the chair or walked to the day room. It was wonderful to see the improvement in her.

'Steele says I should be able to go home next week.'

'How do you feel about that?' Candy asked as she walked with Macey back to her bed.

'I'm looking forward to it very much,' Macey said. 'I'm having some modifications done to the bathroom and kitchen, which my niece Linda is sorting out for me. Things will be a lot easier now.'

'Your nieces seem very nice.'

'Oh, they're wonderful women.' Macey nodded, taking a seat by the bed and putting her leg up on a footstool. She watched as Candy made up the bed. 'You've earned your holiday,' Macey said. 'I wish I could be here to see the postcard.'

'I'll send you one, Macey.' Candy smiled, despite her earlier declaration about not sending any. 'If you're okay with that?'

'Oh, yes, please! It would make my day! Is it just you going?'

Candy nodded.

'Hawaii would be a beautiful place to go with the right man…'

'It would,' Candy agreed, her heart twisting as she

thought how close she had come to sharing a part of her holiday with Steele.

'You don't have a boyfriend, though,' Macey continued. 'If I remember rightly.'

'No.'

'And you're carrying?' Macey said gently, and Candy's eyes filled with tears as she nodded.

'I'm having twins.'

'Congratulations, my dear.'

Macey was the first person to offer congratulations and she said it so nicely that Candy started to cry.

'Pull the curtains,' Macey said.

'No, no.' Candy sniffed. 'I'll go to the staffroom.'

'You'll pull the curtains and sit with me for a while.' Macey's orders were clear and Candy did as she was told.

'Have you told…?' Macey hesitated. She had been about to ask if Candy had told Steele, if that was what the argument the other day had been about, but her sharp mind was returning. Macey sat quietly for a moment, remembering when she had been admitted and had snapped at Steele for being a locum. It had only been his second day here, Macey recalled.

Certainly there had been a romance between Candy and Steele. She had seen it unfold in front of her own eyes.

'Have you told the baby's father?' she asked instead.

'Macey…'

She saw Candy swallow and reached out to take the hands of the younger woman to encourage her to speak on.

'I made a mistake a few months ago, so please don't feel sad for me when I say this—I'm not a grieving widow. The baby's father died a week ago.'

'Gerry?' Macey said, and watched Candy's eyes widen in surprise. 'I hear all the gossip.'

'Yes.' Candy gave a watery smile. 'It was him.'

'That's very sad.'

'It is,' Candy said. 'I don't know how he'd have felt about it,' she went on. 'We wouldn't have got back together but I'm sure we'd have sorted something out.'

'What about Steele?' Macey asked, and she watched the tears spill down Candy's cheeks, though she neither confirmed nor denied there was anything going on.

'You have your holiday to look forward to,' she said, and Candy nodded. 'It's a good job you booked it before you knew.'

'Oh, yes,' Candy said, because it would be her first and last overseas adventure alone. 'I don't think I'll be lounging around on the beach next time I go. It will be buckets and spades...' She shook her head. 'I can't see how I'll manage,' she admitted.

'You know, I can remember being alone and pregnant,' Macey said. 'I expect it's still a very scary place even fifty years on, even with all the choices you girls have these days. I still remember how scared I felt when I got pregnant but I'll tell you this much—by the end of my pregnancy I wasn't scared about having a baby. I wanted him so much and I know you'll feel the same way about your two.'

Candy nodded. She knew Macey was right. 'I'm sorry for what happened to you, Macey.'

'I know you are but don't be sorry. My nieces are getting into contact with him. If I can see him just once I'll be happy...' Her voice trailed off and she looked up and Candy followed her gaze and saw that Steele had popped his head in.

'Sorry,' Candy said, standing up from the bed. She was supposed to have removed Macey's dressing and she was embarrassed at him seeing her cry.

'It's fine,' Steele said. 'I'll come back later.'

He left them to it. He was glad that Candy was having a chat and a cry with Macey and when she came out a little while later and told him Macey's dressing was down, instead of ignoring what he'd seen he addressed it.

'Do you feel better after speaking with Macey?'

'I do,' she said. 'I'm going to miss her.'

And I miss you, Candy thought, but she could not say that without starting to cry again.

'Could we go somewhere after work?' he said. 'Just to talk.'

She didn't really want to say goodbye to him here, not like this, so she nodded.

They returned to the café he had first taken her to, yet it felt so different now—the innocence and fun of before had left them.

'What would you like to eat?' he asked.

'I'll just have a cup of tea,' she said. 'I'm meeting my parents tonight.'

'Have you told them?'

Candy shook her head 'I'll tell them about the twins when I get back.'

'They'll know very soon.' He'd tried not to notice her bump but now that he had he couldn't not see it. 'I'm not a very good doctor, am I?'

He somehow made her smile.

'I think it popped out about ten seconds after I found out…' Candy said. 'I'll just wear a big baggy top tonight. They're not talking to me anyway, because I changed the locks and I'm going to Hawaii, so I doubt I'll be there for very long.'

'Yet you still go.'

'I love them. I don't agree with them a lot of the time but I still love them very much and I know when I do tell them I'll break their hearts.'

'For a little while,' Steele said.

He took a breath. He could do this type of thing so easily for his patients but when it came to matters of a very private heart, things were very different, but he forced himself to step up.

'Would you like me to tell your parents for you?'

Candy frowned. 'Why would you do that?'

'Because I'm used to breaking news to difficult, stubborn, immutable people. I do it every day,' he said, and then made her smile. 'I promise to leave out the part that we've been at it like rabbits. I'll just say I'm a colleague. A doctor...'

Candy smiled. She really understood why he wore a suit and tie for work—the older people liked it. And he was right, her parents would respond very differently to Steele from the way they would to her. If not at first then fairly soon, they would calm down for the *dottore*.

'I need to do this myself, Steele. It's really nice of you to offer and I admit I'm tempted to pass it over, but...no. Thank you, though.'

'Is there anything I can do to help?'

'It's not your problem, Steele.' Then she looked over to him. 'Actually, this has helped and talking to Macey too. It makes it feel a bit more real.'

'Keep talking, then,' he said, but she shook her head.

'I can't really. I mean, I'm upset about Gerry too and I'm trying to work out how to tell his family and I don't think getting upset about Gerry is fair to you,' Candy said. 'I know I felt jealous when you spoke about your wife. I got an Annie burn.'

He loved her openness and he smiled when she admitted to having felt jealous. 'Candy, you *can* talk to me about that.' Ten years older, there were some things he did know. 'Two days before I turned thirty I found out that a woman who I had gone out with for close to six months, just after my divorce, had died. Now, she wasn't *the* love of my life. She was one of possibly too many *loves* of my life…' He saw her pale smile. 'And it hurt. I was stunned and devastated. I was all of the things that you probably are now.'

'It doesn't make you feel jealous when I talk about him?' Candy checked.

'I don't know how it makes me feel,' he admitted, touched that even with all that was going on in her world she could be concerned in that way for him. 'But that's my stuff to deal with. Right now you've got enough of your own.'

'Oh, I do!'

'You know there is one teeny positive,' Steele said.

'Tell me.'

'Well, there was one thing about you that was starting to get on my nerves, a potential deal-breaker, in fact,' Steele said. 'Confirmed bachelors are very picky and selfish, you understand…'

Candy smiled. 'Tell me.'

'Your ability to fall asleep. God, I knew you were tired, we both were, but I was starting to wonder if you had narcolepsy or something.'

She laughed but it changed in the middle and she

fought from letting out a sob because he'd just reminded her how very good it had been between them.

'Candy…' He took her hand but she pulled hers away.

'Please, don't, Steele,' she said. They had always been honest and she was never more so than now. 'Please, don't confuse me now. I miss you very much. I think we both know that it was turning into a bit more than a fling. I think we both know that feelings were starting to run deep.' Which was milder than the complete truth but now was not the time to admit to love. She pointed out the impossibility of it.

'You like the single life.'

'I did,' he said, 'but I very much liked being with you.'

'You've geared your life around not having children.'

'I have,' he said.

'You start your dream job in a couple of weeks.'

'I do.'

'And I'm pregnant with another man's babies.'

It dawned on him then that he had only ever known Candy pregnant. That, really, nothing had changed between them, except that they both now knew and he told her so.

'Candy, since the moment we met you've been pregnant with another man's babies. I think we—'

'Steele,' she interrupted. 'I have to work a few things out myself. I've been raised to share everything, to discuss every decision. I don't want to do that now. I want to think. I want to know that I can do this on my own. I have to know that I can do this on my own…'

'I get that.'

'And please don't pretend this isn't difficult for you.'

He thought back to that morning, sitting on the edge of the bath and crying in a way he never had before, but he felt better for it, clearer for it. He looked at Candy and knew she was right. She didn't need his thoughts now. She needed her holiday, she needed space, she needed to get used to the idea that she was going to be a mother.

'I need to go,' she said. She was on the edge of tears— just one touch of his hand and she wanted more, she wanted his arms, she wanted the comfort of him. She felt as if she had just got off a merry-go-round as they stepped outside. She had felt like that since the news about Gerry's death had hit, since she'd sat in Anton's office, since…

The world seemed to be spinning too fast of late, and Candy took a big breath and tried to steady herself, but big breaths seemed to be working less and less these days. Steele must have seen she was struggling. He wrapped her in his arms, as he had wanted to yesterday but hadn't known how. The shield of him, the feel of him, the tender strength of him brought the first glimpse of peace she had craved, just a tiny glimpse of tranquillity as solo she halted navigated stormy seas.

'You're going to be okay,' he said, and his voice was like the deep bass of a guitar coming up through the floorboards, a rhythm she recognised and understood, and she clung to the delicious familiarity of him and wished it could last. 'I know it's going to be hard, telling your parents, but when you do just remind them that this is their grandchildren they are discussing and that in few months they'll be here…'

'Right now I'm actually not worried about them,' she said. Right now she was wondering how she might ever get over this broken heart, but she daren't be that honest and so, for the first time, she lied to him. 'Right now I'm worried about stretch marks and my boobs reaching the moon and getting fatter...' *And losing you.* 'I'm going to go.'

Still he held her. 'I'll drive you home.'

Still she clung to him. 'I don't want you to.'

'I can drop off your case.'

She hated that he had it in his car.

Steele hated that it was in his car too. He wanted it in his apartment unpacked, he wanted her in his bed, yet he was terribly aware that he must not push her, not confuse her when she was already in such turmoil.

Maybe there was something he could do.

'Do you fancy a day pass?' he said to her ear.

'A day pass?'

'I'm going to Kent tomorrow to look at the new unit and also to look at a few houses that I'm thinking of buying...'

'You're buying a house?'

'I always buy houses or flats wherever I work and I renovate them in my spare time and sell them or rent them out.'

'I'm working in Emergency tomorrow.'

'Oh, if anyone deserves to ring in sick, I think it might be you. Why don't we just have a nice drive, a lazy day...?'

'And no talk about pregnancy.'

'You don't have to pretend you're not pregnant, Candy.'

'I want a day away from it,' she admitted. 'I just want a whole day when I don't even have to think about it.'

'Then that's the day you shall have,' he said, and saw her to the Underground. 'I'll pick you up at eight.'

Candy sat on the tube, looking at all the people, and she saw an elderly woman look at her stomach and then her hand. She glanced up and saw that Candy had seen her and the old lady gave her a very nice smile.

Yes, times had changed.

She didn't feel quite so alone now.

It really was time to deal with what was.

Instead of heading home, she went to her parents'.

They were still sulking about Hawaii.

'Do you remember Gerry, who I work with?' Candy said. 'The one who helped me when I moved?'

'What about him?' Her father frowned. 'Is he going to Hawaii with you?'

'He died last week,' Candy said.

There were all the *How terribles* and Candy took a deep breath. She knew there was no easy way to say it.

It just needed to be said.

'I've just found out that I'm pregnant with twins,' Candy said. 'They're his.'

There were sobs and wails from her parents; her mother actually fell to the floor. As if that was going to change anything!

She had never understood Steele more than she did then. She understood fully how his love for Annie might have died as she watched her parents carry on.

This was about her, this was the hardest part of her life to date, and yet they made it all about them.

She had known they'd be upset but, as Steele would say, that was their stuff. How Candy wished they could give some teeny shred of comfort as she tried to deal with hers.

Candy sat there as her father declared he'd like to kill the man who had taken his daughter's honour and then she stood up.

'*Lui è già morto,*' Candy said, reminding her father

that Gerry was already dead, and then she remembered Steele's words.

'These are your grandchildren we're discussing.' Her voice was incredibly clear and strong. 'And these are my babies and I refuse to listen to you calling them a mistake or talking about shame. In a few months they'll be here and you know as well as I do that you're going to love them. So why do this to me now? I'm going to go and I don't want to hear from you till you've calmed down.' She went to the door. 'And if you want to come to my flat, then you're to telephone before you do. Clearly I have a life you don't know about, and if you still don't want to know about it, then you're to telephone first before you come around!'

She left her parents and she could perhaps have headed for home but instead she did as Steele had once suggested she try.

She bought a single ticket for a movie—the one they hadn't seen that night. It was a real tear-jerker from start to end and she sat there, tears pouring down her face and not trying to hide them.

It was nice, a tiny press of the pause button as she cried over the couple on the screen instead of dwelling on herself.

On Steele.

On what could surely never be.

CHAPTER TWELVE

HER JEANS JUST did up.

Nervous and a little excited, just as she had been the first time he'd come to her door, she opened it the next morning with a smile.

'I'm ready,' she said, 'or did you want a drink first?'

'No, thanks,' Steele said. 'It's probably better that we get going. I've got a lot to get on with today.' He couldn't not comment. 'You've been crying.'

'I had a rather big argument with my parents last night.'

'You told them?'

'I did.' She blew out a breath. 'And I told them a few other things too. Anyway, we're not talking about all that stuff today. I really do want a day off from it.'

'Fair enough.' He smiled. 'But can I just say that I'm really proud of you for telling them.'

'Thank you.'

'You'll enjoy your holiday far more without that hanging over you.'

'I shall.'

They went out to his car and were soon on the motorway. 'First up,' Steele explained, 'I'm going to look at the new wing of the hospital, which might bore the hell out of you. You can go for a walk or to the shops if you like.'

'No, I'd love to see it,' Candy said, 'unless explaining me makes things awkward for you.'

'I never feel the need to explain myself,' he said, and then he amended that slightly. 'Actually, I did cancel dinner with my parents tonight, you would have taken some explaining.'

'Oh, sorry,' Candy said, 'I didn't want you to change your plans for me.'

'I was more than happy to change them. I'm moving closer to them in a few weeks.' He turned and smiled again. 'Though not quite close as you are to yours, but they'll be seeing more of me than they do now.'

'What are they like now?'

'They've mellowed,' Steele said. 'They're much nicer as old people. Though I have to admit that when they start asking questions about my life, my love life, I'm often tempted to tell them to back off, given that they showed little interest in me when I was growing up.' He gave a roll of his eyes. 'I wouldn't do that to them, though.'

Candy knew that he wouldn't. He was too nice.

'You like old people.'

'I do,' he said. 'I don't like *all* old people. It's not a free pass to being a good person but I like how they've let go of the stuff that's not important. I like how they say what they think and share what they know. I like it even when my patients drive me mad with their stubbornness. I learn something every day, every single day, from how to put a brass doorknob on a house I'm renovating to how to face death.'

They arrived at the hospital and Steele shook hands

and introduced her to Reece, a consultant who'd clearly had a lot of input into the new wing.

'Any chance of you starting sooner?' Reece joked. 'Emergency is full.'

'No chance.' Steele smiled. 'I don't need you to show me around if you're busy.'

'You're sure?'

'Of course.'

'I'll see you at the meeting, then.' Reece nodded. 'Make sure you put a hard hat on.'

'I feel like a builder,' Candy said as she put hers on.

'Come on, Bob,' Steele said, and he took her through the building. It was near complete in parts and the roof was going on in others. 'This is going to be the acute geriatric unit,' he explained as he showed her a huge area where the wiring was going in. 'Very high-tech computer system,' he said. 'It has its own occupational therapy assessment area.' He took her in. There were two kitchens and various sets of stairs being built, as well as showers and baths of various heights so that patients could be assessed on how they would manage at home. 'I'm aiming for a forty-eight-hour admission time. Either home afterwards with support or admitted to the correct ward, but most of my patients will first come through here—well, that's the plan.'

'Forty-eight hours isn't very long.'

'Best time frame,' Steele said. 'It gives us enough time to put proper support in place for when they return to their homes.'

Steele showed her the other wards—a palliative care ward and also the acute medical unit—and then he opened a door and they stood in a huge empty space.

'This is the dream,' he said. 'It's not happening yet.

We're facing lots of obstacles and red tape, insurance issues and things, but I'm hoping this space will be a gym.' He smiled. 'Actually, I'm not allowed to call it that. I'm hoping this space will be utilised for healthy living…'

'Sorry?'

'Well, I always feel a bit of a bastard when I know someone's lonely and that a cream cake at three in the afternoon means not only a cream cake but a walk to the shops and some conversation too. Instead of asking them to give it up, I'm hoping that they can come here and have a chat with friends and maybe a bit of exercise. I'm hoping for a slimming or exercise club or something like that. It's all a bit of a pipe dream at the moment, but at least we have the space earmarked for it, if we ever do get to go ahead.'

'How long's your contract for?' Candy asked.

'Two years,' he said. 'They wanted five but I wouldn't agree to it.'

'Because?'

'Because I've never stayed anywhere for more than two years. I like fresh starts. I like putting everything into it and building things up…'

Or rather he had.

They drove to a pub and had a lovely lazy lunch overlooking a huge village green.

'Gorgeous, isn't it?' Candy said, and he nodded.

'Even if we don't get the go-ahead for the gym, I'll probably start a walking club over there.'

'You're going to go start a geriatric walking club!'

'Yep, I walk with my dog every morning that I can. Why not have company?'

'You have a dog?'

'I do.' Steele smiled. 'You have me pegged as a loner—

no friends to go to the movies with, no pets. I have a dog, I have nice furniture and I have, when I'm not sleeping with Nurse Candy, a very busy social life.'

'Where's your dog now?'

'At my parents',' he said. 'He's a chocolate Labrador called Newman.'

'Newman?'

'You'll…' Steele stopped. He had been about to say she would see why when she met him but that wasn't what today was about. *No pressure*, he reminded himself. Today was doing her good, he could see that already. Her cheeks were pink and she seemed more relaxed than she had since…well, since Macey had opened her mouth and knocked their worlds off their axes, but they were starting to spin again, tentatively, though. 'He's got blue eyes,' Steele said instead. 'And he's the love of my life and he knows it.'

'Does he sleep on your bed, Steele?'

Steele shook his head. 'He sleeps on his bed for about seventeen hours a day and graciously lets me share it at night.'

After lunch they walked across the green and Candy laughed as she looked at it through what she imagined were Steele's eyes. 'I have this vision of all these old people doing Tai Chi…'

'So do I.'

She stopped walking. 'And then you'll leave.'

'That was the plan,' he said. 'Though this is a huge project…' He looked around. Since his divorce he had never been able to imagine staying in one place for very long. Here, though, he was close, though not too close to his parents; here was the job he had been working towards his entire career. He looked over as a car pulled up and a man got out and gave them a wave as they walked over to him.

'That's the estate agent,' Steele explained.

'Oh.'

'And that's the renovator's delight I'm hoping to buy, but I'm not telling him that.'

It was a huge rambling house with a small wooden gate, overlooking the green.

'Are you going to come and take a look?' he said.

'I think I might just take another walk,' she said. She didn't want to see his future home, so she walked on the green as Steele inspected the house.

He looked at the cornices and the hanging-off doors; the windows would all need to be taken out.

Don't start on the electrics, he thought as he flicked lights on and off.

And as for the plumbing! The estate agent tried to distract him from turning on taps but Steele was not easily distracted and when he turned on the taps the whole house seemed to rattle. Steele grinned as, in his head, he knocked another five grand off the asking price.

It was magnificent, though.

'Could you give me a moment?' he said to the agent. 'I'd like to walk through it again on my own for a minute.'

The estate agent agreed and Steele took way more than a minute.

The last time he had looked at a home this size had been with his ex-wife. The natural assumption at that time had been that the bedrooms would soon be filled.

The natural assumption as he walked around now was that the bedrooms would be filled too.

It was more than an assumption. It was a feeling it was how it should be. He looked out of a window and could see Candy idly walking around. He wanted to go and fetch her, bring her in, ask her her thoughts, yet her thoughts were cluttered enough now.

His weren't.

He thanked the estate agent and said that he'd be in touch then he walked over and joined her.

'Maybe I can explain you after all,' he said.

'Sorry?'

'I could just say to my parents that you're a friend from work who needed a day out. You can meet Newman.'

'No, thanks,' she said.

'Candy, can we talk—'

'Please, not now,' she said. 'I just need this day. I just need a day of not dealing with it and then I need my holiday to start dealing with it on my own.'

Steele nodded. It was what they had agreed to after all.

They drove back to his flat to collect her case, which was no longer in the car, and Candy needed it as she flew tomorrow.

Candy, of course, fell asleep in the car but now it just made him smile.

She awoke to his lovely deep voice and the sight of his flat and then she turned and there he was.

'I'll go and grab your case,' he said.

'Can I borrow your loo?' Candy said, because, as she was starting to find out, this was something she would be saying rather a lot in the weeks and months ahead.

She went to the loo and remembered the last time she'd been here—when her pregnancy had just started to become a possibility. As she looked in the mirror while washing her hands, she remembered the fear that had been in her eyes then.

The fear was gone now.

Yes, she was confused and exhausted and nervous about how she would provide for two children, but the terror was leaving and, after such a wonderful day's reprieve, she was starting to feel a little more like herself.

'Thank you for a lovely day,' she said.

'Do you want a cup of tea?' he offered, and she nodded.

'Make yourself comfortable.'

'Ha-ha,' she said, and stood and watched him make the tea instead.

Meaning…

She lifted her top and showed him the straining zipper that had simply refused to go all the way back up.

Only Steele didn't really see that. He saw pink lace and a teeny flash of jet hair and the stomach that his mouth had kissed over and over.

And as she put down her top Candy looked at the teabag he was squeezing the hell out of with his spoon and, yikes, there was a sort of gravelly note to his voice as he asked her how many sugars she had in her tea.

'The same as last time,' Candy said.

'Sorry, I'm a bit distracted.' Steele smiled. 'Two?'

'Two.'

'Do you really want tea?' he checked.

'No.'

'Because I don't,' Steele said. 'I want a glass of wine but I'm driving.'

'Poor Steele.' She smiled. 'It really is a problem.' Candy thought for a moment. 'I know!' she said brightly.

'Do tell.'

'Why don't you have a glass of wine and drive me home later?'

He turned and faced her. 'That's so clever, but you're

stuck in those uncomfortable jeans. I insist you take them off...'

They started to kiss, the best kiss ever, because she'd got so lost in babies and feeling massive and unsexy but his tongue swiftly took care of that.

It hadn't really entered her head that he might want her again in that way. Now his fingers were at her zipper and somehow she felt back to the woman she had been.

Out of her jeans, she moaned in relief.

'Nice?'

'Nice,' she said to his mouth.

'That bra looks a bit tight too.'

He unhooked it and took it out through her arms and it was lovely to be all loose and floppy and to rest a moment in his arms.

'Feels so good,' she said.

'It does,' he said. There would be no rushing. He loved feeling her all relaxed against him.

'Get your wine.'

They headed over to the sofa and it was nice to be back there. Steele sat and Candy lay down as he drank his wine and played with her hair. It was good not to talk. She remembered the mornings with Macey and her *nonna*, and the bliss of hush when words could only serve to make you sad.

'Are you all packed for Hawaii?' he said finally.

'Nope.' Candy sighed. 'We're here to get my case, remember?'

This time tomorrow she'd be at Heathrow.

'Can I paint your toenails?' she asked.

'Er, why?'

'It relaxes me and my mum's still sulking at me so I haven't been able to do hers.'

'Do you have some nail varnish with you?'

'In my bag.'

He was so laid back and yet so austere. It was a lovely mixture that made her stomach curl and also gave her a peace that she could be herself.

And she was.

He lay down and she sat on his calves and started on his right foot. 'I like men's nails,' Candy explained, 'because they're bigger.'

'Have you painted a lot of men's nails?' he asked, and then let out a moan of surprise. 'Oh!'

'What?' She smiled as she painted his big toenail.

'I have nail-painting jealousy issues,' Steele said. 'I just felt it burn. I'm looking at your bum and enjoying the view when I suddenly got the Annie burn that you had.'

'I've never painted another man's toenails from this angle.' Candy smiled again.

'Take your knickers off, then.'

She did as told and then got back to painting the toenails on his left foot but she made a terrible mess of his long second toe because she heard his zipper slide down.

'I'm making a bit of a mess here, Steele,' she said.

'I forgive you,' he said.

'Steele.' She was arguably the most turned on she had ever been. She had never thought she'd feel sexy again, had never thought sex would ever be fun again, and yet here they were and it was bliss. 'Can I turn around?'

'You'll finish what you started,' Steele warned.

She gritted her teeth and did the last three toes really quickly. 'Done.' She turned around on his calves to the delicious sight of him and she moved up to sit on his thighs and lowered her head and they shared a long, deep kiss. Her breasts flattened against his chest and she could feel his erection pressing against her stomach.

She brought the kiss to a giddy halt and stared at him. He looked right back at her in a way that had her almost feverish. She started placing small kisses over his cheeks as his hands moved to her breasts, working her nipples.

'Candy...' Steele nearly said something he shouldn't. Today wasn't a day for confusing her, today wasn't a day for declarations, it was about keeping it light and he felt her sudden tension at the tender tone to his voice. 'Time for your hula lesson,' he said, and got the reward of her laugh in his ear.

She lowered herself onto him and he held her hips and had her sway a little and circle, and then Candy could not play any longer and she started moving of her own accord. His hands exploring her breasts had her greedy for more and she leant forward, lowering her breasts to his mouth, dizzy with the sensation of his hands now on her hips, grinding her down a little harder as his mouth worked her tender nipples.

'Steele...' There was almost panic in her voice, a delicious panic because her body wasn't hers any more but was moving into a rhythm of its own.

His mouth left her breast and she looked down at him. His lips were slightly parted and there was tension in his expression, just as there was in hers.

Steele adjusted the angle of his thrust just a fraction and she let out a sob. It was an actual sob as Steele started to come.

And then another sob and it was one of relief as somehow, some way, as she came to him, all she was at that moment was Candy.

Not pregnant, not scared, not worried at all.

The world felt a lot better when she was in Steele's arms.

CHAPTER THIRTEEN

Steele stared at the morning light as she lay in his arms.

It was the last morning they would share in this room.

'Excited?'

'Very.' Candy nodded.

Despite her misgivings at times, now she was looking forward again to going on holiday. There was so much more to sort out now and Candy truly wanted to get on with it.

Right now, though, here was where she wanted to be, and she lay stroking the crinkly hair on his stomach that she loved so.

'What date do you get back?' Steele asked.

It was the first day of his new job.

'Do you want me to see if I can get away this evening and take you to the airport?'

'No, because then we'll have to say goodbye again.' She looked up at him. He'd been so lovely to her. Her time with Steele had been the most wonderful time of her life but she wasn't foolish. Two weeks away from each other, him starting a new job, very soon he might look at things in a very different light. She didn't want to find out a few weeks or months from now that, despite best intentions, they hadn't worked out... A very big part of

Candy wanted it left at this. She wanted it to end while they were crazy about each other, while it was fun and sex and romance—before it all got too hard.

They got out of bed and got ready and he picked up her case and when they got to her flat he carried it in and he laughed when he saw the lock she'd put on.

'How many holes did you put in the door?'

'I'm very proud of my work,' Candy said.

'I'm not sure your landlord will be,' Steele said, and smiled as Candy went a bit pink. 'Did you ask permission?'

'No.'

'Do you want me to fix it up?'

'No,' she said. 'I want to fix it myself.'

'I know you do.'

They had a cuddle in the hall, a quiet one, just stood there and held each other and the moment was theirs.

He drove her to work and as they went to say goodbye it was too hard to do. 'I'll pop in and see Macey and if you're on the ward…'

'Sure.'

He gave her a kiss and they both did their very best to get on with their day.

'Candy…' Kelly said as she came into the changing room. 'How are things?'

'Sorry?'

'You were off sick yesterday,' Kelly fished.

'I wasn't sick, though.' Candy smiled. 'It was a mental health day.'

'So everything is okay?' Kelly checked.

'It will be about ten hours from now when my plane takes off.' She knew Kelly was fishing—everyone was.

And at midday Candy broke her news as they dealt with a multi-trauma.

'I'm stepping out,' she said as they went to do the X-rays. She always wore a heavy lead gown and so she knew it would not have affected the twins, but she just chose to let people know then. 'I'm pregnant, so I'd rather not take the chance…'

She left the room and let out a breath. Steele was right, she'd enjoy her holiday much more without that hanging over her.

And she dealt with the second question on everyone's minds as she stepped back in.

'I'm not comfortable yet discussing who the father is, but you'll all be very excited to know I'm expecting twins.'

There were smiles and congratulations and even a bottle of iced lemonade to toast her at the end of her shift.

'Have fun!' Lydia said. 'Lots of it.'

'Oh, I shall.'

She headed up to the geriatric unit and said goodbye to a couple of patients before she got to her very favourite one.

'Enjoy yourself,' Macey said. 'You deserve to be happy. A rather clever doctor told me that.'

Candy nodded. She had every intention of being happy, but as she gave Macey a cuddle and said goodbye she asked a question, desperate for the older woman's sage thoughts.

'Macey,' Candy said carefully. 'I want to be happy but what if you're not certain that the other person truly is? What if they might be there only out of a sense of duty?'

'Duty?' Macey thought for a long moment and Candy realised she was holding her breath as she awaited her answer, but Macey clearly didn't quite understand her question. 'Duty to who?' Macey asked.

'It doesn't matter,' Candy said, and gave her a smile. 'Stay well and I shall send you a postcard.'

As she left Macey she saw Steele going into his office and she went and knocked at the door.

'Are you off?'

'I am,' Candy said. 'Well, I've just got to see the obstetrician, buy a bikini, pack, take the Underground…'

'You're sure you don't want me to take you?'

'I'm very sure,' she said, and he took her in his arms. 'Thank you,' Candy said. 'I know we only had a short time and I know it was a bit fraught but you really helped and I just…' She couldn't really finish saying what she wanted to say without crying. 'I might write to you,' she said. 'Or call you. I really don't know…'

'You stop worrying about me and just go and have a wonderful time,' he said. 'Do what you have to do. Oh, one thing…' He took out his wallet and peeled off some US dollars.

'Stop!' Candy said. 'I don't need a sugar daddy.'

'I'm not old enough to be your sugar daddy.' He laughed. 'Seriously, I've had these for about five years, since my last trip to the States. Have fun with it.'

'Thank you!' Candy smiled.

'Go,' he said.

'But—'

'Go,' he said again, and she was glad that he did because she wanted to say goodbye smiling and if she stayed a moment longer she might possibly cry.

Then it was time for her official appointment with Anton.

'I told you that you were about to start showing,' he

said with a smile as she walked in. 'Have people started noticing?'

'Yes, though no one had the nerve to ask if I was pregnant just yet, though a patient told me that I was before I even knew. I've just announced it. I also said that I'm not comfortable with telling them who the father is.'

'Well done.' Anton smiled again.

He checked her blood pressure and all was well then Candy climbed up onto the examination table and he spoke to her about twin pregnancies. He said her babies would probably be born at around thirty-seven weeks and that he would see her more regularly than he would for a singleton pregnancy.

'Have you told your parents?'

Candy nodded. 'They didn't take it very well at all.'

'They'll come around.'

'I know,' she said. 'I told them to contact me when they do. I think I'm going to tell Gerry's parents when I return from my holiday. I think that it is only fair to them to know.'

'What about your new partner?'

'He's not really my partner, I don't think,' Candy said as Anton helped her to sit up. 'It was supposed to be just a casual thing. He starts a new job soon and is moving. He'll be gone by the time I get back from my holiday. I don't know what will happen then, if anything.' She smiled at Anton. 'My bad for falling in love.'

'You have told the insurance companies that you're pregnant?'

'I have.'

'Go and have and amazing holiday. Grieve, cry, smile and heal.'

'Thank you.'

They sounded like pretty straightforward instructions and as she packed the last few pieces into her suitcase she called for a taxi to take her to the Underground.

Usually her parents would go with her to the airport to wave her off as if she were going on an expedition for a year but they were clearly not over the news yet so Candy took the Underground and battled with evening commuters and her suitcase.

She caught sight of a pregnant woman's reflection in the window and it took a second before she realised that it was her own.

We'll get there, she said in her mind to her small bump. She loved them already. The numb shock had worn off. The fear had gone. Already Candy knew she'd cope.

They would get through this.

As she checked in at Heathrow and watched her case shoot away she turned and saw her parents.

'Ma…' Candy ran over and hugged them.

'We love you.'

'I know you do.'

'We'll help.'

'I know you will,' Candy said, and they kissed and made up with much relief.

'You move from that flat and come home,' her mother said. 'We can help you to raise them—'

'We'll talk when I get home,' Candy said. 'Thank you so much for coming to the airport. It means an awful lot to me.'

It had but as she sat on the plane she knew she was moving from her flat but not to her parents' home.

She thought of Steele raised by his grandmother. No, she didn't want that for the twins. She wanted to raise her children herself, her way, and not her parents' way.

* * *

There was so much to sort out, so very much, but as she disembarked from the plane nearly a day later and a lei was placed around her neck Candy was the happiest tourist on the planet and knew Hawaii was the right place to be.

'Aloha,' a gorgeous woman said.

Yes, she was happy, yet that evening as she walked along the beach, how she wished Steele was here beside her—dipping his red toenails in the Pacific, making her laugh, making her smile, letting her be who she was.

Candy loved the way he accepted her just as she was.

CHAPTER FOURTEEN

'ARE YOU GOING to a funeral?' Macey checked, seeing Steele's dark suit and tie the following Tuesday morning. 'Wait till you get to my age. I go to one a month.'

'It's a memorial service,' he said. He really liked speaking with Macey. She was so blunt about everything.

'Oh, is it for that nurse in Emergency?' she asked. 'The one Elaine's crying over?'

'Elaine?' Steele glanced across the ward and sure enough a very flat Elaine, very un-bossy of late Elaine, was sitting at the desk when she'd normally be bustling about. 'He got off with her at a Christmas party,' Macey said, 'from what I can make out. Then he had nothing to do with her the next day. I would say he wasn't a good caretaker of lovely young hearts.'

'Oh, he's St Gerry now.' Steele rolled his eyes.

'And I shall be St Macey for a while after I die and then people will start to remember what a cantankerous old thing I really was.'

He laughed and looked into her wise eyes. 'You don't miss anything, do you?'

'Not with the new medication.' She smiled. 'I'm back.'

'God help us, then.' Steele smiled.

'You wouldn't have met him, though,' Macey said, and the smile was wiped off his face at her perception.

'Sorry?'

'He was in Greece, had been there a couple of months when it happened, well, according to the porter who took me for my X-ray… That's what he said to the radiographer anyway.'

'I believe so.'

'So why are you going to his memorial service if you never met?'

Steele said nothing, just gave Macey a small nod and walked off.

He sat at the desk and tried to write notes, but he ached. He actually ached sitting there.

He missed Candy, more than he had ever missed anyone.

He'd never missed anybody really, apart from his grandmother when she'd died.

It felt like grief. It really did.

It was grief because he missed her. He even missed the bump of her twins, or was he just imagining that?

He pulled up his emails and looked at the image of Gerry and it wasn't jealousy he was feeling. Steele understood that now.

It was guilt.

Guilt because this young man had died. Guilt that he might be swooping in and raising his babies because he couldn't have any of his own.

Steele let out a breath and then jumped slightly as a voice startled him.

'I'm here to see Macey Anderson…' Steele glanced up and saw a good-looking middle-aged man wearing a suit and tie and carrying a huge bunch of flowers.

He was nervous, he was anxious and he was hers, Steele knew.

'I'll take you over.' He stood and as they walked to the bed he would never forget the small cry of recognition that escaped Macey as she looked down the ward and for the first time saw her son.

He ran to her.

Those last two steps he actually ran and Steele pulled the curtains around them as Macey held her fifty-five-year-old baby for the very first time.

Some things were private but Steele knew he'd just witnessed love.

Steele checked in on Macey a couple of hours later. She had gone to bed for a lie down, but he found her sitting up, smiling, with a huge bunch of flowers beside her bed and a photo album that her son had brought for her.

'I'm a grandmother,' she said, showing Steele a photo. 'And in two weeks I'll be a great-grandmother. He was a bit worried about telling me that.' Macey gave a delighted smile. 'His daughter, Samantha, is only eighteen. They're coming to visit me when I'm home.'

'You're going to be busy, Macey,' Steele said.

'I shall be. I'd say I'm going to have to hang around for a while yet.' She looked at him. 'Do you know, I always worried what sort of home he'd gone to, more than I worried about what he thought of me. He was raised beautifully. They loved him from the moment they got him and still do… It's a huge weight off my mind.'

'I'm very glad,' he said, and then he moved to go because she was cutting a bit close to the bone.

'I wondered if they'd love him as their own,' Macey said. 'I wondered if he'd resent them if he found out he wasn't biologically theirs, but they were just so open about it…'

'I'm very pleased to hear that,' Steele responded. 'Now, if you'll excuse me, I have to go.'

As he went to do that Macey's words stopped him.

'So she's in Hawaii…'

'Sorry?' he said, and turned.

Macey gave him an odd look. 'Are we going to pretend that you don't know who I'm talking about?'

'I don't,' Steele said.

'Do you think you stop being a matron? I used to know everything that went on in my department. Do you really think I just lie here?'

Steele had never had anyone meddle in his love life, or lack of a love life, and he wasn't going to start now. 'I have to go, Macey.'

'You just interrupted me, Doctor. Why is she in Hawaii and you're here?'

'I don't discuss my private life…'

'But you're fine with me discussing mine?'

'You're my job,' Steele said to her, but she just smiled at him.

'And you're hard work!' she said. 'You're certainly not so chipper these days.'

'I apologise,' he said. 'I shouldn't bring my problems to work with me.'

'How are *you*, Steele?' she said. 'And that's Matron asking.'

Steele remembered Candy sitting here, crying, on this very bed. It had been Macey who had told them both that Candy was pregnant after all. He sat on the bed and this time he was there for himself rather than Macey and he told her how he felt.

'Sad.'

'I'm sorry.'

'I miss her.'

'You don't have to miss her, though.'

'She needs this break.'

'Perhaps, but she'll come back and you'll be gone, living miles away, immersed in your new job. That's not the start that you two need.'

'She needs time to think.'

'Of course she does,' Macey said, 'but you can have too much time and get yourself into a space that it's very hard to get out of.'

She was right. Steele knew that. Of course, Candy's parents would soon come round. From the little he knew about them, he knew that they loved their daughter. They would want to help. They would probably suggest that she move back in with them. He thought about trying to forge a relationship with her parents as gatekeepers.

They didn't need to forge anything, Steele realised.

He didn't need to question himself about his motives towards the pregnancy.

He loved her.

It was that easy.

Macey watched the smile that spread on his face and, yes, some things were private but she knew too that she'd just witnessed the realisation of love.

Steele sat through the long memorial service and heard what an amazing man St Gerry had been, but it didn't hurt him now.

Indeed, he could laugh at a few of his antics.

By all accounts he had been a bit wild, a bit bold, and

now, as the shock of his death started to recede, the real Gerry started to appear.

They all stood as his parents cut a ribbon for the new resuscitation ward and everybody headed up towards Admin for drinks and nibbles and more talk about Gerry, but Steele chose not to go there.

'Steele!' Hugh, a surgeon he had asked to consult on a patient, came over and shook his hand. 'Have you met Rory?'

'I have.' He shook Rory's hand.

'And this is Gina. She's also an anaesthetist here,' Hugh introduced, but Steele couldn't place her.

'I *used* to be an anaesthetist here,' Gina said.

'It's lovely to meet you,' he said, and then watched Gina's features tighten as a man made his way over.

'This is Anton,' Hugh said, and Steele shook Anton's hand as Hugh introduced them. 'Anton's an obstetrician.'

'Well,' Steele said, 'that would explain why we haven't met. We don't have much call for obstetricians on the geriatric unit.'

'I'm also a reproductive specialist,' Anton said. 'Though I guess you don't have much call up there for them either.' He turned to Hugh. 'Are you going up to Admin for drinks?'

'No.' Hugh shook his head. 'I've got to get back to Theatre. Anyway, I've done my duty and put in an appearance but, frankly, he was an arrogant piece of work and I had more arguments with him than anyone else at the Royal.'

Anton watched as Steele gave a wry smile.

'Well, I certainly don't need to be around booze,' Gina said. 'I'm heading for home. I might see you around.' She smiled at Steele. 'I've got an interview next week.'

'Good luck,' Steele said.

Anton, he noticed, made no comment.

Gina walked off and there was an uncomfortable silence for a moment.

'How is she?' Hugh asked Rory.

'How would I know?' Rory said. 'We're not really talking any more.'

The two men walked off, leaving just Steele and Anton.

'Undercurrents?' Steele checked, because around Gina things had seemed incredibly tense.

'Hell, yes,' Anton said, but didn't elaborate. 'I think I might give the drinks in Admin a miss too, although I could use a drink. Do you want to go over to Imelda's?' he offered. Imelda's was a bar across from the hospital and Steele nodded.

'Sure.'

'Have you worked here long?' Steele asked as they gave their orders a few minutes later.

'Just over a year,' Anton said. 'You?'

'I'm only here for a few more weeks. I move to Kent the week after next.'

'My first intention was to be here for a couple of years and then return to Milan, but my wife works here and she's pregnant. I can't see me leaving here any time soon.'

'You said that you worked in fertility?'

'That's right.'

'Is it hard to do both?' Steele asked.

'I set firm boundaries,' Anton explained. 'I first did obstetrics then moved into fertility. I missed it, though, and so when I moved to England I changed back to obstetrics. I still keep my hand in when I can. I would love somehow to do both but they are both very consuming.'

'There are a lot of changes, I guess?' Steele could not believe he was pushing this conversation.

Anton could. 'There are constant changes.'

'What about for men?' Steele asked. 'I mean, you hear all the advancements for women…' He could not believe he was discussing this. He actually wanted to stop because if there wasn't hope then perhaps it would be better not to know.

'Things are different for men also. There is a procedure called ICSE now. Basically, if you can get one healthy sperm an egg can be fertilised. Even if the sperm count comes back as negative, you can go into the vas deferens…'

Steele pulled a face at the thought of a needle in his balls.

'Under local.' Anton smiled.

He'd do it.

And there was the difference, Steele realised. He'd had a lot of loves in his life but never till now 'the one'.

One that meant two hours after taking his first sip of a very welcome Scotch and a whole lot of talking with Anton, he was standing in a room, pants around his ankles, filling a specimen jar.

'That was quick,' Anton teased as Steele came into his office and he took the jar. 'You might want to work on that.' Then he was serious as he prepared the sample. 'You know that if I find nothing in the specimen I can still go into the vas deferens. I might want to do that sober, though.'

'Just tell me.'

CHAPTER FIFTEEN

CANDY CRIED OVER GERRY.

And on days two and three Candy cried quite a bit about finding herself twenty-four years old and pregnant with twins.

Day three she had explored the island and on day four the dam broke and Candy sobbed at the unfairness of it all, that the man she knew she loved had arrived in her life at a time when all the odds were stacked against them.

By day five she gave up on crying and took Steele's money, which she had in a separate purse, and bought a fabulous, seriously fabulous sea-green sarong.

As she handed over the money it felt crinkly and new and she glanced at it and she started laughing.

Liar, liar.

These were far newer notes than Steele had said they were.

He had been to the bank after all!

She loved him.

A lot more relaxed and a little bit sunburnt, in the late afternoon Candy put on her sarong and set off. She sat on a hill, looking out at the ocean, and tried to finally sort her list out.

She dealt with the easiest first.

Job.

She chewed her pen for a full two minutes before deciding that she did love Emergency. No, she didn't want them all finding out that the twins were Gerry's but, of course, they would.

And she'd deal with it.

The Gerry's Wing thing was a bit *ouch*, but she'd just have to suck it up.

She needed the maternity leave.

Which brought her onto the next thing that was worrying her—money. She didn't write that down. Candy didn't even have to think about that. She wrote 'Ha-haha' instead and then moved on to the next one.

Gerry's parents.

Okay, she would telephone them when she returned and tell them the news and, if they wanted to or when they'd calmed down, she would offer to go and speak with them.

Next.

Her parents.

Candy had already decided she was moving, far away so that they couldn't just drop in. Even if it would be easier to have them nearer.

She took a breath. The harder matters were approaching.

Gerry.

'I should have gone to the memorial service.'

Candy didn't know what else to write. She didn't know how to write that she didn't love him but she hated that he was dead and that not only would the world move on without him, but he would have children and not know.

They would know about him though, Candy promised.

'I will tell the twins about you and keep in touch with your family.'

And then she got to the top of the list but she'd left it till last because it was the one that left her so, so confused.

Steele.

She could write to him perhaps. Maybe it would be better in a letter. But telling someone you loved them when you were pregnant with someone else's children came at a huge disadvantage and it was an impossible letter to write.

She never wanted him to think that she wanted him simply as a father for her children.

The natural order of falling in love had for the most part been denied them.

She tried to keep it light, wondering through her words that if it was all too much to deal with for him, maybe they could somehow be friends with benefits. Then she screwed up that piece of paper because given how much her stomach had grown in the past few days she doubted if very soon she would appeal to him.

And so she wrote him a postcard—one she had swiped from the villa and had meant to use for Macey.

Steele,
I wish...how I wish...that you were here now.
Candy xxx

List sorted, she decided.

Now she had to get on with relaxing.

As she walked back she thought she was seeing things because there, sitting on the little chair outside her villa, was Steele. He was wearing dark jeans and a black T-shirt and was very unshaven but very welcome to her eyes.

'I didn't know I had a genie.' She met him with a smile.

This was how he remembered her, Steele thought as she approached. This was how she'd been before it had all happened—here she was smiling, laughing, intuitive and sexy. She handed him the postcard she had written and he read it with a smile.

'That explains what happened, then,' Steele said. 'One minute I was sitting chatting to Macey and the next, *puff*, here I was in Hawaii...' He looked at her and took in the changes, and not just to her body.

She had been right to come alone, he conceded, because it had served her well—she looked relaxed and healthy and happy.

It was very nice to see.

'I've been making lists,' Candy said. 'I'm all sorted now.'

'Can I see?' he asked, and then shook his head. 'Sorry, stupid thing to ask.'

'Go for it,' she said.

'Let's go for a walk,' he said, and he dropped his bag in the villa and took her hand. They headed to the beach and sat there.

She could hear the wind through the palm trees and was all knotted on the inside but in a very nice way.

Steele was here.

'Why are you here?' she asked.

'Because I had this vision of trying to date you from Kent while you were living with your parents,' Steele said as he read through her list.

'I'd already addressed that,' she said, and pointed to her decision on the list she had written.

So she had.

'I feel like the teacher is reading my homework,' she admitted. 'Do I get marked?'

'Verbal comments,' Steele said. 'I didn't bring my red pen.

'Okay, I think moving away from your parents is very brave and very sensible.'

'Thank you.'

'And I think telling Gerry's parents is very brave and very right too,' Steele said, and carried on reading through her list.

'Work…' Steele said, and his hand wavered in the air. 'That's a tough one.'

'I like what I do.'

'I know.

'What's "Ha-ha-ha" for?'

'Money,' Candy said, and he laughed.

He was serious when they got to Gerry. 'As for the memorial service…'

'I feel bad that I didn't go.'

'I went,' Steele said.

'Were there a lot of people?'

'It was packed,' he said. He decided not to mention Elaine and her tears. He had spoken to her the next day and had hopefully helped by listening a bit.

'I met Rory, and Gina…'

'Gina!' Candy's eyes were wide. 'She's been on extended leave. I think she's been in rehab.'

'Well, it looks as if she's coming back,' Steele said. 'Oh, and I met Anton. We went for a drink afterwards.'

He watched as she blushed. 'Is he the doctor overseeing your pregnancy?'

'Yes.'

'Did you happen to mention my infertility?'

'I did.'

'It's fine that you told him. I don't have any issue with that at all. You must have been in the most confused space.'

'So how did you guess that he was my doctor?'

'Heathrow to Hawaii gives you quite a lot of thinking time.' He told her all the questions he'd had for Anton and then he told her why. 'I'm here because I love you, but I never wanted you to think I wanted you for the babies. Does that make sense?'

'Sort of.'

'Anyway, I'm not. I want the babies very much but if it hadn't happened, it helps to know that you very probably can have a baby with me. Not naturally, but the choice and the chance is there.'

She turned and smiled at him. 'Did you do it into a jar for me?'

'I did,' he said. 'And, had it been necessary, I would have undergone a procedure that would involve a lot of local anaesthetic on a very delicate area but, thankfully, Anton seems to think I've got enough swimmers to work with.'

'You asked Anton all those embarrassing questions for me?'

'Yes.' Steele sighed. 'I did. I had no idea at the time that Anton had practically led me to ask them—you've got a lot of fans, you know.'

'Who?'

'Anton, Macey…'

'How is Macey?'

'Meddling. She practically told me to get on a plane.'

Then he got to the hard part. 'Gerry's parents and brother and sister were at the service and they told a few tales.'

'How did they seem.'

'Lost,' Steele said. 'Confused. I think the news of the twins is going to mean an awful lot to them.'

'Why did you go to the service, Steele?' she asked.

'Because I wanted to know more about the man whose children I want to raise and perhaps if they have questions I might be able to answer some,' he said. 'And I'm here because I love you,'

Candy looked at him and her eyes filled with tears. She realised then what Macey had meant when she'd asked her about duty.

Steele had no duty to her babies unless he wanted them.

They had been together for just two weeks when the news had hit.

He had every reason to walk away, to be gone, for things to fade out quietly, and yet he was here, sitting beside her and loving her with his eyes.

'I'm sorry they're—'

'You're going to say that once,' Steele broke in. 'Now. Then it's done.'

He was the most direct person she had ever met.

'You're sorry they're not mine?' he checked.

Tears shot out of her eyes without a sob. They just spilled out with such force that they splashed on her sarong.

'We have to be honest now,' he said. 'We have to have the most honest conversation of our lives and I'm ringing in sick even if it take six months to sort this out because we're staying here till it's done.'

'We've only got five months left till they're here.'

'So we need to talk, right here, right now, and nothing, *nothing* gets left unsaid. My first thought, when you found out you were pregnant, was just that…I wanted them to be mine,' Steele said. 'Then I asked myself what would have happened if the twins weren't already here? My guess is that we'd have made it, because I was already coming to Hawaii and I don't go on holiday with women yet I was about to with you…'

She thought back. Things had been so easy then.

'And if we had made it, would you have wanted a baby at some stage?' he asked.

'I don't know. I think I would want children but if we couldn't…' She looked at Steele.

Did his infertility change how she felt about him?

Never.

Could she love him less?

Not a chance.

'If we couldn't have children we'd have gone for treatment,' Steele checked, and she nodded.

'Or adoption.'

'Okay,' he said. 'Had we adopted, would you have loved them less?'

'No!'

'Would you, in an argument, say that they weren't biologically mine?'

'No!'

'So what's the difference?'

'I don't know.'

'If we had to use donated sperm, would it change how we feel about them?'

'Of course not.'

'I'm going to be there for the pregnancy, the birth, the nappies. The twins will be mine,' Steele said. 'They will know about Gerry and when they turn into feral teenagers and say that I'm not their real father, I won't be hurt, not for a second. Instead, you and I will laugh in their moody, acne-laden faces when they say that, because we know we dealt with all that in Hawaii many, many years ago.'

Candy let out a breath.

'It's not just you that has concerns about getting married,' he said. 'I made a list of my own.' He took out his boarding pass and she read it.

Movies.
Football.
Cricket.

'It's a lot less complicated than mine,' she said.

'Oh, no, it isn't. I like my life very much and there are certain…er…requirements that I swore I would not forgo…'

She looked at him.

'The movies,' Steele explained. 'I like to go on my own sometimes. I just do. I don't want you saying, "But you used to take me"…'

Candy smiled.

'And I know it's horrible and selfish to take myself off when you'll have been stuck indoors with screaming twins, so perhaps you might like to take yourself off now and then to wherever ladies take themselves off to…'

'Like a spa day?' she said.

'I think so.'

'And you'd never say, "Oh, Candy, why do you have so many spa days? Why don't I come with you this time?"'

'Never,' he promised.

'Deal.'

'The football and cricket are one and the same…' He looked a bit worried and so too was Candy as she hated sport—it made her sweat and feel shaky and that was just watching it. 'I don't do romantic holidays,' he said. 'I shall, of course, and I'll do family ones too, but I have a group of friends and we like some big-ticket stuff.'

'Such as?'

'You remember how well we negotiated the movie issue?' Steele checked, because was he really going to land a perfect woman who didn't mind what he was about to suggest?

'I do.' Candy was very curious. She loved their discussions. 'What sort of big-ticket stuff?'

'International cricket events. World Cup…'

'Oh.'

'We don't always all go to everything.'

Candy said nothing at first. It really was a bit awkward. 'Would I be expected to go?'

'Well…' he said. 'There's a lot of drinking and singing…' He waited for her to say that no way would she ever want to go. Yes, this was awkward. 'Might be a bit of bad language, which wouldn't be great for the twins.' Still Candy said nothing and so he told her the real deal. 'There's also a very strict no-girlfriends-or-wives agreement, which I have, over the years, enforced on my friends several times. I'd never be able to live it down if I asked to bring you.'

He watched a little smile play on her lips.

'However,' he said quickly, 'I would think, given I'd be

going away with friends for a couple of weeks now and then and leaving you, that you might need to escape with your girlfriends for a holiday every now and then, and I'd look after the twins and however many others we have…'

'Oh, I think I could agree to that.' Candy smiled and she looked at him, a man so happy in himself he wasn't looking for the other half. It had just turned out that she happened to be it. 'I love you, even without the twins, you do know that.'

'Why isn't there anything written about me on your list, then?' Steele asked, loving the way she blushed.

'I tried to write a letter.'

'Show me.'

'That's so unfair.'

'I need to know you love me, Candy,' he teased, and held out his hand.

It was so embarrassing as he sat there and read how crazy she was about him and then he started to laugh.

'"Friends with benefits." I'm sorry, Candy, this might be insensitive but if I'm having a friend with benefits then I want the blonde, leggy Candy. Not the heavily pregnant with twins one—that's husband stuff.' He looked at her. 'Marry me?'

'Honestly?'

'Honestly,' he said, his heart thumping in his chest.

'I want to be with you but I've never wanted to get married,' Candy admitted. 'I just don't want the big white wedding that my parents would insist on. I don't want to be standing there in a fluffy white dress pregnant with twins…'

'And you'd have to say your name out loud in a packed church,' he pointed out. 'And I'm a divorced heathen…' Then he smiled. 'We're in Hawaii, Candy. We can be married tomorrow, if that's what you want. I know it will upset your parents but I think they will be pleased as well.'

She started to smile.

'Is that a yes?' he checked. 'I'm starting to get worried here.'

'It's a very big yes,' she said. 'But won't your parents be disappointed to miss it?' Candy asked. After all, he was their only child.

'Yes,' he said, 'and I'll be tempted to point out that they missed most of my milestone events growing up, but I shan't do that, of course. They'll soon get over it, especially when they hear about the twins.'

They were back at the villa, all their lists checked and sorted. She loved their honesty, how they just spoke and worked it all out. 'We dealt with that very maturely.' Candy grinned in delight as she congratulated them.

'Oh, I can assure you that I don't feel very mature today,' Steele said. 'In fact, I want to do something very immature.'

He handed her the phone with a text from Annie, asking him if he'd had a think about her suggestion.

'This came through when I landed,' Steele explained. 'Can I?'

'Go on.' She smiled and watched as he started to type out a text.

There's nothing to think about or discuss. I am in Hawaii with Candy and we're about to get married. She's pregnant with twins, which means that she's very moody and volatile at the moment, so it's probably better that you don't text again. Regards, Steele.

He hit 'send' and with that he let go of the past and moved into the glorious future.

'You lied to me, though,' she said as they stepped into the villa and he took her in his arms.

'Never.'

'Yes, you did,' Candy said, and wrapped her hands around his neck. 'You said that the money you gave me had been lying around for five years, but it was only printed two years ago.'

Steele merely smiled at being caught. 'That's because I didn't want you worrying about taking food from your babies' mouths as you looked at that fantastic, sexy sarong.' He stroked her thick nipples through the fabric, and then he ran a tender hand over her stomach and his hand told her how sexy the changes were to him.

His kiss told her that too.

Her fabulous sarong dropped to the floor and Steele undressed with rapid ease.

The only thing missing from her perfect holiday had been her perfect man and now here he was, making love to her.

The doubts, the hesitation about whether or not he should intrude on her time here, were put to rest as he entered her. She wrapped herself around him, moved her body with his and held nothing back.

'I love you so much,' Candy said as she started to come.

No question, no hesitation, they both knew how precious the love they had was. Steele felt the roundness of her stomach press into his and he wanted to say he loved her back but she dragged him in so deep that all he could do was moan.

'I love you too,' he said afterwards as they lay there.

'You've still got red toenails.' She smiled as she looked at his feet next to hers.

'I was too embarrassed to buy nail-varnish remover,' he said. 'We'll need it if we're getting married on the beach.'

'Or not.'

'Oh, no.' Steele shook his head. 'We're getting it filmed for our families and a photo for Macey. I don't want everyone wondering if I'm secretly wearing your underwear.'

'Are we going to live in Kent?' Candy asked.

'We are,' Steele said. 'My offer's been accepted for that house. I wanted to ask you to marry me there,' he said. 'My plan was to do that when we looked through the house, except you chose not to come in.'

'You were going to ask me then?'

'Yes,' he said. 'But I didn't want to rush you.'

'So you gave me an extra five days?'

'I couldn't wait any longer,' Steele said, and then kissed the top of her head. 'So let's go and get the licence and get married so that the honeymoon can begin.'

It already had.

EPILOGUE

It was, for Candy, who had never wanted her own wedding, the perfect one.

It was, for Steele, who had sworn he would never marry again, the best wedding ever too.

Steele opted for sunset, though he didn't tell her why.

They walked to the beach together and stood, their bare feet caressed by the silky sand, Candy nervous, excited and all the things he made her feel as she faced him.

'Aloha,' he said, and she smiled. It was very hard to believe, after all their little teases about her holiday, that he was here with her and that this was their wedding.

'Aloha,' Candy said, grateful when he took her shaking hands.

The air smelt of coconut and frangipani. She was wearing a single flower in her hair. The breeze whipped her hair from her face and moulded Candy's dress to her soft curves. She had chosen a pale blue chiffon that was very simple and tied beneath her bust. He wore a linen suit, which was the colour of damp sand, and a white shirt and no nail varnish. He took her breath away and made her smile just as he had the moment they'd met.

She could hear the roar of the waves as they crashed onto the shore and then hissed back out to sea, leaving the sand as smooth, clean and pristine as their beckoning future.

As the huge crimson sun sank slowly into the sea the service started. They had decided on traditional vows—timeless and classic. She looked right at him as he placed the simple gold band they had chosen on her finger and Candy felt a soft shiver run through her as she heard the gorgeous, deep voice that had come into her life less than a month ago now vow to be with her for ever. 'With this ring I thee wed. With my body I thee worship.'

Then it was Candy's turn and her voice was very clear when she promised the same.

The sun had set, bamboo tiki torches lit the beach and the celebrant told them they were husband and wife.

'You may kiss your bride.'

Steele did and his kiss was long and lingering and then he moved his mouth to her ear. 'I'm the happiest I've ever been,' he said.

To hear those heartfelt words from Steele meant everything to Candy.

'I'm the happiest I've ever been too,' she agreed.

That was how they made each other feel.

With the service over and the documents signed, they walked hand in hand along the beach towards their villa with the waves lapping at their toes.

It was done, she was married and it was exactly as she'd wanted it to be, but as she saw the photographer taking down his equipment, even though they'd had the service filmed Candy felt a niggle of guilt that she had denied her parents this day.

Back in their suite she was determined to push the thought aside, but having again kissed his bride he pulled back and asked for her parents' number. 'You'll feel better when you've told them,' he said. 'You know you will.'

'They'll freak,' Candy said. 'I don't want to spoil today…' But she gave him the number and lay there with her eyes closed as a deep calm voice, one that was very used to dealing with upset, stubborn, set-in-their-ways people, introduced himself and told her father that he was a doctor who worked alongside Candy.

'No, there's nothing wrong with Candy or the babies,' Steele said, and then he told them how he had fallen in love with her, how he was going to take care of her, how he was completely fine about the twins and that they would be his. 'However,' Steele said, 'Gerry's parents will know…' He looked over at Candy. 'Candy and I have discussed it and we both agree that a baby can never have too many grandparents to love them.'

He spoke and listened and then said that he and Candy had got married today. Candy could hear her mother come onto the phone and the rise of drama that she'd dreaded ensued. She'd have to talk to them and deal with their recriminations and the guilt. She held her hand out for the phone but Steele simply listened to her mother and then spoke in that calm way of his and slowly the tension in her uncoiled.

'Candy didn't feel it appropriate, given that the pregnancy is already showing, to get married in a church, but we might renew our vows there.'

He dealt with the drama and examined his thumbnail at one point as they droned on and on and then, finally, he smiled. 'Perhaps you'd like to tell your daughter that.' He handed her the phone. 'Your parents want to speak with you.'

She took the phone and braced herself for whatever her mother would fling at her and closed her eyes.

'*Complimente*...' her mother said, and it was so unexpected, so far from what she'd anticipated, that Candy burst into happy tears as her mother continued to speak. 'He sounds a nice man...'

'A very nice man,' Candy said.

A very nice man who was playing with her breasts and kissing her neck and was ready to get on with his honeymoon.

'Better?' Steele said as she hung up the phone.

'Is that why you wanted an evening wedding?'

'Yep. I didn't want to scare them calling late at night,' he said, 'and I knew you'd be worried.' He gave her a smile. 'Come here, Steele.'

'Steele?' Candy said, and then realised that was her surname now.

'Well, "Mrs Candida Steele", if you want to be formal.'

She was back to her dental commercial and smiling as he took her in his arms.

They were back to *before*.

* * * * *

THE FIREFIGHTER
TO HEAL HER HEART

BY
ANNIE O'NEIL

First published in Great Britain 2015
by Mills & Boon, an imprint of Harlequin (UK) Limited,
Eton House, 18-24 Paradise Road, Richmond, Surrey, TW9 1SR

© 2015 Sheila Crighton

ISBN: 978-0-263-24693-3

Harlequin (UK) Limited's policy is to use papers that are natural, renewable and recyclable products and made from wood grown in sustainable forests. The logging and manufacturing processes conform to the legal environmental regulations of the country of origin.

Printed and bound in Spain
by CPI, Barcelona

Dear Reader,

First of all let me give you a big, fat, juicy thank you for reading my second book! I've been having an absolute blast, diving headfirst into the world of Mills & Boon® Medical Romance™, and will have to be dragged out kicking and screaming.

Writing this book was a no-brainer for me after *The Surgeon's Christmas Wish*, as Liesel was a character who really stayed with me. I wanted to see what happened to her after she moved from America back to Australia—and lo and behold…romance ensues! And a quest for chocolate milkshakes. But I'm jumping the gun here…

Liesel's story is set in an area where I picked grapes (!) during a backpacking trip I had in Australia. I had an absolutely amazing time there, and was impressed by how supportive all those small communities just outside of Adelaide are.

Many thanks to you again, and I hope you enjoy Liesel and Jack's story as much as I enjoyed writing it.

Have fun!

Annie O X

This book is first and foremost dedicated to all of those
who volunteer for the South Australian Fire Service.
You are all heroes and heroines in my eyes.
I would also like to send a special nod
(and a glass of wine) to my fabulous sister-in-law, who
has been an incredible source of encouragement to me.
Lots of love to you, Kymberley.

Books by Annie O'Neil

The Surgeon's Christmas Wish

**Visit the author profile page
at millsandboon.co.uk for more titles**

CHAPTER ONE

"So, DO YOU think we should practice a tiger or a lion roar?"

Liesel was finding it difficult not to laugh as she knelt on the barnyard's baked red earth, eye to eye with the tearful seven-year-old. This hadn't turned out to be the farm visit Devlin had been dreaming of. Or her, for that matter. She'd been nabbed by a harried teacher to come along on the school farm visit as a "responsible adult." The promise of some spring sunshine had won out over the nagging in her head about knuckling down to fill out the school's immunization requirements. The "responsible adult" moniker had made her laugh at the time but now, as she kept Devlin still in the ominously named cattle crush, she knew her nurse's credentials could come in handy.

How Devlin had managed to stick his head through the metal bars designed to keep cows restrained was beyond her. His penchant for showing off might have been the trouble. Now he was paying the price. All of the students had howled with laughter before being shuttled off to help feed the orphan lambs. The farmer, Mr. Jones, hadn't been very quiet with his use of the word *guillotine* when he realized the CFS was going to have to be called. Thank goodness the word was unlikely to be in Devlin's vocabulary. Yet.

If she could just cheer the gloomy-faced boy up a bit as they waited for a CFS crew to arrive, she was sure all would be well. The Country Fire Service dealt with car accidents all the time so would be used to extracting people from steel structures. The thought made her shiver. Blocking out the disturbing images, Liesel gave Devlin's pitch-black crew cut a good scrub with her hand. "Not to worry, Dev, it could be worse. You could be stuck in here with a girl!"

She laughed as Devlin screwed up his young face at the idea of being that close to a girl.

"I could think of worse things."

Liesel shaded her green eyes, squinting hard against the late-afternoon sun to see who was attached to the made-for-late-night-radio voice. Since she'd lost Eric, it took a lot to get her to respond to a man on a primal level—but the rich drawl she'd just heard sent a wave of shivery delight down her spine despite the heat of the day.

Her eyes worked fast to adjust to the glare—quickly turning the silhouetted six-foot-something male into a poster boy for South Australia's volunteer fire service. A thick shock of sandy blond hair had become a sexy tousled by-product of the red helmet he was putting on the ground as he knelt beside her—a pair of bright blue eyes securely fixed on Devlin. Golden stubble outlined his well-defined face. She normally wasn't a fan—but on this guy it looked more Rugged Bachelor than Unkempt Slob. Despite herself, her eyes swept down the golden hairs of his toned forearm and spied a ring-free hand. Not everyone wore a ring, but no ring was a pretty good indication…

"How long have you been caged up in here, mate?"

Devlin flicked his long-lashed eyes up to Liesel.

"Miss, it's been about three hours, hasn't it?"

Liesel threw her head back and laughed. "Hardly, Devlin—I think it's closer to fifteen minutes."

"All right, Dev—is it all right if I call you Dev? Or should I say Dare Devlin?" He paused for Devlin's grin—a show of acceptance of the new nickname—and continued, "My name's Jack and we're going to get you out of here as soon as possible." He turned, putting a hand on Liesel's shoulder, lips parting to reveal a crooked smile. *Uh-oh...that's a knee-weakener.*

"Is it all right if I call you Miss?" He laughed good-naturedly at her startled expression then stood up, putting a hand under Liesel's elbow to help her to her feet as he rose.

Crikey. And he's got manners.

"Miss is great." She tried to force her lips into a casual smile as she silently raced through a quick-fire series of questions. Had her hair seen the right side of a brush recently? Had she unscrewed the lid on her mascara that morning? Then used it? Had her fair skin and freckles already had their daily allotment of sunshine? All too aware of the arrows of heat beginning to shoot across her cheeks, she grew wide-eyed as she spluttered on, "You can feel free to call me Liesel—I mean, Miss Adler. Or Nurse Adler. I'm the school nurse. Registered."

For crying out loud—the man didn't ask for your CV, Liesel!

Jack dropped a slow wink in her direction, simultaneously giving Devlin a soft chuck under the chin. "I think Miss Adler will do perfectly."

Her heart did a quick-fire yo-yo trip across her rib

cage as she dared to look up into his smiling eyes. They were an awfully nice shade of turquoise.

Wait a minute. Did her lashes just flutter? *Get a hold of yourself, Liesel.*

Her eyes dropped back to Devlin, who was looking up at her with a pained expression as he tried to wrangle himself free from his head-locked position.

Clenching her hands into tight fists, she shut her eyes. Just as suddenly as her heart had soared at Jack's sexy wink, it plummeted with a painful twist. Here was this small boy she was supposed to be caring for and she was acting like a love-struck teen. Images of Eric flashed past her closed eyes.

Eric.

Her behavior had been disloyal to him—to his memory. She knew the day for moving on would come at some point—soon even—but this couldn't be the moment. Could it?

"Miss Adler?"

"Yes, sorry." Liesel forced her voice back to the soothing nurse tone she used with the children but kept her eyes fixed on her charge. "What do you need to do to get this little man free?"

Jack was going to have to give himself a ripper of a talking to when he got back to the station. *He wasn't here to flirt.* Or wink, for that matter. Winking was reserved for little old ladies and four-year-olds who needed cheering up, not for cute-as-they-come school nurses. He wouldn't mind running his fingers through a few of those corkscrew red curls of hers. From the shine glinting off of them, they'd feel about as soft as the dark green silk top she was wearing. She wasn't even in a uniform, but his imagination could certainly fill in the— *Whoa! Don't even go there, Jack.*

Ladies were meant to be off the radar, whether or not they were standing right in front of you looking as petite, cat-eyed and creamy-skinned as they came.

Jack heard himself clear his throat a bit too violently as he gathered equipment from the back of the crew truck.

Gear. Work. Much safer terrain.

He was here to help the little boy and from the looks of the heavy-gauge steel, he would need more than a bit of dishwashing soap to get him free. Poor kid. He wouldn't be Dare Devlining for a while, from the mortified look on his face. He'd have to keep an eye on his progress and see if he'd be a candidate for the Country Fire Service cadets in a few years. With the right training, a spitfire youngster could very easily turn into a hero.

Come to think of it, their station could also do with some volunteer nurses on the force. He'd only been at the Murray Valley posting for a few weeks. His assignment was a Class A rescue mission. Its volunteer forces needed some bolstering. Big-time. The lads at the station had told him the school nurse had been someone's granny up until recently so he hadn't even thought of bringing the new one into the loop as regards the station. Now that he'd met Liesel?

Easy there, cowboy.

Then again, she *was* a nurse. He wondered if...

Focus, man.

Jack pushed himself back into action mode.

"I'm going to put some earplugs in your lugholes, all right, mate?" Jack knelt down by Devlin, feeling a little too aware of Liesel's presence behind him. "This thing's a bit loud. It's called a hydraulic spreader. Basically a big set of automated pliers." Devlin looked at him dubiously as he continued, "I'm going to pull these bars a couple of centimeters wider and unless you grow some more brains between now and then, you should be able to get that noggin of yours free and Mr. Jones can have his crush back for the cattle. What do you say to that?"

As Devlin's forlorn face flooded with relief, Liesel felt herself choking back another giggle. This guy was good. He had such a relaxed way with Devlin that any fears she may have had about having to call the boy's parents to explain to them that their son was going to have to spend the night in a barnyard vanished.

Thoughts of her own little boy flitted through her mind. She had imagined the moments he would have spent with his father countless times. Moments like this—well, not quite like this—watching Jack interact with Devlin tore at her heart.

It was still difficult reconciling the fact that her little Liam would not have a single memory of his father. Then again, she silently chastised herself, it wasn't as if falling in love with a ski patroller had been a safe bet. Hazards had been a day-to-day reality with his job. As a trauma nurse in a ski medical clinic she had seen the aftermath of the daily dangers he'd faced.

And now? Now it was taking life day by day in a quiet country town. Her job as a school nurse wasn't crisis free—but skinned knees and the odd sprain were safer territory. Better on her frayed nerves. Not to mention the fact that Liam got free childcare in the school crèche, making her nurse's salary stretch a little bit further.

Surviving the past couple of years had worked by sticking to the day-by-day principle. Trauma centers, extreme sports, high-octane thrill-seeking? All relegated to a no-go zone. Winking, blue-eyed firemen certainly didn't belong on the safe list.

"You might want to pop a pair of these in as well if you're going to hold the little fella's hand while I crank up the pliers."

Startled, Liesel stared uncomprehendingly at the orange foam orbs Jack held in front of her. "Sorry! I was miles away."

"No kidding." His eyes held hers in a questioning gaze. Not accusative, just curious. "It wasn't hard to miss."

Telling him the truth wasn't an option. Neither was acknowledging the tingles working their way up her arm after he'd handed her the earplugs. For crying out loud! She was behaving as if she'd never spoken to an attractive man before. For the first year after she'd lost Eric being with another man hadn't even occurred to her. Nine months later it had all been about Liam. Now, three years later… *Was this really going to be the day?*

"I was just thinking about whether or not I should take a picture for his parents or if it's best to just leave it to the imagination."

Jack unleashed another relaxed smile as he bent to start the small generator for his pliers. "I think this is one best left to the imagination!" He signaled for her to put her earplugs in then checked Devlin's were securely in place before pulling the cord on the generator. With one sharp tug it roared to life.

Curiosity overcame nerves as Liesel watched Jack pick up the enormous pair of pliers attached to the hydraulic hose. He indicated she should shield Devlin's face with her hands as he slipped the pliers between the steel bars. In less than a minute the bars were gently pried apart and the little boy effortlessly pulled out his head, shooting out of the crush at high speed. Above the din she could hear him calling to the other students about his great escape.

Laughing, Liesel turned back to Jack, who was expertly returning the bars to their original position. If Mr. Jones hadn't already seen Devlin's shenanigans gone wrong, he would have never known they were there.

After snapping the generator off, the peaceful cadence of the countryside once again took over.

"Well, thank you so much." Liesel resisted looking too deeply into the blue eyes trained on her. She was in serious danger of mooning. And swooning. She really needed to get a grip. "I'm sorry to have wasted your time on something that wasn't a real emergency."

"What?" Jack stepped back in mock horror. "That wasn't a real emergency? I thought I'd got myself a humdinger of a job there."

Despite herself, Liesel felt drawn to his easygoing nature. Never mind the man was gorgeous—he also seemed to inhabit an infectious sense of fun. She hadn't felt carefree in—well, in a long time, and it was something she missed.

"You know what I mean." She swatted at the air between them. "It wasn't like it was a bushfire or a car crash." She suddenly found herself unable to maintain eye contact. Firemen—especially men who volunteered to go into hazardous situations—were definitely in the no-go zone.

His voice turned serious. "Of course I do—but we take all of our callouts seriously and I, for one, would hate to think anyone would hesitate to call us if we could help."

She looked up into those amazing blue eyes of his as if to confirm that the words he spoke were genuine.

"Truly," he reiterated solidly, as though mind reading the few threads of doubt tugging at her conscience.

"Well, I know one little fellow who will be dining off your heroics for weeks."

Jack leaned back against the cattle crush and nodded appraisingly at her. "So, you think I'm a hero, do you?"

A flush of heat rushed up her throat as he waited for her answer.

"Of course not! I mean, you definitely were to Devlin—"

Jack's easy laughter stopped her inane flow of apologies.

"Don't worry, Miss Adler. I'm always out for a free compliment if I can get one." He tilted his head in her direction, capturing her attention with another one of those winks. *Resist, Liesel. Resist.*

"There is one way you can repay the Country Fire Service if you feel you owe us one."

Liesel crooked her chin up at him, curiosity getting the better of her.

"Murray Valley needs more volunteers. Big-time. A nurse would be a great addition to our local crew."

Liesel felt herself physically recoil from the suggestion.

Not a chance.

She didn't do hazardous things anymore. Not with a son to look after. Not after the loss she'd suffered.

Jack knew in an instant he'd overstepped the mark. Her gentle, sunny personality vanished the moment he'd made his suggestion. There was definitely something painfully private she was keeping close to her chest. Fair enough. It wasn't as if he didn't have his own secrets. Secrets he kept to make his life easier, more honest. Or was that an oxymoron? Keeping secrets to stay honest.

"Liesel! Quit flirting with the handsome fireman," a female voice called from across the farmyard. "We've got to get the kids back to school for pickup!"

Jack and Liesel instantly widened the space between them, staring stricken-faced in the direction of the voice. Liesel looked absolutely mortified and Jack hadn't felt so caught out since he'd been found snogging the headmaster's daughter behind the bike shed when he was thirteen. As if by design, he and Liesel simultaneously looked back at each other, saw their mutual expressions of dismay and immediately burst into unrestrained guffaws.

"Sorry, I didn't mean to look so disgusted! I mean, no—not disgusted." He waved away the choice of words as if the gesture would erase them. "It's not that you repel me or anything—"

"I think you'd better quit while you're ahead!" Liesel laughed, wiping away invisible tears from her eyes. She threw a quick glance over her shoulder toward the growing hubbub of children. "I had better go."

Jack felt a tug of resistance. *So soon?* "Right. Yeah, of course." He stepped forward and offered a hand. "Nice doing business with you, Miss Adler."

What a first-class dill!

Liesel's green eyes flashed up at him, unsurprisingly bemused. He'd really gone in for the bad conversational hat trick. *Nice doing business with you?*

She slipped her petite hand into his and offered him a quick shake of thanks. The delicacy of her fingers instantly made him feel protective of her. Not his usual response to a woman. Normally he wanted to protect himself from whatever she might want from him. Time. Commitment. Less time at the fire station. Too much history in that department had made him wary. But this one, Miss Liesel Adler, something about her told him she wanted nothing more than to stand on her two feet.

"See you around." Liesel threw the words in her wake as she accelerated her brisk walk into a jog to rejoin the group.

Jack watched her retreat round the corner toward the school bus and spoke to the empty barnyard. "I certainly hope so."

It was all Liesel could do to keep the hot burn of embarrassment from her cheeks as she rejoined the group.

"Got an eye for a man in uniform, have you, you naughty thing?" Cassie Monroe—or Miss Monroe to the students—raised her eyebrows up and gave her lips a tell-me-more twist. Her friend and colleague didn't do subtle.

"Hardly!" Liesel shot back at her colleague, a bit more spiritedly than she'd intended.

"Did you get his number?" Cassie continued, as if Liesel hadn't said a thing.

Liesel sent her a meaningful glare. A glare that she hoped said, *Stop talking right now!*

"You're going to see him again, right?"

Nope. Guess the glare hadn't worked.

"I hardly think it's appropriate—"

"Anything's appropriate," Cassie interrupted, "when you're trying to get back on the horse again."

"I'm not trying to get on anything—horsey or otherwise." This conversation was definitely not going in the right direction.

"Liesel." Cassie fixed her with a loving glare, hands planted on her shoulders. "It's time to get back out there and you're the only one who doesn't know it."

"Come along, children." Liesel actively avoided responding. "Let's start getting on the bus. Everyone sure they haven't left anything behind? Rickie—have you got your backpack?"

She felt Cassie sidle up beside her and heard a whisper in her ear. "You're not going to get away with the silent treatment this time, my dear." She felt her arm receive a good solid pinch. "After school. Playground. I want details about the hot new fireman."

Rubbing away the sting of Cassie's pinch, Liesel couldn't help but grin back at her friend. They had only known each other since the beginning of term, when Liesel had taken up her new contract. Cassie's thirteen-year-old son appeared at the nurses' station a bit too frequently— the only plus side being that the two women had become pretty well acquainted. A couple of girlie nights in, a few tips about where to shop, a detailed who's who at the school and Cassie had already proved to be a great friend.

Liesel hadn't known a soul out here in wine country and meeting a fellow single mum, even if Cassie's son was much older than her own, had taken the edge off the anxiety she'd felt at making the decision to move away from her parents' house in Adelaide.

In reality, there had been no other option. A disastrous fortnight at the city's biggest A and E department had proved crisis management was no longer her forte. The other staff had known her situation and had hovered over her, making her feel more paranoid and edgy than confident and comfortable. The two-week tenure had culminated in a disastrous incident where she'd completely frozen over a patient with a gory chainsaw injury. Unacceptable. She'd fired herself before the bosses had had a chance to do it for her.

She'd made the move to Engleton and it just had to work. She didn't have the energy, or the money, for more change. Small-town life and a job she could do without turning into a bundle of nerves were meant to put an end to chaos. To the memories. And maybe, just maybe, one day she and Liam would be more than a family of two.

In truth, she had been pleasantly surprised to discover her new posting as a school nurse was less calm and more "commotion" than she'd originally thought it might be. Mundane had been her goal but, as usual these days, she found she hadn't quite made the right call. Apart from the requisite paperwork, it was great fun to spend time with the children, even if she interacted with most of them when they weren't at their best.

She still had to force herself to take each case as it came, but the occasional heart-racer—a broken collarbone, a deep cut to the forehead, a pencil stabbed into an unsuspecting student's arm—had all been little teasers reawakening the Liesel who'd spent over five years thriving off the high-stakes charge of saving lives. It was a life she thought she'd needed to lay to rest. But now she felt as though it was her personal mission to provide the children with a safe haven in the school. Everyone deserved that when they were in pain—to feel secure.

It was why she had moved back home after giving birth to Liam. Being on the mountain—the mountain that had taken Eric's life—had been just too much. His parents had been amazing, more supportive than she could have ever imagined, and knowing Liam wouldn't be able to see his paternal grandparents as often as they wished made the decision even harder. They did their best to make her feel a part of their own family, but when her own parents had flown over to see her and meet Liam she'd known in an instant where she belonged. Home. Australia. Where the hot sun and burnt landscape provided no memories of the snowcapped mountains where her heart had been ripped from her chest three short years ago.

Liesel skipped up the steps of the bus and grinned at the sight of the children jockeying for the "top spots." Nothing had changed from when she was a kid. Front seats and backseats were still the most popular and now the mayhem of fifteen children organizing themselves in the middle rows played out in front of her.

The seven-year-olds had clearly had a wonderful time at the farm. Some carefully held eggs in Mr. Jones's distinctive red cartons in their laps. A gaggle of children were plastering their faces to the windows to catch final glimpses of the sheep and cattle. Others were talking about helping feed the orphaned lambs, and it was just about impossible not to hear Devlin already bragging about how he'd helped the fireman pull apart the iron bars with his own hands to get free of the crush. A quick glimpse toward the barn and she could just see him swinging into the cab of his truck. Yum. Talk about eye candy!

Liesel felt Cassie sending her a knowing look as Jack's name was bandied about by the children. She sent her friend a smirk and didn't bother to hide her grin.

This was good. She didn't feel she was just convincing herself now. It *was* good. Being around the children all day reminded her of life's endless possibilities. A year ago she could only see dead ends. Now? Now she was ready to slowly start carving out a new life for herself and Liam.

The last thing in the world she wanted for her son was to have his life curtailed by her grief. It had taken every ounce of energy she'd possessed, but when her parents had offered her use of their holiday let—their "retirement fund"—for the first few months she spent out here in Engleton, she'd gratefully accepted. She'd have to move out when the summer holidays came, but that was a bridge to cross in a few months. It was as if fate had been giving her a gentle nudge. *Go on*, it had said, *take a chance*.

Liesel sank into a seat near the driver, a little sigh slipping through her lips. For her son, she would take chances.

This was Jack's favorite stretch of road along the Murray Valley and he'd missed it. No doubt about it. Four years was a long time to stay away from home. There'd been phone calls, but a clean break had been called for and he had made it easy for everyone by packing a bag and leaving.

Intuitively, Jack guided the truck through the sloping hills that spilled into a wide river basin. The land was thick with spring vines unfurling new leaves and clutches of miniature grapes. Next year's wine.

He glanced at the cloudless sky, knowing his background had built in a need to check the weather at regular intervals. His father had done it instinctively and now—well, the apple hadn't fallen too far from the tree. Just a bit farther than usual.

As the moments ticked past he was surprised to see he'd managed to get to the end of the valley without even noticing. It didn't take a brain surgeon for Jack to know he'd been distracted by a certain freckly nose. Or was it the wild spray of deep auburn curls? They certainly didn't detract from anything. A collection of distinctively beautiful parts to make up one heck of a whole. Even with his eyes wide open he could picture those sexy feline green eyes that a certain school nurse had kept tilting up at him underneath a long set of lashes. Liesel was definitely on a par with just about any adorable-one-minute-and-knee-bucklingly-sexy-the-next movie star he could think of.

Meeting a beautiful woman had been the last thing on his mind when he'd received his transfer notice to move back to the Murray River Valley. Confronting his demons had his plate piled pretty high as it was.

He leaned his head back against the truck's headrest, one arm navigating the vehicle along the wide country road dividing the vast tracts of vineyards. The cab briefly filled with a bark of laughter as Jack ruefully acknowledged he knew this road so well he could probably close his eyes and daydream all he wanted about Engleton's new school nurse. As if on cue, his left hand automatically flicked on the indicator and his foot eased off the accelerator before he'd even looked to the right to acknowledge the arched gateway he'd been through thousands of times.

River's Bend Winery.

His family's legacy.

His father's, more specifically. John Granville Keller, locally known as Granville due to his father before him having carried the same name.

He caught movement out of the corner of his eye, a clutch of tourists stepping out onto the veranda of the modern wine-tasting center. He'd seen the plans but had never seen the real thing. It looked good. Becca had done well.

As if thinking about her was strong enough to draw her to him, he saw a familiar blonde figure emerge from the group on the veranda. He slowed the truck to a stop, just remembering to slip the gear lever into Park before jumping out and giving his sister a good old-fashioned bear hug and swing round.

"Hey, there, stranger. I like the new threads! Fireman blue suits you."

Good old Becca. He could count on her for not giving him a case of the guilts. That was his father's specialty.

"You're looking good, sis! And so's your new tasting center." They both turned to give it an appraising look. The sleek modern lines were beautifully crafted to fit in with the lush riverscape surrounding them. He couldn't wait to have a good nosey round—and snag a chilled bottle of the unoaked chardonnay Becca had been bragging about in her emails.

"It beats that old shack you were so fond of." He felt his sister give him a good solid jab in the ribs. He gave her a playful jostle in return before turning her to face him, serious this time.

"How are you? Really? Are you good?"

"Really good, Jack. Just missing you. Staying for tea?" She turned her hundred-watt smile on for him and he couldn't resist pulling her into another deep hug.

"Not today." She pulled back from the hug with a frown.

He tapped the brim of his CFS cap. "Duty calls!"

It might have been true—but it was an excuse he'd used all too often for the past few years. They'd spoken on the phone a lot, emails, texts—but the real thing was something he missed. Staying away from his family had been harder than he had thought—but if he was ever going to prove to his father that he could amount to something then complete focus was necessary.

Thank heavens Becca was such a star. She knew everything there was to know about River's Bend—the crops, the land, their impressive output and, more important, she showed a business acumen that would've been as natural a match to the Australian Securities Exchange. He was proud to call her his kid sister, even though the ponytails and plaster-covered knees were a thing of the past.

"You know you're always welcome. No need to wait for an invitation."

"I know, Bec. I know." He let her go and made a little show of wiping away some invisible dust on her shoulders. "Right, well. Best get on to see Old Man River, then."

"Go gently with him, Jack." His sister's voice was loving but held a genuine note of caution. "It's not been easy for him the past few years."

"I wasn't the one who forced me to choose between a life in the CFS or the farm." He instantly regretted his words when he saw the shots of pain in his sister's eyes and tried to lighten the atmosphere with a playful boxing move. "At least you came out the winner—running a gold-star winery!"

"This was never about winning or losing, Jack."

"I know." He pulled one of her hands into his. "I'm sorry, that was a low blow. You've done an amazing job here, sis. Far better than I would have. I mean it."

He gave her a contrite smile. "Don't worry, Bec. I'm an older and wiser version of 'that wild Keller boy.'" He did a spot-on imitation of the town's former roving police officer and enjoyed his sister's smile at the likeness.

He didn't have a record. No. But he did have a history. Nothing horrible, just the usual teenager-gone-off-the-rails sort of stuff that happened when…when stuff happened.

He climbed into the truck, threw a wave at his sister and eased the truck into first gear. "We'll get that dinner soon, I promise!"

Good ol' Becca. She really was her father's daughter, growing up steeped in the station's quirks and customs. Stubborn as a mule and born to work the land. As a little girl, she was always being retrieved by one of the farmhands from among the vines, where she would spend hours painstakingly setting up her own "wine-tasting" sessions for her dolls. His traditional father had just presumed Jack would take over the business and that his sunny-faced daughter would marry well and be content to enjoy River's Bend from the sidelines.

As a team, they would've made quite a dynamic duo. But life hadn't panned out that way. The winery was her calling and, after his mother's death, the CFS had been his. Too bad his father hadn't seen things that way.

Jack began taking deep, slow breaths. He'd need all the reserves of calm he had to get down the long track past the sleek tasting room, the outbuildings that made up the actual winery, and down the slope into the curved drive fronting the stone expanse of the Keller family home. He may not have spent the past four years here but it was definitely home.

The sprawling three hundred hectares encompassed so much. The eucalyptus-rich expanse of river land he had escaped to as a boy on hot summer days. The exquisitely manicured gardens and orchard where he and Becca had played hide-and-seek. The wooded site near the bridge where they'd spread his mother's ashes after the fateful out-of-control fire so many painful years ago. The new barn built over the burn site as if it would erase the fact Ava Keller had died there. The same barn where he'd had the final, gut-wrenching fight with his father about choosing the fire service over a life on the land.

He stopped for a minute and let himself take in a delicious lungful of the blossoming vines. Coming home was tougher than he had thought. He'd spent virtually every day here until he was twenty-five. He hadn't thought jumping between a life as a CFS volunteer and his duties at River's Bend had been such a wayward existence. But his father had—and had forced him to make his choice.

And he had. He was genuinely committed to the fire service and all it stood for out here in the country. The people out here relied on volunteers to help fight the annual bushfires, pry them out of cars, even rescue the odd kitten—or little boy, as in today's case. Now he was in a position to make it even better. Without this service people would die. As his mother had. Keeping the local station on the map was essential.

Jack slowed the truck to a stop on the hard, iron-rich earth in front of the house, his father already walking out onto the front veranda as if four years hadn't passed and he'd been expecting his son to turn up about now.

Jack hated the look of disappointment creasing his father's face when he saw the uniform.

He would make his father proud. He would understand. One day. He just had to hang on to his principles. Hang on tightly to all he knew was true.

CHAPTER TWO

"I'VE GOT TO hand it to you, Kev. This one's a real corker."
Liesel snapped off her protective gloves and popped them
in the bin.

"Thanks, miss!"

"I should've known you'd take it as a compliment."
Liesel sent the brand-new teen an admonishing glare, al-
beit with a twinkle in her eye. "A black eye and a sprained
wrist on your birthday hardly give you bragging rights."
She secured the brace on his arm before reaching into the
cupboard behind her for a chemical ice pack.

"They are when you finally popped Diggy Reynolds
a good one on the nose. You couldn't have asked for a
better present, miss."

Liesel winced. She'd seen Diggy first. It had been an
impressive nosebleed, but thankfully not a break. Deviated septums weren't killers—but they sure did hurt.
She'd have to talk to Cassie about the incident. Again.
Kev's file was now officially the fattest in her cabinet.

Liesel gave Kev her best "harrumph" as she twisted
the ice pack, felt the coolness flood through the packet
and gently laid it across his wrist. The thirteen-year-old
knew just as well as she did that she had a soft spot for
him. Even if he was permanently in trouble. She was

pretty sure an absent father was the cause, but she was hoping Cassie had things in hand. The counseling training she'd had in Adelaide was setting off all of the alarm bells that Kev was a troublemaker in training.

"Look, you make sure you keep that wrist iced for the next few days, otherwise I'll tell your mother on you."

"Tell your mother what, Kevin Alexander Monroe?"

Cassie's head popped out from around the corner of Liesel's nurses' station, lips pursed, eyebrows raised. Liesel quickly sent Kevin a look indicating it was up to him now and then wheeled her chair out of the way as Cassie entered.

"What is it this time, bud?" Her tone was sharp, but Cassie's face spoke of the volumes of love she felt for her son. "I've got a class to start in five minutes and a hot date with a fireman—so you had better tell me that this week's injury doesn't need a trip to the CMC."

Liesel's attention level shot straight up and, disturbingly, into the a-little-bit-jealous territory as an image of a certain sandy-haired fireman flitted through her mind. Trying her best to quell the heroic poses he was enacting in her imagination, she smiled up at her friend. "A date? You didn't tell me."

"Now, now, my little woodland fairy friend." Cassie laughed, openly pleased she'd piqued Liesel's interest. "We've *both* got a date with a fireman so don't look so envious."

Liesel felt her nose crinkle—her go-to *what are you talking about?* expression.

"Uh-oh, Miss Adler," Kev broke in warily. "You're Mum's latest double-dating victim. Better beware!"

"Right, you two." Liesel stood up briskly, wanting to put an end to the conversation as soon as humanly pos-

sible. "Time's up. I've got an assembly to prepare for."
She shuffled them both out of the nurse's office and shut
the door behind her with a satisfying click.

Discussing her love life, or lack of one, in front of the
students, let alone the son of her new—her only—friend
here in Engleton wasn't on the agenda. She leaned heavily
against the door, allowing a slow breath to escape her lips.
A breath she hoped carried away some of the ache she felt
whenever she confronted the idea of moving on.

Yes. She'd loved Eric with all of her heart, an over-
the-moon-and-back-again young woman's heart, but she'd
never even got the chance to have her wedding day, let
alone share the birth of her son. Now, at the ripe old age
of twenty-eight, Liesel had a daily wrestling match with
the feeling that she was "finished" in the romance department.

It had all happened so fast. A whirlwind love affair in
an American ski resort. The spontaneous proposal. Their
surprise pregnancy. Losing Eric. Never having the family that she had only just begun to imagine.

She started at the *tap-tap-tap* against the door.

"I know you're in there, Liesel. I can hear you breathing."

Despite herself, Liesel giggled. Being friends with
Cassie gave her little glimpses back to the "old Liesel."
The free-spirited young woman she used to be.

Cracking open the door, she allowed her friend access
to one of her eyes. "Friend or foe?"

"*Friend*, you noodle! C'mon," she pleaded. "Open up!"

Liesel pulled open the door while simultaneously grab-
bing a light jumper from the hook on the wall. "Make
it fast. I'm afraid I've got to get going down to the gym

for an assembly. The principal just told me about it fifteen minutes ago."

"Cool your rockets. I'm heading the same way."

"Your class is coming?"

"You could put it that way." Cassie adopted her best nonchalant voice. "Or you could say that my class is coming to your date."

Liesel stopped in her tracks.

"Cassie Monroe! What have you done?"

"Oh-h-h-h…" Her friend was fastidiously avoiding eye contact now. "It might have been me who volunteered you to help with a little demonstration."

"What *demonstration*?"

"The first-aid demo for the first, second and third years. It was meant to be a ladders demonstration, but…" Cassie used her best cheerleader voice.

"But what?"

"Now, that, I don't know exactly. All I know is it has turned into a first-aid demo."

"And who exactly is leading today's first-aid demo?"

"Oh, I think he might have a familiar face."

Liesel felt her body go rigid as Cassie pushed open the door to the gym. Smack-dab in the center of the room a certain sandy-haired fireman was kneeling on the floor, setting up his kit. Seeing Jack again had the same effect on her nervous system as it did on the no-longer-dormant butterflies in her tummy. They were going crazy.

"Oh, no, you don't!" Cassie caught her arm as Liesel tried to turn and leave. "You're the Murray River Valley school nurse and I don't think there is anyone better placed to help our local CFS crew inspire young minds."

"But—"

"Nope. I don't want to hear it." Cassie gave her a quick

hug and a push. "Now, go and put on a good show for my class. They just might be the future doctors of Engleton. Back in a tinkle!"

Liesel watched as her friend hastily retreated down the school corridor. If there was one thing she definitely knew about Cassie, she was persistent.

Jack first caught a glimpse of the familiar auburn curls through the gym door. As Liesel virtually hurtled through it, he felt bushwhacked anew by her fresh-faced beauty. Her petite features instantly made him feel like a klutzy brontosaurus who'd been charged with protecting a tiny and exquisitely beautiful tropical bird. His modus operandi at these gigs was usually big and loud, but something about her made him want to ratchet things down a notch.

"Are you the set of helping hands I was promised?"

"I'm afraid so."

Jack took on board the microscopic flinch as she made eye contact with him. What had provoked that?

"Apologies for the last-minute setup. The CFS are trying to do as much outreach in the local schools as we can and after we met the other day I realized we hadn't done a demonstration here in ages." *Too obvious?*

She squinted up at him, waiting for more information.

"I'm trying to score a few more points locally before I turn in my outreach stats to the big boys in Adelaide." *Too macho. Definitely too macho.*

"What exactly are we meant to be doing today? I heard a rumor it was going to be snakes and ladders." Liesel crossed her fingers behind her back, hoping that demonstrating anything involving body contact was off the agenda. She was beginning to feel a little giddy in Jack's presence and feeling that way—particularly in front of the student body—was definitely not in the rulebooks.

Jack rose to his full height, arms spreading out in front of him as if preparing to sell his wares to Liesel. "Ahh. Well, HQ decided today was the day all the ladders would be checked out by one of their techs. Safety-first bureaucracy, and all that." He gave her a knowing look and she couldn't help but nod along. The world of school nurses was weighed down with thick ledgers of mind-numbing paperwork. It was little wonder his was, too.

"This is what we're going to do today." He waved an arm across everything he'd been laying out on the gym floor. "It's what you find inside a proper first-aid kit— one you'd find at a school, in a restaurant, the science lab. I know these kids are too little to reach one, let alone use it, but we can try and make it fun." His eyes twinkled down at hers and if she wasn't mistaken she saw the beginnings of a wink form, reconsider, then withdraw. *Shame.* Her butterflies were just about ready for another whirl round her tummy.

Liesel knew her eyes were meant to be following Jack's to take in the array of splints, plasters, bandages, wipes and protective glasses—a deluxe edition of first-aid kits. Instead, they were working their way from one of his long-fingered hands along his golden-haired forearm— she had a weakness for a well-defined forearm. Tanned, well-toned, his definitely measured up. Her eyes slid up and over the biceps filling his short-sleeved CFS T-shirt to a set of awfully broad shoulders—

"Like what you see?"

Heat instantly spread across her cheeks. *Obviously.* She hadn't ogled anyone from such close range in years. Three years, to be exact. A twist of guilt knotted up her butterflies and as she looked up at him she realized in an instant he was referring to the contents of the first-aid kit.

Doubly embarrassing.

Even if he hadn't seen her do an ocular tiptoe up his arms and on to the expanse of his shoulders, he would be sure to spy the flush of embarrassment continuing to heat her cheeks. *Say something, you idiot!*

"It's great. You've really got the full Monty here."

She clapped a hand over her mouth. The full Monty! Her brain did a whiz-bang dress and undress of the unsuspecting man in front of her and before she could stop it, Liesel felt herself succumbing to a full-blown case of the nervous giggles.

Jack had no idea what Liesel was finding so funny but was glad to see, whatever it was, that it brought a happy glint to those kitty-cat eyes of hers. He took a swipe at his chin. Maybe he still had some egg yolk on there from this morning's egg and bacon roll.

"I'm sorry." Liesel spoke through her fingers, actively trying to stifle her laughter. "I don't know what's got into me this morning." She cleared her throat and gave her feet a little stomp on the gym floor, as if the motion would add some sobriety to the moment. It worked. For a second. As soon as their eyes met again she burst into another peal of laughter that was about as infectious as they came.

Feeling at an utter loss as to what would have caused it, Jack was relieved to see a flow of students start to make their way into the big gymnasium. He bent his head in their direction and stage-whispered, "Quit your laughing, Miss Adler. You'll take away my tough-guy image."

Hardly. She didn't know a single thing about Brigade

Captain Jack Keller, but there was little to nothing that would diminish from the all-man mojo he was exuding.

Liesel took herself off to a corner to choke down a few more mortified giggles as the students made their way in. Being a few dozen meters away from him made it easier to spy on him. Well, not spy really…assess. Jack had clearly thought out the presentation more than he'd let on and was soon directing the children according to age toward floor seats or the stands.

He was good with them. A natural. He started off the talk with a few jokes that immediately captivated the children's attention. Liesel had to admit it, if there was anyone who could get this boisterous group of young kids interested in first-aid training and the CFS cadets, Jack Keller was the man for the job.

"All right, Miss Adler, time for you to come over here and for us to find out just how smart you are!"

Liesel did her best *who, me?* double take before realizing all eyes in the gym were focused on her and Jack was genuinely waiting for her to join him. The old Liesel would've loved being center stage, playing the jester to his brigade captain. The new Liesel? Not so sure about being in the limelight anymore.

Twenty minutes later Liesel realized she shouldn't have worried a bit. Jack Keller wasn't out to embarrass her—or anyone, for that matter. He really struck her as one of those genuinely kind guys who just wanted to help.

He had devised a really clever game where he would call out the name of an item in the first-aid kit and then he and the children would count how many seconds it took her to find it. Then, when she had found it, he would equate the time it took her to find it with what would have been happening to the patient while they were waiting. The children loved it and at the same time were learning how important it was to get help quickly in an emergency. They were putty in his hands and Jack seemed to be having just as much fun as the students.

"Right. I think it's time to pull out the big guns." Liesel watched as Jack's head turned a quick right, left and back again. Whatever it was he was looking for clearly wasn't there. Liesel thought she might be mistaken…but was he looking embarrassed?

"Right. We've just come onto the CPR part of our demonstration and it appears my good friend Resusci Annie decided to cop out for this particular trip." He scanned the room, his eyes coming to rest on Liesel, complete with that cockeyed smile of his. *Oh, no.* She was in trouble now.

"Who thinks Miss Adler should come and stand in for my dum—my good friend Resusci Annie?"

Jack knew he was going out on a limb here, but he might as well find out now whether or not Liesel gave as good as she got. She'd been great in participating in his game and seemed to know how to play along with him to maximize the learning potential for the children.

The whoops and hollers of the kids were all the confirmation Jack needed to usher a blushing Liesel to the center of the gym floor. He had to remind himself the blushing wasn't for him—it was for the children. Right? Either way, the flush on her cheeks was having a nice effect on his ego.

"Who'd like to see what it looks like when someone faints or passes out?"

Another cheer filled the gym and Liesel gave Jack a

sidelong *thanks a lot, pal* look before performing one of the most melodramatic faints he had ever seen.

Score one to Liesel.

Oh-h-h-h, he's close. Really, really close. Not safe territory!

Jack was right in the middle of explaining the need to check for breathing when Liesel became a little too aware of him kneeling next to her. Then leaning over her. Then whispering in her ear, his soft breath an indicator as to just how close his lips were. His very, very kissable lips. Had her lips just quivered? *Please, say that didn't just happen.*

"I'm going to touch you, touch your head, is that all right?" She tried her best to nod slowly, maintaining the illusion of being unconscious. It was just as well she was lying on the floor. With her eyes closed. The effect of that low voice on her central nervous system seemed to get more results on her than a defibrillator. She felt one of those big capable hands of his gently touch her forehead. It was strange to her that she didn't feel vulnerable. Everything about this man seemed capable, safe. But he was close. Too close. She had to lift her head. *Now.*

"So, to check for breath you just want to lean over and—"

"Oh!"

Jack's mouth swept across hers as if by design. She found her lips breezing across his and meeting his stubbled cheek in virtually the same movement. It was softer than she had thought it would be. Not that she'd thought about it. Much.

His warm scent, a delicious sunbaked salty-sweet combo, filled her nostrils, her body's responsiveness quickly shooting to code red. Cheers and squeals of laughter pealed from the children. Liesel instinctively began to pull back as if she'd been set alight. In a lightning-fast move, she pushed herself away from Jack and up into a seating position. A thousand thoughts clamored for attention as she tried to put together what had just happened.

"That's one way to give the kiss of life, children. Not necessarily approved by the Red Cross, but nevertheless…" She could see him smiling at the children but was more aware of the questions flying through his blue eyes as he locked onto her own.

It's such a good thing I'm sitting down already.

I want to kiss him. For real.

No, you don't!

Yes. Yes, I do.

In front of half the school? And forget about Eric?

Eric.

Liesel was sure you could see her heart beating through her light summer top. Jack extended a hand to help her up. She didn't dare accept it.

"I think we should wait until Captain Keller comes back fully prepared to explore this lifesaving method." She pushed herself up and looked at her watch-free wrist as if willing a timepiece to appear. The not-so-artful dodge. *First-class confirmation that I am* not *ready for this. It seems my body is—but not the rest of me.*

"Looks like I've got to get going." She glanced in Jack's direction but didn't dare meet his eyes. It would've been too easy to call her bluff. "I'm afraid I've got to run. Thanks for the presentation."

She must have looked like a terrified rabbit the way she was hot-footing it out of the gym, but she needed to get out of there. Away from Jack Keller.

Those milliseconds of intimate contact had wiped away the rest of the world for a moment and that wasn't how things needed to be right now. She was a single mum. She had responsibilities. Responsibilities that included putting forward a positive example for the children here at the Murray Valley School.

Heart thumping, she closed the door to her office. It was the perfect sanctuary. A quiet place to process what had just happened. If anything had happened at all.

Her mouth went dry as she realized the whole incident was down to her lifting up her head when she hadn't been meant to. It had all been a mistake and from Jack's perspective she'd just behaved like a first-class lunatic. In the blur of the moment she had just assumed he'd felt the same charge of emotion that had flooded through her as their lips had brushed together. Liesel scrubbed her fingers through her hair. Terrific! Now he knew without a shadow of a doubt the impact his touch had on her.

Oh, this was not good. She collapsed her head onto her crossed arms, fervently wishing her desk could absorb her into the woodwork. This was Class A Embarrassment Central.

"Am I going to have to check for breath again?"

Liesel bolted upright, curls flying everywhere and hands unsure where to come to rest at the sound of the voice that had awakened her senses as if she'd been Sleeping Beauty. Disheveled Sleeping Nutcase was more like it. Could this day get any worse?

Hands firmly planted on her hips, Liesel tried to adopt a casual air, as if she was always almost kissing someone during first-aid demonstrations. "I'm good. Very good. Everything's good here."

If erratic heart rate and jangling nerves were a picture of perfection.

She forced herself to make eye contact with Jack, prepared for the derision he no doubt would have for her ridiculous behavior. What she saw instead was an oasis of calm. A gentle smile played on his lips, little crinkles appearing at the edges of those blue-as-the-sky eyes of his. He leaned casually against the door frame of her office as if he'd been born to fill it, and everything about him said, *Relax. You're safe with me.*

"Glad to hear it. Sorry it was all a bit of a mess today. Organization is generally a bit more of a strong point. I'd like to make it up you—to the school, I mean." He shifted his feet slightly, his smile still as warm as the spring sunshine.

"Sure, that'd be great." Liesel winced. Had she sounded too eager? This wasn't really playing it cool. Or safe. "I mean…I'm sure the children would absolutely love it."

"You know," he continued, seemingly unaware of her internal battle for a bit more personal strength, "it would really be great if you could come down to the station sometime and throw some ideas around. Now that I know you're not—"

He stopped abruptly, almost looking bashful. It was cute. Supercute.

"Not what?"

"The fellas told me you were a granny on the verge of retirement."

"That would've been my predecessor, Mrs. Heissen." She could feel his eyes run up and down her body to doubly confirm she was the opposite of an aging grandmother. The examination wasn't helping her maintain any sort of cool, calm and collected demeanor. His eyes landed on hers. Ping! Crystal-blue perfection.

"I feel I've really missed a trick, not introducing myself to you when I got my transfer here."

"Sorry, I've got an appointment to get to." *Liar.*

She took another glance at her invisible watch. She'd already made enough of a fool of herself.

"Fair enough, but don't think I'm going to give up easily."

She raised her eyebrows at him. Give up on *what* exactly?

"This is a small town and come fire season we genuinely could do with all the help we can get."

Aha. He's still recruiting. Wrong bark, wrong tree, mate.

"I'm sorry, but I'm afraid I just wouldn't have much to offer in the way of free time."

He carried on as if she hadn't said a word. "Not to mention the fact I've only been in town a few weeks and haven't yet found the perfect chocolate milk shake in the area. I'm on a quest. Care to join me?"

Oh. Well, that was quite a different suggestion. Although just as dangerous, given that it meant spending time alone with Jack Keller.

"That sounds like a laudable quest, Captain Keller—"

"Jack."

"Jack." She said the name deliberately before continuing, "I'd really like to help, but—"

"Great. That's settled, then. Things are pretty hectic over at the station for the rest of the week and I've got to get down to Adelaide for a weekend's training session— sometime next week?"

"Sure."

The word leaped past her lips before she'd had a chance to rein it in. Hadn't she just told herself that time spent with Jack Keller was a bad idea?

Jack was still grinning as he lifted the last bits of gear into the station truck. He was feeling remarkably cheery. And a little bit guilty. He was pleased his made-up quest for the perfect chocolate milk shake had worked in convincing Liesel to go out with him. That was a white lie he could live with. The one giving his gut a good kicking was the part about being new in town. Technically, it was true. He *was* new in town if you discounted the first twenty-five years of his life. If you forgot about those and just focused on the past four he'd been away and the man he'd become during those years…then, yes, technically he was new in town.

He was focused. Driven. Making a decision to be a full-timer for the CFS had added the sorely needed rod to his spine. Gone were the days of the noncommitted heir to River's Bend. His father no longer had to put up with experimental fields of hops for a microbrew, escapee pigs destined for air-dried sausage or a pair of Clydesdale horses clearly not meant for work in the forty-degree heat. All well-intentioned ideas with no real follow-through. Now his life was about tangible results. A new Jack Keller was definitely in town.

He coasted down the school drive and pulled out onto the highway, doing his best to surrender his doubts to the beautiful afternoon.

Nope. It was no good.

Everything was too familiar. The road, the tiny cluster of shops, who ran them, the clumps of gum and eucalyptus trees shading this house or that. If he was going to

see Liesel again, he was going to have to come clean—
at some point.

Truth be told, it would be nice to date someone who
didn't have a clue about his history. Someone who just
liked plain ol' Jack the fireman.

He gave a little snort. *Date!* He hadn't dated anyone
properly in years. Girls in Engleton had always had their
eye on the River's Bend prize, while in Adelaide during
training there just hadn't been enough time. Or just not
the right women. Or maybe for once he just wanted to
see something through and prove to his father he had it
in him to talk the walk. Or walk the talk. Or whatever
that saying was.

Liesel definitely had something that spoke to him. Too
bad the timing was shambolic.

He pulled the truck into the station-house drive, smiling at the sight of a couple of volunteers washing down
one of the big rigs. It had just received a whopper of an
upgrade thanks to a ten-grand anonymous donation. All
of the guys had sworn ignorance and he believed them.
They had an angel out there and he, for one, was grateful. The volunteers were great guys. He was just getting
to know them, but already they had him knee-deep in
barbecue invitations and bursting with ideas for fund-
raising drives.

They'd make a success of this station. He was sure of
it. The big guns over in Adelaide had given him a year to
turn around the waning number of volunteers and poor
track record on incident attendance. It would mean a lot
of hard work, being on call 24/7 and his 100 percent dedi-
cation. He pressed his lips together as if to strengthen his
resolve and scrubbed a hand through his hair.

He'd been kidding himself back at the school. He

barely had time to grab a meal for himself, let alone complicate his life with a milk shake quest and a beautiful woman.

Short, sharp shock it was, then. Who was going to feel the pain the most, though, was up in the air.

CHAPTER THREE

"No-o-o-o!" LIESEL DID her best to squelch a few choice words as she wrestled with the steering wheel, the *thud-thud-thud* coming from her swerving car the unmistakable sound of a flat tire.

A quick glance in the rearview mirror showed that Liam, strapped into his car seat, was snoozing away, blissfully unaware of his mother's battle for control with the vehicle. At least one of them was relaxed! She pulled over as quickly and as safely as she could, a glance at the dashboard clock confirming what she already knew. They'd be late. Getting to Adelaide in an hour with a flat tire to fix was out of the question. Not to mention the fact her adrenaline was running at full pelt. Another reminder she didn't—couldn't—do high octane anymore. Just the few seconds it had taken to pull the car over had been more than enough to set her heart racing. Her hands shook as she put the car into Park and rested her head on the steering wheel to collect herself, before getting out to assess the damage.

"That was a well-controlled skid, Miss Adler. I didn't have you pegged for a rally driver."

Liesel nearly jumped out of her seat at the sound of the male voice—the exact same male voice attached to the exact same pair of lips that had been doing reruns in her head since yesterday afternoon.

"Hello again." Liesel managed a feeble wave through her open car window, heart still racing but for a completely different reason now. "Fancy meeting you here."

"It's one of the perks of living in a small town."

Mmm...he wasn't kidding. Then again, these run-ins were beginning to accrue quite a high count of embarrassment in her camp. Why couldn't he ever see her when she was doing something normal? Or, even better, laudable? Not that it mattered. Not really.

"I hope you weren't racing off to find a chocolate shake without me."

"At nine in the morning?" She couldn't help but laugh. "Even *I'm* not that keen!"

"Shall we take a look at your car?"

"I'm sure it's just a flat—I'll be fine." Liesel ran her fingers through her tousled hair. This guy sure had a knack for showing up when her hair and a comb were distant strangers.

"Oh, I never had any doubt about that."

Liesel felt herself being appraised by him and wished for the second time in as many seconds that she'd looked in the mirror that morning and perhaps even bothered to pop on a bit of lip gloss after brushing her hair. She was only going to housesit for her parents so hadn't bothered with the whole dolling-up routine.

Who was she kidding? Dolling up had been the last thing on her agenda for the past three years. Yet under Jack's gaze she suddenly felt the need to look her best. No. Not "the need"… No, that wasn't it. She *wanted* to look good. For him to like what he saw. And the collateral wake of feelings that went along with that little revelation was throwing her nerves into a right old jumble.

"First things first, Miss Adler." He squatted down so his head was level with hers, a long index finger reaching out to pull a couple of wayward curls out of her eyes. "Any bumps or bruises?"

Liesel shook her head, praying he hadn't noticed the lightning bolt shooting down her spine at his touch. It was obvious he hadn't done it as a flirtatious move—she'd made the same gesture along Liam's forehead countless times. Although somehow she didn't think her two-year-old got butterflies in his stomach when she did it.

"Would you like me to take a look at your car?" Jack pressed, standing up with a nod toward the back of her car.

Not really. Basking in that crooked beam of a grin of yours is working pretty well for me.

Rescuing damsels in distress had to be his true calling. Seriously.

He had already proved he was good with schoolboys in distress, and from the spray of goose pimples shivering up her arms in the morning sun he wasn't going far wrong with the damsel part, either.

"That'd be great." Liesel made her decision, clicking the door open and hoping it would signal to Jack that she needed a bit of space. Close proximity to this guy was unnerving. In a good way. *Far too good.*

She got out of the car and joined him at the offending rear tire.

"Looks like I won't be getting to Adelaide anytime soon."

"I'm afraid you won't be getting to Adelaide at all with that. It looks like a cracked tire wall—not just a flat."

Liesel stood in silence, her mind working through all the possibilities. She'd promised to look after her parents' "replacement child," Moxy, the toy poodle, while they spent a weekend with her sister in Melbourne. Their neighbors were a bit too elderly for the walks and if anything went wrong—well, she was hoping nothing would go wrong. Their train left in just a couple of hours and after all their amazing support she couldn't let them down.

"I'm headed to Adelaide."

"Are you staying long?"

"Overnight." Liesel looked up at the sky in frustration. She had to sort this out. "I'm meant to be housesitting for my parents."

"Why don't you catch a ride with me? I'm doing a weekend course with the Metropolitan Fire Service. I'm not heading back until late Sunday afternoon. Would that work for you?"

Jack let the words hang between them in the fresh morning air. They were out there before he'd had a chance to really think about what would happen if she said yes. But seeing the stricken look on Liesel's face had instinctively made him offer his help.

"Oh, I couldn't let you do that."

"Why not? I've got a perfectly good truck with a spare seat."

"That's really kind of you, but…" Her mind raced, knowing there was a lot he didn't know about her, a lot she wasn't ready to share. "I don't even know your full name."

"Officially it's Brigade Captain John G. Keller, but given that we're both technically state employees—

meaning we're colleagues—I'd say you should still just call me Jack. And I'm warning you now—" he waggled a finger at her "—you'll *never* get to know what the *G* stands for!"

There was that laugh again. A smiling Liesel was definitely better than the one who'd looked utterly panicked when he'd arrived. He wasn't sure what it was about this woman, but being around her brought out a deep need to protect her. Not to mention a whole slew of other things he'd already decided were not options for him. Like finding out what it would be like to really kiss those ruby-red lips of hers.

Lust aside, he reasoned with himself as he held open her car door, as one of the few salaried members of the CFS he was a civil servant. It was his job to help.

Shaking away the idea his protective impulses were anything more than a fireman's gut reaction to any human in distress, he gestured toward the truck. "Grab your stuff and hop in, Miss Adler."

"Oh, no, really. I couldn't accept." Her eyes darted to the backseat of her car. "It's not just me."

Jack's eyebrows shot up at his oversight. "Right, well, who have we got back here? You have a dog?" He tipped his head so he could get a glimpse of the backseat passenger.

Liesel moved in between him and the car as if by instinct. "He's my son."

"And what a good-looking little fellow he is." Jack peeped over her shoulder, trying his best to give her a relaxed smile.

He sure hadn't seen that one coming.

He felt sucker punched. Liesel was taken. She wasn't wearing a wedding ring and certainly didn't have a mumsy aura about her—but a son was a pretty good indicator she wasn't available. True, he hadn't considered dating someone with children before, but—honestly? He hadn't even considered *dating* in a long time. It might take a little while to shake off the effect she had on him but—big picture—it was probably just as well she was off the market.

"Should we give his dad a ring and have him come collect you two?"

Ice flooded Liesel's veins. She still hadn't found a way to tell people about Liam's dad. Not without wanting to cry or subjecting the other person to huge waves of embarrassment.

"No, it's just us, I'm afraid."

She felt Jack's hand rest lightly on her shoulder. It was all she could do not to press into the warm comfort of it. Lean into the strength he offered.

"Not to worry," Jack said gently. "Guess it's a good thing I showed up. Let's get you two packed up and hit the road."

As if in a daze, Liesel followed Jack's lead. She was so grateful to him for not prying. Not asking more. Just a few short years ago she'd been a girl who loved to hash out emotional affairs in minute detail, but keeping things neutral was her survival mode now. In fact, accepting a ride from a virtual stranger was a leap out of her current comfort zone, but it wasn't as if she had a lot of choice. Her parents were expecting her and what harm could come of it? They were both state employees. Colleagues. *Right?*

Jack gave her the number of a local towing company, who, after a quick chat, agreed to pick up the car and drop it at the school on Monday morning when they had finished. Everything fell into place like a well-laid plan. Living in a small town definitely had its advantages.

As she spoke to her parents to let them know about her change of plans she watched as Jack expertly unclipped Liam's travel seat, a single muscled arm smoothly moving him from car to truck before securing all of the appropriate buckles in his backseat with barely a flutter from her son's sleeping lashes. She grabbed the enormous tote bag she'd hurriedly packed moments before they had left the house. It contained more of Liam's things than her own. Looking after herself had come a distant second over the past two years and this morning had been no different.

"You're going to have to forgive the mess, I'm afraid." Jack sent an apologetic glance toward the front cab of the truck. "Regulation dictates we keep it free of excess materials, but regulation doesn't take into account a man's hunger when on call twenty-four hours a day!"

"Don't worry about it." Liesel found herself strangely relieved to see the jumble of empty soft-drink cans and tomato-ketchup packets lying about the cab. It took the superhero edge off, making him the tiniest bit more human.

"Here, let me take that for you."

She felt her mega-sized tote being lifted out of her hands as if it didn't weigh a thing and watched as Jack deposited it in the backseat on top of what looked like a regulation issue CFS duffel.

"It's not all mine, I promise." She scrunched her face at the memory of going through Liam's room at high speed this morning, covering every single option for what her son might or might not need for the next forty-eight hours. She liked to be prepared. Some would say overprepared, but this morning's tire disaster was proof you just couldn't plan for everything. Not even a run-in with a handsome fireman who'd danced in and out of her subconscious last night.

"Right!" Jack smiled across at her as she climbed into the front of the cab. "Where are we headed, Miss Adler?"

"The Northern Hills, if that's all right. Near the Kangaroo Creek Reservoir."

"No problem. The station where we're doing the training is just across the reservoir from you, at Houghton. You all buckled up?"

Uncertainty flickered through her eyes as he spoke and Jack tutted when he saw her glancing at the door handle, as if second-guessing her decision to accept a lift into town.

"Don't worry, love. I don't bite. You're getting a certified rescue." Turning off the jokey voice, he continued, "If you like, I can call it in to the station. Just so we're all on the up-and-up." He reached for the in-cab radio.

"It's all right. Sorry, sorry. It's just been a bit of a mad dash this morning and now with the tire—"

"Even better that you're catching a ride, then. Not good to be behind a wheel when you're stressed. Just sit back and enjoy the ride."

Much to her surprise, Liesel found herself doing just that. Conversation with Jack was easy and after a few more "Miss Adlers" she managed to convince him to call her Liesel. Despite her initial reservations in riding along with him, she found her trust in this man deepening as the kilometers glided past.

"Will you and the little fella be hitting the town tonight? There are some nice places around where you are."

Liesel laughed at the idea of going out. She couldn't

remember the last time she'd been out for dinner, let alone feeling as if she was "out on the town."

"Hardly. It's just going to be me, Liam and some Saturday-night television, I'm afraid. All very boring."

"Why don't you let me take you out?"

Liesel caught her breath at the words, eyes widened in surprise.

"Both of you, I mean. Training stops at five. We could go for an early tea and I'll get you back before the little man's bedtime."

Liesel checked her instinct to immediately say no. The butterflies soaring round her tummy were already clinking icy glasses of Pinot Grigio on a restaurant patio with him. The scared, desperate-to-be-wrapped-in-cotton-wool side? Firemen were still in the no-go zone. For her son.

"Thanks, but I don't think we should. The whole reason we're going to Adelaide is to look after Mum and Dad's cherished poodle." She found herself embellishing the task, detailing for him the great attention to detail her parents lavished on Moxy.

"Sounds like they should have called her Cleopatra or the Queen of Sheba."

Liesel laughed in agreement, treating herself to another sidelong glance at Jack. He was a good guy and the fact he wasn't pushing her was something to appreciate. Actually, it went beyond that. For the first time in ages Liesel was enjoying the simple pleasure of having a normal conversation.

Normal.

She'd been craving that sensation for a long time now. Since Eric had died it was hard to know what normal was. Hard to know when someone wasn't treating her like a bereaved single mum or just as her old self—footloose, worry-free, globe-trotting, fun-loving Liesel.

If someone had told her she'd find "normal" sitting in the cab of a pickup next to a ridiculously fit fireman in the heart of Australia's wine country, she would have laughed herself silly.

She leaned against the window, hoping he couldn't tell she was looking at him through her dark sunglasses. Again.

No doubt about it. He was gorgeous, of the good old-fashioned hunky fireman variety. He probably had girls hitting on him all the time. She was guessing her permanently rumpled appearance made her "friend" material rather than a possible girlfriend. Not that she had imagined dating him. Or kissing those full lips of his, or rubbing a cheek along that silky-soft stubble lining his face before stealing another cheeky kiss... *Liesel! Stop it!*

She pressed her lips together. Hard.

"C'mon." She heard Jack's teasing voice from the other side of the cab. "It'll be fun. We could even start our chocolate shake quest early. I know a place Liam would love."

"Sorry, Jack." Liesel fixed her gaze straight ahead. "I really think we ought to stay in."

Jack gave his head a quick shake. She sure was making asking her out difficult. And given the fact he wasn't on the hunt for a girlfriend, it was pretty weird he was pushing so hard. No. That wasn't true. He knew exactly why he was pushing so hard. He wanted to get to know her. Plain and simple.

His let his fingers run round the leather steering wheel, before glancing in the rearview mirror at Liesel's peacefully sleeping son. A son. He'd hardly thought about having a girlfriend, let alone a wife. Children, future heirs to the Keller dynasty? They were all wisps of cloud in his imagination. There was nothing plain and simple about his life right now and, from the looks of things, not in Liesel's, either.

He should let it go. Leave Liesel in peace to have her quiet night by the television. They drove on in silence, each seemingly absorbed in their own thoughts.

"What's that?" Jack's eyes darted around the cab at the sound of a popular sixties tune coming from the footwell.

"It's my ringtone, sorry." Liesel dug furiously in her bag to end the blaring tones, glancing back anxiously at Liam, whose eyes only blinked open and closed quickly before he drifted back to sleep.

"Bit of a hippie, are you?"

"Used to be." Liesel glanced up at him, a flicker of mischief flashing across her feline eyes before she pushed the "accept" button on her phone. "Hello?"

Jack glanced across, unable to hear the words of the caller, but the high-octane delivery and Liesel's raised eyebrows indicated it wasn't a pleasure call.

"Cassie, I need you to slow down. How big is the burn?"

Jack's attention level shot up a few notches. Burns went with fires. He tapped Liesel's arm, gesturing that he could turn around if she needed. She shook her head, clearly focused on the caller's rapid-fire explanation.

"We've got to establish the depth of the burn, all right?"

Jack was impressed with the calm in her voice. She had initially struck him as quite a timorous, shy little thing, but the steady, capable voice he heard now showed him a whole other side to the enigmatic Miss Liesel Adler.

"Is it just red and glistening or are there any blisters?"

Jack pulled the truck onto the hard shoulder. Liesel shot him a quick look of gratitude. It was fleeting, but just the grateful glimpse from those expressive eyes puffed up his pride a bit. He wasn't sure how she did it, but he wanted to make sure he earned the gratitude her look had expressed.

"Have you put anything on it yet, Cassie?"

Cassie. The name rang a bell. One of the teachers up at the Murray Valley School?

"It doesn't sound too bad, Cass—but if I were you I'd make sure you give it a good clean and then wrap it loosely in a light bandage. You need to be careful not to pop the blisters." She paused and Jack smiled as her soothing voice turned into that of a strict schoolteacher. "Tell Kev he is, under no circumstances, to pick them open. No gaming devices if he does, and I don't care if he's thirteen and knows everything."

She paused to listen and offered Jack an apologetic smile. "All right, Cass? Call me if there are any problems, or take him straight to the clinic if it gets infected. Speak soon."

"Everything all right?"

"Sorry, yes. I didn't mean to delay us. It's my friend Cassandra Monroe—up at the school?" She raised her eyebrows in question and he nodded—he did know Cassandra. And her son, Kevin. He'd heard through a couple of the guys at the station that the boy had become a bit of a tearaway since his dad had left town a year or so ago. One to put on his cadet recruits list. Being a cadet had given him focus—now he was trying to pay it forward.

"He's one of the most accident-prone kids I think I've ever met. This time it's a mishap with the grill pan."

Jack's eyes opened wider. "Is he trying to become a chef?"

"Hardly!" Liesel gave a hoot of laughter, her fingers flying to cover her mouth as she glanced back to make sure her son was still asleep. "Cheese on toast," she whispered, her attention now fully captured by Liam.

They both watched him in silence, the previous conversation forgotten.

Jack had never been one to coo over babies, but he had to admit Liesel's toddler was a handsome little chap. It was incredible to him how trusting the boy looked, deeply and comfortably asleep in his car seat as if he hadn't a care in the world. Building his own family was something he had always imagined happening one day. He cleared his throat. Getting broody was *not* on today's agenda.

"Shall we hit the road again?"

Liesel flicked through the TV channels, finding it difficult to believe the hundred-plus channels her parents received contained absolutely nothing worth watching. It would have to be a cooking show. Maybe that would inspire her to get something to eat. Liam had nibbled at her uninspired offerings before ultimately abandoning them for a game of tug-of-war with Moxy the Wonder Poodle, leaving Liesel with her own listlessness to contend with.

It didn't take a brainiac to figure out she had no attention span because of some not-so-idle daydreams about dining with a certain fireman. Too bad she couldn't take her advice as easily as she dispensed it. The number of times she'd encouraged Cassie to shake off a bad date and to keep on trying! Now here she was turning down a date—no, not even a date really, a casual dinner with the first man to stir feelings in her that she thought had died with Eric.

She flicked the channels again. Doughnut-making.

Nope. Still not as interesting as thinking about Jack. About that one, perfectly still moment when his strong hand had held her—well, held her shoulder, at any rate. Or back in the gym when just the brush of his lips had—

Stop. It. Now.

She looked across the room at her son, happily sharing his teddy bear with the poodle.

Liam. He was who she needed to focus on. Not Jack.

A knock at the door pulled her out of her reverie.

She jumped up from the sofa, tightening up the drawstring to her tracksuit bottoms as she went to the door. One of the neighbors must have popped round.

"I couldn't resist." Two enormous chocolate shakes worked their way round the door frame.

Most decidedly *not* a neighbor.

Jack handed her the ice-cold drinks, his wrists weighed down with two very full bags of takeaway from a local rotisserie.

"Hope you haven't eaten yet."

How he'd divined roast chicken was one of her favorites she'd never know. Liesel felt a smile creeping onto her lips.

Was this another little nudge from fate?

Or a supersize push?

CHAPTER FOUR

"You're making it very difficult to resist your charms."

"You think I'm charming now, do you?"

Jack scooped out the final dollop of potato salad for Liesel then leaned back in his patio chair, highly aware of feeling a bit too eager for her response.

She made a noncommittal noise, took a huge forkful of potato salad to her lips, smiled coquettishly, then devoured it in one go. He watched as the tip of her tongue captured the last miniature dot of mayonnaise resting on her upper lip.

And another point to Liesel for winning sexiest eater of takeaway rotisserie!

There was no keeping an appreciative smile under wraps. From where he sat, Jack felt he'd come out the true winner. A genuinely relaxing evening with a woman he could get used to spending a lot more time with. Not to mention her son. Talk about an infectious laugh.

He had to admit to being shocked by the fact Liesel had a child, but as the idea grew on him, and having seen them interact like the natural twosome they were, it would now seem strange to imagine her without him. Liesel never mentioned the father but Jack was pretty certain that was a topic better left for her to bring up.

The boy was a testament to his mother—fun-loving and relaxed. Just a happy little toddler enjoying life, the way it should be.

Jack rested his chin on a temple of fingertips. With the sun behind him, he had the perfect position to enjoy watching the remains of the sun dance through Liesel's auburn curls. It was all too easy to imagine slipping his fingers through her hair, brushing a thumb along the soft down of her cheek before drawing her in closer to him for a…

He shifted. He was staring, a move unlikely to be found in the rulebook for *playing it cool*. He pulled a hand through his own hair and tried to turn the gesture into a casual stretch. Nope. No good. He was just succeeding in looking like an idiot.

"If you consider this morning's heroics—"

"A hero *and* charming," Liesel interrupted with a burble of laughter. "This is a red-letter day for Captain Keller, isn't it, Liam?"

The two-year-old, tightly curled in his mother's lap, responded by snuggling in even deeper and emitting a little boy-sized snore.

"Clearly my charms aren't working on your son."

"I guess you're going to have to try a bit harder." Liesel cocked an eyebrow with a playful smirk, and then just as quickly averted her gaze. *Had he seen a glint of flirtation there?* Good.

"That is a challenge I will happily accept." Jack pushed back his chair and started collecting what remained of the takeaway. The milk shakes were long gone. Scored seven out of ten. "Why don't you get the little man to bed and I'll sort these things out?"

Liesel accepted his offer with a silent smile. Jack

watched her slip through the patio doors into the comfortable bungalow her parents had moved into a decade earlier—a downsize, apparently, after their daughters had moved out of the original family home. It had a nice family feel about it. Loved and lived-in. The same feeling River's Bend had had before his mum had died.

He dragged a hand through his blond thatch again, giving his scalp a bit of a knead as if it would stop the memories from shifting into high gear.

Jack turned his attention to the handful of scraps left on the picnic table. Chicken? Gone. Potato salad? The tiniest smudge of mayonnaise lurked in the corner of the takeaway container. Veggies? *Nada.* They'd made mincemeat of the "family meal" he'd ordered. Demolished the lot.

Scrubbing at his chin, he realized anyone looking over the fence would've seen the three of them as just that—a family. Not really what he'd had in mind when his eyes had first lit on Liesel in the barnyard the other day, but he had to admit, learning she had a son hadn't detracted from his response to her. She brought out the all-male side of him in a big way. He'd been showing off for the past couple of hours and there was no doubt in his mind if any of the lads from down the station had seen him being used as a jungle gym by a poodle and a two-year-old with an insatiable desire for "More!" then the ribbing would have been long-lived.

The entire evening had been fun. Good old-fashioned fun. And he knew he'd come back for more. If Liesel was up for it.

Pulling the light blue duvet over her son's shoulders and tucking his favorite cuddly tiger under his arm, Liesel couldn't stop herself from lingering a bit over her son. His cheeks were still flushed from a full evening of chase with Moxy, enough airplane rides from Jack to last a lifetime and another first, eating grilled vegetables. She didn't know why she hadn't thought of barbecuing them before. Cranking up the barbecue for just the two of them had seemed excessive. She'd have to reconsider. Liam had devoured a pile of veg that normally would have been ignored whether they were diced, sliced or shaped into flying saucers.

Her lips slipped into an easy smile. Jack definitely knew how to tantalize the right things into a young boy's tummy.

Who was she kidding? He knew how to tantalize *her*, too. The number of times she had caught her gaze lingering on his hands, wondering how it would feel if he slid his fingers along her hip, round to the small of her back… She looked back down at her son. She'd have to squelch those feelings for now. No matter how irresistibly tingly an effect he had on her, Liam had to stay her priority. She couldn't stop her smile from broadening. At the very least, knowing Jack would be an asset to the weight loss she'd suffered over the past couple of years.

She and Liam had attacked Jack's takeaway like a pair of starving wolves. And Liam had already had his tea! It was as if Jack's presence had given them both an extra jolt of energy, reminding her that life did have its footloose and fancy-free moments. She giggled a little.

Fancy-free was for sure. With his unerring ability to catch her at her worst, she had given up worrying about the fact that her couch-potato outfit hardly flattered her petite figure. She was just having fun with a new friend—right? Well, a new friend who flirted, gave her goose pimples from ten meters away and lit up her tummy like a lava lamp for the first time in—well, a very long time.

Liesel's fingers ran through the fine waves of her son's blond hair. From the looks of things, it didn't seem as though he'd share her thick, corkscrew curls. It was definitely Eric's hair.

Her stomach clenched. Eric. Her son's father. Her first love. And had she really just spent the past couple of hours flirting with another man as if he had never existed?

Her body gave her the answer before her mind dared confirm it.

Yes.

Liesel felt her lips thin as she tried to press away the fact that not only had she kept Eric and their history out of the conversation with Jack, but she hadn't even thought about him. They'd been having so much fun and the time had flown by. How could she have let this happen? She needed to knock some sense into herself—and she definitely needed to give herself a good mental talking-to.

Tipping back her head, she closed her eyes as tears prickled at her lashes.

Would it ever end? The guilt? The need to hold on to the past knowing full well the only way to give her son a future was to let go? And how much? Were there guidelines? How much of the past could she let go of before safely moving on?

"Liesel, you need to come now."

Jack's low voice sounded urgent. He was halfway back down the corridor before she'd swatted away the stray tears he hopefully hadn't spied trickling down her cheeks.

"What's going on?"

"Your parents' neighbor has just had a nasty fall on her back patio. Pretty sure it's her hip but she's nonresponsive. Her husband's with her now. I'm going to call an ambulance but the first aid required is beyond my terrain. See you there in a few minutes?" Jack grabbed the wall phone, not waiting for an answer.

Instinct took over. Liesel bolted out of the back door and through the adjoining gate between her parents' and the Daleses' backyards. The two sets of parents were longtime friends; they'd known each other long before their children had been born and had moved next door to each other for this very reason—to be there if they ever needed help.

Liesel's heart lurched into her throat at the sight of Mrs. Dales sprawled on the hard tiles of their patio, a small pool of blood forming along the slate stone beneath her head. Mr. Dales looked up at her, eyes stricken with panic. "What do I do? She's barely conscious."

This was exactly the sort of situation Liesel had been trained to deal with. Extreme trauma. And exactly the type of scenario she'd been actively avoiding since she'd frozen in the Adelaide trauma unit.

She had a duty of care. And her head was spinning.

She had a duty of care.

Her instinct was to run and curl up in Jack's arms, hands pressed against her ears, blocking it all out. She'd feel safe in his arms.

She had a duty of care.

He was here. Close by. She could do this without freezing. Steeling herself, Liesel stepped forward, placing as reassuring a hand as she could on the elderly man's shoulder. It had worked for her when Jack had done it so she hoped it had the same calming effect on her neighbor.

"You're doing a great job, Mr. Dales. My friend is ringing for help." She let herself feel the invisible squeeze on her own shoulder.

"Would you run into the kitchen for me and grab some clean towels, ice and some warm water? Don't try and get it all in one trip, all right?" He nodded wordlessly and disappeared into the kitchen as she knelt, turning her full focus onto Mrs. Dales. Her fingers automatically dropped to the woman's slender wrist to check for a pulse. Her skin was deathly pale and she was now unconscious. A sharp trauma could cause that. Liesel knelt closer, tipping her cheek to the side to check for breathing. The faintest of breaths stirred the fine hairs on her cheek. Uneven. Slight. But breathing.

Thank you. Thank you. Thank you.

As if on autopilot, Liesel started working her way through a mental checklist she hadn't used for a long time. She wouldn't move Mrs. Dales at all. That would be a job for the SAAS team when the ambos arrived. They would have neck braces, immobilization backboards, the lot. Her job now was to stabilize Mrs. Dales as best she could. The possibility of a break bordering on a key arterial route was often lethal. The slightest of movements could cause paralysis if the break was in the neck or spine. Equally, a sudden movement could loosen a blood clot, sending it on a fatal path, ultimately blocking the blood supply to the brain.

Liesel scrunched her eyelids together as tightly as she could, a heavy exhalation gushing past her lips. It felt as if she was short-circuiting.

Breathe. Focus. Jack thinks you can do this. You know you can do this.

Liesel opened her eyes, blocking out everything but

Mrs. Dales. From the placement of her legs and her sprawled arms, it was clear she had taken quite a fall. Broken hip, leg, back, arm, wrist—one or all of them were possibilities. Intrascapular fractures, breaks along key arterial routes of the neck, were also a possibility. Much more likely in a woman than a man, but from the placement of Mrs. Dales's body, she guessed it was more likely to be a hip injury than anything else.

She'd encountered quite a few broken hips during her tenure on the slopes, young people usually—daredevil skiers losing a game of chicken with a pine tree or such-like. They were extreme traumas but youth was on their side.

For the elderly? Life wasn't as kind. Particularly with someone who was suffering from osteoarthritis—an affliction shared by both Mr. and Mrs. Dales. Her parents had laughingly told her about how their lives were reduced to swapping notes about medications over the garden fence. It was no laughing matter now.

The elderly were highly susceptible to these types of injuries and Liesel knew more than most that a broken hip for someone in their seventies could easily result in death. If not today, the chances of it happening over the next year were high. Too high.

It was the cut to the head that needed immediate attention. Head injuries always bled heavily but weren't necessarily as bad as they looked. Infection could be the real problem.

Liesel made a quick scan of the patio. A plate of raw sausages was strewn over the crisscross of slate and stone tiles. The squared edge of the barbecue side tray was just to their left. A small stain of red and a couple of white hairs on the corner betrayed its status as the culprit for the head wound. Liesel's instinct was to stem the blood flow as quickly as possible but, well aware her hands weren't sanitary, was relieved to see Mr. Dales appear alongside her with a pile of immaculately clean dishcloths.

"We were just going to cook a few sausages and she—" Mr. Dales stopped as if just describing how the accident had happened would make the situation worse.

"Thanks, Mr. Dales. These are exactly what we need." Liesel gave his arm a gentle squeeze, before pressing a cloth to the wound, using another to carefully dab at the trickle of blood running down Mrs. Dales's face. "Would you mind going to your medicine cabinet? Any gauze bandages, antiseptic—anything like that would be a great help."

He nodded silently, his softly jowled cheeks betraying a slight tremble.

Liesel stemmed the flow of blood as best she could. It was not too long a cut, about seven centimeters, but it was jagged and had been lacerated by the aluminum of the barbecue side tray, which probably contained an untold number of germs. She had to get some antiseptic in there before applying a bandage. The cut most likely required a couple of butterfly stitches or adhesive strips. Again, things she didn't have to hand.

Liesel felt her heart rate begin to speed up again. She wanted order, precision and calm. Without all the appropriate kit to hand, how was she going to help Mrs. Dales to the best of her ability? The buzz began in her ears again.

Stop it, Liesel. Stop it! The old you wouldn't be freaking out like this! You'd improvise and make the best of a bad situation. Focus, focus, focus.

"Ambos should be here in under ten."

Liesel's eyes shot up at the sound of Jack's voice. There it was. The injection of calm she needed.

"Don't worry." He pulled Liam's baby monitor out of the back pocket of his worn jeans and waggled it between his thumb and forefinger as he opened the clasp of the gate between them with the other hand. "I've got you covered."

She believed him. Right here, right now, kneeling on the patio in an old pair of sweats and an oversize T-shirt, hands mechanically swabbing away at the blood on Mrs. Dale's forehead, she believed him. And she was grateful for the strength emanating from him because it was taking every single teeny-tiny morsel of concentration she possessed to keep her cool.

"What can I do to help?" Jack crossed the lawn to the patio in two long-legged strides—poised for action.

Liesel blew a fine stream of air past her lips. She wasn't going to let him hear her voice shake.

"There's not too much more to do until the ambulance arrives. Without proper immobilization, I think it's too dangerous to move her." Just hearing her old voice say the words as she connected with those pure blue eyes of his and—*ba-bump ba-bump*—her heartbeat began to steady itself.

"You're the expert." He gave her a mini-salute of respect.

"Hardly." Liesel shook away the compliment. "I haven't been around this sort of injury in a while."

"Looks like you're doing all right from where I'm standing."

He was good. Almost too good. Could fate have sent him to help restore her confidence in life? In living?

She heard a low buzzing and followed Jack's hand as

it automatically slipped the beeper off his belt loop and pulled it up for inspection. His change of demeanor was instantaneous.

"Liesel, I've got to get this. House fire in the hills at the back of a small estate bordering on dry bushland."

Her head didn't turn. Was she angry? Focused? *C'mon! Give me something to work with here!*

Leaving wasn't his style—but fighting fires was. Jack winced, simultaneously scanning the yard as if one of the blossoming rosebushes would offer him a solution. On call was on call. He was already wasting precious seconds. The longer a fire burnt, the more harm came of it. He had to go.

Mr. Dales came through the patio doors, using both of his hands to carry a wicker basket overflowing with multicolored medicine tubes, bandages and cotton swabs.

"Anything here of use? How is she?"

"That's great, Mr. Dales, thank you. She's still unconscious, but she's got a steady pulse. Not long now." Liesel's voice was tight, her eye line fastidiously restricted to her patient and the basket of first-aid items.

Jack stayed static, his impulse to help Liesel overriding his professional duty. It was an entirely new feeling. He knew his behavior was entirely personal. Professionally? Lingering wasn't an option.

Mrs. Dales was in good hands. He watched as Liesel's slender fingers swept through the basket brought by Mr. Dales. Were they shaking or just hurried? Maybe he should wait until the ambulance arrived.

"Go on, I'll be all right."

She flicked her eyes up at him. Her voice was solid. He guessed he had his answer. He had to go.

* * *

As she heard Jack's truck pull away from the curb, Liesel let Jack's words run through her mind in a loop. He was right. She knew how to do this. It was scary, especially on her own, but she could do it. She let her fingers slip down to Mrs. Dales's wrist, a religious check on her pulse rate. Liesel held her breath and waited.

One.

Two.

Where was it?

Her fingers flew to Mrs. Dales's neck, just below her chin.

Where was the pulse?

She knelt directly over the elderly woman, fingers moving from the papery-soft skin of her wrist to the same position on her forehead where Jack had touched her just a few days previously at the first-aid demonstration.

She shifted her cheek to feel and listen for breath. "Mrs. Dales?"

There was nothing.

"Mrs. Dales?" It was all she could do to keep the panic out of her voice. She could sense Mr. Dales approaching. They'd been married just shy of fifty years. The same as her parents. The couples were going to share a golden wedding anniversary cruise to New Zealand via the South Pole in a few months. A group of adventurers, they'd told her, smiles spreading across their faces at the thought of everything life still held in store for them. The type of future she hoped for herself one day.

No, no, no, no. She wove her fingers together, intuitively beginning to perform the perfectly timed compressions essential to bringing back breath. Bringing back life.

In the distance she thought she could hear— Yes! She could hear the faint sound of an ambulance siren. *I can do this. I can do this.*

Jack's conscience gnawed at him. He'd been flat out for the past seven hours and hadn't had a moment to call Liesel to check on how things had gone with her neighbor. With the moon ready to make its descent and the sun teasing at the horizon, he was pretty sure a phone call would be an unwelcome intrusion. Liesel was one tough cookie, but she had looked as white as a ghost when he'd left. Not to mention seeming none too impressed with him when he'd announced he had to race back to the station. She worked in the public sector—surely she knew it wasn't personal.

Attend a fire or stay with a medical emergency he couldn't assist on, with an ambulance en route?

These were the types of decisions he had to make all the time now. Staff numbers were short. Decisions had to be made. Prioritizing crises—the bureaucracy of fighting fires.

"Drink this before you drop off, Jack. It'll do your muscles wonders."

Jack put up his hand and caught the flying bottle of colored liquid. "This one of your magic vitamin drinks, Chief?"

"Precisely, mate." Jack's commanding officer sank onto the bunk beside him and began to peel off his socks. "Get that down you and you'll feel better than new."

"Better than that house we just doused at any rate."

"I've never seen a place go up so quickly. Like it was made of kindling or something." The regional chief officer shook his head. "Such a shame."

Jack shook his head in agreement as he bent over his knees to unlace his leather boots. It never ceased to amaze him how quickly a house could be reduced to a pile of ashes.

"How was your date?" His boss jigged his eyebrows up and down for effect.

"Sorry, mate?" Jack thought he'd been discreet about nipping out of the station for a bit.

"I saw how quickly you hightailed it out of here earlier. Never seen anyone go for a quick bite to eat 'with a mate' with such well-combed hair." He reached across the space between bunks and gave Jack a light punch on the arm. "Looks like love-'em-and-leave-'em Casanova Keller is back on the scene!"

"Hardly!" He winced away the moniker from his training days. Liesel was in an entirely different category from the girls he used to date. If you could call two or three nights maximum dating.

"Was she worth almost getting a reprimand for?"

"Reprimand?" Jack felt his forehead crinkle in consternation. He'd arrived at the station before the callout.

"I'm just joshing you, mate, but you'd better watch it. The higher-ups are getting more strict about personal lives taking precedence over station business. Especially when we're short on staff and belts are being tightened. It wouldn't take much for them to close down Murray Valley in the blink of an eye."

"They said I had a year."

"They say a lot of things."

Jack sat back in his bunk, stuffing a pillow between his head and the wall.

When he was working he liked to be entirely focused. That's why his cavalier approach to "dating" during his training days had earned him the Casanova nickname. The theory was, if he didn't get serious with anyone then he could keep his eye on the prize—running his own station. The fact that his assignment was in his hometown only doubled the stakes.

The station and its success was his main aim right now. It had to receive his full attention. Failure was, quite simply, not an option.

He could hear his father's voice as clearly as if he were sitting next to him, *"You have always been an either-or fellow, haven't you, Jack?"*

He'd been right.

Either he joined the rugby team or he joined the Aussie rules team.

Rugby.

Either he put Engleton Station on the map or he turned down the posting.

Map.

Either he accepted responsibility for his mother's death the day of the fire or he—

No. That hadn't been his fault. That's what the facts said anyway. Too bad his father didn't see things the same way. If he hadn't run round the back of the barn, outside his mother's sight, she might not have entered the barn. Then again, she might have. She'd loved the horses as much as he had. It had been their secret meeting point. If ever Jack had been escaping another how-to-run-the-winery lesson from his father, his mum had known exactly where he'd be. The stables. He hadn't ridden a horse once since then. Or discovered the love his sister had for running River's Bend.

Either he ran the winery his father's way, turning his

back on the CFS, or he left River's Bend, leaving his sister to pick up the reins.

Even that seemed to be going wrong.

Seeing Liesel had been a bad idea. He was 100 percent certain he had not been 100 percent focused tonight. He just couldn't keep his thoughts away from Liesel. What it would be like to run his fingers through her hair. Tasting her, touching her, falling into a first-class sensory overload. Having Liesel in his life simply wasn't going to work if he couldn't focus.

"Earth to Jack."

"Yeah, mate—sorry?" Jack tried to snap himself back into the room.

"Who is she?"

"Who?"

"The girl—the woman—you're mooning over. I haven't seen such a dopey expression on your face in— well, ever." The chief tugged a blanket over his shoulders, appearing visibly amused with himself for having hit all the right buttons.

"She's not— It's not what you think. She's a nurse I'm trying to persuade to volunteer down at the station. Just putting in a bit of personal time with her to talk her through how it all works."

Yeah, right! Who's going to buy that load of malarkey?

"Don't worry, mate." The chief stuck a ringed finger out from under the khaki blanket and wiggled it in front of Jack's dumbstruck face.

Obviously not the chief.

"Twenty-two years in February. She made us get married on Valentine's Day so I wouldn't forget the anniversary."

"Clever." No way he was going to contribute more to

this conversation. Holes were getting dug everywhere and he didn't have the energy to dig himself out.

"That she is, mate. That she is." The chief rolled over toward the wall, throwing a few words over his shoulder as he went. "Just make sure your girl can handle your lifestyle—because the fire service is in your blood. That's one thing about you she won't be able to change."

Jack pulled his unlaced boots off and tugged on a fresh T-shirt but his guaranteed shut-eye from a few minutes ago was off the radar now. From a casual night out to advice on long-term wedded bliss. *Thanks a million, Chief!*

CHAPTER FIVE

IT HAD BEEN four days and…Liesel flicked her eyes up
to the office wall clock clicking away the slow-motion
seconds…ten and a bit hours since Jack had dropped
her and Liam off and she hadn't heard a peep since. Despite her best efforts, each time the phone rang, her entire body responded with a whoosh of adrenaline and an
accelerated heartbeat.

A huge chunk of her wanted to shake off her concerns
and ring him or at least drop him a thank-you note—to
just go for it and see what sparks might fly between them.
Maybe even have a good old-fashioned snog!

The other part? Not quite ready to part with her fears
over his chosen profession. If she was truly being sensible, Jack Keller wasn't an option in the romance department. She didn't want to date. Didn't want to hang
out. She wanted to fall madly in love and start a proper
family with someone. How did you put all of that in a
greeting card?

Maybe she should just choose the teenager way of
dealing with it and blank him. Out of sight, out of mind—
problem solved!

She tipped her chin up and closed her eyes to try it
out. A vision of Jack in his formfitting CFS T-shirt tan-

goed past her closed lids. He moved in closer, took her face in his big man hands and lowered his mouth to—

Hmm. That plan might need some work.

"What's got you so blue?"

Cassie's high-beam smile failed to lighten her mood. Liesel pointed at a stack of paperwork on her desk.

"More data entry." She made a stab at returning the toothy grin still shining away at her from the doorway. "The joys of nursing!"

"Not enough excitement for you out here in the back of Bourke, Miss Adler?" Cassie waggled a reproachful finger at Liesel then placed it on the side of her nose, her face settling into a reflective pose. "Or could it be there hasn't been enough action with the local fire department?"

Liesel scrunched up a scrap of paper and threw it at her friend, trying her best to laugh away the accusation. "Don't be ridiculous." *Was she that easy to read?*

Cassie's attention shifted abruptly from Liesel to someone behind her. "What are you doing out of class, mate? I hope it wasn't another fight." Liesel couldn't make out the mystery boy's muttered response. "Are you all right, love?"

Liesel shot out of her chair. Cassie's tone was not good. Neither was the scene playing out in front of her office door.

"Kev? Kev, what's going on, love?"

Cassie was on the floor, kneeling by her ashen-faced son, who was doubled up in obvious agony. Cassie's face was wreathed in terror. Liesel felt the familiar coils of fear start to constrict her own breathing. She knew part of her job was to provide calm in a situation like this, to embody common sense and active pragmatism, but seeing

Kev gasping for breath was overreaching the parameters of her remit of scraped knees and brushing a few tears away. It wasn't outside her training, though. And there was no time to lose.

"What's going on? He doesn't have asthma!" Cassie's voice was low but the tone screamed volumes. Kev needed help. "Call an ambulance, Cass. Now."

Liesel dropped to her knees, fingers flying to Kev's carotid artery to check his pulse. It was racing and anyone could see he was barely getting any breath with each painful attempt to inhale. She placed hands lightly on either side of his chest. One definitely responded more than the other as he fought for breath. Collapsed lung. It had to be.

Primary spontaneous pneumothorax.

Liesel had seen it before. When a fast-growing, lanky teen like Kev had yet another growth spurt not all of the organs had a chance to catch up and occasionally a tiny tear in the outer part of the lung allowed air to escape, which would then get trapped between the lung and the chest wall.

"Hurts…" Kev wheezed the word out.

"I know. You're going to be all right. We're going to patch you up but you're going to have to stay as calm as possible to help slow your breathing down. I think you're just working on one lung right now, okay, Kev?"

Kev's eyes flew wide open, a sheen of sweat visibly breaking out on his forehead. Liesel wanted to bite her tongue the moment the words were out. She was there to calm him down, not distress him more.

The truth of the matter was this was a dangerous situation and, without help arriving soon, any number of problems could arise. His heart rate was fast and if it went over one hundred and thirty-five beats a minute Kev could quickly begin to suffer from tachyarrhythmia. He was young, but even a teenager needed a steady flow of blood and oxygen to the heart and body. Without it, permanent tissue damage to the heart and brain could begin to occur in as little as three to four minutes. Next came the kidneys—

"He's on his way."

"Who?"

"Jack Keller. The closest proper ambo is an hour's drive away."

"What?"

"The hospital always uses the CFS when they don't have anyone around."

"We'd be just as well driving to the hospital ourselves, then. What is it, about twenty minutes away?"

"More. He said he's bringing the station's paramedic SUV. It's part of the Community Emergency Response Unit and we can put on the lights and siren. He'll get us there faster."

Liesel sat back on her heels, mind racing. If Kev did, in fact, have a collapsed lung, he must have waited some time to come to her for help. He would've felt some tugging in his chest, tightening, possibly a whoosh of air and further tightening until the condition began presenting itself as it was now. Very seriously.

She locked eyes with Cassie. "We've got to keep Kev as calm as possible. Technically, as a school nurse, I am not allowed to administer aid to him but, in the same vein, I have a duty of care to help him if there is no one around to do so. I believe there's air in his pleural space—"

"What's that? I don't know what you're talking about, Liesel!"

"It's air trapped outside his lung by the chest wall." She gave Cassie a moment to steady her own breathing and blink back some tears. "We're going to get through this, all right?"

"That's right, Cassie, you couldn't ask for a better trauma nurse. I've seen this one in action."

And there he was. Brigade Captain Jack Keller. Filling the doorway with his six-foot-something good looks. Capable, calm, ready for action and completely off-limits.

"Is the gurney locked in?"

"Securely." Jack gave Liesel a quick nod and glanced at Cassie. "You're going to want to buckle up for this, Cass. All right?" Without waiting for an answer, he closed the back door of the enormous SUV, quickly jumped in the front, threw a few switches, and, lights in full swing, they shot past the school principal, who was soberly waving them off.

"What's our ETA?"

Liesel was grateful she didn't have to shout over any sirens. The roads were relatively clear out here and the lights on their own should give other drivers ample warning.

"Ten to fifteen minutes, traffic pending. Are you going to be all right?" Jack's eyes were firmly on the road but Liesel knew his mind was on the patient. It wasn't looking good. Kev was presenting all the signs of a tension pneumothorax, a life-threatening condition. This was different from a spontaneous pneumothorax, which often occurred when just sitting or resting. Kevin had managed to tell them he'd been out on play break with the other students when the pain had started.

She looked down at him, an oxygen mask secured loosely to his mouth. There were no telltale signs he'd been in another fight. That would've been her first guess. His last set of black eyes had faded and he showed no other external injuries.

She gave the elastic band a small tug, ensuring Kev could get maximum airflow. The large SUV was kitted out to the nines for emergency medical scenarios, just the sort of vehicle she would've wanted if she'd— Nope. Not going there. At the very least she could thank her lucky stars they hadn't attempted the drive on their own. Avoiding face time with Jack wasn't worth risking Kev's life. The teen was definitely going to need more assistance than she could offer and the oxygen tank was vital. She knew they'd be safe in Jack's hands. Whatever her personal feelings were, he was a professional you could depend on.

When they arrived at hospital, she was certain Kev would need immediate attention—specifically, a needle aspiration. Liesel had only witnessed it being done, had assisted. It was generally a doctor's job to insert the needle into the chest cavity in order to release the trapped air. Some doctors preferred to use tubing in the chest but research she'd seen in her nurses' journal had proven it to be more traumatic for the patient and generally increased the hospital stay. She hoped the Murray Valley Hospital was up to date on that front, for Kevin's sake.

"Do you think it was the other kids? The ones from last time?"

"Sorry, Cass?"

"Do you think he was roughed up by those lads again?"

Liesel shook her head at her friend, confused. "I don't think this has anything to do with a fight. Besides, I thought it was the other way round."

Cassie huffed out a solitary "Ha!" before letting her head fall into her hands.

"What's going on Cassie?"

"They're bullying *him*, Liesel." Cassie's eyes were filled with anguish as she continued. "He puts on such a brave face, trying to be the man of our family, but the boys are relentless. I told him to be bigger, better than they are by not fighting back, but if I've put him in danger..." A ragged sob filled the closed space in the back of the SUV.

Liesel reached over Kev and squeezed her friend's shoulder. "You don't know that. Let's wait until we hear the whole story."

Returning her focus to Kevin, Liesel's eyes shot wide open, alarm bells ringing dangerously. Kev's chest had become distended and after a quick check she confirmed his trachea had deviated to the opposite side of the collapsed lung. This was a sign ER teams usually only found when examining X-rays. But Jack was thin enough that she could see the shift of location despite the fact it was located behind the sternum. She pulled off Kevin's oxygen mask and checked for breath. They didn't have time to wait anymore.

"Jack. Pull over."

He didn't wait to hear it a second time.

"What do you need?"

"I am going to have to aspirate Kevin's chest. The risk of the car hitting a bump while I'm inserting the needle is too high." She heard him snap back the seat belt and pull open his door as she signaled to Cassie that she would be best out of the car while she did it.

"I want to stay here."

"Please, Cassie—you'll be right outside the car. Just give us a few minutes. It's all we need." Liesel felt horrible as she made her friend climb out of the back of the SUV, but this was a first-time procedure for her and Kevin's life depended on it. She needed absolute focus. Jack was in her place before she'd taken in Cassie's absence.

"What can I do?"

Liesel was already pulling on gloves and protective face- and eyewear, which had been easily visible in the vehicle's storage boxes.

"Can you find a fourteen-gauge over the needle catheter that's about three to six centimetres long?"

"Give me a minute."

"We don't have a minute."

"I'm here to help, Liesel. Not hinder." His voice was quiet, reassuring. He handed her the needle catheter with hands already sheathed in the precautionary blue gloves. One glimpse into his clear eyes and she knew it was true. Knew Jack's presence added to her confidence. He was the one her mind had leaped to when she'd needed confidence with Mrs. Dales. And he was here for her again. She felt a charge of the old Liesel flash through her. She could do this.

Liesel made a lightning-fast scan of the storage boxes. She couldn't see any devices for creating a one-way valve, an essential part of the procedure. She'd have to use an EMS trick Eric had taught her. She grabbed a protective glove and ripped off a finger, quickly inserting the IV catheter into the sterile nitrile.

"Is there any saline solution?"

"Just over here." They had a rhythm now, a cadence to their work. Fluid, swift, focused.

Liesel pulled a ten-millimeter syringe out of its sterile packaging, quickly drawing five millimeters of the saline into it. Here, on the side of the road with traffic passing by, she couldn't be sure she'd hear the gush of escaping air when she inserted the catheter needle into Kevin's chest. If—*when*—she hit the right spot, the air would create bubbles in the saline, giving her a visible indicator she had done the job properly.

"Can you cut open Kevin's T-shirt, please?" She would need full access to his chest. Inserting the needle in exactly the right spot was vital. The midclavicular line. Inserting it into the medial sternal or axillary lines could only worsen an already bleak scenario.

"Stay with us, Kev. We're going to help you, mate."

Jack's rich voice was like a soothing tonic in the charged atmosphere of the SUV. She knew the words were meant for Kevin, but they were just what she needed as she palpated her fingers downward from the teen's collarbone to his third rib. There was no messing this up. She held the loose "finger" of glove over the needle, having wiped antiseptic over the midclavicular line she'd marked with a pen. She needed to direct the needle into the intercostal space just above the third rib and nowhere else.

She glanced up at Jack, his eyes the only thing visible above the protective face mask he'd pulled on. She could see the confidence in them as he nodded at her. She felt a charge of readiness and pulled herself into a strong-seated position.

Poising the IV needle over the small "X," she held her breath, steadied her hand and inserted it through his skin with a quick, sure movement. Almost instantaneously the fluid in the syringe began to bubble. It wasn't over yet, but they had won the first major battle. She lifted her eyes up to Jack's questioning gaze, only trusting herself to answer him with an affirmative nod.

She waited until the bubbling stopped then withdrew the needle, leaving the "finger" of glove in the puncture wound to act as an exit valve until they got to the hospital. She disposed of the needle in the sharps box attached to the wall of the cab and quickly taped the blue glove finger into place. It wasn't pretty—but it was functional and that's what counted.

"Can I look?" Cassie's head peeped round the corner of the back door.

Jack's long legs unfolded themselves from the back of the vehicle to make room. Liesel resecured the pure-flow oxygen mask to Kevin's mouth and, out of the corner of her eye, saw that Jack had folded the worried mother in his arms.

"He's going to be all right, Cassie. I'm sure of it. Why don't you jump in the back again and we can get your boy to Valley Medical?" She could hear the relief and conviction in Jack's voice that Cassie's son would be all right. If there was some way she could tap into his confidence and let it refill her own depleted resources, she would do it in an instant.

The women rode in focused silence in the back of the vehicle, each holding one of Kevin's hands, after Jack gave them a seven-minute ETA.

Liesel caught Jack's eye every now and again in the rearview mirror. She'd tried to stop herself from looking, but found she couldn't help herself. What was she, seventeen again?

It seemed ridiculous, but Liesel felt as though she was drawing new stores of confidence and positive energy each time their eyes locked. The surges of certainty she felt about her nursing skills when she was with Jack were

ANNIE O'NEIL

exactly what she'd been missing at the A and E unit. It felt amazing. Was this what change felt like?

Liesel suddenly felt like turning a thousand thoughts into action. Finding a permanent home for herself and her son. No more relying on her mother and father. She wanted to push the limits on her nursing skills, really find out what she was capable of. Maybe even reconsider Jack's offer to go down to the CFS? At the very least, she knew she wanted to explore whatever it was that was zinging between her and Jack. A glimpse, a light touch, a brushing of lips… She pressed her eyes shut, the memory of their aborted attempt at displaying CPR pinging front and center in her mind's eye.

Her body felt as though it was awakening after a long, long winter. Her loose cotton top made of eyelet fabric played over her skin, bringing out a shiver of heightened awareness. When she had pulled on the royal-blue top that morning, the last thing in the world it had seemed was sexy, but now, fully aware of Jack's glances back into the cabin of the vehicle, it suddenly felt sensual. The tiny holes in the fabric exposing miniature flashes of skin. Had he noticed? Her eyes pinged wide open. She really wanted him to notice. She felt like dancing. And kissing. Was he feeling the same way? Or was she just hallucinating this entire "thing" between them?

Her eyes intuitively flickered to the vehicle's rearview mirror. There they were. Those bright blue eyes. Watchful. Assured. And giving her a long, slow wink.

Jack loved moments like these. The successful handover to the emergency department. A moment to know you'd done your job and done it well.

Cassie was at the reception area, giving her son's details, and the emergency department doctor was giving Kevin a once-over before shifting him onto a hospital gurney.

"Looks like you saved this young fellow's life. How long have you been an emergency medical responder?"

"I'm not." Jack shook his head regretfully. "I started the training in Adelaide, then got a transfer before I could complete it."

"Then how did you learn this trick?" The doctor pointed at the tip of the rubber glove, still doing its job in Kevin's chest.

Jack shifted his eyes from the ED doctor's approving gaze to Liesel. He tipped his head in her direction. "It was this talented young woman here."

"Impressive." He nodded approvingly at Liesel then called behind him for a couple of medics to help with a transfer. "Have you been in the Country Fire Service long?"

Jack watched Liesel stiffen at the question then try to laugh off her reaction. "Not me. I'm just the school nurse."

"But where'd you learn that technique? I've seen it on the internet, but only from North American sources."

Liesel went quiet for a moment, her fingers playing along the rail of Kevin's gurney. "Someone from America taught me."

Jack didn't know who that someone was, but from the change of her tone they had been pretty important to her. He'd heard she'd worked in America through Cassie, but had she also left her heart there? He hoped not. He knew a relationship was the last thing he needed right now, but logic didn't stop him from hoping Liesel was available. If he were a finger-crossing man, he'd be doing it right now.

"You've got a lot of valuable training behind you for a school nurse. We could easily use you here at the Valley Med or on the EMR team. Blimey, I'm surprised Jack here hasn't recruited you yet."

"Believe me, I have tried. She's rebuffed my every advance." He leaned against a nearby pillar, crossing his arms over his chest and hoping he looked more casual than keen. Because he was more than keen. On a number of levels.

"Did that include convincing this young man to detach a lung for you?" The doctor grinned down at his new patient, who, to Jack's surprise, gave him a half-wilted thumbs-up.

"Deal's a deal, mate." Jack played along. "You're guaranteed a spot on the cadet force as soon as you're up and running."

At that Liesel nearly choked. She knew it was a fiction, but still! Besides, the reminder of Eric had served its purpose. She was giving this sort of stuff a wide berth for a reason. Right?

"I appreciate the effort, Kev, but I could've saved you the trouble. If I wanted to be recruited, I would be in uniform already. Keep it low level next time, all right?"

"He's all checked in." Cassie breathlessly appeared by her son's hospital gurney.

"Right! Let's get to an exam room, see about getting this glove out of Kevin's chest and try to reinflate that lung." The doctor gave Jack and Liesel a final nod of thanks before wheeling the gurney down the hall.

If he had thought he'd stood a chance to get her into the CFS before, Jack was hearing loud and clear that she wasn't interested. What was stopping her, exactly?

She obviously had the skills and her crisis management was top rate. He watched as Liesel's feline eyes followed Kev's gurney through to the double doors leading to the surgery department. Pure class. And seemingly intent on turning him down.

She was clearly talented. What was holding her back? Was it worth one final push? He'd have to test the waters with care.

He shook his head. What was wrong with him? Was he doing this for the station or for himself? Both, definitely— but the fact that he kept pursuing her was a pretty big clue that the scales were definitely weighted in one direction. If he recruited her, then he was guaranteed to see her all the time and that was an idea he liked the sound of. A lot. Then again, if relationships were off-limits, having her in his crew would be like having the best bottle of wine in the world uncorked in front of him and being told he couldn't have any.

He tried to shrug off the maze of conflicting thoughts. Fine wine, he concluded, was worth waiting for.

"I guess I'd better get you back to school, miss." Jack unfolded his arms, pushing himself away from the pillar with his foot.

"We're back to 'miss,' are we? After all we've been through?" He could tell she'd been going for a jokey tone, but there was more meaning behind the light words and her bright smile.

"Liesel." His voice had gone deeper than he'd anticipated and the space separating them suddenly seemed minute. He could smell the wildflower freshness of her skin as the whir of activity surrounding them seemed to still to a slow-motion hush. In seconds he could be holding her in his arms, willing whatever made her so very sad to go away. He watched as a soft flush rose to her cheeks and as suddenly as the moment had come between them, it flashed away.

Liesel glanced at her watchless wrist, laughed and then scanned the room for a clock.

"It's just past four," Jack interrupted, even though her search for a clock had given him more time to drink her in.

"I think I've missed the final bell." Liesel threw him a *yikes* expression and shrugged.

"Good." Jack scooped up her small hand and tucked it into the crook of his arm. "That means I can take you out for a congratulatory milk shake."

"I really should get back…"

She wavered just enough to give him the confidence to have another go.

"C'mon, we can pick up a couple of shakes and I'll show you my favorite spot on the river."

He could see she was tempted. Even though he saw the hints of that pinky blush coloring her cheeks again. He could guarantee that if she really knew what he was thinking, her color would definitely deepen. Him, Liesel, a warm spring evening down by the river. Anything could happen…

"I've got to pick up Liam."

Jack stopped in his tracks. Liam! Of course. He was an idiot to forget. "Where is he? We could pick up the little man and bring him along."

"Really?"

Jack nodded his head in the affirmative, loving it when he saw the sparkle in her eye. If just a fraction of that was for him—

"You're sure you wouldn't mind? He's just at the school nursery. The latest they can keep him is four-thirty."

"I guess we'd better hit the road, then."

Liesel felt as if she was floating on a big, bouncy cloud of happiness. She tried to wipe the dreamy expression off her face as she tucked in Liam but as she replayed the evening's picnic down by the river, keeping the smile off her lips proved impossible.

She pulled the door to her sleeping son's room shut and began to tiptoe back to the veranda. Jack had insisted on waiting out there, settling into a cushioned deck chair to "keep an eye on the river," even though she'd insisted he was welcome to come in.

"It wouldn't be proper," he'd said, as if he were a character in an English costume drama. Old-fashioned manners, straight-up-her-alley good looks… He'd even wiped a dab of mustard off her chin after a particularly greedy mouthful of artisan sausage. Who knew a tiny gesture could get her all shivery?

It was absolutely ridiculous how she reacted to his slightest touch and how spending time with him seemed to blur the rest of the world into a fuzzy haze. Considering she'd had just about every single one of her danger-zone buttons pushed that day, it was a wonder she hadn't just accepted his last-minute offer to opt out of the picnic, be dropped off at home and crawl into bed with Liam curled up beside her and a hot mug of chamomile tea.

It appeared Jack knew her better than she knew herself. A picnic by the river, her son whooping it up with all the kookaburras before devouring his tea, not to mention a first-rate chocolate milk shake to recharge her batteries. Maybe it was as simple as having a couple of hours off not to think about Kevin and the high anxiety she'd felt as she'd dealt with his collapsed lung.

As she looked back on the afternoon, she was beginning to see that instead of feeling a terror that she'd stepped into hostile territory by reverting to her trauma nurse days, she should feel confident and proud of what she had done. This was twice now that she'd been forced out of her comfort zone and had found herself...comfortable. And, truthfully, she hadn't been *forced* out of her comfort zone. She just hadn't fled—which had been her default position up to now. She was a good nurse and using her skills came naturally. Kevin could have died if it hadn't been for her quick diagnosis and treatment. A technique she wouldn't have known about if it hadn't been for Eric.

She pressed her eyes shut, willing herself to have the strength to always love Eric but somehow move forward. She knew she had to. Not just for Liam but for herself. It was just a question of *when*.

Ha! So much easier thought than done.

She opened her eyes again, quietly making her way into the kitchen to drop off Liam's nighttime bottle. She turned in the growing darkness of the kitchen, eyes adjusting to the remains of the evening's light.

She could see Jack's silhouette through the screen door. He'd hitched a hip up onto the veranda's railing, his long back supported against a post, looking as happy as could be, while the sun set beyond him among the tangle of gum and eucalyptus trees.

If time were her plaything she would've stayed there for ages. Just looking at him made her feel all zingy with feminine response. Not bad for a five-meter gap. She had never seen someone who looked more comfortable in their own skin. He stretched an arm across his body, pulling his knee up along the railing. The movement cinched up the T-shirt, which didn't do a very good job of disguising his well-defined biceps. Her eyes ran along the broad spread of his shoulders and slipped up to his face. As if he felt her watching him, he turned and met her gaze. She felt herself soften, a warm swirl of heat gathering in her belly.

"This is an amazing place you've got here."

"I wish it were mine." Liesel pushed the screen door open, praying he hadn't seen how much she'd been ogling him.

"It's my parents' place. They bought it a few years ago to be their retirement fund." Jack raised a curious eyebrow. "You know, a holiday cottage for people wanting to spend some time out in wine country, or enjoy the river."

"Wise move. They sound like good folk."

"They're great. I can't imagine what I…what we—I mean, Liam and I—would've done without them these past few years."

"Oh?"

Jack raised an interested eyebrow. Liesel wavered. They were having such a lovely evening. She didn't want to go there. She didn't want to rehash recent history when all of the sudden the future seemed like something she could begin to imagine.

"They're brilliant grandparents!" *Good dodge, Liesel!* She shifted her gaze away from Jack's. "Anyhow, we need to move on come summer so they can collect their holiday rent—but I can't tell you how grateful I am for their generosity." Liesel smiled warmly.

Before Eric, before Liam, she'd been the opposite of a planner. She'd traveled all around the world, seeking out youthful thrills, pushing her nursing skills to the limit and scraping the bottom of her savings account to make ends meet.

It was hard not to feel wistful about the young woman she had been not so long ago. Young, brave, ready to make a difference. Undefeatable. So much had changed.

"They say you don't choose your family, but it seems your parents did a pretty good job of endowing you with their sensibilities. You're lucky to be so close."

Was that a hint of sadness in his eyes? Or the setting sun? Hard to tell, but something flashed there.

"They do a mean yabby bake. My parents."

Jack swung round, planting both feet solidly on the wooden floor. "Do they now? That sounds like a bit of a challenge."

"I thought you were a city boy." Liesel accepted the dare, relieved just to be having fun again. "What do you know about a good old-fashioned yabby bake?"

"I've spent a bit of time on the river."

"Oh, yeah?" Liesel dismissed the second twitch of darkness she thought she saw flash across his eyes.

"Yeah. I live on a houseboat."

"Seriously? I always wondered what type of person lived on a houseboat."

"Well, you're looking at a Class A example."

Liesel couldn't help but give a snort of laughter. She doubted there was anyone alive who could make living on a houseboat seem sexier than Jack.

"You doubting my status as Old Man Murray River?"

"You bet I am."

"Then you'd better prove it to me."

Liesel merrily crossed the veranda toward him, hand extended. "I bet you I can out-yabby you any day of the week."

Jack rose to his full height, reaching out a large hand to meet her much smaller one. A crackle of electricity zigzagged up her arm and played across her chest as their fingers connected.

"Winner picks the prize?"

Had his voice gone husky? Liesel's eyes met his. The deep lake blue of them was so inviting she felt as if she could dive straight in. If she could stop the world right now, she would.

"Within reason." Her voice was barely a whisper.

"What kind of man do you take me for?" He closed the space between them with a deliberate step. The honeysuckle breeze wove between them, almost tangibly filling in the ever-decreasing pockets of space. Liesel felt her breath quicken. Her eyes flicked to his chest. Still gorgeous, but safer than his eyes.

"A pretty nice one." *Lame! That was pathetic, Liesel!*

"That's a relief." Jack reversed his stride, still holding her hand as he sat back down on the veranda railing. She found herself willingly responding to the gentle tug on her arm and stepped into the opening between his legs. She and Jack were at an easy eye level. Tiny crinkles appeared round his eyes as his face softened with a slow smile. Her fingertips twitched with a desire to trace along them. The air between them felt alive with the pleasurable tension of sexual attraction. Her gaze dropped to his lips. She felt another ribbon of heat tease its way through her, swirling in slow undulations below her waist.

A parrot called in the distance. A burst of laughter sounded from across the river. A family playing a board game? It was all a blur. The only thing Liesel was fully aware of was Jack. It was all she could do not to slip a hand, both hands, into that thick blond hair of his. Explore it with her fingertips then draw them down along his neck, thumbs grazing the strong angles of his jaw before feeling her way toward the well-defined spread of shoulders.

Her eyes flickered back to his. She felt her lips part, her tongue wetting her bottom lip then retreating, unprepared to make the first move. She hadn't done this for a long time. Standing here, in the thickening silence, everything felt incredibly new. A first-time experience. A sudden longing flooded her entire body. A desire to move forward, to experience new things. Jack's bright blue eyes sought—what was it, permission? She didn't know what hers were saying in return, but as her back made the smallest of arches toward him, as if being tugged in his direction, he tipped his head down and, oh, so gently rested his forehead on hers.

They stood like that for a moment, as if each of them was trying to let their mind catch up with what their body was calling out for.

He was so close. *So perfectly close.*

Liesel felt Jack's fingers unwrap themselves from around her hand then slip one by one onto her waist. It was all she could do not to roll her hip toward him and whisper, "More." She felt his breath on her cheek. A physical ache began to pulse through her. As if reading her mind, Jack's fingers guided her in closer, her hips grazing the sides of his parted thighs. The fabric of her skirt suddenly felt incredibly thin, hot sparks of heat on her hips and thighs teasing at her very core.

Her back arched instinctively more fully toward him as, in a single fluid moment, his lips met hers. She drew in a breath and began to tentatively explore. His full lips moved in complete synchronicity with her own. Soft, curious, intimate. She didn't know how, but he tasted like the beach.

Any doubts she'd had about kissing Jack slipped through the floorboards as if she had shed an overheavy winter coat. All she could feel now was Jack. His lips tasting, teasing her own, not into submission but into a sensual communion. He spread the fingers of a broad hand across the small of her back, the other slipping up her spine, his thumb shifting along the delicate curve of her neck until it came to rest in the shallow hollow at its peak, where his fingers tangled themselves among the curls at the back of her head.

She felt tiny in his arms, delicate, safe. Her breasts grazed lightly across his chest, her nipples responding with a lightning-quick response. She felt her hips push into his hands as he wrapped his fingers round them, firmly holding her in place. Unable to resist, she pressed into him, her lips seeking more, her fingers finally able to thread themselves through that deliciously thick, sun-bleached hair of his. She had to stop herself from tipping back her head and letting out a full-throated laugh of delight. She was kissing Jack Keller! It was better than she had let herself imagine. He smelled amazing—like burnt-sugar caramel—he tasted sexier and she wanted more.

Jack had to resist the urge to scoop Liesel up in his arms, carry her into her bedroom and have his incredibly wicked way with her. As each moment passed, resisting was becoming a greater challenge.

A low moan escaped his lips as he felt her breasts sweep against the thin cotton of his T-shirt. There was little doubt her body was responding to his touch. If she were to press in much closer, Liesel would be just as aware of the effect she was having on him. A full-blooded, inescapably male response to her incredibly sexy figure.

Her slim waist? Perfect for tracing with an index finger. He felt his thumb graze the underside of her breast and her body tipping toward him at the sensation. He buried his head in the crook of her neck and shoulder, as pure white as the driven snow, fighting the urge to relieve her top of its bright red buttons.

Willpower, Jack. She's worth the wait.

He couldn't resist tracing his lips along the creamy length of her neck, his teeth taking a cheeky tug at her earlobe as his hands made a slow-motion journey from her collarbone, down her sides to her hips. As he kissed her, he could feel a low groan of satisfaction vibrate along her throat, a soft rush of air crossing her kiss-swollen lips.

He drew both his hands along her back, his fingers tracing upward as he teased more soft kisses out of her. Suddenly unable to resist his body's desire for more, he pulled his thumbs along her jawline, drawing her even closer to him, daring her to meet the passionate intimacy of the kisses he wanted to give her. His teeth tugged softly at her lower lip. He took a deep breath of her sun-warmed meadowy scent, tongue tracing the deep red contours of her rosebud mouth. Her tongue met his in teasing little suggestions that she could give as well as receive. He felt her small fingers slip away from his hair, her fingertips playing along his time-enhanced five o'clock shadow. He tipped his chin up as first her lips then her tongue teased its way down his throat toward his Adam's apple.

He heard himself respond with a deep moan of carnal approval.

Crikey. She was really bringing out the caveman in him. And he liked it. Jack captured both sides of her face in his hands and held her back for a moment, eyes caught in each other's gaze, each of them taking deep lungfuls of river air. Did she want him as badly as he wanted her? This could go further—much further. Her eyelids quickly shifted from a sexy feline smolder to a wide-eyed question. It was then that he felt the beeper buzzing against his leather belt.

Fire. He had to go.

CHAPTER SIX

GIVING A GRIN and a wave to Jack as he headed off to the fire had taken incredible willpower. Liesel knew she had only just managed a halfhearted attempt to look cheerful at best.

She flipped the security hook onto the screen door and let herself sink back into the deep sofa cushions. Evening over!

Her fingers lifted to her lips. She could still feel the heat in them, the tiniest of pulses waiting, wanting more. Who was she kidding? Her whole body was virtually vibrating with desire for the man. Desire unfulfilled and, from the looks of things, likely to stay that way. She tipped her head back against the headrest, willing herself not to cry.

You are bigger and better than this. It's what he does for a living so just...just...just what?

Get over it?

Hard to do.

Don't see him ever again?

Possible, but not easy, considering the local population head count.

Suck it up and see where this goes, even though it's facing all your fears at once?

And we're back to "get over it."

Her fingers dangled over the edge of the sofa and grazed the surface of the telephone. Cassie! She would know what to do. Bless her, the poor woman had been left high and dry by a no-goodnik husband a couple of years earlier and she had hit the dating train—such as it was out here—as if it was the last caboose out of town. She was always positive, open to new ideas and didn't seem to get knocked back when things didn't work out. "Aim high and stay true!" Her familiar motto rang in Liesel's ears as she dialed her friend's number.

"And how can I help you tonight, Miss Adler?" Liesel laughed at her friend's greeting. She always forgot about caller ID.

"Hey, Cass, I'm in a bit of a bind. I just…um…" How should she put this exactly?

"I knew it! I knew it would be today!" Cassie interjected.

"Knew what?"

"You kissed the fireman!"

"Are you sure Kev doesn't mind?"

"Are you kidding? He is living the life of Riley up at Murray General. He's their star patient." Cassie dipped her finger into the cookie-dough bowl and took a swirl of the mixture onto her finger as if it were icing. "Plus, he's got the promise of some of your delicious baking first thing tomorrow. We both love it that you bake when you're upset."

Liesel couldn't help sticking her tongue out at her friend.

"Besides, he gets a whole hospital full of doctors to make sure he doesn't go all crazy deflating-lung boy on me again." Cassie concluded her statement by licking the remains of the dough off her finger with a wide smile of satisfaction.

Liesel laughed, happy to see her friend back in good spirits after the day's extreme stresses. Talk about wrenching! She was surprised Cassie looked as energetic as she did.

"This is a ripper of a recipe, Liesel. The boys are going to love these."

Liesel felt an awkward twist in her stomach. It was just one large blond-haired man she cared about. And that was going to have to stop. Cue: more baking!

"I was thinking of doing a batch of my pecan cinnamon rolls, as well. Those are good anytime of day so it doesn't matter when they get back. I could just drop them off tonight and they could heat them up whenever." Baking for Jack was one thing. Seeing him when she didn't really know where she stood? That was a whole other kettle of fish.

"You know, I was chatting with Jack the other day—"

Liesel's eyes shot up and she felt herself tense. *Oops. There goes my poker face.*

"About *Kevin*," Cassie emphasized heavily, unable to keep the amused grin off her face. "For their CFS cadets thing. I thought it might help give him some confidence. Anyhow, it came up that they are still looking for volunteers."

"No." Liesel's response was solid. "I told you, now that I have Liam, it's just not an option. He's already lost one parent to—"

"I know." Cassie laid a hand on Liesel's arm, steadying her frenzied stirring. "I wasn't talking about going out and fighting fires, you dill. I was talking about the odd shift, cooking for the boys when they come back from a job. You know, make 'em all feel like heroes with your fluffy cinnamon rolls."

Liesel shot her a reluctant look and shook her head. She knew she was being petulant but how was she going to make it clear that she just did not want this in her life? She wanted Liam to have a father again one day—and a guy who went out and fought fires for a living? Not going to work.

"Do you want to see him again? It's not like you've had a fight. He got a call to work." Cassie pressed on. "Do you want a relationship with Jack or not?"

Liesel's nose began to tease her with the telltale prickle and she forced herself to retrain her eyes on the well-beaten cookie dough. It had had enough of a beating and so had she. Cassie had a point. It wasn't as if he'd kissed and fled the scene. He'd held her and caressed her and unleashed a heated swell of sexy feelings she hadn't experienced in a long time. But she still had to play it a little cool. Right?

"Who wouldn't?" Or not so cool. She pulled baking sheets out of the cupboard, actively trying to avoid eye contact with Cassie.

"I really like him. I can't even begin to explain to you how nice—more than nice—it was to be with him. And tonight…"

"Tonight?" Cassie tried to gently tease more out of her.

"Tonight, when we kissed, it was— Oh, I don't know—this is going to sound nuts."

"Takes one to know one," Cassie shot back, encouraging her to continue.

Liesel sent her a teary grin, wiped at her eyes with the

back of her hand and began spooning lumps of cookie dough onto her baking trays.

"Tonight, when we kissed, it was as if the universe was saying to me, 'It's all right to move on. You'll always love Eric and the times you had, but it's all right to move on. Especially with a guy like this.' And then Jack's beeper went off and I knew he was going to a fire and all of the sudden the universe was saying exactly the opposite!"

"I think you're giving the universe too much credit."

"Yeah? Well, look where it got me last time I didn't listen!"

Liesel snapped out the words, slapped the tray into the oven, clapped the door shut and began on a second batch. It was all she could do not to scowl at the fluffy combination of butter, flour, eggs, chocolate chips and dark brown sugar. Her love life, or lack of one, might be a disaster, but if she had anything to do with it, the whole of Engleton would be enjoying fresh cookies in the morning.

"Liesel." Cassie softly broke into the silence. "I am listening harder than I ever have. I almost lost my boy today. My son would've died if it hadn't been for you. *That* puts things in perspective."

Tears sprang to Liesel's eyes afresh. How could she have been so thoughtless? She turned to her friend, ashamed of her petulant behavior. Ditching the cookie-dough spoon, she threw her arms around her friend in a big bear hug. "I'm so sorry, Cass. That was a horrible thing for me to say."

Cassie returned the hug with a big squeeze then held her friend out at arm's length. "Look, I can't tell you what to do with your life. But from where I'm standing, you've been itching to get back to the business of *living* for a while and, as far as I can make out, the universe—if that's what's talking to you—is saying here's a perfect chance. Jack couldn't be more gorgeous, he obviously fancies you and, yes, he has a dangerous job. But that's what you're drawn to, Liesel, men who live on the high-octane side of life. It's who *you* are, as well. I saw you today."

Liesel's eyebrows shot up. "I was just doing my job."

"It's a lot more than a job to you. It's your passion— and you like to push it to the limit. I saw the pride in your face when your rubber glove valvey thing worked. You saved my boy and not everyone could have done it. Face it, love, life with an IT guy just wouldn't cut it for you."

Liesel couldn't help but giggle. The local computer genius had tried to ask her out a couple of times, but her gut instinct had said, *I don't think so*, in the blink of an eye. Despite everything, she knew she was more adrenaline junkie than computer geek. She embraced Cassie again, this time with a happy laugh. It was pointless to try and contradict her friend. Cassie had her down to a T.

Jack was bone-tired. He leaned his head against the cool tiles of the shower, grateful to feel the jets of water shooting down his back. They'd been twenty minutes late to the fire. Twenty minutes late meant an easily containable bushfire had nearly spread out of control. Luckily, the wind had been on their side this time. Next time? Luck shouldn't play a role at the CFS. If he hadn't been with Liesel—

"Hey, Cap'n! Get a move on. Breakfast is here!" The shout came over the shoulder-height shower curtain.

"What?" He quickly rinsed the soap off his face. "We don't have anyone scheduled on today."

"Looks like one of the Jack Keller fan club has come to the rescue once again! Hurry up, mate, or I'll eat yours, as well."

"What are you talking about, Nate?" Jack pushed aside the shower curtain, wrapping a towel round his waist.

"Don't play bashful, Captain. Surely you know—"

"Know what?" Jack cut him off, pretty sure he knew what was coming.

"Hey, don't get me wrong." Nate's voice went serious. "We all appreciate how hard it must be to be Ol' Man Gran—I mean, Granville Keller's son. It's a lot of weight to take on your shoulders."

"Right." Jack tried to keep from clenching his jaw. "What was the fan club crack about, then?"

"Nothing, mate. Honestly." Nate raised his hands in surrender. "Us married blokes think it's great you've got the ladies flocking over to cook for us after a big fire, that's all."

Jack tilted his head in the direction of the dining hall. "You best get out there, then."

He toweled off quickly, his hunger diminishing by the second. So the boys saw him as Granville's son before they saw him as captain, did they? He wondered if they still imagined him in short trousers. Was he going to have to prove to his father and the entire population of Engleton that he had grown up and was making something of himself?

He squared himself up, ready to play it cool to whoever the woman was who'd shown up to cook breakfast. He hoped she had a thick skin because today wasn't his day—and if TLC was what she was after, it didn't look as if it was going to be hers, either.

"Smelled so good, I couldn't wait for a shower."

"Please—" Liesel gestured at the laden trestle table

just outside the kitchen hutch "—help yourself to as much as you like."

She grinned as the soot-covered man accepted a plate of fresh-off-the-grill eggy bread with a side of bacon. She couldn't help but shoot an anxious look over his shoulder to see if a certain someone had entered the dining hall.

At the very least, she knew her stress baking had come up trumps. Cassie had taken Liam to the hospital to visit Kev so she had been free to chop, dice, bake and scramble in the station's catering-sized kitchen.

Steaming cinnamon rolls, eggy bread, a huge bowl of fresh fruit and a platter of scrambled eggs surrounded by thick-sliced, locally made bacon were all being demolished by the crew. They'd been out all night and were obviously famished.

Liesel gave a chagrined chuckle at the empty kitchen. Cassie may have railroaded her into serving up breakfast to the exhausted volunteers, but she could see from the smiles on their faces she had done the right thing. She hadn't met a lot of people in Engleton these past few months, but it was easy to see these men were part of a proper community. It looked fun out there, all the laughing and gentle joshing despite the obvious fatigue they all felt. Like family.

She couldn't help but wonder what Jack would think of her efforts, if he was there at all. She hadn't seen a single golden whisker since the crew had returned. A little shiver tickled its way down her spine as her fingertips remembered tracing along Jack's soft shadow of stubble.

Before Cassie had come over and knocked some "straight talk" into her, Liesel had been ready to give up the ghost on pursuing a romance with Jack. Stupid or not, she didn't need her innermost fears thrown in her face every time the man's beeper went off.

Yes, she really, really liked him. More than a lot. And so did her son. And Jack seemed to like him, too. Something she didn't take lightly.

In between making batches of baked goods she'd sat down and thought about it. Hard.

Eric had always said she had one shot at "being Liesel" so she'd better make the most of it. She knew she wasn't going to be able to shrug off the past in one fell swoop, but step by step, day by day…

From the snippets of conversation floating through the kitchen hatch, it was clear it had been a tough night but one when no one had been hurt.

Thank you, universe!

An unexpected sexual charge surged through him when Jack laid eyes on Liesel, looking so natural in the station-house kitchen. Her clingy sundress didn't help calm his body's response, either. Every fiber in his body wanted to vault through the kitchen hatch, pull the shutters down, lift her up to the counter, dispense of her flimsy dress and begin to kiss and caress her the way he'd wanted to last night.

He tried shrugging off the heated sensations. One thing was for sure. His response to her told him everything he needed to know. If the station was going to work, Liesel was too big a distraction to be in his life right now.

She turned around and spied him, those emerald-green eyes of hers bright with expectation—with hope.

"This is a surprise."

"A nice one, I hope." Her lashes dropped, hiding her expressive eyes, a light pink flush playing along the curves of her cheekbones. *Strewth.* She was about as beautiful as you could get.

"What are you doing here?" *Open mouth, insert enormous boot.*

"I thought I'd see what the CFS was about—but if you'd rather…"

She wasn't flushing with pleasure anymore.

"It's not really the best—"

"You're right," she hurriedly backpedaled. "I shouldn't have come. This was a bad idea."

"No. It's not that. The guys are loving it." He shot a glance over her shoulder then lowered his voice. "Look, I'm sorry about last night—"

"Oh. I see." Her voice was level but were her cheeks flushing a deeper red? Liesel moved as if to turn away.

"Not the…before. The after." This was not going well. *C'mon, Jack. Man up!* "This isn't really the best place for you to be right now."

If he could wipe the hurt from her eyes he would, but he had to get her out of there and clear his head. His gut churned with an overwhelming need to keep Liesel as far away from all of this as possible—the dirt, ash, smoke, fire. As strongly as he'd hoped to get her involved in the station, he now felt a more powerful drive to ensure she was as far away as possible. The thought of putting her in harm's way, of coming into contact with the danger that automatically came with the job, his job? *No.* Not a chance. He didn't think he could bear it if anything happened to her.

Was this how his father felt every time he heard the sirens? How he'd felt after he'd lost his wife? Powerless? Well, Jack had the power and the position to say no. No to all of it. Even if it did feel like stopping one of the best things that had come into his life.

He shot a look at the volunteers, all hard workers who could do with even more support. Liesel was the answer to a professional prayer. But her presence tore at his focus. Not professional.

Lack of focus cost lives.

Lack of focus meant the station would close, endangering the lives and homes of a lot of locals. After losing his mother because there hadn't been enough hands on deck, there was no chance he'd see that happen again. See someone go through the grief his family had endured. His father in particular.

He had to make a choice.

"You have always been an either-or fellow, haven't you, Jack?"

His father's voice rang in his head. A persistent chiseling away at his ability to make the right decision.

He felt as if his heart was being ripped in half.

"Sorry, Liesel, I've got to run."

Liesel inhaled sharply as if all the air had been sucked out of her. She stood stock-still, staring out into the dining hall at the receding back of Jack Keller, certain she looked little short of a first-class idiot.

What had just happened? She couldn't have misread his signals. Could she?

Suddenly feeling acutely aware of the glances being thrown her way, she wondered what she must look like to all of them. A fire station groupie hoping to bring a smile to the lips of the big hunky firemen? Well, fire*man*. And from the way Jack just spoke to her, she'd just been summarily dismissed.

Talk about humiliating! Were there boundaries she was supposed to have known about? Was she supposed to be a secret? The idea made her feel sick.

She watched dumbly as he threw a quick glance over his shoulder and without so much as a smile grabbed a cold drink from the dining hall and left the room.

Liesel felt her cheeks flame up, not with embarrassment this time but anger.

How dare he treat her like that? How *dare* he?

She hadn't been the one popping round with chocolate milk shakes, suggesting spontaneous picnics, pushing her to her professional limits and back again. She hadn't been the one pulling him into her arms and giving her just about the most perfect set of kisses and knee-weakening caresses she could have ever imagined. How *dare* he dismiss her like this?

Liesel curtly turned her back on the dining room and surveyed the kitchen. It looked as if the breakfast fairy had exploded in there.

Fine.

If he didn't want her around, it jolly well wouldn't look as if she'd been anywhere near his precious fire station. Just like a fireman to blow hot and cold. The irony would've made her laugh if she hadn't been so cross. The counter began to appear in moments. Then gleamed. The cupboards? Scrubbed inside and out.

Despite her Herculean efforts, scrubbing Mr. Tall-Blond-and-Way-Too-Handsome out of the kitchen was proving hard. Far too hard. Little thoughts niggled away in her mind. None of Jack's behavior that morning rang true with the man she'd been spending time with. It was well and truly out of character. Or was it? What did she really know about Brigade Captain Jack Keller? She could just howl with fury! It wasn't as if she was falling for the guy or something.

Oh.

Wait a minute.

Was she falling for him?

Hardly. He couldn't have made that much of an impact with his perfectly winning personality, supersexy kisses and too-good-to-be-true good looks. She scrubbed at the long-neglected corners of the refrigerator, certain that steam was pouring out of her ears. The *nerve* of that man!

She had finally thought she was taking massive strides forward. Finally feeling brave enough to move forward with her and Liam's lives—moving out of the fragile egg-shell existence they'd been living. It really was a good thing she couldn't scream in here because she was building up to a proper old-fashioned tizzy.

How *dare* he treat her as if she was some sort of love-sick puppy, desperate for his attention? Lovesick puppy. There it was again. This wasn't looking good.

"Wow, you can do mine next if you like!"

Cassie's voice was a welcome extinguisher to her over-heated thoughts.

"Oh, what happened to *you*? Jack not show up for your big breakfast bonanza? Or did he hate your cooking?"

Liesel knew it was meant to be a joke but it didn't feel anywhere close to being funny. She sat back on her heels, trying to slow her thoughts to a lower gear before responding to Cassie. From the looks of things her friend was already reading her like a well-thumbed book.

"Here's someone who can cheer you up!" Cassie swung Liam's car seat into view, complete with her son, the most committed nap-taker in the southern hemisphere. She felt her body soften, the anger slip away.

"Ohh, it's Liam the Super-Sleeper!" she stage-whispered, before nuzzling her face against the crook of his neck. He smelled like a new beginning. This little guy was the light of her life. He was who she was living for, fighting her demons for. And she couldn't let herself forget that. Not for a second.

"Li-e-se-e-l…" Her friend drew out her name as if it had several syllables. "What's going on?"

"It appears the bushfire wasn't the only fire that was put out last night." Liesel threw a crinkly browed glance in the direction of the dining room.

Cassie lowered herself to the floor alongside Liesel and Liam.

"Spill it."

"C'mon, let's get out of here!" Liesel grabbed her friend's hand. "I've got a better idea."

Jack hit the empty country road, his feet taking full-length strides, temples throbbing with a grade-A headache and thoughts running at full speed. He knew he should be trying to catch up on his sleep but he had to physically work the stresses out of his system.

He couldn't believe he'd just blown Liesel off like a casual fling—and the moment he'd left the station he'd known she meant more to him than that. A lot more.

Up until now it had been easy—too easy—to keep women at arm's length. Throughout his teens he'd never trusted anyone because he'd never known if they'd liked him or if they'd liked John Granville Keller III, heir apparent to River's Bend Winery. As he refocused his energies into making something of himself at the CFS, relationships were the last thing on his mind. Making good on his silent vow to his mother was key to ensure more people didn't die because there wasn't a fire service.

Not that his decision had helped things with his father. Far from it. Granville Sr. had been a changed man after his wife had died. Utterly grief-stricken at the loss of his true love. Jack hadn't understood it at the time, but he was getting a firsthand glimpse into what it was like to lose someone you cared for. The look on Liesel's face after he'd made it clear she wasn't welcome? Awful. It was as close as anything had come to the moment Jack had told his father he'd chosen the CFS over the winery. His father had taken his decision to leave as a full-frontal blow to the legacy his son was meant to have accepted like a golden mantle.

Jack kicked up his speed.

Why couldn't things be easy? When he'd been in Adelaide, he'd been driven—as though his divided energies had finally found a home base. He had been right to have chosen the CFS over running the winery. Becca was amazing at steering River's Bend into the future while he, on the other hand, had been born to fight fires. And then along had come Liesel. Delicate and strong, cream-skinned and flame-haired Liesel, forcing him to confront his either-or existence. He'd made a choice that morning and it didn't feel right.

He forced himself to sprint, enjoying feeling his lungs strain, his legs burn, his arms pump against the warm spring air. When he couldn't take it anymore he stopped, hands falling to his knees so he could catch his breath. When he looked up he started with surprise at seeing where his body had automatically taken him: River's Bend.

Home was where the heart was? There was definitely

something to that. Until he fixed things on this front, he didn't know how much good he'd be as a boyfriend to Liesel. *Boyfriend?* Yeah, right. He choked out a laugh. As if she'd let him anywhere near her after his performance that morning. Looked as if his habit of burning bridges was getting even better.

It was the most extraordinary feeling. Being in the hospital. Just wandering the halls was like visiting an old friend.

Liesel had left Liam and Cassie chatting away with a very animated Kevin showing a newfound confidence now that he had a top-of-the-range personal injury story.

She had to smile as he told his mother and the new shift nurse about how all the doctors had deemed his the "coolest pneumothorax" solution they'd ever seen.

Now, strolling the corridors, she could hear snippets of conversation floating from patient rooms, drifting above the high desks of the nurses' stations, snapping rapid-fire from doctor to doctor. All the talk, the hospital banter, had once filled her up like high-octane fuel. It had also been exactly what she'd been avoiding like the plague for the past three years. What had she been so afraid of?

Today it felt like a dose of the perfect medicine. The simple truth was the hospital was familiar terrain and had never failed to assure her she had chosen the right profession. There were so many people to help and to care for—and she knew she was good at it. Working at the school was great, but the electric atmosphere of an emergency department had always been more her style.

Maybe this would be a better place to start putting her fears behind her. A hospital was every bit as much of a community as a fire station. She'd even seen the notice boards filled to the brim with Harvest Festival notices, film nights, exercise classes, all sorts—all promises of things to come once the patients had healed.

All those things were out there for her, too. But had *she* healed?

Realistically, things wouldn't—couldn't—work with Jack. Her main priority was her son and Jack's was the station. He obviously wanted to compartmentalize things in his life—and that was the last thing she wanted. At the very least, she should just enjoy the fact that a deeply gorgeous man had found her attractive enough to pursue—at least for a little while. Despite everything, the grief, the rebuilding, today's supersize disaster, she was still a woman. A desirable one. Which was a good feeling. And if she was going to try to lavish everything with icing, Jack had helped rekindle her passion for medicine. So maybe…

She took a big breath and pushed through the double doors into the ED waiting room. She eagle-eyed a corner seat that would be perfect for surreptitiously watching the action. She glanced at the wall clock. Fifteen minutes. She'd give herself fifteen minutes.

CHAPTER SEVEN

"Excuse me, miss?"

Liesel didn't have to turn around to identify the young male voice.

"What is it?" She swung around to face Kevin, thankful that she'd bitten back the *this time* she had been going to tease the teenager with. "Wow! Look at you!"

It was probably the first time she'd seen Kevin look shy. And clean-cut. And a part of her felt like begging him to change back to the ragamuffin kid who was in her nurse's office a bit too frequently.

"What do you think of my new threads?" Kevin put on a pose as Liesel took in his immaculate new Country Fire Service Cadets uniform.

"I think you look fantastic!" She didn't have to like the uniform, did she? It seemed ridiculous to admit, but complimenting the uniform was just a bit too close to complimenting a certain Captain Jack Keller. Or Captain Persona Non Grata, as she liked to think of him these days.

"I hate to be a party pooper—but has your doctor approved this?"

"He already said I have to wait to do the ladder training."

When had Kev seen Jack? She'd seen neither hide nor hair of him for five days. Not that she was going to admit to anyone she was missing him. At least her house had benefited. It was sparkling clean. If she could have spring-cleaned her own son, she would have.

As if reading her thoughts, Kevin continued, "Jack came to see me at the hospital after work. He said he's been really busy and would like it if I could be his second in command. You know, in charge of the clipboard, checking all the cadets in and out, that sort of thing, until I'm ready to begin training. Be, you know, like a manager."

Oh. So Jack had thought of everything. And Kevin looked so very proud. The first time she'd seen him this confident in ages.

"So what can I help you with, mate?"

"Mum says would it be all right if you took me to cadets this evening, please? She's got parent-teacher conferences tonight and has to prepare."

"Oh, did she, now?" Liesel raised a suspicious eyebrow.

"Yeah." Kevin looked back at her blankly. He obviously didn't see the thoughts whirling round her head at turbo speed or know his mother's fine-tuned ability for setting Liesel up on dates she had no interest in going on. *And* on the day a seven-year-old had vomited all over her top. Perfect.

"She didn't say anything else?" There had to be more to this than met the eye.

"I don't think so," Kev replied hesitantly, already accustomed to his teenage brain letting him down in the messenger department. His eyes shot up to the ceiling, as if that would help, then returned to Liesel. He gave her a small *I don't know what you're talking about* shrug.

Typical teenager.

Why didn't you tap your mother for the real *reason behind this trip?*

Five ludicrously long days had passed since that ridiculous morning in the fire station and not a peep from Mr. Hot-and-Not-So-Nice. Guess it was time to start up more tutorials at the school of hard knocks.

She tried unsuccessfully to shake away the sensation of being in Jack's arms.

How could she? Kissing him had made her feel incredibly, beautifully, wonderfully alive.

And had she heard *anything* from him?

Nada. Zilch. Nothing.

She'd recapped the morning at the station again and again as the hours had turned into days. Jack didn't seem the type of man to kiss and run, but, for all she knew, he could have disappeared off the end of the earth and she'd be none the wiser.

Cassie had tried playing Twenty Questions with her—or more like Twenty Excuses of Captain Keller.

"Fire season's kicking into full throttle."

"The man has a phone."

"So do you."

"He blew me off when he last saw me."

"Is that what really happened or is that what you think happened?"

"I'm a girl—I know these things."

"Are you still in high school?"

"Doesn't matter how old you are, a blow-off is a blow-off." Then she had stuck her tongue out at Cassie. It had seemed the right thing to do.

"He's very busy recruiting for the station." Cassie had returned the gesture.

"And he suddenly doesn't need nurses anymore?"

"Yeah, because you were chomping at the bit to take him up on that offer!"

Good point.

Liesel had tried out some of her own.

"He doesn't want a premade family."

"Don't be stupid. You said he had an amazing time with Liam."

"He made a mistake and thinks I'm ugly."

"As I said, don't be stupid. Look in the mirror!"

"He's just not interested."

And Cassie hadn't had anything to say to that. How could she? It wasn't as if either of them had a hotline to Jack and his thought processes.

Served her right. She knew falling for—no, not falling for, just having a crush on…or whatever it was—a guy in the fire service was definitely not for her, and Jack Keller was in the fire service, so out of sight…out of mind?

She felt the wind fall out of her self-righteous sails—he was definitely not out of mind.

"Are you all right, miss?" Kev's voice snapped her out of her reverie.

"Of course! Just having a little daydream!" *A rotten one.*

She scooped up her keys from her desk and grabbed her handbag. Better get it over and done with. "Ready to go?"

Jack recognized the car as it pulled into the station and felt an instant shot of remorse. He was overdue, long overdue, in apologizing to Liesel for his stupid behavior. There was no excuse—well, there were excuses but none that made up for pulling her into his arms, sharing mind-blowing kisses with her and then virtually writing her off the next day at the station. And the one hundred and seventeen or so hours since then. He was going to have to do some serious backpedaling.

He strode toward the car, intent on making things up to her.

"Kev! You sure look sharp, mate."

Was that Liesel already sticking the car into reverse? Wasn't she even going to say hello?

He grabbed hold of the passenger-side door before Kevin could slam it shut.

"Hey, Liesel. How are you going?" *Lame. Lame and pathetic. And cowardly.*

"Late to pick up Liam. Do you mind?" Her head tipped toward the door he was holding open, clearly not interested in chitchat. *And she's back in the ring!*

"Liesel, hang on a second." He held on to the car door, despite the fact he could feel her moving the vehicle slowly back down the sloping station drive. "Blimey, what happened there? Are you all right?"

"What do you mean?" He watched her turn bright red as she took in what he'd pointed out—a huge stain covering most of her body-hugging blue top.

"Work."

She's not really giving away much, is she? Or does she think I'm just staring at her breasts? Which is exactly what I'm doing. Stop it, Jack!

"What happened?"

"Too much chocolate birthday cake for one of the youngsters."

"Crikey. Not really a job perk, is it?"

Her face showed she was doing anything but enjoying his stab at casual banter.

"Sorry. I'm late and I'm not going to let my son down. He likes consistency." And another hit! A palpable hit! *Suck it up, Jack. She's in the right here.*

"I owe you an apology."

"You don't owe me anything."

Her eyes flicked up to his and he felt the same electric jolt of attraction he had the very first time he'd laid eyes on her. Feisty, gorgeous and trying her best to run him over.

"I do, Liesel. An apology and an explanation." A clutch of cadets gathered outside the station house were openly watching as his walk turned into a jog as he tried to hang on to the car door. He looked like a stalker. *Way to lead by example, Jack!*

"I was a jerk. Please. Just give me a few minutes to explain."

Her car shook from the quick application of brakes.

Good! She was softening. No more playing hard to get. He closed the passenger door he'd been hanging on to, leaned down and stuck his head through the window. Perhaps a wry grin would put things on a better note...

"Listen to me, Captain Keller. I don't play games. Never have, never will. And I will not let some daredevil fireman wreak havoc with my life or, more important, my son's. So *back off.*"

Ouch. He wasn't entirely sure how she made a clenched jaw and words bit out through gritted teeth appealing, but it was just about all he could do not to jump into the car with her and prove the last thing he was was a fly-by-night. Wrestling with priorities? Absolutely. Game player? Not anymore.

"Liesel, please." He couldn't help a moment's distraction by some poorly timed laughter from the boys. "Give me a chance?"

"I'm sorry, Jack, I have to keep my priorities in order and being treated like a hanger-on is most definitely not one of them. Please let go of the car. I have to collect my son."

Jack took a quick glimpse up at the cadets and waved them toward the ladder tower, where they'd be running drills. "Get yourselves a bottle of water from the cool box, boys. I'll be with you in a second."

He dipped his head back into Liesel's car window. "Liesel, I know I don't deserve it, but let me explain." Her expression remained neutral. "Over dinner?" He saw her tip her chin up ready to make an excuse but before she could start he jumped in, "I'll make it for you—at yours—once the little man's gone to bed."

She narrowed her eyes, clearly reluctant to agree. She sure did make mad look good. Really good.

"I make a mean lemon tart."

He saw her lips twitch a bit.

Was that a smile she was fighting? He hoped so.

"C'mon. Say yes. Fighting with you is no fun."

"Is that what we're doing, Captain?" She quirked an eyebrow at him.

"Not if I have anything to say about it." He thought he would plunge forward and take her lack of a refusal as a yes. Just about as tentative a yes as you could get but he was pretty sure if—or *when*—he showed up at her house tonight he wouldn't get the door slammed in his face.

As she glanced in the rearview mirror, Liesel was surprised she didn't see steam coming out of her ears. And goofy cartoon love hearts. How mortifying. Covered in a child's vomit and trying to play it cool? Disasterville! Or was it? Did she have a date with Jack tonight? It seemed like it, didn't it?

Even so, Cassie should count herself lucky she was in parent-teacher conferences or they would most assuredly be having words. Sharp ones.

And Jack Keller? She didn't know whether to close her heart for good or let the cartoon lovebirds swirling around her carry on with their chirping.

Tonight! Her heart skipped a beat. *Traitor!*

She drummed her fingers along the top of the steering wheel. What was there left to be angry about?

I know, she thought facetiously: *child abuse!* How dare Cassie use her own son to get her within spitting distance of the one man in the whole of Australia who had her every nerve end smarting with embarrassment. And frustration. Not to mention a healthy dollop of regret that things hadn't taken a fairy-tale course.

Then again, lots of bad things happened in fairy tales—evil witches, danger-filled woods, charming wolves dressed in sheep's clothing…

These days the dangerous bits of the old-fashioned stories were edited out. But this was real life. No director. No editor. Just good old-fashioned making it through day by day.

If she hadn't known better, Liesel would have sworn all the blood in her body was churning its way up to a storm-force hurricane. Hurricane Liesel! It had a nice ring to it.

Common sense was telling her to cut Jack out of the picture. Kissing him had unearthed a big fat pile of psychological laundry she could hardly begin to sort through, let alone press, fold and put away in the attic. If only she really could stuff all her feelings in the cupboard and close the door. That'd be the life!

Being angry with Jack had been easy when she hadn't seen him. The second those bright blue eyes of his had met hers? Putty.

She flicked on the radio for the five-minute drive back to the day care to pick up Liam. A little smile played across her lips as she imagined her son running toward her and jumping into her arms as he did every day at pickup. He was getting more handsome every day and—curiously—more of an amalgam of herself and Eric. The first year or so he had almost exclusively looked like Eric and now he was definitely a product of the two of them.

Her thoughts shifted a bit too quickly back to the dangerously blue eyes and thick thatch of blond hair her fingers had itched to run through just a few short days ago. The stubble outlining that pair of cheekbones a model would be happy to sport. Tanned forearms propped on her car's window frame. Well-defined muscles nicely visible as they went taut and then relaxed beneath a light spray of blond arm hair. The man was gorgeous.

She'd let Jack make her dinner but would play it cool. He'd just be a nice bit of fireman eye candy she could enjoy from time to time. From now on they'd be friends.

Her eyes flicked down to the car clock.

Four twenty-seven.

Liam went down at seven.

Two and a half hours. And three minutes.

Not that she was counting. Or worried about if she had time to take a shower, not smell like little kid puke and tame her curls in some way. This time Jack was going to know what he was missing. She wasn't some naive country school nurse he could play mind games with. She'd traveled the world and worked on some of the most difficult trauma cases a person could imagine, for heaven's sake! Frankly, he could come over and apologize until the cows came home, but this time she would stay strong—remain immune to his sexy, firemanly charms.

She was woman!

"Hear me roar!" she shouted out into the car, unconcerned if anyone saw her. She cranked up the pop music on the radio for good measure. "Roaaaarr! Take that, Captain Keller! Let's see you take on the she-lion tonight!"

Jack felt his shopping basket getting heavier by the minute. He knew he couldn't buy his way back into Liesel's good books but he sure could try to cook his way there. Lemons... Where did they keep the lemons in this place?

"Why, Captain Keller, what a surprise, meeting you here."

Jack looked up and saw Cassie Monroe sending him a Cheshire-cat grin over a pile of artisan bread.

"G'day, Cassie. How are things?" He felt like a character in a soap opera. Mysterious but charming. He hoped.

"Good. Good." She nodded along with the words. "Haven't seen you around much."

The words were loaded with meaning and he knew what they were saying.

You treated my friend poorly. Really poorly. And us girls stick together.

"It's been mad at the station." It was true, but even as the words left his lips he knew they sounded weak.

"Right, of course. Fire season." Cassie nodded along with an earnest expression. "I guess you fire blokes don't use telephones during the high season for safety reasons?" Her facial expression read like a triumphant picture book.

"Cease-fire! I'm on a rescue mission tonight!" Jack lifted up his basket for Cassie to inspect. He was relieved to see her nod approvingly at the collection of fresh groceries. He was going for a lemon and asparagus risotto, roasted tomatoes, all topped with a nice bit of grilled fish.

She gave a sniff of approval. "At least you didn't pick up a packet of snags for the barbie." She went on tiptoe to make a more detailed inspection. "If my ex-husband had cooked this well, he might have stood more of a chance." She laughed good-naturedly, the tension of their previous banter dispersed into the early-evening air of the open-walled farm shop.

"Hopefully Liesel's ex wasn't up to much in the kitchen. I might know my ingredients but I—" Jack stopped in midflow, acutely aware Cassie had shifted into yet another mode: protective mother hen. She threw a furtive look over each of her shoulders before joining him on his side of the bread display.

"Has she not told you?" Her voice was low, concerned.

"Told me what?"

"About her ex?"

"Not a word. I thought Liesel had a don't-ask-don't-tell sort of thing going on."

Cassie fixed him with a serious glare. He could practically hear the invisible seconds ticking past. What was going on? He'd just presumed it was a loser boyfriend or husband who'd cut town when a kid had arrived on the scene, so he hadn't pressed for details. His only thought had been that the guy must've been an idiot to let her go. Not to mention Liam. He was up there on the cute-kid meter.

"Cassie," he gently prodded. "What is it? If it will help me make things up to Liesel for being a first-class berk you've got to tell me. As I said, I'm on a rescue mission here."

She motioned him over to a quiet corner of the country store.

"This didn't come from me, but if you really want to make things work then you need to know the truth. I'm doing this for Liesel's good because I can tell you this—that girl is her own worst enemy."

Cassie fixed him with a burn-holes-through-your-head glare. He nodded, not interested in the politics of her confession, just the content.

"You'll have to ask her yourself."

"What?"

"You want Liesel in your life? You earn her trust—and then you'll win her confidence." Cassie was well into her mama-bear role now.

"Can't you even give me a hint?" *Youch. If looks could kill.*

"Ball's in your court, Jack. Time to kick up your game a notch."

"Are you sure I can't show you around?"

Jack shooed Liesel away from the kitchen, handing her a cool glass of what looked like very fancy wine in the process. "Positive. You just go get yourself settled out there on the veranda and enjoy the sunset. Before you know it, dinner will be served!"

More time to wonder what on earth was going on with this chameleon of a man. *Thanks for nothing!*

Her fingers played across her lips. Lips a bit too keen to pick up the action from the last time she'd been out on the veranda with a certain someone. Maybe gnawing on them would put them off. Kissing was *not* on the agenda tonight.

Her teeth released her lips. No good. Pillar of strength or not, Jack still sent her tummy's butterflies into a tailspin.

She chanced another peek into the kitchen. It struck her how at home he looked in her kitchen. She could hear him humming quietly to himself. Steadily chopping, frying, cleaning as he went—what a plus! He had changed from his uniform into a faded pair of jeans that hung loosely off his hips. Maybe he was hiding a secret past as a jet-setting jeans model. He looked just a bit too good.

His trim waist was visible above the wooden countertops, swiveling here and there to hunt for a pan in a cupboard, a knife in a drawer. The broad reach of his shoulders extended farther as he stretched to pull a pair of plates down from a shelf. This was like chef porn. Or something. She really needed to get a grip.

At the very least, she had to congratulate herself for agreeing to let Jack work his way back into her good books. She was well and truly intent on making a life for herself and Liam here in Engleton and, like it or not, Jack was part of the small-town package.

She took another sip of the delicious wine. It was quite unlike anything she'd had before. "This wine is great, Jack. How did you hear about it?"

"I just keep my ear to the ground. I know a thing or two about wine."

"Well, color me impressed—this is great. It's local, right? You sure I can't give you a hand?"

"You bet. It won't be long now."

* * *

Jack didn't feel right withholding information from her. It officially bugged him now that she didn't know everything about him. He would get there. She'd know his whole story one day—when he had everything in place. Sorting things out with his father was just another bridge to cross and he wouldn't be ready to go there until he had Engleton CFS station firmly placed on the map and his father's stamp of approval.

He looked up from his chopping, the gentle curves of Liesel's silhouette just visible through the screen door, backlit by the final rays of the day's sunshine. It was all too easy to imagine running a hand along the soft swoop from her waist to her hip and he felt his body respond. It would take less than a second to cross the room, pull her into his arms and kiss her as deeply and completely as if the world were about to end.

Actions spoke louder than words?

Most of the time. But that wasn't what tonight was about. It was about respect. And a healthy slice of humble pie.

"Why don't you come on in? Dinner's just about ready."

He should have been focusing on his risotto, but found watching Liesel cross the room, fingers playing through her auburn curls, a better option.

"That's not a burning smell, is it?" She wrinkled up her nose and tilted her head, trying to pinpoint the source.

Jack looked down and realized the risotto was the culprit. Staring doe-eyed at Liesel hadn't done it any favors.

"Is that smoke?"

"Oh, no! The fish!" Jack whirled around to look in the

grill. He reached in to pull out the grill pan, realizing too late he didn't have an oven glove on.

"Ow-w-w!"

"What happened?" Liesel was by his side in an instant.

"The fish!"

"What about your hand?"

"Burnt." He held it up for her to inspect.

"Whoops." Liesel's voice held a barely contained giggle. "I'll just grab some ice for— Is that pot meant to be boiling over?"

Jack whirled around, burnt hand cupped in his good one, only to find his asparagus turning to mush in a sea of frothy, boiling green water.

"Go." Liesel was handing him a tea towel filled with ice and pointing to the veranda.

"But—your dinner."

"I think we can agree this might not be the night for me to sample your home cooking."

That had better be a twinkle in her eyes.

"Here, take this. It'll help dull the pain." Liesel went to the fridge and pulled out the bottle of wine he'd brought and poured a few healthy glugs into a glass.

He gratefully took the glass, feeling the chilled wine cool the red mark already rising on his hand. He lingered a moment, watching as she swiftly and efficiently switched off the oven, the stove, the grill, and removed all the burning and boiling kitchenware from the offending heat sources.

"Would you believe this isn't really the fine-dining evening I'd envisaged for us?"

He watched the smile on her face grow even larger. Had he noticed how full her lips were before?

"Maybe not, but it's been pretty fun watching a fireman incinerate every single course of a meal."

"You know—" he sidled up to her, hoping he looked like a sexy cowboy "—not every man can turn a meal into a three-fire alert."

She gave him her best *wow, I'm impressed* face then rummaged through a kitchen drawer next to the phone until she found what she was looking for. Triumphantly holding up a colorful piece of paper, she waggled it in the air between them.

"Pizza?"

CHAPTER EIGHT

"Yum. That was just what the doctor ordered." Liesel lay back on the sofa, hands appreciatively rubbing her full belly. Pepperoni always hit the spot.

"You mean you didn't fancy a beautiful asparagus risotto with river trout tonight?"

"Uhh…" She eyed him dubiously. "I'm not entirely sure how to answer that."

"How about like this?" Jack leaned toward her on the sofa, looking very much as if he was going to kiss her. Her body reacted as though she'd just been filled with recharged batteries. Everything was tingling. Everything wanted to say yes.

She felt herself stiffen.

"Sorry, Jack. I…I can't."

He pulled back, a freshly bandaged hand raised in a gesture of surrender. "That's cool. I just thought you might like to know you've got a bit of pizza left over for later just here." He wiggled a finger by the edge of his own mouth, signifying she was wearing a face snack.

Sexy, Liesel. That's the way to play it. Turn a man down for a kiss he wasn't going to give you.

"Sorry, I thought—"

"I know." Jack shook his head, more at himself than

at her. "I did—I do want to kiss you. I just covered like a bloke. Don't worry. Your face is still the same beautiful picture of perfection it always is."

"Hardly!" Liesel tried to laugh away the compliment while simultaneously swiping at her cheek. He was right. There was nothing there.

She looked across at him, suddenly aware of how quiet he'd gone.

"What? What is it?"

"I mean it, Liesel."

"What, about the pizza?"

"No, you silly thing—about how beautiful you are."

Oh, no! You're not meant to make me feel pretty—like a woman again! We're supposed to be friends!

"I'd say right back at you but that's not really what a bloke wants to hear, is it?"

"Liesel, I'm being serious." She could see it in his eyes—but the only way to survive this was to carry on playing the fool. Or was it time to take a breath and act like a grown-up?

"So am I, Jack." He nodded for her to continue. She felt like squirming or, better yet, running away and pretending none of this was happening. But that wasn't who she was now. She was a grown woman and a mother. *Bite the bullet, Liesel!*

"Look—I don't know how much you're going to like this but I need to let you know where I stand. For myself and for Liam."

He leaned back against the sofa cushions, brows raised and wearing an open expression that invited her to continue. Lordy, he was sexy. He didn't make a "friends' night" easy in any way.

"Okay—here it goes. I've felt as though there has been

something between us—at least, there seemed to be a few days ago." Then the words began to pour out. "It's obvious the fire department is your priority. You and me—and whatever we are or aren't—it's clearly something you don't have room for in your life. I don't want you to think of me or Liam as things competing for your attention—something you have to choose between."

"You're right, the station *is* my priority right now."

Liesel felt her heart sink. That had ended more quickly than she'd thought.

"But," he continued, a hand slipping over to rest on her knee, "once I've got it secured on the map, I don't want to look up and find you're not there."

Liesel gulped. Hard. She watched as Jack's eyes implored her to believe him. Holy cow! What was he saying exactly? He wanted her to wait for him? But that meant being put on hold. No. That wasn't right, either. They'd be better off deciding on a friendship now. A really sexy, hormone-fueled, abstemious friendship. With benefits?

"I think…" He gathered her hands in his, a thumb skimming along her wrist. "I think there's something else that's frightening you. I know I work crazy hours and the lifestyle is a bit nuts—but you're no stranger to that world. You're a strong, amazing woman. I've never met anyone like you. It's one of the reasons I'm over here incinerating dinners, trying to get back into your good books! I know I'm not ideal boyfriend material but would you be willing to give it a go?"

Ping! Ping! Ping! He was hitting all the marks. You bet there were other things that frightened her.

Him dying, for example. That was the best example—no need to continue.

"I don't know, Jack. It's just not what I imagined. Waiting around for someone."

"Are you saying I'm just anyone?"

He put on just about the most gorgeous hurt expression a man could muster.

Boyfriend material?

He wasn't hanging up his fireman's hat—but wasn't pulling his punches, either. He wanted her in his life. Could that be enough to risk loving him? Risk losing him?

"I just think it's a lot to ask of someone." *You're dodging the real issues here, Liesel!*

"C'mon, love." His voice was all low and sexy now. He was playing emotional hardball. "I've felt the sparks between us, too."

Liesel allowed a cheeky smile to begin to creep onto her lips. *Boyfriend material.* It made her skin all shivery. In a good way.

What was Liesel's smile suggesting? Three seconds ago he'd felt like an onion—freshly relieved of a new layer. Exposed and on his way to the frying pan. She'd called a spade a spade. But that thick-lashed twinkling set of emerald eyes looking up at him… His fingertips were itching to pull that cute little body of hers closer to him. Really close.

"It would be much easier to believe what you said if you found a way not to give me the cold shoulder for showing up at the station with a tray of cinnamon rolls."

"I was a pretty big jerk the other day, wasn't I?"

He watched as Liesel's smile grew toothy. This whole bare-bones thing was a bit less painful than he'd thought.

"You were a super-big jerk."

"Anything I could do to make up for it?"

She put her best coy face on. Those cat eyes of hers did their magic. Stirrings of a distinctly male nature were coming to the fore and he hoped she was experiencing the same lusty call.

"Oh…" She planted a finger at the side of her rosebud mouth. "I could think of a thing or two."

Jack didn't need any more prompting. From the saucy look in Liesel's eyes he knew it was time to let actions speak louder than words. He cared for Liesel. Deeply. If she was willing to try things with him despite his commitment to his job, he would do his red-blooded best to thank her.

Pushing himself forward on the sofa, he started planting soft kisses on Liesel's neck. From the way she tilted it toward her shoulder he knew he was on the right track. "How's this? Any closer to working my way back into your good books?"

"A little." The words might've been bland but her voice had purred them. He took them as a cue to continue. They might have things to work on, but if access to Liesel's creamy smooth neck was the payoff, he was going to be a rich man.

A sigh escaped Liesel's lips as Jack brushed his lips along her forehead, her cheeks, each touch sending a warm flush of pleasure straight through to her very core. His fingers teased their way along her jawline, drawing her chin toward his expectant lips. She felt her breath catch in her throat until Jack sealed the moment with the most tender of kisses. A kiss that soon turned hungry, more demanding.

Caution, playing it safe, fear—all of them faded into the background as the need to respond to Jack's kisses consumed her. Liesel pulled herself up onto her knees, still kissing him, teasing, nibbling, her hands beginning a tentative exploration of his chest. Through the cotton top she could feel his nipples harden. She couldn't resist giving them a playful swirl and tweak before moving on, exploring him, his body. His perfectly sexy body. A wash of pure animal lust rushed through her, turning thoughts into mush and physical contact into explosions of pleasure. Thank God Liam was a good sleeper. She could feel a moan of pleasure rolling through her throat.

She wanted him. She wanted Jack more than she could have imagined possible. Her hands slipped below his waist, onto his thighs and round the back for a cheeky squeeze of that jeans-perfect bum of his. He felt so good! So male. Everything shifted into primal responses. The touching, the soft moans of pleasure meeting in midair between them. She pressed her breasts against his chest, unable to resist nestling into his neck. Jack's scent flooding her senses, heat passing between them as if they were unclothed.

Why were they wearing clothes? Everything was in the way now. His shirt, hers. His jeans, her skirt. An urge to rip the buttons off his shirt shot through her fingers. As her hands continued to explore there was no doubt Jack was feeling the same way she was. A strong arm slipped round her waist while another possessively slipped below her hips. In a single swoop Jack pulled her legs up around his waist and was carrying her toward the bedroom. "You ready for this?" His voice was urgent, full of need.

"More than I thought possible!"

If Liesel could've made her legs more like a human pretzel she would have. It was still early morning—the perfect time for a sexy snuggle. She nestled into the human spoon Jack had wrapped round her and wove her legs between his. The night of lovemaking had gone beyond anything she'd imagined. He had, by turns, been passionate, gentle, insatiable, patient. She felt like a first-class sex kitten.

Thank goodness she wasn't facing him. Just thinking about the fact that his beeper or radio could go off at any moment brought a salty sting to her eyes. She clamped them shut. Making love with Jack had dug just about the biggest hole she could've imagined. Here they were, not even twenty-four hours into trying out the boyfriend-girlfriend thing and already she was nervous about him being called out.

This wasn't going to work. The painful twist in her heart was proof she was going to have to break things off. Now. If it was going to be painful today, it would be even more so in a week, a month, a year, when Jack might or might not have things the way he wanted them. If she'd learned anything, it was that life didn't wait around for things to be perfect.

This? Lying in Jack's arms? It was pretty close to as perfect as a girl could get. So she'd just have to cherish this memory and move on.

Jack obviously needed to focus on the station and having her moping around was hardly going to help things. Not that moping was her style. Thanks to him, she was seeing more clearly than ever that she might have been hasty in vowing never to work in the trauma wards again. She thrived on it as much as Jack was charged by putting out a fire or rescuing someone. They each had their calling. But for right now? Her main calling was to roll over and see what sort of early-morning kisses she could elicit out of a sleepy Jack Keller. She teased and nibbled at his lips and from the press of his hips against hers, both their thoughts were clearly headed in the same direction.

The sound of the telltale buzz of his mobile phone brought a distinct moan of displeasure from Jack. Despite her vow to try and chill, Liesel stiffened. Could she really do this?

Jack reached across Liesel's shoulder and grabbed his phone from the side of the bed, where they'd hastily discarded their clothes the night before. He took a glimpse at the screen. A text.

How about coming to River's Bend tonight? Casual barbie. Dad's coming. I forbid you to say no. Love Bec.

Great. A fence-mending night. Jack knew it was long overdue but he wasn't quite ready. Not to mention the fact he still had to tell Liesel his family lived just down the road. He pulled a hand through his hair and flicked the phone back onto the jumble of clothes. Something was bound to come up. As much as he hated letting her down, he'd let his sister know his excuse in an hour or so. But for now he had some more kissing to— "What's up, buttercup?"

Liesel was actively wriggling her way out of his arms. She'd spent the entire night getting about as close as a woman could to a man and now she was beating a retreat?

"Was that the station?"

"No." Jack felt himself drawl the word to try and buy some thinking time. He knew they hadn't gone deep and dirty in terms of discussing their lives last night, but Liesel was obviously worked up about the station. He tried to pull her back into his arms but she pushed herself up to a cross-legged position and folded her arms solidly across her chest.

"Is there something more than me prioritizing the station that bugs you?"

"How about everything?" Liesel tried her best to laugh off the comment, but knew her raw voice betrayed that it came from a very real place. All of it was scary! His job, how he prioritized it over everything else, how he didn't want to include her in it and, most important, the real possibility he could be injured or worse. That about covered it.

The salty sting of tears began to threaten. *No!* She pulled her hands from his and scrunched them into fists. She wasn't going to succumb.

"Let's try and break it down. What's really bugging you?"

I'm falling in love you with you, you idiot.

"Look, it's just not going to work, is it? Us. Me waiting. I'm hardly going to spend a year pining while you run off and act the hero."

The words tasted acrid. That was what Eric had always done—acted the hero. And if he had, just that once, been sensible, thought of her—he might be alive.

Jack pressed his hands down as if to calm her. "I'm not asking you to do that. Not at all. You know me better than that, don't you?"

She could feel herself bite away a response. She thought she knew him—knew his character—but there were a lot of gaps.

"I'm not entirely sure what I'm asking, or how we can make this work…but I think it's worth it—the wait." He dropped her one of those hard-to-resist winks. "We've got sparks, baby!"

Obviously! But it's such a big risk!

Jack slipped out from under the sheet and pulled on a T-shirt and boxers then sat down solidly opposite her on the bed. It was a good move because having this discussion with a naked Jack Keller was taking a boatload of concentration.

"You say you're scared—so let's break it down. Just start with one thing and we'll go through all of them." Jack looked around the bedroom. "You got a pen and paper? We could make a list if you want."

Despite herself, she smiled, appreciative of his gesture of trying to make it a more comfortable atmosphere for her. She loved lists. How he knew her so well after such a short time was beyond her. She reached over to the bedside and pulled on a long T-shirt. *May as well make this even.*

"I think I already got one in here." She tapped her head.

"Okay, shoot. Number one?"

"Number one..." Lordy. All her reasons jostled for pole position. "Number one—your job scares me."

He nodded. It was no secret firefighters lost their lives in Australia—hell, everywhere—every year.

"I'm not going to change jobs. I can't do that." The words could've sounded belligerent, but coming from Jack they were just the truth. The fire service was part of him, she knew that instinctively.

"I know. I'm not asking you to. It's just that..." She bit her lip. If she told Jack the real reason behind her hesitancy he might just agree it was too big a hurdle to leap and they should call it quits. But that was what she wanted anyhow, right?

Wrong. Right now she wasn't entirely sure what she wanted. She took a big breath, swallowed her tears and began, "Liam's father died in a terrible accident. He was a ski patroller and I knew he faced danger every day, but we were young—we took risks. I just didn't ever imagine his risks having such permanent repercussions. The same week he died I found out I was pregnant with Liam and—well, I don't think I need to say how awful the next year was. But in so many ways it was great! Liam was such a happy baby—he brings me so much joy. I moved back to Australia and my family could not have been more amazing in supporting me." She shook her head in wonder. "I don't know if I could have dealt with Eric's loss as well if I hadn't had them."

Her hands flew to her eyes. Staunching the flow of tears just wasn't working. But she wanted, needed, to get the rest of her story out. Jack needed to know why this was all so difficult for her.

"When I met you, I… It was nice."

He raised his eyebrows.

She smirked back at him, despite herself. Fine. They were telling the truth here, right?

"Better than nice. But with your job and everything it—" She had to stop. She didn't want to sob, didn't want to lose it. This was all part of growing up, moving on, taking charge of her life. She squeezed her eyes shut and blew a slow breath between her lips, willing herself to stay strong. Lashes flecked with tears, she finally braved opening them and there he was, steady and solid as ever, Jack and his bighearted smile.

"Liesel, I'm so sorry. I wish I'd known." He moved a

hand up to her cheek, brushing a few curls behind her ear. It was strange how being touched by him when she was telling him about Eric didn't seem like any sort of betrayal. It was crazy! She and Jack were sitting in bed after a mind-blowing night of hot sex and she was telling him all about her dead ex-fiancé. And it felt okay. She certainly hadn't anticipated that. Had she moved further ahead in the emotional stakes department with Jack than she'd thought?

Taking advantage of Liesel's faraway thoughts, Jack jumped in. "You're right about me, you know," he began, then quickly qualified, "to an extent."

"That sounds ominous."

"It's not meant to." His voice softened. "Look, I didn't join the fire service because of a great calling to be macho and fight against Mother Nature's fiery wrath. She's a powerful force and I can assure you I take every precaution available to me. I want to live as much as the next guy." And he meant it. Looking into Liesel's eyes, her emotions laid bare before him, he knew in his heart he would do everything in his power to stay safe for her.

"Then why? Why do you do it?"

"The truth?"

"Yeah. That's what we're doing here, isn't it?" Liesel couldn't keep a bite of punchiness from her voice. It wasn't as if she had just bared her soul to him or anything!

"I joined because my mother died in a horrible barn fire when I was a kid and while everyone around me was doing everything in their power to put the fire out, I ran round the back of the barn to see if I could get my pony out. My mother ran in front. I'll never know if she was going in for me, the horses or both. Either way, my idiot move…" He cleared his throat and punched some air back into the pillows before continuing. "Since then, I'd always thought if I'd known what to do—had had some training—she would still be alive today."

Liesel's mouth went dry, her fingers covering her lips as she nodded at him to carry on. Jack knew loss as well as she did. Horrible, gut-wrenching, life-changing loss.

"Surely, though, the CFS was there."

"That's just it!" Passion ignited his words. "They weren't! There weren't enough volunteers, or they were out doing something else—I don't know. It doesn't matter now—they just weren't there."

"And you're trying to make up for it by running the Engleton CFS station?"

"In part. I can never make up for it. Not in my father's eyes."

"What does that mean?"

"He blames me. Holds me responsible for her death."

"What? Surely not. You said you were only a boy."

"She went into the barn and I wasn't there to stop her."

"You can't think he blames *you* for that, though?"

His father had been in a rage when he'd joined the CFS cadets straight after his mother's funeral. He'd never seen him so angry. Asked him straight-out what good he thought learning about fires would do him now—now that the damage had been done. It hadn't been an outright accusation. But it had been enough. "It's complicated. But losing my mother—well, he's never been the same. His grief consumed him. I swore I wouldn't let that happen to anyone else if I could help it."

Those clear blue eyes of his tore at her. How Jack spoke about all this without crying was beyond her.

It explained his drive, his ambition with the CFS. She reached across and gave one of his hands a squeeze. "If what I've seen is anything to go by, I know you'll do your best."

"That's kind of you, Liesel, but my best doesn't seem to stretch far enough. If I was proper boyfriend material, I'd find something else to do—something that didn't scare the daylights out of you."

"I can't imagine you giving up the CFS."

"Nor can I." Jack hung his head, shaking it as if he was trying to find a way out of the situation.

A fug of gloom hung between them as Liesel's upper teeth gripped her lower lip then shot it out again, her thoughts fighting for order. Being in the CFS was every bit a part of Jack as nursing was in her. She couldn't believe for a second he'd ask her to give up nursing, so she could hardly ask him to give up his profession. Cassie had already called her kettle black anyhow. Accountants and IT guys weren't her style. Men on the front line, helping people in times of need, were. And that was Jack to a T.

The truth was, he had a lot of irons in the fire and she just couldn't risk putting herself and Liam through the heartache of another loss. She pressed her hands onto her face, hoping it would help silence the roar of blood rushing through her ears.

Friends only?

They had such a connection!

She peeked at him through her fingers. Just a glimpse of that tousled blond hair and her tummy went all fizzy. She couldn't believe how powerful an effect he had on her, and now she'd have to give it all up?

She sucked in a sharp breath, held it, then made her decision.

If only he didn't smell so good! And feel so good. And—

Stop. Giving up Jack Keller was going to be a mammoth task, but she had to find the strength to do it.

"It sounds a lot to me like we've both got some demons to tackle."

"You're not wrong there, love."

Love. Boyfriend material. He was making this tough!

"So-o-o—it's probably best that we call whatever this is a day and just be friends."

If she'd slapped him, he couldn't have felt a more vicious sting. It was all Jack could do not to give her a disbelieving double take.

"Are you kidding me?" He gestured at the rumpled sheets, their discarded clothes, himself. "After last night? You want to just be friends?"

"No. I want to be a lot more than friends—but I just don't think it's possible. Not for me. Not for Liam."

"Liam?" He stopped before he stuck his foot in it. Of course the little boy factored into this whole thing. Whatever it was. *Nothing*, from the looks of things. He felt as if he was splitting in two. "I think Liam's great! You can't doubt the fact that I care for him, would look after him." *And you. I'd look after* you.

"I believe you—I do." She pulled her gaze away from his, obviously as unhappy as he was but determined to stick to her guns. "I just have to make sure he has someone in his life who will be there for him. And I— We—" She stopped, visibly wrestling with her words. "We need someone in our lives whose life is straightforward, who we can rely on."

He felt his nerve endings go dull with sadness. Sadness that she was right. She had the same clarity his father did. She saw him for what he was: a man on a self-imposed mission. And until he saw that mission through, he wasn't the man she wanted—or needed—in her life.

"And I'm not that guy."

"Not right now, Jack. I wish to God you were, but you're not."

"Friends?" He put out a hand, wishing it was to caress her but knowing the best he would get was a handshake.

"Friends."

CHAPTER NINE

"You going to the Harvest Festival?"

Cassie was using her teasing voice. The one that was saying one thing and meaning another. Since the great unsaid involved Jack, Liesel didn't feel like playing. The past few weeks of "just being friends" had been tough. She had feelings for him. Big, huge, undeflatable feelings, and this whole being sensible thing was turning out to be harder than she'd thought. Particularly when anytime her thoughts veered in a certain tall, blond and incredibly gorgeous direction her insides turned into happyville. What a disaster.

"That's the plan."

"Planning to meet up with any special friends?"

Liesel suddenly felt the hairs on the back of her neck stand on end.

"Sorry, Cass. Did you catch that? Do you mind...?" She gestured at the radio playing on her friend's kitchen counter.

"What?" Her friend flicked the volume up a notch and leaned in to hear the announcer.

"That's right, folks. In case you haven't heard, you'll want to avoid the high street in Engleton. Looks like one of the vintners is out of luck as a lorry has lost its entire load and taken out quite a few other vehicles—"

"Switch it off."

"I thought you wanted to hear it."

No. This could not be history repeating itself.

"Jack was just heading into Engleton. He messaged me to see if I wanted to meet him for milk shakes."

"Ooh! Still keeping in touch with Mr. Pants-on-Fire, are we?"

"Cass, you're not hearing me!" Liesel heard her voice rising. "He could be in that crash!" Panic was setting in. This was exactly what had happened with Eric. Exactly how she had learned he was in trouble that day. Had her pulse raced this fast? Had her heart lodged as high in her throat? She couldn't remember. All that mattered now was that Jack could be in trouble and she could help. This time she wasn't going to stand by and wait to hear what was happening. She was going to be there.

Jack hadn't lost consciousness but the past few seconds had played out as if they'd been hours.

He'd pulled into traffic behind a large truck hauling grapes from the harvest and remembered thinking the heavy vehicle was taking the corner into town a bit fast for such a huge load, and then—jackknife. He'd pulled the emergency brake and whipped the wheel round in a one-hundred-and-eighty-degree safety turn—but he'd had to pull in sharply to avoid oncoming traffic and had tipped his truck. The passenger side of the truck had seen better days, but he was all right.

Jack unclipped his belt, bracing himself as he did. He'd have to climb out of the cab. His truck was on its side but he was unharmed. He'd had a narrow escape. From the sounds coming through his open window, not everyone had been so lucky.

* * *

"He'll be fine with us." Cassie held Liam on her hip and gave Liesel a grim smile. "Go."

Liesel swept her son's fringe aside and gave him a quick smooch on the forehead. He was why she was doing this. There was no chance she was going to raise him to believe you had to be fearful of life. Life was about making the most of it—the good and the bad. Even if it did make your blood run cold with fear at times. Jack had given her strength to face her fears and conquer them.

"Just friends" or not—it was her turn to help.

"Mr. Jones, it's Jack—Jack Keller. Can you hear me?"

The front of the farmer's truck might as well have not even existed—it had crumpled into nothing. The haulage truck must have caught it head-on from the looks of things, and now Mr. Jones's legs were trapped in the lower cavity of his cab. His air bag may have saved his life, he had a pulse, but Jack wasn't so sure about his legs.

"Help! Over here!"

The call was thin, a child's.

Jack looked up from the unconscious form of Mr. Jones to the car on the other side of the haulage truck, a blue estate car. Flames were shooting through the sides of the bonnet. And they weren't taking their time about growing.

He felt something wet on his face and swatted it away. The sky was as blue as they came today—it couldn't be rain.

"Help!" The child's cry came again.

"What do you need me to do?"

Liesel. It was the salve he needed to bring order to the blur of chaos threatening to engulf him.

"You came!"

"Of course I came. That's what friends do, right?" Worry threaded through her eyes, but so did something else. Something stronger than the friendship they had shaken hands on those two long months ago.

"Liesel... I'm sorry, I...." He scanned the crash site. This wasn't the time. "Can you stay with Mr. Jones? I've got to run—"

He watched as Liesel's face turned a ghostly shade of white.

"Jack, your forehead." Her voice wavered as she spoke and he watched her physically regroup before continuing. "You've got to get that seen to before you do anything."

He lifted his hand to his forehead again, the smear of blood on his palm helping him to connect the dots.

No. Children in burning cars came first.

Liesel's mind went into overdrive.

Head wounds bled a lot. Common knowledge. It didn't necessarily mean he was concussed, but Jack had definitely looked confused when he'd seen her.

Her eyes made a quick scan of the scene, as if she were making an incident report. They were both trained in mass casualty management, but if Jack had been concussed during the crash he definitely should not be taking part in the rescue efforts. But timing was just as crucial. Seconds counted in a scenario like this.

Establishing scores for each of the cases needed to come automatically, otherwise lives could be lost.

Extreme cases first, secondaries put into order in a temporary triage unit until additional support arrived. Jack needed to be on that list and he... *Where was he?* He had been standing there just a second ago.

Flames leaped from the car on the far side of the haulage truck. She saw a figure running toward the vehicle—a familiar athletic figure.

"My mummy's stuck! Please can you help?" A little girl tugged at Liesel's arm, pulling her in the direction of Engleton's general store, now an open cavity. The haulage truck must have sideswiped the brick structure, taking the entire storefront along with it. Liesel shot a backward glance toward Jack, but thick smoke blocked her view. Her heart leaped to her throat. If she wanted any more proof that he was the wrong man to fall in love with, she had it right here in front of her. *Love?* Her skin began to feel clammy, the buzz of indecision drowning out her thoughts.

The insistent tug of little fingers on her hand brought her round. Her teeth clenched in frustration. This was the nature of their work—hers and Jack's—their individual callings. It wasn't about being a hero; it was about saving lives, and right now lives were at stake. Clarity hit her like a lightning bolt. This was precisely why Jack felt he couldn't have her in his life. Love made you lose focus and lives were lost.

"Where's your mum, sweetheart?"

"In here." The little girl tugged her across a pile of bricks and a cascade of tinned food that must've been on display at the front of the store.

A man staggered over the pile of debris, heading toward the street, holding an arm close to his chest. From the limp manner in which it hung, there was little doubt it had been broken. At least the bone hadn't pierced through the skin. Infection was often a compound fracture's worst enemy. She turned toward him to offer help.

"Over here." She felt the sharp tug on her hand again.

Right away Liesel saw the girl's mother prostrate, face down on the floor, lower limbs trapped under a tall grocery shelving unit. She immediately dropped to the floor.

Liesel's fingers instinctively located the woman's pulse along the side of her throat. Thready. The woman was lucky she and her daughter hadn't been directly under the shelving. They could've been killed in an instant. Even so, it wasn't looking good.

"I can't feel anything." The woman's voice was hardly a whisper.

"Don't move your head, it's very important." She lowered her own head to be as close to the floor as possible.

"My name is Liesel. I'm a nurse. We're going to get you out of here, all right?" As she said the words she felt her strength grow. She was a nurse and she knew how to help. This was what she'd been trained for. She was prepared for this.

"What's your name?"

"Marilyn."

"Marilyn, that's a beautiful name." Liesel took in the pool of blood forming around the woman's head. Could be a head injury or, more likely, a broken nose. She threw a quick look over her shoulder toward the woman's daughter. She shouldn't see this. "Darling, do you mind doing me a favor?" The little girl nodded, desperate to be of some use. Liesel's eyes tore across the front of the store. Astonishingly, the structure of the building seemed sound. "Do you see that fire extinguisher there? I need you to find an adult outside to help carry it to the fireman, all right?"

"Which one?"

Jack. He needs it.

"There's only one out there now, darling, all right?"

My Jack. "You're a clever girl. Can you do that for me?" Liesel knew it was heavy—too heavy for a little girl. If she couldn't find anyone to help, she'd have to drag it.

Liesel tilted her head up to listen for the telltale whine of sirens. Someone surely would have responded by now. They had to know at the station, if the call had gone out on regular radio, right?

Then again, the local CFS was made up of volunteers, except for Jack and he was already here. Her heart twisted with a need to ensure he was all right. She clenched her eyes shut.

Focus, Liesel.

"Marilyn, I'm going to try to shift these shelves, all right?"

"I can't feel anything—I can't move."

"As little movement as possible is a good thing right now." Liesel prayed her words wouldn't have any lasting impact. Worst-case scenario? The woman could end up a paraplegic. Best case? Some nasty bruising.

If she'd had time to cross all her fingers, she would have, but right now she needed to relieve the pressure off Marilyn's spine.

Liesel scanned the shop to see if there was anyone left in the building who could help. Deserted. The man with the broken arm must have been the last one out of the store. The unit wasn't massively heavy, but she was petite and it would take some effort. The longer the shelves pressed into Marilyn's body, the more profound her injury could be. One false move...

She grounded her feet as best she could at the corner of the unit. Her hands gripped the sides of the shelves, stomach muscles tightened, and with a big inhalation of breath she began to lift.

* * *

Jack barely took the time to register the figure of the young boy at the side of the road. He knew the lad wouldn't leave with his mother trapped in the car. He wouldn't have, either. The side of the car had been struck by the swing of the second haulage trailer, landing the vehicle perilously close to the milk bar's oil storage tank. The door wouldn't budge and neither would her ankle. Flames soared from the bonnet of the car to the wooden veranda.

The look of terror on the woman's face tore at him.

He either had to get that fire extinguished or get her out—but he didn't have his tools. Half of the town was out at work. His crew hadn't arrived yet. She wasn't going anywhere.

"In the back." The words came out as a ragged half scream.

"Where?" Through the fear, Jack could see she was telling him something. Emergency kit. Many people carried aerosol-style fire extinguishers these days. That had to be what she was telling him.

He bolted to the back of the car, thankfully unharmed by the crash, and popped the rear door open. A small puppy lay cowering in the corner on top of a couple of wool blankets. The family pet. The poor woman's car was on fire and she was worried about their family pet. The selflessness of the move doubled his drive.

The vehicle was lodged in the veranda of the local milk bar and already the beams along the tin veranda roof were aflame.

Jack swiftly lifted the dog in his arms, turning to bring him to the little boy. His eyes widened in amazement at the sight of the boy helping a young girl of around seven years old drag a huge fire extinguisher across the road toward him.

"Good work, guys." He handed over the puppy, simultaneously signaling for them to run back to the far side of the road. He spread the blankets for the boy's mother, helping her to cover herself before he lifted up the fire extinguisher. If the flames got much hotter, the blankets would protect her somewhat. From there, he went into autopilot to extinguish the flames coming from the car bonnet. He needed to sever the connection between them and the burning storefront.

A lone teenage employee came hurtling through the front door with two jugs of water.

"No! Get out of there, mate. Don't throw that water!"

Water and oil didn't mix. Ever. There was no guarantee the flames crackling up along the veranda beams hadn't caught their fair share of oil from one of the vehicles caught up in the incident. His eyes snapped to the pin on the fire extinguisher, with a built-in triple check it was the right type. Dry powder was best. Everything slipped into slow motion. The teenager moved across the patio toward the flames. Jack tore to the front of the vehicle, slamming the gearshift into Neutral, willing himself to have the strength to move the car. There was no time to get the woman out.

"Cover your face with the blanket!"

The woman in the car looked terrified as he pressed onto the frame of the burning car with his back and shoulder and began to push. This was mind over matter. He had to move the car away from the storefront. He didn't care what it took, but he was damned if he was going to let another little boy lose his mother to a stupid fire. Not on his watch.

He saw it first. Then heard it.

The teenager had ignored him and had thrown the jugs of water onto the flames.

Liesel collapsed on top of the shelving as the unit fell away from the woman with a crash. The force of what must have been an explosion outside the store had sent her flying. Or was it adrenaline? Or both?

Jack was out there.

She scrabbled to her feet, fighting the urge to run out onto the street. She needed to make sure Marilyn was stabilized.

Where was Marilyn's daughter? Liesel's gut clenched, knowing she had been the one to send the child out into the street—the scene of an accident. She'd thought getting her out of the building had been a good thing.

Where was Jack?

A swell of nausea turned her stomach.

She heard voices shouting. It was impossible to distinguish one from another. A small girl appeared in the doorway. Marilyn's daughter.

She looked shocked, but she was alive. Liesel heaved a sigh a relief. Thank God.

The wail of sirens filled the air as Marilyn's daughter ran toward her. Liesel held her in a tight embrace. The noises outdoors became more distinguishable. The guys were here. The CFS. Whatever had happened in that explosion could be dealt with now. If anything had happened to Jack...

No. It was one night only. Nothing more. They were just friends now. But you could still love a friend, right? Just not be in love *with them.*

"Marilyn, can you hear the sirens?" She released the

woman's daughter from their hug and knelt down on the floor. "Marilyn?"

No response.

Liesel moved her hand to the woman's lips. A soft breath tickled her fingers. She was breathing. Okay. Good. "What's your name, hun?"

"Kirsty."

"Okay, Kirsty. I need your help again. Could you please hunt down some frozen peas for me? As many as possible."

Help was coming. But she needed to tend to Marilyn up until she was officially handed over to the emergency services. Each moment that passed meant more swelling around the damaged areas of her spinal cord. There was no chance she could conduct therapeutic hypothermia properly but a few tactically placed bags of peas would help. As soon as a crew arrived she would see if they had any methylprednisolone. The steroids could help reduce inflammation.

Her eyes shot to the open front of the shop. Where were the guys? Her view was blocked by one of the haulage truck trailers. The sirens had stopped and a steady hum of activity had replaced the eerie silence after the explosion.

Would anyone know they were in there? Or was what was happening outside so big they didn't have any spare resources? She couldn't believe how alone she felt. Not knowing… It was just like that day on the mountain.

Tough. She had to pull it together for Marilyn.

Liesel scanned the standing shelves of the shop for anything to help. Diapers. Not ideal, but it was an emergency. She grabbed a few packets of diapers using them as soft braces to keep Marilyn's neck in place. They weren't heavy enough. She needed something to weight them down.

"Is this enough?"

Kirsty's arms were stacked to her chin with frozen peas. Perfect. She could place them along Marilyn's spine—but she'd have to be incredibly careful. If the cold made her shift at all...

Don't panic, Liesel, you can do this.

"What do you need?"

The voice rolled through her like a longed-for drink of water. Her instinct was to run and jump into Jack's arms and smother him with kisses. His face was a smear of soot and blood, a small clot knotting up at his hairline—but he was alive! Her heart soared with relief. Jack was alive!

One night only. It was your choice.

There was work to do. This was what she had to do now. Pour her passion into her work. It was the only way. Her focus sharpened.

"We need a backboard. Possibly two."

Jack sent a questioning look. God, she loved those blue eyes of his. *Keep your eye on the ball, Liesel, not on the hot fireman you thought you might have lost.* The hot fireman who tugged at her every heartstring.

"We're going to have to roll her and I can't do it on my own. She's presenting possible neck or spine injuries."

"I'll get one of the lads to bring you a backboard and lend a hand."

As swiftly as he'd appeared, Jack vanished around the corner, still managing to leave in his wake that incredible sensation of confidence and strength he always seemed to infuse in her. He was a man who could handle a crisis. And he clearly trusted her to the same level. Professionally. And that was the only bond they would share from now on. Work. It'd take a while, but she could suck it up. Eventually.

Jack was so engrossed in supervising Mr. Jones's release from his truck that he jumped at the light touch on his arm.

"Sorry! I didn't mean to freak you out."

Liesel. A sight for sore eyes. "No worries. Looks like I've got a case of the jitters, eh?"

"A big strapping fireman like you? Unlikely!" Her eyes teased but he could see the concern creasing her brow. His fingers itched to smooth away the worry, kiss away the fear. But he needed to make sure Mr. Jones was all right first. The poor man had been knocked out by the impact of his air bag hitting him, but miraculously he hadn't received any leg injuries. From the look of the front of his truck, Jack would have sworn some sort of higher power must have been on watch. It had been demolished. The EMTs would take him to hospital for a once-over just in case. Sometimes a frontal blow from an air bag could cause a broken rib or, in some rare cases, a heart attack. The hospital would definitely need to run a few tests before sending him home.

"The EMTs have it covered. It's your turn now, pal. Move it!" Liesel crooked a finger at him, making the come-here-now gesture look more sexy than he was sure she'd intended.

Jack followed, presuming she was heading toward the flashing ambulance lights just visible beyond the haulage truck. If he had a right to stop her from turning the corner he would. His gut clenched as she came to an abrupt halt, his eyes soberly following hers. The milk bar was a cinder shell, three of his guys still at work tamping out the smoldering remains. The half-burnt-out body of the estate car in front of it lay abandoned like a sun-dried carcass left for the scavengers.

"Were there—"

Her fingers flew to her throat as if the words were lodged there.

"No. No, there weren't. By the skin of our teeth there weren't."

He ground out the words, unwilling to tell her how close it had been. Death. He wasn't ready to hear the words spelling out the plain truth. She had been right to have backed off from him. Today had been dangerous. Too dangerous.

An understaffed station was to blame for all this. He could have easily been killed, along with several others. And now Liesel was staring at the proof that her worst nightmares could, in fact, have come true. Today.

"What happened?"

"The kid who worked at the milk bar tried to lend a hand—he threw water onto the fire coming from the car. The water reacted with some oil in the flames and, I know it's hard to believe, looking at this mess, we were actually incredibly lucky—" he scrubbed a sooty hand along his chin as Liesel stared at him dumbly in disbelief "—instead of igniting the burning vehicle, the flames were sucked into a fireball under the tin roof of the veranda. The milk-bar kid suffered his fair share of scrapes and bruises but is otherwise injury-free. Unbelievably lucky for such an incredibly foolish move."

He knew he sounded harsh and tried to soften his words. "He should have been educated. If we had more than one donor angel, we could afford to hire someone else. A part-timer, maybe, who could have come round town and taught everyone and made sure the proper extinguishers were in place."

"Donor angel?"

"Someone's sent in a couple of checks over the past year. Big ones. It's been incredibly helpful, but the station was in very bad shape when I inherited it. Maybe if I hadn't spent the last chunk on re-kitting out the truck…"

Liesel ached to see him in so much pain. It wasn't right that he accept all the responsibility for what had happened here. One man couldn't predict every accident that was going to happen in what was an expansive rural area. It just wasn't possible.

Jack turned to face her, his large hands taking hold of her shoulders. His eyes seemed to be searching for some sort of evidence that he couldn't have done more. "You were right to worry, Liesel. I shouldn't have ever have asked you to wait for me. At the rate I'm going, it could take years for us to get the sort of support we need."

"Jack, I—"

"Shh…don't worry, darlin'. This is on me. It's too much to ask, taking on all this." He nodded toward the smoldering high street then gave her shoulders a quick squeeze before releasing them. "Still friends?"

"Of course." The words came out as a whisper, followed by a silent *always* as he turned away from her.

Jack knew he was letting emotion cloud his logic. If only he could give up his professional calling, make friends with his father and go back to a nice, safe life at the winery. Then he'd be able to give Liesel the fairy-tale ending she deserved.

If. There were so many ifs. He raked a hand through his hair, a masculine stab at keeping emotion at bay. No good. It was still charging through him like a herd of wild elephants.

"Jack, if you ask me, I can't believe you did so much *good* work today. On your own, no less."

Liesel's voice broke through his rampaging thoughts.

"You think this is good?" He swept a hand along the small high street. It looked like a film set in a disaster movie. After the disaster.

Liesel took a step back, shocked at the harsh tone of his voice. This wasn't the Jack she knew. Today couldn't have changed him that much, could it? "I think the good really outweighs the bad here. Surely you can see that? There were no fatalities, right?"

He shook away her comment with a brusque wave of his hand. "Can you imagine what would've happened here if we weren't around? If the station didn't exist anymore? Today would've been a one hundred percent disaster. Can't you see that?"

Liesel felt herself suck in a deep breath. She wasn't going to use Eric as a cheap playing card to get ahead in this conversation—but Jack was alive, and so were all of the other casualties here. They were *alive*! There was no way she was going to let him call this situation a failure.

"I think I'm in a *very* good place to know when good outweighs bad." She put a hand on his arm, wishing she could stroke his face, wipe away some of the soot, hold him in her arms. "Jack, remember, I know more than most how bad a situation can get, and I for one am amazed and pleased with today's outcome."

"A mother almost died today, Liesel. Because of a

careless mistake. I almost got her killed because I took my eye off the ball for just a few seconds!"

The grief in his eyes went deeper than what was happening today. Much deeper.

"Jack, what are you *really* talking about?"

"I'm talking about my mum…" He raked a hand through his soot-laced hair. "I swore I wouldn't let this happen again."

"But you didn't! You saved her, you numpty!" The words may have been teasing, but Liesel's heart was in her throat. How awful for him. She wanted to hold him, soothe away the grief that was so clearly eating away at him, but saw he was too charged to be held, comforted.

"I didn't really lay any of your fears to rest, did I?"

"Not particularly." Her lips set and she shook her head sharply. "But let me tell you this right now—if I hadn't been so worried about you, I wouldn't have come out and helped the people I did. You've helped, Jack! Many people. That woman in the store could be paralyzed for life if I hadn't helped her—in the same way the woman in the car might not be hugging her son right now if it hadn't been for you."

Jack glanced over at the mother and son then looked back into Liesel's clear eyes, sparking with intention. "You were worried about me?"

"Of course I was! Can't you see I'm nuts about you and the whole reason your job makes me crazy is because I can't face the idea of losing you?"

"Come here, you." Jack pulled her in close to him, soot, filth and all, so she wouldn't see the tears in his eyes. Liesel was nuts about him! He hadn't wanted to admit it, but he'd been blindsided when she'd announced she just wanted to be friends after their very X-rated night together. And now she was saying their struggle to be friends hadn't been because of an absence of feeling but because of so *much* feeling.

Jack pulled his fingers through Liesel's hair and held her tight to his chest. He ached to kiss her. Tip that little chin of hers up and taste that strawberry-red mouth again and again. If she was nuts about him, he was positively cuckoo about her. Full steam ahead sparko. He was going to have to get some order in his life. Put things into a better place so he could make sure she had the life— and love—she deserved. Today was proof you couldn't change the past. But he did have something to say about the future.

First step, John Granville Keller. Mending fences with his father was a tall order, but essential to becoming the man he wanted to be for this woman he held in his arms. If healing old wounds couldn't be done, then Liesel was better off facing the future without him.

Liesel clapped her hands with a big laugh when Marilyn wiggled a toe on departure. The ambulance crew had the young mum safely strapped to a hard board, and if the toe wiggle was anything to go by, then any trauma she'd received on her spine might not be permanent. She crossed her fingers behind her back and gave a wink up into the heavens for good measure.

She reached out a hand to run down Jack's shoulder and just as quickly as he'd been so present with her, he was gone again. A few meters up the road, she could see his eyes trained on the burnt-out scene in front of them. It stung, but she knew it wasn't personal. At least she understood him now, knew his whole story. The CFS was Jack's life, whether or not he had a lovelorn school nurse on the scene.

And, sadly, he was right. Without the local station, the accident could have left far more destruction in its wake. Other emergency services were a good hour away. She chanced a look at his profile. He was an incredible man. Strong, passionate, committed. His drive to help was catching. He'd definitely reignited the flames of community service within her. But what would be enough for him to lay his own demons to rest? She knew talking it out over a bottle of wine was not really a "guy" thing but maybe someday…when the chances of them ending up naked in bed again weren't quite so high. A quick shake of the head was required to get that little picture out of her head before she approached him.

"Why don't I make us dinner tonight?" If he wanted to talk, she'd obviously listen, but something told her it might take a while. At the very least, he could chill out and let her be there for him.

He turned, slowly running a thumb along her jawline, as if tracing it gave him strength. "No, darlin', not tonight." He bent down and planted a soft kiss on her lips. A kiss so gentle she could've sworn she could float. A kiss so perfect it soared well out of "just friends" territory. Just as the whole world around her began to disappear he pulled back, nodding at the devastation of the high street. "I'm afraid I've got something else I have to do."

CHAPTER TEN

"HELLO, SON."

"Hey, Dad."

Scintillating start to a life-changing moment.

Jack covered his eyes, squinting against the late-afternoon sun to look up at his father, stationed at his usual post on the veranda. Rocking chair? Check. Steaming cup of coffee by his side? Check.

"What did I do to deserve the pleasure of Fire Brigade Captain Jack Keller all the way out here at our humble vineyards? Come to check our extinguishers?"

And we're off! Thanks for rubbing salt into the wound.

"C'mon, Dad, I was hoping we could have a talk."

His father's tone remained defensive. "Forgive me for being surprised, son. It's not like we've seen an awful lot of you since you've been back in the Valley."

"Fair enough." And it was.

Either-or. That was how he did things. And now the tactic was isolating him from everyone he cared about. If he didn't get his life in order he'd never be in a place where he could have—well, it all. Friends, family, loved ones…Liesel. Accident cleanup had kiboshed his plans to see his father straightaway and it was probably just as well. It had given him clarity. Perspective. And not just about his father—about Liesel, as well. In the days following the crash, it had become as clear as day to him that life with her as a friend was— It just wasn't good enough. He now understood firsthand how frightening it was to think of losing someone you loved in a dangerous situation.

He shook his head as he clumped up the steps and joined his father on the veranda. No wonder his father hated his life in the CFS—he was terrified of losing his son.

"This chair all right?" Jack pointed to the Adirondack-style chair next to his father.

"Suits me fine."

They were perfectly situated to look out on the sprawl of vines and outbuildings sloping down to the river's edge. It was beautiful. It was home. He wanted Liesel to see all this, love it as much as he did. He could sit here all day if...

"Well? Cat got your tongue? I need to get over to the shed and service the harvesters."

Jack took a sidelong look at his father. He wasn't really the mean old curmudgeon he was playing to Jack now. He was a good man. A traditional man who wanted the very best for his family, and he'd been dealt a raw deal.

It had been a long time ago, some twenty years now, when Jack's mother had died in the fire. She had been the love of his father's life. He'd never once hinted at remarrying. She had been his father's one and only and she was gone. Until now, Jack had felt he'd been on a quest to make up for it. And failing. Now he realized that by trying to make up for it he'd been making things worse. Only problem was, it had turned out his professional passion really was in the CFS. The trick was to find a balance.

He took a deep breath and lifted his chin in his father's direction.

"How's everything going with River's Bend?"

Not neutral territory, but it was a place to start.

"Your sister's keeping everything in order. Could do with a second pair of hands, though."

A compliment for Becca. That was a change. An insult for him. The usual.

"Dad, I want to talk to you about something. About the CFS."

"What about it?" His father's mouth thinned and his gaze stayed fixed on the horizon.

"I think I have a pretty good idea now why you're so dead set against me being in it."

"Oh, you think you've got it all figured out, do you?"

"No, but I've got a pretty good guess. I've done some soul-searching lately and I have a feeling my joining the CFS was about the cruelest thing I could have done to you after losing Mum."

He watched as his father registered what he was saying.

The scowl on his father's face deepened then relaxed a hair.

"Dad, listen to me." He pulled his chair around so that he faced his father. When he felt he had his father's reluctant attention he continued, "We've got to lay this to rest. I know you think I'm full of extremes and that my world is black and white, but since Mum died…" He took a ragged inhalation and continued, "Since I ran round the barn that day, I swore I would dedicate my life to making it right. Turning inaction into action. And after years of hard work and training, it turns out I'm not just good at it but I love it. It's work I was born to."

"So what is it you want me to say? That I support you? I think you'll find I have been supporting you."

"By making me choose between the farm and the CFS?"

The scowl returned. "Am I meant to congratulate you for choosing a life in the CFS over the generations of hard work and development that went into creating all of this?" His broad hand indicated the hectares of old vines bursting with fruit. "All of this—" he punched each of the words out as if they were weapons "—ready and waiting for you on a silver platter."

His father stared at him glassy-eyed. Jack couldn't tell which way the conversation would go.

"I just want you to be safe, son!"

Jack reached across and took what was now an old man's hand in his and gave it a firm squeeze. God, he'd been an idiot. An idiot not to see a father's desire to keep what remained of his family safe and secure after such a horrible accident. It was the same thing Liesel had said. "What we need to figure out now is how you're going to forgive me. *If* you're going to forgive me."

Granville's eyes snapped to attention.

"Is that what you think? That I despise you?"

"It's been a little difficult to believe otherwise, Dad. The last thing I've felt here is welcome."

"Of course you're welcome. This is your inheritance! I wanted you and your sister to be able to raise your families here, just as your mother and I did, until…"

Jack flinched. At the rate he was going he would never have a family. He'd been sure he could have had a ready-made one with Liesel. One they could add to and make bigger and more rambunctious than the trio they could be now. If she would have him. He wasn't so sure he deserved her faith—her love.

He watched as his father's hand ran along the horizon. "Son, this is your history! My history and your grandfather's! And you just want to throw it all away on sorting out other people's problems. Putting out other fires that will never ever bring your mother back. Can't you see I didn't want that for you? A life reliving the horror of her death each and every single day? I wanted you to focus on the winery so you could let go of the past, have the future I'd built for you!"

"I would love to be part of the winery's future, Dad—but I can't give up the fire service."

"Well, it doesn't take a brainiac to figure that out." His father sat back in his chair.

Jack shot him an inquisitive look.

"Don't think I haven't heard about all your heroics on the radio. That's why I've sent those checks over to the CFS."

"What?"

"You don't think I'd just let my only son come back to rescue a two-bit fire station and not get some support from his old man?"

Now it was Jack's turn to swallow a heavy wave of emotion.

"That was you?"

"'Course it was! Who else do you think wants that place as well equipped as it can be? I'm not having you run round in a half-clapped-out tin pot! If my son's going to run a fire station, he's going to run a proper one. You're a Keller. We don't do things half-baked."

His father loved him. Had been there for him. Jack pulled his father out of his chair and hugged him. Tight.

"I don't know what to say, Dad. I really don't—other than thank you."

He felt the hug being returned. "Well, why don't you make your face a bit more of a familiar commodity out here in return?"

He was welcome at River's Bend. Could things really change in an instant? A life, a future here at the station was something he hadn't let himself consider. Jack's mind flooded with a wash of possibility. There was so much to consider he fell into a stunned silence.

His father gently pushed him out of the hug. "Why don't you go on in the kitchen and get something cold to drink, son? You look a bit parched. Clearing up that mess in town must be tough work."

"How d'you know?"

Granville pushed himself up out of his rocker and nodded his head in the direction of a radio sitting on the window ledge. Of course. What Granville Keller didn't know about Engleton wasn't worth knowing.

"Have a nosy in the fridge, too. After you get something to eat, maybe you can give me a hand with one of the harvesters. I've got to replace some old valves."

"That'd be great, Dad. I'd like that."

"So, you think they'd go for it?"

"We'll do everything we can!" The chirpy Murray Valley hospital rep gave Liesel a hug right there in the middle of the busy ED. "We need the Engleton CFS as much as you need us. We'd be delighted to help.

"That's great. I'll just jot down all of the details for you and we'll see you on Saturday night, then."

"Running a CFS recruitment stand doesn't sound like

the most fun way to enjoy the Harvest Festival. Are you sure you're going to be able to do it all on your own?"

Liesel waved away the rep's concerned expression. "Don't worry, I've got a couple of spare pairs of hands in town to help and it's not as if I won't benefit from more people on the crew." *And Jack.*

She waved goodbye to the rep, scooped Liam up onto her hip and took a last look at the buzzing ED. Yup! It still gave her a buzz. Truth of the matter was, since the Great Grape Spill, as she'd been calling it, she hadn't been able to keep away from the hospital. She'd been popping by for the past week after school to check up on Marilyn, her patient from the crash. A full examination along with some dedicated rehab and she was going to be fine. She'd suffered a lot of bruising but no permanent damage. The same was true of the rest of the victims of the spill. Everyone who had sustained some sort of injury looked as if they'd come away from it largely unscathed.

Joke names aside, there were still a lot of serious issues to be dealt with. The wrecked shop, the burnt-out milk bar. Thank goodness the haulier was from a reputable company and had been fully insured. It might take a while for everything to come out of the wash, but once it did Engleton and her residents would be all right.

Especially if her plan worked.

She took a glance at the wall clock above Reception. Time to get a move on. She'd promised the volunteers down at the station some freshly baked muffins in exchange for keeping the recruitment stand at the Harvest Festival a secret from Jack. Just a few more days and he would know she was well and truly going to be there for him.

She didn't know if grand gestures were his thing—

but it was time to show him she meant to battle her demons head-on. He had been open and honest with her about his life so it was time to lay her cards on the table. She loved Jack and wanted him to be in her and Liam's lives. Better to enjoy life day by day and as fully as possible than to live her life in fear. Fingers crossed, Jack still had room for her in his life.

"What are you doing down here?"

Not quite the greeting she'd been hoping for... He did look happy to see her, those blue eyes of his bright with surprise. It was hard to see him hold himself back from her when all she wanted to do was give him a hug and a kiss. Well, a lot more than that—but they *were* in public.

Liesel held up the plate of warm snickerdoodles in response. "Want one?"

"Love one." Jack took a cookie but kept his gaze fixed on Liesel. "How's the little man?"

"Well! He's well." *Missing you almost as much as I am.* "Busy! I never knew a two-year-old could have such a full social schedule." She laughed to fill the awkward silence. "I suspect you are, too."

"Not half!" Jack swept a hand through his hair. It took all her control not to do a follow-up caress. He looked tired. She hadn't seen him in over a fortnight and if she were a betting woman, she would've laid money on the fact he had been putting in twelve-hour-plus days. Maybe she should just tell him now she wanted to help, wanted to be there for him. Why keep it a secret?

"The high street is a mess. It's going to take a lot of work to get it back together, not to mention we're heading into peak fire season."

"Well, if anyone can make a bad situation good, you can."

"Jack! Mate!" one of the volunteers called out from the station house. Liesel watched as Jack's body went taut with attention. "Someone's just rung in a bushfire over at Cooper's Pass. Ready to saddle up?"

"Liesel...I'm sorry."

"Don't worry. I understand." She did, too. If there was a medical emergency she would've been running by now. Now wasn't the time to tell him he'd helped her find the strength to believe in love again. To believe taking risks—no matter how scary they were—was worth it. "I'll just pop these in the kitchen for when you lot get back. See you at the Harvest Festival?"

"I'd like that."

From the look in his eyes, she could tell he meant it. And that was enough to help her believe she was doing the right thing. At the very least, if Jack decided he only had time and energy for the CFS she would have been honest with him. Played her true hand. And honesty was vital.

"Mate, are you ready?"

"Sorry?" Jack looked up from the telephone receiver at the volunteer leaning into his office.

"It's getting on for seven o'clock. We got to get the rig ready for the festival."

Jack felt his forehead crinkle in confusion. "What are you talking about?"

"The rig, you know..." He watched as the volunteer clapped a hand over his mouth. "Forget I said anything. Uh...wheels up in ten minutes, all right, Captain?"

"Sure thing." Jack shook his head in confusion. The

guys had all been a bit weird around him the past few days. He knew he wasn't a master at reading body language but it was hard to miss the sotto voce conversations, the sidelong glances.

He pushed himself up from his desk and tried to shrug it off. The past forty-eight hours had been a whirlwind and there was no doubt he'd been in his own world for most of it. Ten minutes? Right. Better get a move on.

Liesel could hardly believe her eyes. River's Bend Winery was absolutely beautiful. It was hard to believe she'd lived in Engleton almost a year and hadn't been out to see this place yet—it was amazing. She and Liam stood hand in hand, trying their best not to gape at everything.

A few days after the crash River's Bend Winery had announced its decision to volunteer its tasting rooms as the location for the Harvest Festival, rather than it being held in the main street, where it had originally been scheduled. By the looks of things, the winery had pulled out all the stops. Fairy lights swirled around a parade of gum trees leading up to the property. Bunting was strung along the veranda of the tasting room—an incredibly beautiful structure in its own right. A massive marquee, complete with an expansive dance floor, was floodlit and already thick with revelers.

The lawn had several huge vats with little staircases leading up to them where punters could kick off their shoes and enjoy a bit of their own winemaking. Local artisan cheese, sausage, bread and cured olive makers had set up a long stream of trestle tables and enormous washtubs filled with ice showed off wines from across the valley.

River's Bend management had made it clear one and

all were welcome. So that was why she'd made the telephone call. If they were about community, they were about the CFS.

She gave Liam's hand a little tug. It was time they manned their stand—the Community Fire Service recruitment and baked goods stand. Her oven had been working overtime the past two days as she'd baked up more cookies, cupcakes and other delectables than she had in her entire life at one time. A few of the emergency staff at the hospital had said they'd share the roster with her to help raise money and recruit volunteers for the Engleton station.

It had taken all her powers of secret-keeping in order to not spill the beans to Jack. Being friends was tough, but watching him struggle was harder.

Her heart rate slipped up a notch when she saw him arrive amid a throng of firemen. They may have all been wearing the same uniforms, but no one filled it better than Jack Keller. In the slick black lines of the suit, he embodied the role of Engleton CFS Station's brigade captain. The commanding officers at HQ in Adelaide would've been impressed. She couldn't believe the pride she felt swelling within her. He was an amazing man. A small twist of pain began to tighten within her.

The time they had spent together over the past few months had filled her with such happiness. Her son had grown in confidence—and he wasn't the only one. She was a changed woman. She could feel it in her very core. Elements of the old Liesel had definitely come back— but the woman she was now? Fun, confident, a nurse, a mother. He'd made an impact. A big one.

"Are you the one in charge?"

An elegant gentleman approached her desk. She smoothed the skirt of her green dress and gave him her best smile of welcome.

"Absolutely. There are a variety of jobs down at the station—all volunteer, of course. Would you like to take a look?"

"No need, love. I think I might be a bit past running up and down ladders." He gave a rueful laugh and made a playful show of being a bit rickety. She laughed along with him, although she thought for a silver-haired man he looked pretty vital. And familiar. There was something about the way his eyes—

"The winery would like to make a donation, as well."

"Of course. Do you mean—"

"River's Bend." His eyes ran warmly around the premises. "This is our place and we'd like to put our continued support behind the CFS in the form of a memorial fund. I'm thinking somewhere in the neighborhood of ten thousand dollars. A month. I presume you'll take a check."

"Absolutely!" Liesel couldn't believe it. What an amazing start. She had hoped to have a good list going and at least a few dollars in the pot before Jack came—but this was even better than she could have imagined.

"My son works for the CFS but he's going to invest in his roots again."

"Oh?"

"Yes, he's thinking of moving back here, to the winery, to be with family."

"How lovely! You're a lucky man!"

"You bet I am. He's one in a million, my boy."

The gentleman looked so happy Liesel couldn't help but send him a wide congratulatory smile in response.

She wondered which of the volunteers was his son. This gentleman seemed so familiar.

"Now, where do I sign?" The man lifted his pen in anticipation.

"Just here," Liesel spluttered, pulling the appropriate clipboard across the table toward him. "Just down here." She put her finger to the line where he should write his name. Just as quickly she was withdrawing it as if she'd been burnt by the words formed by the man's pen: John Granville Keller.

He noticed her sharp movement and looked up with a warm smile, eyes twinkling. Bright blue eyes.

"Liesel—"

She knew that voice. And there wasn't a chance in the world she was going to look at the uniformed man who had just approached the CFS stand. Not now. Not with shock turning her smile into a stupid fixed grin. Jack hadn't told her the truth. His whole story. She'd told him everything and despite their promise of friendship he'd still kept her compartmentalized. As if she was a dirty little secret to keep hidden away.

How could she not have seen it? She felt like such an idiot. And humiliated. She'd been so open with her own life, allowing Jack full, unfettered access to herself, her son. She had plans in motion to change her *life* for this man and he couldn't even tell her his father lived down the road? And that he was going to give up his all-important CFS? The very same CFS he had wanted to put her on hold for?

Blood was thicker than…than whatever feelings she'd thought Jack had for her. She could feel her face burn with indignation.

Was she so off Jack's true radar that he had to keep

her secret from his past? Apparently so. She forced herself to look up. She could do this. She could.

And there they were. Side by side. Father and son.

If Jack could have prevented her confusion, her pain, he would have. Correction. He could have, but he hadn't. So Jack did the next best thing he could think of...backpedal. Like crazy. "I see you've met my father."

"Yes, we've just met." Liesel had put on her best bubbly party voice but her eyes told another story. "He's going to make a very generous donation to the CFS. In the name of..."

She let the sentence hang for Mr. Keller to fill in.

"In the name of Ava Keller. It'll be an annual donation." He turned and clapped an arm along his son's shoulders. "Better than ad hoc. Your mother would've wanted it that way."

Jack rocked back on his heels. He knew he and his father had set the wheels of repairing old wounds in motion—but this was one heck of a gesture. He was truly touched. "Thanks, Dad." He pulled him into a strong hug. "I mean it."

"Well," Liesel began briskly, "it looks like you two have some catching up to do."

"Actually..." Jack broke in quickly. He had to stop any conjecturing Liesel might be doing right now. He could practically see the wheels whirling in her head. "We *all* have a lot of catching up to do." Jack reached out a hand, indicating he wanted her to join them.

Liesel tossed a quick look over her shoulder. Liam was happily playing away with a group of supervised toddlers. He looked happy, content. He was the one "man" she could rely on these days. Which was just as well, as it looked as if it would be just the two of them from now on. She just needed to get this over with, this whole horribly planned night, and then go about the near impossible task of putting Jack Keller out of her mind.

Liesel stiffened as Jack reached across and took her hand in his. His long fingers slipped through hers, instantly infusing her with that incredible feeling of warm protection she'd felt the very first time she'd met him. How could someone who made her feel so safe be such a master of deceit?

Relief flooded through her that she hadn't turned in her own CFS form yet. Maybe it wasn't too late to talk to the hospital about working there. Living closer would be a good idea, as well. Farther away from Jack.

Why had he kept all of this secret from her? Made a life decision to move on—away from everything she had thought he wanted to do? Had the whole CFS-is-my-life thing been a lie? Was it because she was a single mother? Or was he ashamed of her? As an heir to one of the region's most successful wineries, he could no doubt have chosen from a huge pool of adoring women.

She felt her mouth form into one of those crazy upside-down smiles. The good news was that if he was leaving the CFS to work at the winery, she wouldn't have to see him at the station when she encountered the team. He wasn't going to take away her newfound confidence on the nursing front. Not a chance. She felt the lines of her mouth grow firm with resolve.

See? There's a plus side to everything!

As she stomped reluctantly behind him, trying her best not to stare at that backside of his, she afforded herself a small snigger, grateful that Jack at least had the courtesy to bring her and his father to a quiet part of the sprawling lawn. Her humiliation wouldn't be completely public. Not to mention the fact that stomping in high heels was bloody difficult. She shot a glance back toward the toddler playgroup at the sound of Liam's laughter. She could still see his little blond head happily at play. She'd been that happy just a handful of minutes ago.

Ignorance had been bliss.

"Just thought you'd like to keep an eye on the little guy."

Good old Jack! Thinking of everything again. Too bad I'm trying my best to squelch any feelings I have for you!

"Dad. Liesel." His eyes played between the two of them as if he was expecting them to start a sparring match. Or possibly use him as a punching bag. "You're the two most important people in my life and I think… I know I owe both of you an explanation."

Liesel and Granville opened their mouths simultaneously to concur then muttered that the other should go ahead, their voices melding into a verbal jumble. They laughed nervously, turning to Jack in a joint appeal as if speech was no longer one of their skills.

Jack couldn't help but throw his head back and laugh. This was all a first-class disaster.

"Son, I don't really see what's going on here."

"Jack. You don't have to do this. I understand everything now and I'll just get going."

"No! That's just it." Jack raised his hands in a hold-it-for-a-minute pose before continuing. "Neither of you have the full picture…and the truth is I don't think I did until now."

Liesel looked at him uncomprehendingly. What was he going on about?

Jack turned to his father. "Dad, I love you and I would

love to be part of life here at River's Bend again one day, but there are two pretty big conditions I have."

His father raised his forehead appraisingly and tipped his head, indicating Jack should go ahead and name them.

"One, Becca continues to run the winery and you use me as an ad hoc odd-job man. I will stay full-time with the CFS and continue to try and make it the best station in the region. From the looks of things—" he dropped a wink at Liesel "—there appear to be some new volunteers I hadn't counted on." He raised a hand as Liesel made a move to interject.

"In the meantime, I would love to help with the harvest and any other busy spells when Becca might need me. I promise you she won't be left alone. But I won't abandon the CFS. Do we have a deal?"

His father pushed his lips out, tentatively started to nod and then reconsidered. "I think I need to hear the other condition first."

Liesel cocked her head to the side. This was going to be interesting.

"Actually, Dad, I might need a bit of privacy for this one. Can you give us a minute?"

His father gave him a knowing nod and that all-too-familiar wink. "All right, son. I'll go get us a glass of something sparkling, shall I?"

"That'd be perfect." Jack waited a moment as his father worked his way back toward the booths before he turned to Liesel.

The wheels in her mind were spinning like mad to catch up with all this new information. How could Jack have kept all this from her? He had a whole family just sitting and waiting for him right here in River's Bend! A family he'd chosen to keep at arm's length until he sorted things out. Just as he'd done to her. Well, that just wasn't good enough. That wasn't love. That was… All thoughts disappeared as Jack turned the full force of his bright blue eyes directly onto her, clasping both of her hands in his, and began to speak. "What's more important to me, Liesel, more than the CFS, the winery—all of it—is you."

She drew in a swift breath. *What? Was this for real?*

"If my job has taught me anything, it's that life is so very precious and that you need to make the very most of it. I love you. I love you and I don't want to spend another day in my life without you. Liesel Adler, will you do me the honor of becoming my wife?"

Liesel's blood ran hot and cold.

"Is life so precious, then, that you keep your family hidden away from me? Or was it the other way round? You didn't want them to know about me?"

"No, that's not it at all," Jack protested, but she could see she'd hit a nerve.

"What about Liam?"

Jack laughed and squeezed her hands. "Well, I don't want to *marry* him, but I'd sure love it if you'd allow me to be the best father figure to him I can be—and maybe give him some brothers and sisters along the way."

"I don't know, Jack." Liesel tried to tug her hands free, her mind buzzing with too many thoughts. "This is a lot to take in. If you keep people you claim to love at a distance until you've got all your professional ducks in a row, then how can I know you'll be there for me, for my son, when we need you?" Liesel's eyes stung with the tears she'd been trying to keep at bay. The smile on Jack's face faded, his fingers keeping a firm grip on hers.

"I love you, Liesel. With everything in my heart. What would make you think I didn't?"

"Keeping your whole life a secret, for starters!"

"Not half!" Granville burst in, hands juggling three glasses of sparkling wine, the broad smile on his face betraying the stern words he was trying to impart. "How could you have kept this beautiful woman a secret from us for so long?"

"If she'll answer my question, we'll have the rest of our lives to explain."

Jack turned expectantly to Liesel, his eyes bright with anticipation. He loved her. He *loved* her. There was nothing to fight here—only a lifetime of happiness with the man she loved to gain.

Or more secrets to unravel. More time to wait until Jack decided he was truly ready to take part in a real family life. She couldn't live that way. All these conditions he kept putting on things! It shouldn't be like that. Love didn't work like that! It was big and powerful and overwhelming and exactly what she felt for Jack, but if he needed to live his life by a set of rules only he had access to—it just wasn't good enough.

"I'm sorry, Jack. I love you, too. You know I do, but I think in our case it's just not enough."

"What do you mean? I know I was late off the mark in telling you about my family but surely that's not a deal breaker?"

"You know my history, Jack, and you knew I didn't want any more mysteries. No more waiting, wondering. I just can't do this." She swiftly pulled her hands from his and ran as fast as she could across the lawn, stopping only to pull off her ridiculous heels so she could run faster. Chest heaving, she picked up Liam from the playgroup and wound her way through the buildup of cars to her own. She could hear Jack calling her name.

She needed to get out of there. Now.

Fumbling for her keys, she could hear Jack's voice getting closer.

Alone. She just wanted to be left alone. She and Liam had been doing perfectly fine before Jack Keller had come into their lives. The last thing she'd needed was to be railroaded this way or that by someone who, it had turned out, she barely knew. She quickly opened the side door and buckled Liam into his seat.

"Liesel, wait!" She could see Jack appearing from behind a truck and slammed the driver's door shut as if it would help stop the entire situation from happening. How could he have expected her to accept a marriage proposal from a man who only wanted her in one part of his life? The sidelines! Was he mad? Or was she crazy to have become involved with him in the first place?

"Liesel!" He was right by her window. Those dear eyes she adored were so close, silently pleading with her.

"I'm sorry, Jack." And she was.

Liesel put her foot on the gas pedal and pulled away from the manicured lawns, the beautifully decorated acreage, all of which could have been hers to enjoy if she'd just said one little word. She looked in the rearview mirror and saw Jack's silhouette against the fairy-lighted trees. Her gaze slipped down to her son, whose eyes were wide with bewilderment. She shifted the car up a gear and drove away.

"Have you gone completely stark-raving mad?"

Cassie stopped her from throwing yet another perfectly gorgeous floral bouquet into the rubbish bin.

"Hardly. I've got a son to look after and there is no chance I'm going to marry a liar."

"He's not a liar, Liesel. He's sorting out some issues."

"By keeping things secret from me. By partitioning me off. Hardly the foundation for a loving relationship." She handed the bouquet to her friend with a firmly set smile. "Here. You take it. I have to finish packing."

"You've got three weeks to pack and you still haven't found a new place yet."

"Common sense is not going to prevail right now, Cassie! I'm…" Liesel felt her voice about to break and she didn't want to give in to tears. Again. Her heart was absolutely broken and the only thing she had to rely on now was her own strength of character. That and the promise of a new job at the hospital come summertime. She had given notice at the school and just needed to set about finding somewhere for her and Liam to move into before her parents let out the house for the summer.

"Have you told your parents?"

"No."

"And that's different from what Jack did to you on what level?"

She turned to her friend, tears firmly swallowed. "It's incredibly different. He lied to me about his background, his present, his future, and then thought he could just drag Liam and me along whichever way his current mood took him. One minute he wants me in his life, the next he doesn't. Flip-flop! It's not acceptable. Not for me and definitely not for my son."

"Even if that future involves living on several hundred hectares of Murray Valley's finest winery with a blond hunk?"

"I fell in love with a plain old fireman."

"Ha! As if. And I seem to remember someone who was pretty dead set against falling in love with a man in a hazardous profession."

"People change."

"Exactly."

Cassie pulled her into a tight hug, flowers still in hand. The perfume of the wildflower bouquet filled Liesel with scented memories of being with Jack. Now she'd have to start hating flowers to boot. Terrific.

"Liesel, I know you're angry with him but you're obviously still in love with him."

Liesel stiffened. *So? Was that against the rules?*

"No one goes to this much effort to avoid someone they're indifferent to. I'm not asking you to forgive him this minute. I'm just saying maybe you owe him a second chance. A chance to explain himself. That's all he's asking for."

Liesel eased herself out of the hug and opened the back door of the house for her friend. She needed more alone time. "I don't know, Cass. Jack has done a pretty good job of burning his bridges."

"Just don't do anything you'll regret. Never is a long time to stay away from someone you love."

Liesel closed the door with a halfhearted wave and let herself slide to the floor. She propped her elbows on her knees and held up the card she'd managed to steal from the bouquet before Cassie left.

Poppies are red, cornflowers are blue, chocolate milk shakes mean nothing when I'm not with you.
I love you,
Jack

She tried to squelch the smile slipping to her lips and scrunched her fingers along her temple. Cassie would make a brilliant agony aunt. Of course she was still in love with Jack. Days were better knowing he'd be part of them. As things stood, days weren't very good right now.

Yes, she'd picked up the phone a dozen times and then hung up just as many after each bouquet had arrived. But she had her son to think about. He needed someone reliable in his life. Besides, she'd set the wheels in motion to move on. And that's what she was going to try and do. It wasn't running away—it was progress. At least that's what she'd keep telling herself. Maybe one day she'd actually believe it.

"She'll love it."

"You sure?" Jack grinned at his sister, a woman blessed with brains and good taste.

"Positive." She fiddled with his uniform collar for a minute then leaned back and returned the grin. "Who could resist my handsome big brother?"

"Liesel, apparently. I'm running out of silly rhymes!" He offered her a wry smile as he slipped the small box back into his pocket. He was on a mission. A long-term one if need be. Patience was something he was good at and he was determined to win Liesel back. If it took until he was as craggy and aged as some of their finest cellared wines, then so be it. After hearing through the town's very short grapevine that she'd handed in notice at the school and was accepting a job at the hospital, he needed to let her know he was in this for the long haul. He couldn't let her move on without trying again.

If he was really honest with himself, he knew she had every right to be angry. If he'd been in her shoes, he'd definitely need some cooling-down time. And a good old-fashioned apology.

So far he had sent a dozen bouquets. That made it twelve days since The Dark Night, including a Sunday when the florist had been closed and he'd had to improvise. He hadn't realized how difficult it was to make a bouquet. Thank God Becca had been around to help him. Being able to go to his family for help was incredible. They had his back—and he would need their support as he sorted out the cataclysmically large mess he'd made of things.

"So. Is that next on the agenda?" Becca tipped her head in the direction of his pocket.

"No, I've got something I hope will be a bit more persuasive in mind."

"More persuasive than Mum's vintage diamond-and-emerald ring?"

Jack rocked back on his heels and looked out of the tasting room toward the river. "Mmm...on a par, on a par."

Her office couldn't have sparkled more if it had been brand-new. Liesel popped the box of personal effects onto her immaculately clear desk, ready for her replacement. She'd already met the young woman, an Adelaide native like herself, and thought she'd be great. She would miss the children, but knew her new job at the hospital was a better fit. Leaving Engleton, that was going to be harder than she'd thought.

"Miss! Miss!" Kev appeared round the corner, urgently gesturing for her to join him.

She fell into a jog beside the teen, who had fully recovered from his collapsed lung. "What is it? Has someone been hurt?"

"You've got to come quickly, to the car park."

"What's going on, Kev?" Her brow crinkled with worry. A serious incident was not the way she was hoping to say goodbye to everyone on her last day at the school. She was hoping to leave everyone in good health. Then sneak away like the coward she was beginning to feel like. Dodging her problems wasn't usually her style. Oh, well. People changed.

"Just hurry!" Kev furrowed his brow in frustration, then broke into a run toward the double doors leading out to the back of the school.

She raced after him, heart pounding. There must be something really wrong.

The moment she burst through the doors she turned to go back in. Kev got there before her, blocking her entrance. "Miss," he cautioned with all of the gravitas a teen could muster, "my brigade captain needs to have a word."

And there he was, chocolate milk shakes in hand, as knee-weakeningly gorgeous as ever. Her dream come true, her worst nightmare. Jack Granville Keller III.

At least she knew what the *G* stood for now.

"Care for a ride in the country?" His too-kissable lips tipped up into a slow grin.

"I can't. I've got Liam."

"I've got Liam, actually." Cassie appeared beside her. "Kev and I are going to take him to the pictures."

"He's two." Liesel was grateful for the fleeting distraction from Jack's blue eyes. She'd missed them so much, the additional spark of life they seemed to give her.

"Going on three and he likes a good cartoon as much as the next person." Cassie dropped her a sassy wink before turning on her heel. "It starts any minute so we'd better get a move on."

"C'mon." She felt Jack's fingers thread through her own and give them a light squeeze before she'd realised he was beside her. She had to fight the instinct to return the squeeze. "Let's go for a ride."

"Jack, I really don't want to. It's my last day and I—"

He lifted a finger to her lips. "If you give me a chance, today could also be a day of firsts."

She resisted the urge to swat his hand away. She might be angry with him, but there was no need to be nasty. Besides, his finger against her lips was a teasing reminder of the sensual pleasures Jack had once released in her. Not that she wanted those anymore. Well, she did. But she *shouldn't* and that was going to have to be enough.

"On you go!" She felt Cassie give her a little shove. Looked as if she wasn't going to have much choice in the matter.

"A short one." She arched what she hoped was an assertive brow up at Jack. He gave her one of his crooked grins and all at once she was back in the barnyard, her body turning into a butterfly-filled lava lamp all over again. She retrieved her hand from Jack's and reluctantly followed him to the truck, where he'd placed the milk shakes in the beverage holders. For a man who thought of everything, he certainly had a knack for not explaining anything! Which was precisely the problem.

She chewed on her lips as he climbed into the cab and pulled the truck out of the school's car park just as they'd done dozens of times before over the course of their—whatever it had been. Friends didn't hide friends from their families. And she needed to remember that.

"Do you mind a little music?"

"Not at all." It would cover up the fact she couldn't think of a single lucid thing to say to him.

She watched as Jack flicked on the CD player then took in a sharp breath of surprise as the first song came on.

"This is—"

"Your favourite hippie music."

She couldn't help releasing a hint of a smile.

"Where are we going?"

"I'd thought of making it a secret, but figured we'd had enough of those." Liesel shot him a sharp look. Was he taking a dig at her or himself?

"River's Bend," he continued, his eyes trained on the road. "We're headed to River's Bend. I want you to see why I love it there and explain, if I can, what happened in the lead-up to the Harvest Festival.

"Jack, I just don't know. A lot has changed in my life."

"If you're talking about taking the job at the hospital, I heard." He saw her eyes widen in surprise.

"I have my sources!" Her cat eyes narrowed.

No more secrets.

"Cassie. Cassie told me. And I can't even tell you how proud I am of you. The hospital is lucky to have you. Truly." He placed a hand over hers and gave it a little squeeze.

"I know you don't owe me a thing, but I would do anything to win back your trust."

"It's not just my trust you need to earn, it's Liam's." A surge of emotion shot through her like a lightning bolt. "I can't bring someone into his life who changes his mind on a whim about who he is and whether or not he wants us around." It was difficult to keep the hurt out of her voice, not to mention the anger, but she tried her best. Despite herself, she loved this man.

"Believe me, I know."

"But how could you?"

"Because I didn't think I had my father's trust all these years. And that hurt. A lot."

"You two seemed pretty chummy the other night." This time she knew she sounded unkind. And it felt wrong. Hurting Jack was the last thing she wanted to do.

"That's thanks to you, you know."

Uh, what was that? I thought I was being a jerk.

"Meeting you changed my life in ways I'd never imagined possible. At the very least, I owe you an enormous thank-you." He slapped the steering wheel gleefully. "Maybe you having a right old go at me. Blow off some steam. What do you say?" He was chuckling now, obviously delighted with the idea. "Do you fancy giving me a good old-fashioned telling off?"

"I don't really think that's necessary," she answered primly, before taking a sip of her chocolate milk shake. Delicious. A ten. Or was that Jack?

Quit softening my resolve, you...you picture of perfection!

He waggled his brows at her and spun out a toothy grin. "C'mon, darlin', you know you want to."

"Hardly. I'm more mature than you."

"That's what they say about girlies."

It was hard to stop the giggles from burbling forth. "Well, it's true." She pointed a decisive finger at him. "And I'm hardly a girlie."

Jack took his eyes off the road for a moment to appraise her. "No, darlin'. You are definitely all woman."

And *whooooosh*! There went the butterflies.

Jack turned the truck into the impressive entry gates of River's Bend. Her eyes scanned the seemingly endless rows of fruit-laden vines, the various winery buildings dotted along the left side of the drive and, as they wended their way along the dirt track, the classic country farmhouse sitting among a grove of gums. It was breathtaking. And off-limits. *Right?*

Jack clicked off the ignition and tipped his head in the direction of the trees. "C'mon. Let's take a walk."

Her resolve was softening by the second. And the seconds were flying past.

"Jack, I really don't think this is a good idea."

In a flash he was on the other side of the car, taking her hand in his. "I think you'll find it is. The future mistress of River's Bend really should know her way around the property, don't you think?"

Her fluttery tummy turned into a hard twist.

"No, Jack. I can't."

"Can't or won't?"

"Both. Not if you think compartmentalizing your life is a way to live. I've been through too much already. I'm not going to beg you to find out more secrets—nor am I going to sit around waiting for you to surprise me with another mind-blowingly huge plan for the future you 'forgot' to tell me."

"C'mon." He gave her hand another gentle tug, succeeding, this time, in guiding her round the side of the house into the sun-dappled woodland. They strolled for a few moments in silence, Liesel's head busy fighting the urge to turn into a pinball machine. When the thoughts settled a little, she still reached the same conclusion.

"Jack, I am so sorry for all you have been through, but you didn't trust that I would have been there for you."

"The way you trusted me with your history with Eric?"

Ouch. That hurt.

"That's not fair."

"Nor is keeping me in your bad books forever for the same mistake."

"It wasn't a mistake. It was…" Liesel hesitated, knowing Jack had made a legitimate point. "It was a tactical omission."

"Tactical omission?" Jack's eyes widened with disbelief. "Seriously?"

No. It was more than that.

"I thought I was waiting until I was ready to say goodbye to Eric."

Jack's expression softened. "Oh, darlin', you'll never say goodbye to him. He's the father of that great kid of yours. I was just hoping there was room in your heart for you to say hello to me."

Liesel felt tears prick at her eyes. She'd already said hello. Quite some time ago. And saying goodbye to Jack? It was proving near on impossible. Still. Her heels had been dug in, she might as well hash the whole thing out with him.

"It still would have been nice to find out you were a local boy and heir to a…to all of this before the Harvest Festival." She gestured at the beautiful woodland and expanse of riverfront that peeked through the bushes at the end of the path they'd been walking along.

"So you're telling me you would've gone for Jack the winery heir more than Jack the brigade captain?" His tone had turned brusque. He'd obviously had a lot of that growing up and it wasn't at all what she'd meant.

"No! Not in the slightest. I just felt like an idiot—everyone there knew who you were except me, the supposed object of your affection." She glared at him then felt her willpower weakening at the memory of him in his dress uniform. "Besides, I quite like Jack the fireman."

"Quite?" Jack's lips parted in a slow, sexy grin.

"A bit," she replied coyly, a finger working its way round one of her curls.

Obviously sensing he had some emotional purchase, she saw his confidence grow as he continued. It wasn't helping her resolve that a confident Jack was about as sexy as they made 'em.

"It would be an understatement to say the way things panned out at the Harvest Festival was the total opposite of how I wanted them to be."

"So I wasn't meant to find out anything at all?" Liesel stopped in her tracks, hands flying to her hips, chin quirked to the side. Sparks may actually have been shooting out of her eyes but she was too astonished to be sure. This was one heck of an apology! Resolve? Back into set-cement land.

"No, you noodle, the total opposite. I wanted you to know everything about me, but with the crash and all, everything went pear-shaped. It was meant to be a Liesel dream night! There was supposed to be wine, delicious food, formal introductions to my family and me on a bended knee in front of the entire town with a beautiful ring and an accordion serenade."

Liesel couldn't help herself. She burst into hysterical laughter. "An accordion serenade?"

"Okay, maybe not the accordion serenade but everything else was true." Jack opened his arms wide, beckoning with his fingers that she should come in for one of his bear hugs. She wanted to, every pore in her body wanted to. But they still weren't quite there yet. She folded her arms as if they would help protect her from the answer to the next question.

"Are there more? More big things I need to know?"

"I once ate a worm on a dare from my sister then threw up in my dad's combine. It took him a week to clean it."

Liesel laughed softly, but kept her arms folded tightly across her chest. God, he made her laugh. She loved that about him.

Who was she kidding? She loved *him*. But she needed to know who the real "him" was. "Jack—be serious. I don't need a blow-by-blow account but a nice round nut-shell version of the man I love would do before—"

"Before what? Wait!" His eyes went another notch up on the sky-blue barometer. "You love me?"

"Of course I do, you dill. Why do you think I was so upset?"

"Hang on. You said you needed a nutshell version of my life before—before what?"

"Before you can think about bending that knee of yours again." *Uh-oh.* She'd softened. *And we're back to putty!*

"Well, that, my darlin' redhead, is fair enough." He took a big breath and as he began to speak, ever so slowly began to lower one knee to the ground. "Nutshell version—I was born John Granville Keller the Third to Ava and Granville Keller. Lived an idyllic childhood here at River's Bend Winery with my sister, Becca. A fire, the details of which I have hashed over for the past twenty-odd years, took the life of my beloved mother and my father's true love. I blamed myself and, subsequently, thought my father hated me so I threw myself into a life of wild-child silliness that didn't really suit me until I eventually came to roost in the barracks of the CFS training HQ in Adelaide, where I found focus. Drive."

He took her hand in his and continued, his knee hovering inches above the ground. "I led a life of purposeful improvement with the fire service and active avoidance of my family and then one day—*pow!*—I met the most beautiful woman I have ever had the pleasure of laying my eyes on. She was smart, funny, has a cute-as-can-be kid who melts my heart every time I give him an airplane ride. She—her name is Liesel, by the way—gave me the strength to heal old wounds with my family and, more than anything..."

Liesel watched silently as Jack's knee met the ground and his hand slipped into his trouser pocket. He withdrew a small black box and flipped open the lid. "More than anything I wish she would agree to be my wife."

Her eyes widened at the sight of the glittering diamond flanked by two beautiful emeralds. It was the most gorgeous ring she had ever seen.

"Liesel Elizabeth Adler, will you please do me the honor of becoming my wife?"

If someone had told her your heart could actually get lodged in your throat, Liesel would've believed them at that moment. The man of her dreams was down on one knee, asking her to marry him, and she couldn't speak!

"Liesel?"

"There's just so much to process!" She knew she was just buying time—and she also knew what her heart was telling her.

"I'll do you one better, then. Would you agree to be my fiancée? I will give you a one-year warranty on any faults or problems you find with me." She raised a dubious eyebrow. "Within reason, of course."

"Well, that certainly is an interesting offer…"

"Liesel." His tone was insistent now. "Please, say something. Please, agree to spend your life with me."

Liesel dropped to her knees in front of him, wanting to look directly into those eyes of his when she answered. "Yes. Yes, I will, Brigade Captain Keller."

Jack threw back his head and let out a huge whoop. They were going to get married! Before she had a chance to take it in fully, Liesel felt Jack's hands slip along her waist, gently pulling her toward him. She couldn't believe a lifetime of butterflies and hot-blooded fireworks awaited her. And a man to rely on. Jack.

As his lips began to explore hers, she surrendered to the enjoyment of the sensual pleasures and promise of things to come as the future Mrs. Jack Keller.

* * * * *

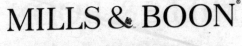

MILLS & BOON®

The Chatsfield Collection!

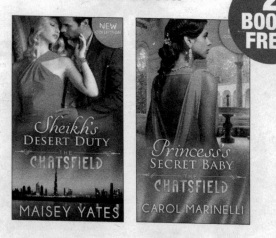

Style, spectacle, scandal...!

With the eight Chatsfield siblings happily married and settling down, it's time for a new generation of Chatsfields to shine, in this brand-new 8-book collection! The prospect of a merger with the Harrington family's boutique hotels will shape the future forever. But who will come out on top?

Find out at
www.millsandboon.co.uk/TheChatsfield2

5_INSHIP2

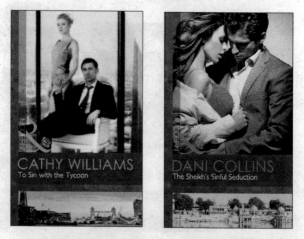

THE ULTIMATE IN ROMANTIC MEDICAL DRAMA

315/03